Burst

H. C. Daria

Created and Published in Spartanburg, SC.
Printed in the United States of America.
ISBN: 978-0-578-64593-3

Library of Congress Control Number:
2020906634

Dedicated to my Aunt Kirstin.
Thank you for everything, for the kind words and
encouragement you gave (and give) every step of the way.
Vielen Dank

TABLE OF CONTENTS

Chapter One	1
Chapter Two	14
Chapter Three	25
Chapter Four	34
Chapter Five	44
Chapter Six	51
Chapter Seven	61
Chapter Eight	73
Chapter Nine	80
Chapter Ten	95
Chapter Eleven	102
Chapter Twelve	108
Chapter Thirteen	111
Chapter Fourteen	120
Chapter Fifteen	135
Chapter Sixteen	141
Chapter Seventeen	149
Chapter Eighteen	155
Chapter Nineteen	173
Chapter Twenty	186
Chapter Twenty-One	194
Chapter Twenty-Two	201
Chapter Twenty-Three	211
Chapter Twenty-Four	225
Chapter Twenty-Five	233
Chapter Twenty-Six	237
Chapter Twenty-Seven	253
Chapter Twenty-Eight	266
Chapter Twenty-Nine	269
Chapter Thirty	290
Chapter Thirty-One	298

Chapter Thirty-Two   312
Chapter Thirty-Three   324
Chapter Thirty-Four   332
Chapter Thirty-Five   341
Chapter Thirty-Six   357
Chapter Thirty-Seven   369
Chapter Thirty-Eight   376
Chapter Thirty-Nine   383
Chapter Forty   389
Chapter Forty-One   397
Chapter Forty-Two   401
Chapter Forty-Three   408
Chapter Forty-Four   417
Chapter Forty-Five   420
Chapter Forty-Six   432
Chapter Forty-Seven   438
Chapter Forty-Eight   445

About the Author / About the Illustrator

CHAPTER ONE

I heard the wind through the thin schoolroom walls, and I could imagine the red and orange leaves racing through the air to who-knows-where outside. The visual was a perk for having an autumn birthday, I guess, but it didn't matter if I couldn't see through the filthy window. If only someone would wipe the grime off the glass, then I would actually be able to look beyond it.

"Well, Pasin?"

I jerked my head away from the window and turned it toward the man at the front.

"What?" I asked. One side of the teacher Slate's mouth curled up, and he crossed his arms, still smirking.

"Pasin," he said again, drawing out the word, "if you are too absent-minded to pay attention—"

"No! I mean…" I shook my head, grit my teeth at the jab. Brock Copper at the desk next to me snorted, and Slate chuckled to himself. I continued, "King Dante's most important contributions to Falleon were an annual census and the identification pieces still used today."

Slate's smile faded, and he pursed his lips.

"Stop daydreaming in class!" he said and turned back to the board. "Dante's reign might have lasted longer if he had not passed the following laws…"

I hated the sound of my name spoken by Slate. It hadn't mattered to me as a child when everyone only had one name, but as the others developed their Elements, changing from Curro to Curro Gust or Ulena to Ulena Earth in a shining moment of fulfillment, I remained Pasin. Just Pasin.

With Slate's back to the class, Copper leaned toward me and whispered, "Answer all the questions you want. You're still an Absent."

My muscles tightened at his statement. It was bad enough to be the only person called by their first name, but the generic name for people without Elements was worse.

"Shut up, Brock."

"Pasin!" Slate spun around and pointed at me, chalk in hand. "That was uncalled for. After-school detention tomorrow." Slate's earlier smile returned to his face with the new development. I snorted, though not loud enough to be noticed. The detention didn't bother me though; it happened often enough that it wasn't a surprise, and maybe if Slate left during the detention time, I could work on writing my story.

"For homework," Slate called out while erasing the board, "write a page about one of Dante's policies. I don't care if it's the census, identification, whatever, just write a page." He put down the eraser with a thud. "Class dismissed."

"Speaking of Element identification," Brock said

to me as everyone moved to leave, "when's your level test?" He smirked and his friends guffawed as I threw my things into my bag and left before I did anything else to get me in trouble.

I stopped by the library on the way out and checked out a book about the previous rulers of Falleon. The books at the orphanage where I lived were almost fifty years old, so they didn't include the recent rulers like Whestor Light, Dante Blaze, Gaeron Zinc, or Oramus Void. I could understand not including Oramus, seeing as he had only been in power for the four years after Gaeron Zinc had died, but really, the books needed to be updated.

I exited the school, avoided the groups of other students, and started making my way down the road away from the Andor sector of Falleon City. I passed a couple of farms, the different Earth-type workers shifting the soil while Water manipulators directed the water's flow, and Brock's taunt echoed in my mind. Even if it was a tradition after someone's sixteenth birthday, how could anyone expect me to take the level test? I had no Elemental power to gauge.

I shook my head and looked around instead. Even from this distance, the Caeltactus Mountains loomed over the landscape far to the north and west, their peaks reaching into the clouds just as they did around the land perimeter of Falleon. A dense forest burning in its fall colors stretched down the mountain all the way to the edge of Falleon City and throughout most of the kingdom. A book I had read years ago said that elves lived in the forest, but I didn't think many people tried to verify this. The forest and mountains were settings to too many horror tales for many people to explore them themselves.

Finally, I passed the farms and clumps of trees. After the last line of trees, I slowed down to take in the view to my left.

An enormous golden field stretched uninterrupted from the side of the road to the edge of the real Falleon City. Not just an outlying sector of the city–no, it reached all the way to the core of Falleon's capital city, to the edge of the sector that contained the palace. The distant turrets of the castle defined the skyline, and I let out a small sigh at the open space. I didn't want to be chastised for being late though, so I quickened my step.

The orphanage appeared behind another grove of trees, the building's earthen walls pockmarked by the passage of time. The stone wall surrounding the orphanage, however, showed no such decay.

I made it to the iron gate just as one of the matrons exited the building with the matching iron key.

"Cutting it a bit close aren't we, Pasin?" Matron Water asked, raising an eyebrow while simultaneously smiling. I didn't smile back.

"I had to get this book from the school library," I answered, waving the Dante book in her direction.

"Even so," she replied, "rules are rules. Now put a smile on that face and get to your homework!" Despite her sickeningly playful tone, I managed to lift the sides of my mouth in what could almost be called a smile.

I passed through the gate into the courtyard, hurrying to the door. Despite my effort, I could still hear the metallic clang as the gate was shut and locked for the night.

Once I entered the building, a pebble promptly

hit me in the forehead.

"That's not Matron Water!" a little girl yelled to the boy across the room. "That's Pasin, you dirt clod!"

"Then you do it next time!" the boy hollered back, and he proceeded to physically throw the few other pebbles in his hand at the girl, who manipulated most of them away from her.

I made my way to the staircase as other kids joined in the pebble war. Despite Slate's aggravating demeanor, at least school gave me time away from the herd of children who lived here, most of whom were ten or younger. I began climbing the stairs when I heard a voice louder than the rest.

"What's going on in here?" Matron Water yelled over the din. Everyone fell silent and a smile played on my lips.

I climbed to the third floor and walked to the room at the hallway's end. A battered sign on the door read, "Pasin," and a newer, shinier one below read, "Arina Wood." Arina was the latest roommate in a long line of girls; I lost count after the thirteenth, I think. I opened the door and was surprised to see Arina in the room for once.

Arina looked up from the book she was reading.

"Hi," she said quietly.

I shifted where I stood. Normally Arina spent her time in the back garden. She came about two months ago, a twelve-year-old who lost her parents in an accident upon which the matrons didn't elaborate.

"Hi," I replied, still standing in the doorway. Realizing how silly I probably looked, I entered the room and placed the Dante book on my desk in spite of Matron Water's homework command.

"How was your day?" Arina asked, putting her own book down. Once she put it down, though, she started fidgeting with her fingers. We had never really talked, and despite the simplicity of the question, I had difficulty coming up with an answer.

"Fine, I guess," I finally said, tracing the wood pattern on the desk. I had wanted to write more of my story in the quiet of the room, but I really wanted to be alone. I grabbed a fresh sheet of paper and a pencil, leaving the already written portions in my desk drawer.

"I'm, um, going back downstairs," I said, not really looking at Arina as I walked past her back to the hallway.

"Bye," she said.

"Bye," I replied, though probably not loud enough for her to have heard it.

I felt a combination of anger and guilt on my way back downstairs. Arina couldn't help it, but I was jealous of her. Even though she was older than most of the kids here, it wouldn't be a problem. She'd get adopted soon enough with her silky straight brown hair and pretty face. I had blue eyes and dirty blonde hair that I either wore down or up depending on whether I wanted to hide my acne-prone face or the sheer bushiness of my hair. Also, it definitely helped that she had an Element. Not having an Element killed any chances I might have had of getting adopted as I got older and the odds of developing an Element became slim. But even before then, prospective parents just seemed to steer away from me.

She had parents once. I mean, so did I, but I never knew them. Matron Water said I was a doorstop child, a found child. I had lived at the orphanage for as long as I could remember. At least Arina had parents once, right?

"Stop it," I muttered to myself. I mentally shoved the thoughts away and made it downstairs. The pebble war had disbanded, but the kids were still being loud, vaguely annoying, and…just kids, I guess. I headed toward the dining room, hoping for some kind of quiet, but another matron accosted me.

"Oh, hello Pasin," she started, a large smile stretching across her face. "Why don't you go outside? It's such a nice day." Before I could say anything, she guided me to the entrance, opened the door, and all but pushed me outside.

I sighed in the outside air. They were probably doing something for my birthday in the dining room. They did it for every person, but I really wanted to just write. I sat down on a bench facing the iron gate, so I could look beyond the walls of the orphanage even if I couldn't go there. I heard the front door open again, but I didn't look to see it was, and the footsteps faded quickly. I turned my attention to the paper ready to be filled.

When I read for fun, I preferred fantasy, so it made sense that I would write it. At the time, I had been working on the story for four months or so, and I knew what the defining characteristic of the world and the story was. Absolutely no one in this world had Elemental abilities. It stretched the imagination, trying to figure out how people could work and function as a society without these abilities. At the same time, it almost felt like research for the future, because I had to make a living doing something at some point, and I didn't have a natural backup. Time was running out. After I finished this year of school, the orphanage wasn't obligated to host me anymore.

I wrote about a quarter of a page to add to the collection of papers upstairs, but the sky kept distracting me. A flock of birds erupted from the nearby wood. As they flew away, I thought I saw words in the flock's contorting shape, but the birds wouldn't stay in the same place long enough for me to read what they said.

The footsteps returned behind me.

"Pasin?"

I twisted my head and saw Arina. She looked down and back up and was holding something behind her back.

"Can I sit with you?" she asked. I had no reason to say no, so I nodded. She sat down next to me and looked at the paper and pencil in my hands.

"What are you doing?" she asked.

"Writing," I replied. Or trying to.

"What are you writing?" she asked. I fidgeted in my seat a little.

"A story."

"What's it about?" My fingers twitched, and I twisted my wrist just a little so she couldn't read the words.

"A girl," I said, "She…it's hard to explain." After a moment of silence, I continued, "Sorry." Even as I said the word, I hated it and the cop-out before it.

"It's fine," she replied, her hands still behind her back. Another moment of silence passed, and she continued this time.

"I heard it's your birthday," she said.

"It is," I replied without looking at her, my finger rubbing the paper in my hands.

"I got you a present," she said, and I looked over. She held out her hands in front of her, and the cupped hands held a single flower, a fire red bloom with little white specks spread across it. I knew the plant; it was an ignis flower, one of my favorites, and I even knew which bush she plucked it from in the back garden.

I took it from her hands, saying nothing at first as I stared at it. A smile spread across my face.

"Thank you," I said, looking her in the eyes.

"You're welcome," she replied and gave a small smile back. I opened my mouth to say more, but the front door opened again, and Matron Water called to us.

"Dinner time, girls!"

I pocketed the flower, and we walked into the building together.

When we entered the dining room, about thirty kids and a handful of matrons yelled surprise and congratulated me on my birthday. Everyone was smiling, but that was probably just because we typically had better food on birthdays. The food was tastier than usual, but it was difficult to enjoy the meal with the young children yammering. At the end of dinner, Matron Water came up to me.

"Are you ready for your presents?" she asked. I nodded, and we left the dining room and walked into the matrons' office. There was no great precedent for presents, but it did intrigue me that she used the plural. That didn't happen often.

"Let me get the first one," she said and grabbed a covered dish. A little hope bubbled up in me. Could this be a cake or a pastry of some sort? That would be wonderful.

"This might come as a surprise," she said, her hand hovering over the cover, "so let me explain it, all right?" I nodded, just ready to see what it was, and she pulled the cover off to reveal a plate of ash.

"What's this?" I asked.

"The papers we found in your desk," she replied. It took me a moment, but I realized…my story.

"What? Why?" The words shot out from my mouth, a cry I didn't even try to restrain. The magnitude of what I had lost, the hours spent scribbling in my room and at school, hit me like a blow to the chest. The edges of my sight became dark red like the anger I felt boiling within me. I opened my mouth again, but Matron Water raised a finger.

"Like I said, let me explain. When I read through these, I was disturbed by the utter disregard you showed for our society." She lowered her hand and sifted her fingers through the ash while I stood there, mouth agape and hands balled into fists at my sides. Even in the papers' current state, I wanted to shove her hand away from them.

"This is the world you live in, Pasin," she continued. "It won't do you any good to try to escape it."

"But it's mine!" I blurted out, gesturing toward the remains. "They were mine! You can't just go and—"

"Now that you're sixteen," she interrupted, "you are an adult in the eyes of law and society. We want to help you transition into that position of responsibility instead of dreaming." She took a deep breath and smiled, and I could tell by her smile that she really, truly thought she was doing me a favor.

"It might hurt now," she added, "but it will get

better. I promise."

I couldn't look at her. I turned my head away from the plate and felt tears gather in the corners of my eyes. Matron Water put the plate down on the desk and sighed.

"Well, now that that one is out of the way, let's get to something more fun, shall we?"

I didn't answer, and I guess she didn't expect an answer, because she continued.

"As an official adult, we agreed that you can be trusted with some more responsibility." Out of the corner of my eye, I saw her face, and it looked like she was regretting that decision.

"Therefore," she continued, "we decided you can go to the Andor marketplace tonight. Alone."

Even though the fire within didn't fade, I did react to this news.

"Really?" I asked, my voice shaking just slightly. I could barely believe it. Normally the other children and I couldn't leave the orphanage alone for anything except school.

"Yes," she answered, smile broadening. I stared at her then, torn between the pain and rage I felt about my papers and a tingle of excitement I felt about being able to leave the orphanage alone. My gaze shifted to the pile of ash on the desk, and the rage boiled up within me again.

"Now come along," she said and grabbed my arm to lead me outside. My muscles tightened at her touch, but I followed.

We walked up to the gate, wind making fallen leaves lash around, and Matron Water reached into her pocket then paused.

"Before I forget," she said, taking something out

of her pocket, "here's your last present. Be sure not to lose it." She placed something in my hand and went back to the gate. I looked at the item and my breath caught in my throat.

A coin sat in my palm, and I realized what it was immediately. As Matron Water had said, I was an adult from that point forward, and part of being an adult included the government-issued identification piece. I closed my hand around it without further inspection, because I knew what it said already. Each identification piece included the person's name, birthday, and Element. The coin is given at sixteen, because sixteen is the age when a person's Element is considered set.

"There you go," Matron Water said, opening the gate only a little bit before the wind swung it open all the way. I walked through it, ready to leave the orphanage behind.

"Also," Matron Water added as I walked down the path to the road, "your level test is this Saturday at ten."

"What?" I stopped and looked back at her. "But how—"

"Every sixteen-year-old has to go through it," she replied. "It's a royal mandate."

"But that doesn't make sense!" I protested. "What the pont do they expect me to—"

"Saturday at ten," Water repeated. "You will be there, and you will be there on time. Now," she continued, "enjoy your time at the market. Be back before dark." And with that, she smiled once more and closed the gate behind me.

I stared at her retreating back for a few moments before turning away. Only then did I realize my fists were clenched again. Something cut into my palm, something hard and solid. I opened my hand and extracted the coin identification piece. Bronze and perfectly circular, it shone with nearly sickening newness and brightness. I rubbed the piece between my fingers; I felt the ridges spell out my name and birthday–nothing else. I looked at it once again and registered the blank space on one side of the coin where my power level would be recorded. I squeezed my hand around the metal piece, just as my eyes squeezed shut. Hot tears ran down my face, and as much as I wanted to leave, I also wanted to take Water's smile and burn it as she had burned my happiness.

After a moment, I wiped the tears away, but I could still feel their heat on my cheeks. I looked down the road, felt the air rush around me, and then I ran, ran with all my might away from the bleeding sun towards town, my anger blending with the fiery leaves flying by.

CHAPTER TWO

I ran all the way to the school before I had to slow down, and I shoved the identification piece into my pocket without looking at it again. My heart pounded as I reached the edge of the Andor sector of Falleon City, the exertion and recent revelation merging to create a fire in my chest that I tried to extinguish without success.

Being Falleon City's artisan district, the shops lining Andor's streets mostly sold creations, from simple clay pots on tabletop displays in the walkways to metal sculptures sold in the actual shops. As I entered the sector, I stopped and admired the nearest building, its exterior marked by alternating light and dark grains of wood whose lines looped and spiraled across the surface. My gaze followed one line until it ended up at a metal plaque reading, "Designed by Floran Wood."

I had never noticed the intricacy before, because the matrons normally hurried us along any time we visited Andor. Another wave of heat flared inside me at the thought of the matrons. I turned away from the building and followed a mother and daughter into the central square.

Similar buildings surrounded the square while tables and carts dotted the stone paths covered in spiral incisions. Some purple and black flags waved in the breeze, each bearing an O overlaid by a V for King Oramus Void. As I walked closer to one of the flags, a man far ahead of me glanced at the symbol for a moment before hurrying on in the other direction, head ducked.

The little girl, jumping from one stone swirl to another, ran ahead of her mother, and I stopped at one of the glass figurine stands. I didn't have any money, but I still wanted to look. I was peering at a phoenix figurine in my hand when I heard a high-pitched shriek somewhere on my right.

"Mama, Mama, look!"

I turned my head to see what the commotion was about. The little girl stood in front of a shop's window and was pointing at her reflection.

"Look!" she repeated, "I'm shining! I'm getting my Element!" She threw her hands out in front of her as if expecting a burst of flame to erupt from them. Her mother grabbed one of the girl's arms and lowered it.

"Stop that! You're not shining," she said. The girl opened her mouth, pointing at the window with her other hand, and the mother continued. "It's just the light on the glass. Look." She pointed at my faraway reflection, trapped in the same ray of sunlight. I looked away, but I could still hear her.

"She looks like she's shining too, but she's not. It's just the light."

My hands tightened around the phoenix's wings, but I caught myself just before the glass broke. The little girl let out a whine, but the mother interrupted her.

"Marisa, stop." She paused, then her voice softened as she continued. "You'll get your Element someday. Want to go to the Solluna shrine for now?" The girl agreed and the two left my field of sight entirely, but I did hear the mother add, "What did you plan to do anyway if you were a Fire? Burn the shop down?"

"Hey."

My focus returned to what was in front of me, and I looked at the stall keeper.

"Plan on buying that?" she asked, gesturing toward the phoenix figurine still in my hand. I shook my head.

"No, ma'am," I replied, putting the figurine back down. The woman scowled at me, and I added, "I mean, not today at least."

"Oh yes, sure," she mocked, waving her hand at me. "Yes, you must be quite the big spender with—"

"Hey!" I interrupted, and she stopped speaking, her widened eyes focused somewhere to the side of my face. "I didn't break anything. You don't need to—"

"Is there a problem here?"

I spun around at the sound of the new voice and took a step back.

A tall man with black hair stood maybe five feet away, flanked by two other older men. Each person wore black tunics with King Oramus' seal on the front, but while the purple seal dominated the older men's garments, the central one had the O.V. as a small silver symbol over the upper left of his chest. He scowled though, looking incredibly disinterested in the events before him. I was taken back by how young he seemed. Despite appearing no more than three or four years older than me, something in his demeanor froze the heated anger I felt moments before.

"Well?" he asked. His right hand held a silvery ring of sorts, large enough that he put four fingers through it, twisting it around his fingers with his thumb.

"No, sir," the woman behind me said in a much milder tone. "We were just talking a little back and forth."

The man looked straight at her for a moment then turned his gaze upon me.

"Do you have anything to add to that?"

His russet brown eyes unnerved me. I looked down and replied.

"No, sir."

A couple of tense seconds passed, then he tightened his fist to stop the twirling ring.

"Let's keep it that way, hmm?" he asked, still with the bored tone.

"Yes, sir," the stall keeper said. I nodded. The central man moved first, and the others followed. I finally lifted my head again and felt a hand on my shoulder. I turned and saw the woman.

"Best be going now," she said quietly. I nodded again and started walking in the opposite direction of the trio.

As I walked across the square, I noticed the girl and her mother kneeling in front of the local Solluna shrine honoring the sun and moon. I didn't know anyone who regularly visited the shrine, but it made sense for the girl to be there. Many people believed the sun and moon gave each person their unique Element. I passed without stopping.

Before I could get very far, another man clad in a black tunic came out of an alley and began walking in my direction. I stopped in front of another shop, its sign reading "Mendor's Fine Watches and Charms," hoping the dark figure would turn again before passing me. As he came closer, my nerve gave out, and I ducked into the shop.

A flood of ticking noises barraged me as I walked in. Clocks covered all of the walls and even hung from the ceiling, their individual voices mingling with each other so that no one was distinct. I paused just beyond the door, taking it all in before a voice interrupted my musing.

"Are you looking for something special today?"

I looked up. A white-haired, stooped man stood behind the counter, waiting for a reply.

"Um…no sir," I said, "I'm just looking around."

His eyes narrowed. "If so, then I suggest you leave." I glanced out the front window and opened my mouth to say something, anything so I wouldn't have to go back out yet, but another voice stopped me.

"Cheb! Behave yourself!" An equally white-haired woman stepped out of the door behind the counter and hit the man's arm mock-seriously. "There's no need for that." The woman turned to me and smiled.

"Sorry about my husband. He's a bit grumpy today, because the King's guard came through earlier and searched the shop. Old Cheb always gets a headache when they're about." She went up to her husband and rubbed his back. I shuffled my feet, averted my eyes, then finally spoke.

"How much is your simplest piece?"

The woman removed her arm and gestured toward one of the chokers under the counter.

"We have this engagement necklace for one silver piece. It doesn't bond when you clasp it, but between you and me, I think that's for the best." She gave me a wink, and I tried to smile at her joke. Hardly anyone could afford the bonding engagement necklace, the one where the two ends of the chain never separated once placed around the neck. If the cheapest nonbonding necklace cost a silver, I didn't want to think what a bonding necklace would cost.

"I'm sorry, I meant one of the pocket watches," I replied, pointing to the collection next to the engagement necklaces.

"Oh. Of the watches, the least expensive is that one right there." She pointed to a bronze watch. "It costs three silver pieces."

"All right," I replied. "Thank you, but I don't have quite that much today." The man scowled at me, but I focused on the woman.

"It's fine," she said. "Stay as long as you want." She waved and left. Her husband however, kept glaring at me. I turned away from him to glance out the front window. I didn't see the man from before, so I left the building.

Shadows of the western buildings spread over most of the square, and my heart sank with the realization that I would have to return to the orphanage soon, back to the matrons and back to the people who knew what I lacked. The internal fire sprang back to life and a building headache joined it. I closed my eyes for a moment, but the headache stayed. When I opened my eyes, I surveyed the area with the knowledge that I could only go to one more place before heading back. A bookshop across the square received that honor.

The moment I walked up the steps into the shop, I felt an aura of kinship with the hundreds of books lining the walls and bookshelves. At the same time, however, I felt a kick in my stomach as I thought of all of my pages reduced to ash. The anger inside grew stronger, but I tried to ignore it as I walked through the shop.

I stopped in the fiction section and looked for where my book would be placed once I could rewrite what I had lost. Two women sat nearby, and I couldn't help but hear their conversation.

"Well, I heard that Oramus is sending men to search for dragons in the mountains. The word is he wants them for rebellion calming." In the corner of my eye, the lady in green leaned closer to the lady in purple for emphasis. "But," she continued, her voice lowered, "some say he's trying to find a way out of Falleon. That he wants to go over the mountains."

"What is he? Twenty?" the lady in purple replied. "Why would he want to leave when he has everything here?"

"He's looking for a queen, isn't he? I guess the ladies at the palace aren't good enough for him." The woman in green snorted after saying this.

"Well," the lady in purple said, "there's no shortage of girls at the palace. He must want something different, I guess. No lowly Earth for him." She looked at the lady in green and laughed. "No offense."

"I wouldn't want to be with him anyway," she said though her body language said differently. "He's power-hungry and—"

The woman stopped short as the other lady shushed her. They didn't speak again until a lone man passed and disappeared into the back room.

"You shouldn't be so loud," the woman in purple chided. "You never know these days."

"I know, Hespa," the green one said, though with half the volume of before. "I understand why—can I help you?"

This unknown woman targeted these words at me. It was then that I realized my observation had moved from peripheral vision to near straight-out staring. I jerked back, heat flaring in my cheeks. Their eyes turned hawk-like, suspicion tainting their gazes.

"N–no ma'am," I replied. "I'm sorry, I'm just looking for a book…" My voice trailed off, and they continued to glare at me. "I guess it's not over here," I ended lamely.

"Then I suggest you keep moving," the woman in purple said and waved her hand like she was sending off a pesky beggar, though she seemed much more on edge as she did so.

I ducked my head and turned away, moving toward the staircase just as a large man descended it. He blocked my path.

"We're closing now," he said. "Are you going to buy anything?" He looked at my empty hands and answered for me. "No? Then please leave." His voice still echoed in my now-aching head as I stumbled out of the shop, cheeks burning.

I looked up to the sky to estimate how much time I had left and overshot a step on my way down. I fell forward on my chest and skidded on the stone ground. Nearby, a group of teenage boys guffawed, and I stood up, face nearly scalding. I heard something beyond their laughing. I looked down, saw my identification coin roll into one the grooves in the stone, and watched it follow the groove over to the group until it bumped into one boy's boot. I walked over to the group, but the boot's owner picked up the piece before I could. Gritting my teeth at the continuing laughter, I held my hand out.

"That's mine," I said. The boy grinned but didn't give it back.

"And?" he asked, flipping his hair out of his face. "Obviously it wasn't important enough to hold on to." The other boys cackled, and I took a step closer.

"It's mine," I repeated. "Give it back."

The boy stood his ground and turned to his friends.

"What do you think I should buy?" he asked them. "This is worth what, how much?"

"It's not mon—" I started, but he turned the piece over, and a huge grin spread across his face.

"She's an Absent!" he crowed. "Check it out!" He threw the piece to another boy and the others surrounded him.

"Give it back!" I called, cheeks flaring with embarrassment and anger. My head pounded and red flickered in the corners of my sight. People passed by, but no one stopped as the setting sun all but disappeared.

The person with the piece moved his arm to throw it back to the first boy. I lunged forward to grab it, but the intended receiver turned on his heel and pushed his arms forward toward me. A burst of wind blew me back nearly fifteen feet, knocking the breath from my chest, and by the time I looked up, he had the metal piece in his hand and a smirk on his face.

"It's...mine," I panted, one knee on the ground, the other knee raised with my hand planted on it. The boy walked forward a few feet toward me and flipped the piece in his hand.

"Yeah?" he asked, raising his eyebrows and looking down at me. "What are you going to do about it?" He laughed again, turned around, and began to walk back to the others.

My muscles tightened. The hints of red in my vision scorched across my sight, and I stood, trembling not with fear, but with anger and something more, something so much more. The injustices of the day flashed through my mind and fell into my chest like a ball of firewood. I took a deep breath, and in that moment, the ball ignited.

The red filled my vision, my feet left the ground, and with a force I didn't recognize, I roared at the thief.

"Give it back!"

He turned his head toward me and through the red filter, I didn't see but sensed his smile melt. Wind rushed around me, and I couldn't hear him as he threw the piece at me. I barely registered it bounce against my leg, and though I couldn't see him, I felt him flee—he and his friends and the other people nearby. The pain inside me rushed out and I flung out my hands, willing the rage to leave, but it didn't. The fury built, and I barely heard the screams over the howling in my ears.

Blind, nearly deaf to the world, I hardly noticed

the feeling of one figure sprinting toward me. In the midst of the raging crimson blinding me, I didn't see the person as they reached me and grabbed my arm. A second later, blackness blotted out the red, and my mind plunged into darkness.

CHAPTER THREE

When I was finally able to open my eyes, the darkness didn't dissipate. My breath caught in my throat as I stretched my hands out and felt nothing but wood forming a box around me. The box swayed back and forth, and I heard muffled voices conversing and hooves hitting the ground. Where was I? Where were we going? And what...what happened back there? I couldn't remember seeing anything after the boy walked off.

Minutes passed. Something more terrifying than my lack of memory descended on me. Fear. Crawling, scratching fear. My heart rate increased as it had in the square, and I felt around in the darkness for an escape, any escape. I felt the groove of what I hoped to be a door, but my fingers couldn't grasp the edge. Panic overcame fear and began to wreak havoc on my mind. I pounded on the door, scratched and clawed like the fear within me, but it would not give way. During that horrible episode, I discovered something foreign on my wrist. A bracelet, a bangle cold to the touch, wrapped around my wrist and hugged it tightly. Unlike the door, I felt no groove on it at all, and every attempt to remove it yielded nothing.

I sat on the ground, panting and unable to push the panic out of my mind. Some time later, the rocking stopped, and the voices rose in volume. I turned toward the door and heard chains rattling. Then the clanking stopped, the door swung open, and moonlight bled into the darkness around me.

I felt hands grab my arms and drag me out of the cart. Two darkened men, both wearing Oramus' seal in purple, pushed me forward towards a stone building. Three large words glared at me in the moonlight– "Falleon City Prison."

"You done with this then?" a voice asked from behind us. I peeked over my shoulder and saw a plainer-dressed man gripping the reins to the horse. One of the men holding me answered.

"Yes," he said. "You're done."

The man with the horse nodded and started to move away, and the men pulled me forward through the prison's door.

The first room was little more than a dim foyer, but the men turned and dragged me through another door leading to a brightly lit room. A crowded desk dominated the space, and a large, muscular man stood behind it.

"Sit," he said to me, nodding at the chair in front of the desk. The two men loosened their grip, and I did as he said, even as the fear pounding in my ears threatened to cancel out his words. As I sat down, the two stepped back, but I didn't hear the door open again. The man in front of me peered over my head.

"You can leave now," he said. The men didn't

move.

"We were told to remain with the prisoner until otherwise instructed by our superior," one said. The man before me scowled, but he didn't respond. Instead, he spread his arms out on the edge of the desk and leaned toward me.

"Can you talk?" he asked. I almost nodded but caught myself at the last moment.

"Y–yes."

"Good," he said. "I am Stone, captain of Falleon City's police force. You are under arrest for disturbing the peace in the Andor sector of Falleon City. Anything you say will be regarded as truth. If found otherwise, severe punishment will result."

I nodded mutely at the warning, but my mind raced in anticipation of the questions I knew I wouldn't be able to answer. Stone sat down, and I opened my mouth to tell him this lack of knowledge, but he cut me off.

"Name?" he asked, dipping a quill into an inkpot.

"Pasin," I replied. He wrote down my name and looked up. A couple of seconds passed before he raised his eyebrows and spoke again.

"Full name," he said. He looked straight at me, and I couldn't help but look away from his stare.

"Pasin," I repeated. A few more seconds elapsed without him moving his body or gaze, and I continued.

"It's just Pasin," I said, each word spilling out faster than the last. "I don't have an Element."

I looked back into his eyes, but I found no understanding there. If anything, he seemed irritated.

"All right, Pasin," he said, overemphasizing my name. The old spark of anger at hearing my first name rose in my chest, but it fell at once. "How old are you?" he asked. I took a steadying breath.

"Sixteen."

Stone snorted at this and put down his quill.

"After reading the report, do you really expect me to believe," he asked, elbows on the table and leaning forward again, "that you are of age and still an Absent?" I was about to answer when he continued, "Where's your identification then? That should clear this up."

"I don't have it!" I answered, voice rising. "I don't know where it is. I don't know what happened—" As I spoke, one of the men behind me let out a hushed expletive and stepped forward.

"Sir, this was found at the scene," he said. He extended his hand, and I watched my identification coin pass from one to the other. Stone raised an eyebrow and examined the piece. A couple of moments later, he put it down.

"That would have been nice to have to start with," he said, eyeing the men over my shoulder, but they didn't reply. He grumbled and looked at me again.

"Why don't you have your power level listed?" he asked. I looked at the empty side of the coin, a little scratched and bent from earlier, but still without the marks he asked for.

"My level test is Saturday," I replied, "so I haven't—"

A single knock rapped against the office door, and Stone stiffened. He looked down at his papers.

"Come in," he said, still looking down. I turned my head to glance at the new visitor and my throat tightened.

The third black-clad man from the marketplace stood in the doorway, his silvery-gray version of Oramus' seal glinting in the numerous candle lights. He wore the same bored expression as before, but it was added onto with a slight pulling up of his upper lip. He took two steps and stopped at the edge of Stone's desk. He didn't look at me, but I turned my head in case his gaze did glance my way.

Stone scribbled something on the papers before looking up at the man.

"I have this under control, Corinth," he said. "You don't need to be here."

I took a sharp intake of breath after Stone said the man's first name instead of his Element. Corinth took it in stride though.

"Just like in Andor?" he asked. His fingers hung just over a foot away from my face, and I fought the urge to lean away. "I didn't see any local law enforcement during our inspection. Good thing we were there today, isn't it?"

A spot of pink appeared on Stone's cheeks, but he replied quickly enough.

"Even so, she is under my custody now."

"Yes," Corinth replied, "and I want to see how you handle it. Continue."

He crossed his arms over his chest, but he didn't move from his position. Stone's muscles tightened, but the middle-aged man did as Corinth said. He picked up his quill again and asked, "Where do you live?"

"Andor Orphanage," I replied, "on the road west from Andor."

Stone wrote this down and put the ink-covered paper aside. Corinth picked it up and began to look it over.

"Do you know why you are here?" Stone asked, picking up another paper.

"You said something about disturbing the peace," I said, and I heard Corinth snort, "but I don't remember what happened." The fear rose in my throat again.

"According to the report," Stone replied, "you injured a Gust and a Darkness and caused property damage to two of the vendors in the square."

"But how?" I asked. "I don't remember anything!" My voice rose, but Stone's expression remained unchanged.

"Oh, stop it," Corinth said idly. "I saw what you did, and I know this—" he said, holding out my identification piece, "is a lie." The fear within boiled into anger with his accusation. I turned my head to him, but he was looking at the paper again.

"It's not!" I said. "I don't have an Element!"

Corinth put the paper aside.

"Fine," he said. "Let's check."

He jerked his body to the side to lean over me and caught my gaze straight on. His eyes widened, and I couldn't look away from the muddled brown irises, neither light nor dark, neither ugly nor beautiful. My chest swelled with each breath I took, but it didn't feel like enough. I felt like a dead leaf suspended in space with neither ground nor air to support it.

Corinth blinked, and I let out a great breath as I was released. I started panting again and looked away from him, but I still saw his expression out of the corner of my eye.

"You two," he said, pointing to the men behind

me, "are excused." The men left the room, and Corinth straightened up.

"That's enough for today," he said to Stone. He barely glanced at me before continuing. "Lock her up for tonight."

"Wait, what?" I pushed back my chair and stood, but before I could take a step toward Corinth, I felt the stone floor slide over my feet as Stone moved his hands.

"Don't try that again," Stone said. He reached under his desk, grabbed a pair of handcuffs, and walked over to me.

"But I don't even know what I did!" I cried as he placed the handcuffs on me and grabbed my upper arm. He undid the stone around my feet and looked at Corinth.

"Let's go," he said.

Corinth opened the door, and Stone dragged me through it. I jerked my body around, but his grip didn't shift. We moved through the first room again but turned away from the entrance toward a larger pair of doors.

On the other side of the doors, a narrow stone corridor stretched in front of us. Lamps hung from the walls every twenty feet or so, but there were no windows to be seen except for the narrow-gated vents between each set of lamps. We walked almost a third of the way down the corridor and stopped. Stone trapped my feet again, and then turned to the blank wall. He moved his hands and feet in a sharp motion, and part of the wall split, revealing a hollow cube maybe six feet tall. Stone undid my feet and pushed me into the room. I fell to the floor and whipped my head around, but the last thing I saw as the wall

31

moved back together was Corinth's expressionless face. I gasped in a breath of air, on the verge of crying, when I heard the men's voices through the vent in the wall.

"I need you here early tomorrow, Stone," Corinth said.

"I'll be here," Stone replied, his voice trailing off like their footsteps, "but tell me, what's going on?"

"I can't tell you," Corinth answered.

"Sir, as the captain here—"

"No."

"Sir—"

"No."

"I need to know in case—"

"She was telling the truth, all right?"

The footsteps stopped, and I could barely hear Corinth's voice, but I knew it was seething. After a moment, the footsteps resumed.

"She was telling the truth," Corinth continued, and I heard the doors open, "so even she doesn't…"

The doors closed, and I sucked in air when I realized I had been holding my breath while they talked. I leaned forward and pressed my body against the stone, but I couldn't feel a consistent groove of any kind. I tried to stand up, but failed and slipped, falling on my back and hit my head against the ground.

Sprawled on the ground, my eyes adjusted to the nearly complete darkness, and the stone was everywhere–around, below, above. My foot shied away from the wall. I curled up on the ground, surrounded by the darkness, the solid walls looming above. Tears formed in the corners of my eyes from the pain, first from my head, but then my thoughts returned to whatever happened in the past few hours. The tears intensified, and in moments, I was sobbing.

My chest rose and fell against the hard, stone floor, and my previous headache came back with a fury, and yet, and yet…at some point the crying changed. Sobs softened and changed from inhalations to exhalations. The exhalations became higher and faster, and though I was still curled on the floor of a stone box, I began to laugh. Hysterics echoed in the room and shook my chest, making the handcuffs clink in unison. But even as my laughter grew louder and louder, the tears came back, and the cackles and sobs became indistinguishable as I fell into an exhausted sleep.

CHAPTER FOUR

The sound of scraping rock woke me up, and I heard Stone and Corinth's voices.

"...but for precaution?" Stone said. "Two is just—"

"It's an order from the top," Corinth grumbled. "Get up." The tip of his boot prodded my shoulder, and I tried to rise, but I couldn't stand. Stone moved forward and pulled me up, and Corinth took a step forward as well with an unamused look on his face. I saw a silver bangle spinning in his hand, just as I had seen him with one the day before. He walked behind me and snapped the bangle on my wrist. A couple of seconds passed, but nothing happened.

"What are these?" I asked, eyeing my wrist.

"It's time for your trial," Stone said without preamble, eyeing the bangles. My mind shifted to the new, startling information.

"What?" My heart raced. I could barely stand I was so cramped from the night's sleep, and my near empty stomach and full bladder didn't help matters.

Corinth let out an exasperated sigh from beside me.

"What did you expect?" he asked.

"I don't know!" I replied, voice rising. "More than a night…something…" Anything but an actual trial.

"It's happening now," Stone replied. "We are taking you to the palace now."

"The palace?" My breaths shortened as I saw where this was heading.

"Yes," Stone said. "Now follow me and—"

"But who?" I asked. "Who at the palace is judging…"

"King Oramus."

…what?

"King Oramus?" I repeated, voice even higher and heart beating even faster. "King Oramus?"

"Yes," Stone said. His fingers twitched. Corinth shifted where he stood.

"But I didn't…I don't know…don't remember…"

"Maybe he'll cut her head off to make her shut up," Corinth muttered.

"Cut my head off?" my voice squeaked.

"Quiet!" Stone spoke over us. "Both of you," he added. Next to me, Corinth straightened up and turned his head straight toward Stone.

"Watch yourself," he said quietly. An uneasy quiet, interrupted only by my panting, filled the place until Stone grunted, placed handcuffs on me, and gruffly took my arm.

We left the cell and walked to the far doors. I managed to stay silent, but my body trembled all over and my steps faltered as I thought of what was before me. As we went through the doors, Corinth put his hand on my shoulder.

"Wait," he said. Stone and I stopped, and Corinth moved around and looked at me.

"Do you need to…relieve yourself?" he asked with an expression of idle disgust clouding his face. My stomach lurched at his words.

"Yes," I said, sweat beading at my temples. Corinth grimaced, led me through a nearby door into a windowless latrine, and took the handcuffs off.

"Two minutes," he said and closed the door behind him.

I did what I needed quickly enough, but the whole time, my body kept shaking and the sweat began to pour down my face. Why Oramus? Why me? What in the world could I say to him, king of the world? I stood and almost opened the door, but I turned at the last moment just in time to vomit.

"Oh shining," Corinth's muffled voice swore through the door. Something snapped within me.

"I'm dricking terrified, all right?" I yelled through the door, voice quivering. This time Stone replied.

"Hurry up!"

I tried to clean my mouth and finally opened the door to leave. Corinth stood right on the other side, his disgust not so idle anymore. He looked me over.

"Do we really need the 'cuffs?" he asked, though I couldn't tell if he addressed me or Stone. My eyes darted to the exit door, but I knew it would be pointless to try.

"She's not going anywhere like that," Stone answered. My body, still trembling, seemed to agree with him.

"Well, put her in the back at least."

Corinth motioned for me to step forward. He moved behind me, careful not to touch me, and Stone led us outside. I paused at the sight of the morning sky, but Corinth stepped on my heel to keep me going. They loaded me into the back of an enclosed wagon, closed and chained the door, and left me, once again, in darkness.

#

The drive to the palace passed in a haze of racing thoughts, darting from questions to anger, cries to terror. I rubbed the bangles on my wrist, but each piece was smooth, though I had felt the new one wrap around my hand earlier. I scraped the tight bracelets against the sides of the vehicle, but to no effect. Smooth and neither warm nor cool, the pieces didn't change.

At some point during a crying stage, I stuffed my hands into my pockets just to further myself from the foreign objects on my wrist. Something scraped against one hand, and a tiny smile reached my face when I recognized what it was.

The ignis flower from Arina felt brittle in my hand, but it didn't crumble when I pulled it out of my pocket. Though I couldn't truly see it in the darkness, the memory of the one bright spot in the day before lit my heart for a moment. The bright spot faded as Corinth's words echoed in my head though. *Maybe he'll cut her head off...* this flower was probably the last flower I would ever touch. I held it in my hand during the rest of the ride.

As the wheels eventually slowed, I put the flower back in my pocket, and the fluctuating emotions solidified into one feeling in my chest–fear. Fear vibrated through my body and seeped into my mind when the wagon stopped, the door opened, and I was dragged back into the light.

I didn't have the chance to look around at the palace exterior before being steered to a small door in the stone wall. The men's movements were brisk and precise, and I had great difficulty keeping up without stumbling. The initial halls boasted no adornments, and we passed few people as we turned and twisted through various corridors. Of the people we did encounter, none let their eyes rise to meet Corinth's for more than a moment. At one point though, after ascending a flight of stairs, a large, glass window revealed a sight beyond anything I had seen before.

A magnificent hall, stretching far and branching off into countless exits, was spread beneath us. A thousand colors crawled in the hall, the silks and velvets of people hurrying to who-knows-where. An amazing forest scene covered the walls with fantastic creatures peeking from behind trees, and a mirror stood in every crevice in the walls, magnifying the depth of the painted trees down the hall before it curved out of sight.

As Stone and Corinth rushed me forward, my mind lingered on the beauty I had just seen and the stark difference it held against my normal life.

The bare hallway ended, and we went through another door, leading into a giant foyer of sorts. Keeping up with the previous splendor of the forest hall, this room seemed to be as tall as the three-story orphanage in Andor. Strong white marble laced with veins of gold made the floor and trailed up the walls. We entered the room from a side door, and as we walked around, the scene unfolded.

A grand staircase swept up from the floor and led

to a landing. From the landing, two staircases, one left, one right, led to higher levels above. Centered between these two staircases was a set of double doors reaching halfway up the wall. The dark wood was intricately carved with images of mythical creatures and regular ones. Dragons, peacocks, griffins, and others besides crawled across the wooden piece. The rest of the room with its gold statues and marble columns all complemented the centerpiece.

No one stood in the room except for our threesome and two men standing on either side of the massive doors, wearing the black tunics laced with Oramus' purple seal. Noises could be heard coming from behind us—probably from the forest hallway; at least seven doors lined the wall opposite the door wall.

Stone's and Corinth's strong, brisk steps echoed as we walked across the intimidating empty floor space, but my steps faltered. My feet barely seemed to support me. Only one person could be on the other side of that door. The guards on either side of it nodded at the men flanking me and swung the doors open.

My jaw dropped. The throne room was an extension to what I had already seen but with a majesty surpassing everything before. A vast forest mural covered the walls, dotted with hundreds of platforms laden with unlit candles. On the marble floor, inlaid peacocks with amethyst, gold, and emerald wings smiled regally from beneath my feet. Rays of light shone through the windows ringing the tops of the walls. Every item in the room, every leaf, peacock, person, faced the same direction, where a man sat and stared back.

Before I could notice much else, a hand slammed me down so my knees hit the floor and my head bent forward, looking directly into a peacock's cold sapphire eye. A seething, whispered curse came from my left, and I realized my mistake. Forgetting to bow before the king…despite the pain in my knees, I silently thanked Stone for correcting me.

"Stand," a distant voice said, and we obeyed. I lifted my eyes and looked directly at the ruler of the world.

Compared to the brightness of the room, King Oramus looked dark as the night sky. Deep purple and black clothes trimmed with pallid gold covered his long frame, and his pale skin contrasted them like the moon behind clouds. His black hair seemed too long; in fact, most of his face seemed a little too long, from his nose to his chin. Even his mouth was elongated, a straight line across his face. Oramus sat on the throne on a platform off the ground, both elbows on the throne's arms, holding his head in place with a single finger. He looked straight back at me.

"Tell me your name," he said. It was clearly an order and not one to be defied. I opened my mouth, but nothing came out at first. A tickle of anxiety shivered up my spine.

"P–Pasin," I finally choked out.

"Pasin," he repeated back at me. I waited for the inevitable question of my Element, and my stomach clenched and quivered in anticipation. His stillness seemed to emphasize my shaking.

"Just Pasin, yes?" he continued. I nodded. He finally moved, though only his hand. He waved it in my direction and spoke to Corinth on my right.

"And you're sure about this?" Oramus asked. Corinth nodded with confidence.

"She's telling the truth, Your Majesty."

Despite the circumstances, a flash of irritation shot through me. What was that supposed to mean anyway? Of course I was telling the truth; I didn't have anything else to say. I snorted under my breath, and Stone jabbed me in the side, but neither Oramus nor Corinth reacted.

The sheer absurdity of the situation hit me. There I was, standing in front of the most important man in the world, and he was talking about me. Even if I didn't understand whatever he was talking about, the whole situation struck me as ridiculous, even funny. A smile spread across my face, and a titter escaped my lips before I could think.

Stone moved to prod me again, but I wouldn't have any of that. I stepped away from him, toward the king, and the dynamic of the room immediately changed. Corinth lunged forward to grab me, but I sidestepped his arms and laughed outright at the look on his face. The ground beneath me moved, but I jumped aside before Stone could trap my feet again. I leapt away again and again, and with each spring, my laughter grew louder.

In those fleeting flashes of movement, I felt free. The shouts couldn't stop the pure exhilaration racing through my limbs as I bounded from peacock to peacock. No concern for the future bloodied the moment. I spun and danced while I could, tears blurring the room around me into nothing more than a riot of color. I cried from laughter at the ludicrous situation and from a rising panic, because I knew I

41

had made a terrible mistake.

I stepped again, and the floor swelled, covering my foot. I fell hard on my back, and three more ground swells covered my hands and other foot. Unable to move, I stared up through tear-blurred eyes to the top of the throne platform I lay at the foot of. Oramus stood at the top of the platform, one hand at his belt and a grimace on his face. Even through my tears, I could see the brightness of his blue eyes. He glared at me, then looked up.

"What was that?" Oramus shouted at the two men rushing to where I lay. Stone's face was red, but Corinth was livid. He stood by my head, one foot on top of the stone encasing my hand, one hand rubbing the end of his sleeve.

"Your Highness," Stone sputtered, dropping into a kneel, "with this floor I'm not—"

"No excuses!" Oramus said, his words echoing in the empty space. He glowered down at Stone and then glanced over at me. I averted my gaze immediately. Whatever remaining internal laughter died, and fear came back to the forefront. Oramus didn't move for a couple of seconds, and when he spoke, his voice was lower, quieter, darker.

"If you are unable to perform what is required of you—" Oramus began, but an urgent rapping on the distant door stopped him. I peeked up and saw Oramus looking straight forward toward the noise. His eyebrows gathered together and without looking away, he said, "Get the door, Stone."

The man hurried to comply, leaving me with Corinth. Corinth didn't look at me; he kept his gaze on Oramus. I turned my head, saw Stone open the door, and watched a teenage girl enter and collapse into a bow. Oramus' mouth twitched, but otherwise, his face didn't change.

"Yes, come," he said, and in one fluid motion, the girl stood, strode across the room, and climbed the steps of the throne platform to Oramus' side. She had to stand on her toes to speak into Oramus' ear in tones too hushed for me to hear. After a couple of seconds, she came down on her heels and waited. Oramus' gaze flicked my way again. Seconds passed agonizingly slowly, but finally, he nodded.

The girl bowed again and walked down the steps to my side.

"Release her," Oramus said. Stone hesitated, but then moved his hands and the ground shifted away from my hands and feet.

"Come with me," the girl whispered to me. She alone helped me up; Stone stood nearby, face still red, and Corinth remained perfectly still next to me, a sneer marring his face.

"Come on," she said urgently, and she grabbed my hand and led me back across the room, past Corinth and Stone to the door.

As she opened the door, I chanced one last glance. Oramus stared back, a fist covering his mouth, and his gaze didn't waver as the door closed between us.

CHAPTER FIVE

We turned left outside the throne room and ascended the stairs. After another left turn, the girl stopped and looked at me closely.

"Are you all right?" she asked. She peered into my eyes almost suspiciously, her own pear-colored eyes partially hidden by her brown hair.

"I think so," I replied. My mind couldn't quite grasp what had happened, but at the same time, I didn't want to question it. I was just happy to be out of the throne room. She leaned forward and squinted at me, and I didn't know where to look.

"What?" I asked. After a moment, she relaxed.

"Never mind," she said, shaking her head. "Let's go."

She grabbed my hand again and led through the hallways. Her frizzy straight hair, pulled into a loose ponytail, stretched halfway down her back, and her skin reminded me of a light brown fallen leaf. Even though she seemed younger than me, she walked with an enviable purposefulness, though one without the authoritarian overtones of Corinth and Stone.

She stopped in front of a dark, wooden door similar to the others that lined the walls and let go of my hand. As she fished a key out of her pocket, I noted her garb. She wore a tunic and pants like the guards, even though the women I saw in the forest hallway had all worn dresses. What caught my eye, though, was the sword hanging from her belt.

She unlocked the door, opened it, and entered.

"Come in," she said with a smile, waving her hand toward the room. I did, and she closed the door behind me.

The room had the same items as my room back at the orphanage, but there was no similarity in quality. I gazed longingly at the plush, pillow-laden bed, and my body ached remembering the previous night. Two windows illuminated the rest of the room, and dust motes danced in the beams of light. The girl sat at the desk chair and looked at me.

"Sit down," she said, but her tone implied it wasn't an order. I sat on the edge of the bed and closed my eyes for a moment as some of the past twenty-four hours' stress lifted. When I opened my eyes again, the girl was observing me, her face serious again.

"Are you sure you're all right?" she asked. I thought about it for a second.

"Not entirely," I answered, "but I am a lot better than before." I laughed, again at the absurdity of what happened. She smiled as I laughed.

"I'm Spark," she said, "and I want to tell you some stuff before Pearl comes, because Pearl's not really one for questions if you know what I mean."

I nodded, partly out of ignorance of who Pearl

was and partly because I was just appreciative that someone proactively offered information. She continued.

"Actually, let's start there." Spark moved forward to the edge of the seat as she spoke. "Do not ask questions. I mean, I don't mind if you ask me, but others will. It's a fast way to get into trouble. As a lady of the court, asking questions is not your place." Any little movement of mine stopped. "Now, it doesn't matter if it's something minor, but beyond that, no," she finished. My mind tried to process the implications of what she said.

"But I can ask you questions?" I asked. Spark nodded.

"Yeah," she replied, "but I might not be able to answer them." I pushed forward anyway.

"Did you just say I'm a 'lady of the court'?" I asked. The phrase felt odd on my tongue.

"Yes, I did," she replied, her lips still turned up at the corners.

"But what does that mean?" I continued. Spark pulled her legs up from the floor to sit cross-legged on the chair.

"It means that you are going to live at the palace, partake in activities with the other ladies and gentlemen, and be a part of the general 'court.' That means dinners, outings, a bunch of stuff." She grinned. "You'll find out more about that with Pearl."

The inevitable follow-up question sprang to my lips.

"Why? Why am I a lady of the court?" I asked. It didn't make sense, though neither did most of the recent occurrences in my life. Spark's grin didn't disappear, but it did fade.

"Now I can't answer that," she said, slouching a bit. "I can't answer the why questions. Even if I knew the answer, there are some things I can't talk about." I started twirling a strand of hair in my hand and tried to hide my disappointment.

"I wouldn't tell anybody," I finally said, but Spark shook her head.

"It's not that, it's just...well, that's one of my points, so let's get started with that." She straightened up and held out her hand.

"One," she said, lifting her index finger. "Do not cross Corinth. He is the head of security at the palace, and as you've probably experienced, he can read minds." I thought back to the prior night and the weightlessness I felt when he looked into my eyes with his own muddled irises.

"That's why I can't share my theories," she continued. "Just in case. And before you ask, no, I have no idea how he's able to do that." She shook her head. "Any questions about that?"

"Yeah," I answered. "What's his Element then?" He clearly wasn't an Absent like me.

"No one knows," Spark said. "I wish I did. He's got something, but he just goes by his first name, like you or King Oramus." So Corinth was kind of like me without an official Element. Oramus was called by his first name because of the tradition of retiring rulers' names, so I didn't think it counted.

"Ready for the second one?" Spark asked. I nodded. She raised her middle finger alongside the index finger.

"Really this should be the first, but...two, do not cross King Oramus." She leaned forward, opened her mouth, but closed it again before speaking. After a moment, she continued in a steady, measured tone.

"Obviously," she said, "as king, he has complete authority and can do as he likes, which is his…right." Even as she said the words, her mouth was a straight, tight line, her earlier playfulness gone. "So whatever happened in the throne room, I suggest you don't do that again. As a Void, he has a wide range of abilities that would make it unwise to get on his bad side." I almost asked her what those abilities were, but I had a feeling she wouldn't be able to tell me.

"Third," Spark said, raising her pinky finger. "Don't cross Pearl. She is head of the ladies of the court and surrogate queen until King Oramus marries. She has a lot of influence on the court, so once again, it would be a bad idea to get on her bad side." The seriousness on Spark's face evaporated as she continued, "Pff, as if she has a good side." She chuckled and I joined in, happy to see her smile again. "Just don't become her enemy," she added.

"Any other questions?" she asked. Out of the dozens floating around in my mind, how could I pick? Well, taking out the "why" questions cut the number down, and I settled on one.

"Can you tell me what these are?" I asked, holding up my hand to show her the silvery bangles on my wrist. Spark leaned forward and seemed to chew on the inside of her cheek, but she shook her head.

"No I can't," she said. I lowered my hand and looked away, trying to hide my disappointment.

"Also," Spark continued, "even though what we are doing is not forbidden…" She said the last word gingerly. "…It would be best not to talk about it outside this room. All right?" As I looked at her face,

I saw an odd mixture of anxiety and hope.

"All right," I agreed. I opened my mouth to thank her for the information when my stomach decided to speak up instead. A rumbling growl broke the silence, and I clasped my hand to my mouth in embarrassment. Spark's head tilted toward the noise.

"How long has it been since you ate?" she asked. If it was currently the time I thought it was, then...

"Seventeen hours?" I answered. "Maybe."

"Wow. No wonder you're hungry." Spark glanced at the door. "Pearl should be here soon, and I'm guessing she'll bring food. If you need to," she continued, pointing to a door in the wall, "there's a washroom in there. Also, if you have anything with you that you'd like to keep, I suggest you stash it somewhere, so it doesn't get lost or taken."

I entered the washroom, washed my face, readjusted my bun, and otherwise tried to look somewhat better. I observed myself in the mirror. I saw no change except for the background behind me, but so much was different, nonetheless. Amazing what could happen between mirror visits. Before leaving the room, I extracted the ignis flower from my pocket and placed it on the counter. Besides my clothes, it was all I had left of the past. I had no idea where my identification piece went, but honestly, I didn't care. I preferred the faded red flower to the shiny metal coin.

Spark was nibbling on her fingernails when I reentered the room, but she stopped once she saw me.

"We only have a little bit left before Pearl gets here, and I need to tell you one more thing." I nodded and Spark continued, "I know it's confusing and stuff, how you got here, what you're doing here, but…you're just here for now. I think it's best to just accept it and keep going, you know?" She looked me in the eyes, anxiety showing up on her expression once more, and I nodded again. Even if nothing about the situation made sense, it could have been a lot worse. I was still alive. I wasn't in prison. I didn't have to see the matrons or Slate. At the current moment, it seemed like things were looking up for me, though I had no idea where this "up" would take me.

"I hope everything works out for you Pasin," Spark added. She seemed a little awkward, as if there was more she wanted to say but couldn't.

"You too," I replied, not sure what else to say. I did venture a bit more though.

"I'll be able to see you again, right?"

Her smile broadened and she replied, "Yes, I think we can do tha—"

A knock on the door silenced Spark, and my nerves returned in expectation of whatever stood on the other side.

CHAPTER SIX

A woman advanced through the door followed by another younger woman carrying a tray covered in food. The sight of food made my tongue salivate. Oh, and the smell? My nose basked in the scent of chicken, basil, and freshly baked bread.

I tore my gaze away from the food to the new people. The first woman stood strong and rigid. Her short, dark gray hair framed her face in a stately fashion, and her dress was also a deep gray, firm in its own way. Her face showed the front line of attacking wrinkles, not too many but promising more. All in all, her appearance strongly reminded me of a tooth. Not a sharp one necessarily, but pointed, nonetheless.

The other female was a short, nondescript girl. Her brown hair hung in a short bob; the bangs nearly covered her dull eyes. She wore a pale green dress, which even in its plainness made my clothes look like trash. Her face revealed nothing about her, though that might have only been in comparison to the intense woman watching me from her right.

The stern, gray one spoke.

"You may leave now Spark."

"Yes, ma'am." Spark gave a short bow and left.

Pearl's steely gaze looked me over and made me shiver. Her demeanor suggested urgency, but her eyes told me it was on her terms.

Finally, she spoke to me.

"Pasin, correct?"

I nodded mutely.

"I am Pearl. I am in charge of the ladies of the court. Welcome to the palace."

Was I really welcome? I wasn't quite sure about that.

"This is Grass," Pearl said, gesturing toward the other girl. The girl curtsied, still with the tray in her hand. "She will be your servant. Now eat."

Her words flew swiftly. I gladly accepted the tray and tried to eat as quietly as possible without seeming completely unmannered. I bit my tongue several times (mostly metaphorically) and managed not to ask any questions.

While I ate, Pearl sent Grass away. When she returned, she carried a dress that I changed into. It was a soft purple velvet, smooth to the touch. The shoes were a soft leather too.

"Now it is time for you to be initiated," Pearl said. "Follow me."

With trepidation, I followed her out the door and back through the maze of hallways. I tried to focus on remembering the path we took, but my mind kept wandering back to wondering what it meant to be "initiated."

There were more people about in the hallways this time. They quickly gave way to Pearl, and Grass and I followed in her wake. It was terribly exciting when we walked through the forest hall I had seen earlier. The colors were so much brighter and bolder than I had remembered. The mirrors seemed to extend it into forever.

The next room we entered was entirely white, hard and sterile. I could almost feel every imperfection of my own standing out against the whiteness. We went through one more door, and my discomfort grew.

Assembled before me on ten layers of seats sat a multitude of women. They were so colorful, like a collection of flowers or gems or…bugs. Shiny bugs. They sat amphitheater-style, each row higher than the last. Five women occupied each row and with ten rows that was fifty people. My skin itched at the thought of a hundred eyes' gazes crawling over me.

Grass left us to stand against the wall behind us with a group of other plainer-clad people. Servants, I guessed. The thought of being somewhere with servants, let alone having a servant, was vaguely mind-blowing. Pearl led me to the center of the room and left me there as she walked forward to address the crowd.

"Ladies of the court. You have been brought here today to induct a new lady into our midst. It is up to us to make her fit for such a position."

If any of those hundred eyes had been focused on Pearl, they adjusted their focus on to me. I felt as if I was being visually picked apart, and I was sure that the verbal would come soon enough.

"This is Pasin," Pearl said, "And she will be referred to as such." Instantly, whispers rippled through the women.

Pearl ascended the stairs and took a seat on the tenth row.

"Begin."

The other four women from the tenth row descended and circled around me, still standing. No one touched me, but their gazes were like little rays of piercing light, uncomfortably hot. After a few minutes, they all returned to their seats, and the next two rows came down. The same procedure occurred twice more, next three rows then four. So many eyes. Watching. Judging, I was sure.

Soon, but not soon enough, it was over.

"Now that we have all had a chance to take stock of the girl," Pearl called out from her seat, "does anyone have any suggestions?"

"Well..." One voice from the crowd drew out one syllable just long enough to let everyone turn around and look up at the speaker. The voice was bored, haughty, and had the air of someone who thought the room was full of idiots. The owner was a girl in the ninth row from the bottom. She had porcelain skin, bloody lips, and deep green eyes. Her brown hair rested in waves, framing her face. Her fingers were linked and rested lightly on her crossed legs that showed under her short green dress.

"Yes, Emerald?" Pearl's tone implied that this sort of behavior was usual for the ninth-row female.

"I wasn't finished." Emerald looked at Pearl with annoyance before inspecting her nails. "I think that this Abse...Pasin." Emerald smirked at me wickedly, "If she wants even the slightest chance of fitting in, then she must do something about those heinous red splotches on her face." Another wicked smile and another nail inspection.

"Better than a heart-shaped hole in my chest," I muttered. No one in the stands could hear me, because Pearl admonished Emerald in the same moment I had insulted her. However, I did hear a few snickers from the servants behind me. I bit my lower lip, trying valiantly not to grin. As I looked at the other women in the room though, I could tell from their faces that many agreed with Emerald.

A petite woman dressed in light brown in the seventh row raised a hand. Pearl nodded and the lady spoke.

"I'm not trying to be rude by asking this," she started. Her voice was soft but held a hint of power behind it, like a gentle push. "But what color is Pasin going to wear?"

I took a second look around the room. Emerald was wearing deep green; Pearl was wearing gray...I felt silly for not making the connection sooner.

"Maybe she shouldn't wear anything since she's naked of a classification." Emerald's voice jumped to answer the question. Why was she doing this? Blood rushed to my face. Pearl glared coldly at Emerald and answered the other lady's question.

"Pasin will wear black, purple, and green. If there is no natural color choice, then the royal colors will be used. Good question, Topaz." Pearl nodded her head slightly and Topaz nodded back.

In the third row, a younger lady wearing a pale red dress raised her hand. Pearl pointed, "Yes Ruby?"

"What level is she starting at?"

I didn't know what to think of that question; I had no idea what she was talking about.

Pearl's jaw tightened a bit, and she answered, "That is still to be decided." A few whispers danced on the still air before dying under Pearl's gaze.

After that, I lost track of the women asking questions. It was fascinating to see the array of Elements in front of me. There was Gold, Turquoise, Mist, Vine, Breeze, and even a Frost. However, most of the ladies' Elements were gemstones or precious metals.

I really tried not to listen to what was being said. Most of it was about my appearance, and though I knew I didn't look great, my ego still took a big hit. It didn't help that they debated each subject at length. Several minutes were spent squabbling over whether or not to shorten my hair. It was a relief when they decided to leave my hair's length as is.

Quite a while later, the group finally finished discussing all the nuances of my appearance. My feet were killing me. Luckily, Pearl was wrapping it up.

"Thank you very much for your time and input ladies. You may leave now." Pearl herself stood up and started descending the stairs.

Yes, I must have looked stupid just standing there, not knowing what to do. Pearl passed me without a second look and the other ladies likewise hurried by. After the room was nearly empty, Grass walked up to me.

"Please follow me, Miss."

And I did. It's not like I had much of a choice.

#

The passageways felt endless. Thank goodness Grass knew how to navigate them. It made me wonder how long it would take me to figure them out.

The next few hours were full of different methods of hygiene that I will not go into. The bath was nice, yes, but I wasn't too fond of the hair plucking.

After that ordeal, I was brought into yet another room. It had the usual palace opulence, but one wall was entirely covered in mirrors, reflecting every imperfection of mine I could ever imagine. Racks of clothes, mostly dresses, filled most of the room, and in the far back, I saw a mess of fabric and ribbon. From the mess, a disheveled woman emerged with a large, warming smile on her face. Her dark skin seemed the perfect complement to her impeccably messy and shockingly large yet stylish hair. She shook my hand and started talking immediately.

"Hello! I am Vine and this is my wonderful realm of clothes-making!" She clapped her hands with excitement, and her golden bracelets clanked. They were different than the ones around my wrist, first in color, but more importantly, they looked wide enough that she could slip them on and off. Lucky.

"Okay, so you're Pasin, and you're going to be wearing purple, black, and green, right?" I nodded. "Can I get some measurements from you?"

Before letting me reply, Vine whipped out a notebook. At her request, I stated my height and mumbled my weight.

"Age?" Vine asked.

"Sixteen years," I said. "And one day," I added.

"Really? Happy belated birthday." Vine gestured with her pencil-holding hand to a folding screen. "I need to take some measurements; please come this way."

She gave me a thin shift to change into, just a little white thing with really thin straps.

"Ready?" she asked from the other side of the divider.

"Yes," I replied. She walked around the screen, paused once she saw me, and then pulled out her tape measure. As she measured the width of my shoulders, she lightly touched a spot between my neck and left shoulder.

"What happened here?" she asked. I knew what mark she talked about without looking.

"I got burned when I was younger," I answered but didn't elaborate with her. When I was eight, Hex Blaze got mad at me when I didn't believe that he was distantly related to King Dante the Victor. He told the teacher he only meant to singe my hair, but I didn't believe him.

"Don't you worry, I'll make sure it's covered." Vine gave me a reassuring smile and got to work.

She took my measurements and then sent me to another woman, a quiet Leaf who didn't try to make conversation as she worked on my hair, but that was fine with me. When she finished, my hair did look a lot better, but the pile of trimmings in the trash was larger than I expected.

As Grass led me out, Vine let out a cheerful assurance that the dress would be magnificent, and that the sheer beauty of it would leave me speechless. If it was anything like the ones I had seen on the other girls, then I had no doubt. For the moment, I was still garbed in the velvet dress from earlier.

When Grass and I traversed the forest hallway again I felt a twinge of recognition. As we walked the hallway leading to my room, I felt as if I might know the way. Maybe I could get used to this. Maybe.

So I sat on my bed, thinking. Grass had gone to

the kitchen to get dinner for me. She was serving me because that's what she was supposed to do. Because somehow, I went from convict in the morning to lady of the court at night. Quite remarkable. No, that was not even close to the storm of emotions I felt. Excitement, confusion…terror. But then more excitement and maybe even a dash of hope for a better tomorrow. It was insanely inconceivable, and yet, there I was, sitting on a bed in the imperial palace and smiling like an idiot as the reality finally sank in.

So yes, I spent the next five to ten minutes in a sort of happy daze. It might have been odd, but it was one of the best happy dazes in my life.

I enjoyed the soup Grass brought, and we ate mostly in silence. I tried to engage in light conversation, but Grass' replies were guarded. When I finished, I looked at the clock. Six-thirty.

"Grass?"

"Yes, ma'am?"

"Um…you can leave for the night." I wasn't sure if that was the right way to handle the situation, but Grass bowed her head.

"Yes, ma'am," she repeated. She curtsied, took the dirty dishes, and left. For the first time since the prison, I was alone.

I looked around the room again, and the desk drew my attention immediately. I moved toward it, then stopped as another thought crossed my mind. I went into the washroom, picked up the ignis flower, and then sat at the desk. I placed the flower inside one of the drawers and picked up a pencil and some paper.

For the next two hours, I worked on rewriting the story the matrons burned. Despite the betrayal I still felt over the loss, the scratching of pencil on paper soothed me, and as the familiar characters took shape on paper, I smiled.

At some point, the sunlight outside faded. I put the papers back in the drawer and stood up. Even though exhaustion dragged at my eyelids and I knew it was pointless, I stood still, took a deep breath, and pushed out with my hand as I had seen the Gust do, as I had seen Blazes do. Nothing happened. I tried again, harder, just in case, but still nothing.

"Don't be silly," I muttered.

I changed into a nightgown, blew out the candles, and got into bed. In the darkness, under the blankets, I curled into a ball and let sleep take me.

CHAPTER SEVEN

The morning light shone softly through my eyelids, and smooth sheets and blankets cradled my body. Even before opening my eyes, I smiled, because I realized that the past two days were not a dream. I was not in prison and I was not in Andor anymore. When I opened my eyes to fully realize this new reality, the first thing I noticed was a person sitting at my desk chair.

"Oh good, you're awake." Spark stood up and stretched.

Uhhh...

"So, how did your first day go?"

Uhhh...

"Fine, I guess." The feeling of awkwardness lightened a bit as I rubbed my bleary eyes. When I looked back up, Spark had a coy smile on her face.

"You've got a bit of drool right about here," she said and gestured. She rubbed her left lower chin, and I rubbed my right lower chin.

"No, other side."

What?

"Well that's just odd." I finally located the spittle. Yuck.

Despite mannerism differences, Spark's relaxed demeanor was refreshing compared to the ramrod behaviors of others.

She shrugged. "I'm not a mirror you know. If I point to my left, I mean your left too."

"Well fine." I lay back on the cushions but grinned nonetheless. I saw Spark roll her eyes but smile back. It was nice.

Wait a second...

"Why are you here again?"

Spark seemed somewhat abashed. "Well, I don't have to be here if you don't want me to—"

"No, no, that's not what I meant." I looked around for a clock. Seven thirty. Ten hours of sleep. Wow. Must have been pretty sleepy. Though a lot did happen the day before.

I turned back to Spark. "How long have you been in here?"

She too glanced at the clock. "Oh, about half an hour or so."

Wow.

"Sounds boring."

She sat back down and examined her fingernails. "No, not really. It's relaxing actually. First morning in a while that I haven't had to wake up at five to train."

"What do you mean 'train'?" I asked.

Spark looked up from her nails.

"I'm one of the weapons trainers, and we have early practices," she answered nonchalantly. Well, that explained the sword.

"Wow, that's really cool," I said. I didn't really

know how to answer, "But the early practice sounds terrible."

Spark nodded. "Yes, yes it is. I'm happy it's my day off."

I yawned and rubbed my eyes again.

"It's still kind of early though, isn't it?" I asked.

Spark glanced out the window.

"If it's light outside, I don't think so." She stood once more to stretch, this time the other way. "Anyway, I wanted to make sure I could talk to you this morning before the day really starts."

Spark sat down, crossed her legs, then continued, "So, how was your first day? Besides 'Fine'."

I considered her question. How could I fully communicate how I felt about it?

"It was exciting," I said. Spark frowned.

"Anything else?" she asked. Now it was my turn to cop a coy smile.

"It was absolutely indescribable." She raised her eyebrows.

"That's cheating." Her eyes narrowed, which made a hilarious combination with the raised eyebrows. "And you know it."

A beat passed, and then I replied.

"I guess you'll have to...fine me."

Spark stared at me, and I burst out laughing, falling back onto my bed. After a moment, she smiled too, though hers was more bemused than anything.

"I think you need more sleep after all.".

As I pulled myself back up, she continued, "No, I'm just here for some moral support if you need it. My first day was terrifying so I thought I'd drop by in case you needed a jump-start, I guess."

"Was yours really that bad?"

She laughed. "I got so lost in here...I was twenty minutes late for training."

"Oh. For me, it feels like I've been led around on an invisible chain," I said. Neither of us said anything for a moment.

My question broke the silence. "Spark, how long have you been here?"

"Let's see," she started. "I'm fifteen so...about four and a half years." I sat up again.

"You've been doing sword stuff since you were eleven?"

"No. I was a servant for six months, but my employer passed away, so I left the palace. I picked up a sword at some point and something clicked, I guess. I came back and offered my services when King Oramus came to power." At no point did Spark mention her parents. Despite my curiosity, I didn't bring it up, just as I wouldn't want someone to ask me about my parents.

"Elves are traditionally good with swordplay and weapons in general," Spark continued. "I guess that helps."

"Wait." I shook my head. "You're an elf?" Spark grinned and shook her head.

"No, I'm not an elf," she answered. "But I am half-elf." She tucked her hair behind her ear, exposing its pointed tip.

"Whoa, that's awesome!"

"Thanks," she said and replaced her hair over her ear. "I don't normally show or tell people." She shrugged. "Just in case it upsets them, or something."

I shook my head, and she twisted around to look at the clock.

"Now servants usually come around eight thirty,

so we still have some time. Can you tell me more about your day yesterday?"

I told her the big picture of what happened and filled in the details where I remembered.

"Oh yeah," I said, "and while that was happening, and I felt embarrassed enough already, some girl kept making snide comments about my face. Her Element was Emerald, I think."

"Which level?" Spark asked. What was this level thing people kept mentioning?

"I don't know?" I replied.

"What row was she on?"

"One from the top," I said. Spark nodded knowingly.

"Yeah, that Emerald is like that. Her dad is governor of Mint Leaf Bay, I think." Spark picked at a nail for a moment and continued. "Most of the ladies here are from noble families or something similar, though some got in by pure looks." I didn't respond, because it brought up the nagging question–why was I there? I didn't come from a noble family, and Emerald made it clear that I didn't have the superior looks required for court life.

"What about you?" I asked. I wasn't entirely sure if she would answer, but I could try. "Where are you from?"

"That," she answered, "will have to wait for some other day." I looked at the clock. It was almost eight fifteen. Pont.

As she started to rise from the chair, I swiftly blurted out "Thanks for coming. I really appreciate it."

She smiled. "You're welcome. Good luck with today."

"What's going to happen?" I asked eagerly. Her smile turned mischievous.

"You'll find out." That smile was infuriating.

"Yeah, that's helpful," I replied, rolling my eyes. "Thanks."

"See you later!" She waved goodbye with a ridiculous smile and departed.

#

When Grass came in ten minutes later, she brought breakfast and another dress, a dark green silk one with long sleeves that clung to my arms. As I ate, Grass stood silently and unobtrusively nearby. She didn't fidget or anything; she just stood like a polite statue. Despite her manners, her silent presence made me uncomfortable. When I finished breakfast, she spoke again.

"I have been informed that you are to meet your tutor now. If you are ready, please follow me." Grass dipped her head and moved towards the door. I, of course, followed.

We walked through the hallways and down a small flight of stairs into the central hall. As quickly as we entered the hall, however, we ascended the stairs on the other side of the throne room door. Unlike the day before, other people moved through the central hall as well. It might have been my imagination, but I thought I felt the lingering of gazes on me. I didn't look at anyone; I just followed Grass to the western wing.

Darker woods decorated this part of the palace, but I didn't get the chance to fully take in the differences before Grass opened a narrow set of double doors and gestured for me to enter. I went in and almost gasped at what I saw.

The room was a library. Not a second-rate school collection of books or a single bookcase at the orphanage, but a beautiful, well-stocked library. Hundreds, maybe thousands of books lined the ornate bookshelves, their spines beckoning me to come and take a look at the knowledge held within. Or that's what it felt like, at least.

A little distance from the entrance, a man with iron gray hair sat stiffly in front of a table covered neatly in books and paper. His crossed hands sat on the table without moving. As we came closer, I noticed his eyes were closed.

When we were within five feet of the table, the man spoke.

"Thank you, Grass. You may leave now."

Even though the man could not have seen it, Grass gave him a curtsy and then did the same to me before leaving. I turned back to the man as he spoke to me with his eyes still shut.

"I am Water." Water spoke with more tenor than bass, but his speech was deliberate and precise. His skin looked slightly worn and a few wrinkles darted around his eyes, but all in all, he gave a presence of silent authority and vitality.

"Please sit down across from me and do not speak." I obeyed as quietly as possible and he continued, "As you can see, there is a small stack of papers along with a supply of writing utensils. That stack of papers is a small examination of your knowledge in areas ranging from mathematics to Elemental knowledge." I found it difficult to not laugh, because Water's face seemed so serious and moved so expressively with his words, all while his eyes remained shut. I knew the danger of laughter though, and managed to keep it in.

Water continued still, "You will have one hour to complete the test. If you have finished before time is up, tap your inkwell on the table three times. The hourglass behind me will track the progress of time. For the duration of the test, neither of us will talk. If you understand these instructions and are ready to begin, please tap the inkwell twice against the table."

Yes, I understood the instructions, but not the instructor. Nevertheless, I tapped the table with the inkwell twice and looked at the paper expectantly. It might sound silly, but I was excited. Excited to prove myself finally, and maybe to be judged on ability instead of inability.

"When I turn over the hourglass, you may begin." Water swiveled around in his seat and set the hourglass over with a definitive thud. Smiling in anticipation, I flipped over the packet and started reading.

Some sections were hard. Some were really easy. I was pretty sure I aced the history section (at least up through Dante the Victor). Mathematics was okay, but the Elemental stuff...I hardly knew anything. How was I supposed to know the temperature at which Ices lose their ability to freeze liquid? However, I did know the one question about Absents. Huzzah.

My hand ached terribly by the time I completed the test, but I felt confident in what I did. I set the quill down and looked at the hourglass. About seventy percent of the sand was gone. Pleased, I tapped the inkwell three times.

Immediately, Water tapped his fingers on the desk

and asked for the test. I obliged and leaned back in my chair. Something told me that one, I shouldn't talk, and two, this was going to be a long wait.

As the little voice in my head guessed, the remaining sand in the hourglass had been drained for many, many minutes and still the man had his back to me. I noticed that during the entire duration of the grading, Water wrote continuously in a little booklet. The script proved indecipherable because of the distance, but the handwriting was a beautifully arachnid style, the lines as thin as spider's webs. He wrote straight up and down, filling pages with his silky strings of words. I had absolutely no idea what he was writing about though.

As time marched on, or rather dragged on, at some point the pen's scratching stopped. I looked up again as the man put down the pen and turned around.

His gaze hit me right in the eyes. His eyes reflected every bit of my face, every blemish and imperfection. Under this mirror, I encountered the deepest, darkest blue irises I had ever seen. His eyes widened almost immediately.

"Oh." He seemed perplexed. "I had deduced from your answers that you were a Fire. Yet due to the green hue of your clothes, I suppose you are an Emerald or an Earth?"

"No sir," I replied, shaking my head. As if. "I don't have an Element. I'm an Absent."

Water's eyes did change, but not in any way I could understand. It was hard to see under the shine though; maybe they hadn't changed at all.

"I see." He leaned back in his chair slightly and brought his clasped hands to his face. The moment of silence allowed me to register more of his facial demeanor. His iron gray hair was short and flared away from his face. His eyebrows sat bushy and stern. He broke the silence.

"Let me make a better introduction. Once again, I am Water, and I am something of a behavioral expert and Elemental researcher. This is my first time meeting someone without any Element, so please excuse any odd questions." He repositioned himself and continued. "I have been assigned as your personal tutor during your stay here at the palace. I can see you are well versed in grammar and mathematics though you seem to have little knowledge about recent history and Elemental studies. Though of course, that is only what was apparent in your answers on the test. Now tell me," he asked, leaning forward a tad, "what is your name and age?"

"Pasin, sixteen."

"All right. What was your home life like? Your family?"

I didn't take long to answer. "I was raised in an orphanage. I don't have a family."

At this, Water raised his eyebrows for a split second and wove his fingers together as he leaned forward, elbows on the table.

"Really? Could you elaborate on that?"

Seeing my hesitation he amended his request. "Perhaps not now. That information is not necessary for your schooling; it was more out of curiosity. Maybe some other time. However I do need to know some other things. Please tell me everything you remember learning in school as far back as you know. I realize this is strenuous, however it is necessary." He picked up his quill and notebook once more and readied himself for writing.

I dutifully recounted what I could, trying my best to remember just what I learned and not the experiences that went with it. Early on, school wasn't bad. Even up to age ten, I was still considered a late bloomer almost ready to blossom. After that year though, as the odds of me developing an Element became terribly slim, I was treated as the outsider I was in a world where nearly everyone had some ability to define them.

The information came out rather sporadically and more disjointed than I wanted it to, but I tried. Water didn't seem to mind; he looked sincerely interested in what I had to say. I couldn't really tell though; his eyes were too glossy to read.

It was almost an hour before I finished, and if my calculations were correct, Water filled about ten pages in his book with his arachnid script.

"So you have learned history up to Dante the Victor?"

"Yes, that's the last thing I learned in Andor." Because later that day, I got arrested and thrown in prison. The next day I laughed in the face of the ruler of Falleon, and the day after that I'm sitting in front of a behavioral expert in the palace library. You know, no big deal.

"I see that your education has been particularly deficient concerning Elemental Studies. Let's see—" Water rose and moved lithely across the floor to a distant bookshelf. He moved with surprising grace for such an older man.

He skimmed over the titles and picked out a leather-bound tome using only the last segments of his fingers. As he came back, I marveled at the intricate gold detailing on the cover. Tiny leaves twisted around thick brambles and stood out against the rich brown leather binding.

"Are you impressed by this cover?" Water inquired.

I nodded.

"This book is fairly old, fifty years or more I believe. The newer volumes are much grander." The man laid the book in front of me, *An Exhaustive Lexicon of Elemental Classifications*. Now that I looked closer, signs of wear were apparent.

"Wait." Water took back the book and flipped through the pages. To my horror, he tore out one of the pages and folded it neatly. Without explanation, he slipped it into his little notebook.

"Find five Elements that interest you. Write a page about each by tomorrow. You are dismissed." With that, he looked away and began writing once again in his notebook.

I retrieved the lexicon and started to head to the door. With the distinct feeling I was missing something, a feeling I was starting to get used to, I exited the room.

CHAPTER EIGHT

Grass immediately joined me outside the library. She curtsied before speaking.

"Vine has given notice that your dresses are done. Pearl wishes to see the changes. If you would please follow me."

As I tailed Grass to Vine's area, I made a promise to myself. Someday, I would be able to find my own way around. Someday, I would know where I was going. Because, despite knowing it wasn't a big deal, my pride was beginning to bristle following around someone so much shorter than me.

When we arrived, Vine came up to us with flushed excitement on her face and something hidden behind her back.

"It's done!" Vine said and whipped out the said piece. My jaw dropped.

"Wow."

Plum-colored satin made up the main part of the dress, the fabric draped from the bust to the floor. At the top of the bust, lace work crept up and covered both of the arms all the way past the wrists.

"Come and try it on now." Vine passed the dress to me. After I handed the Elemental book to Grass, Vine gently shoved me into a changing area. When I came out and looked at myself in the mirror, it was hard to believe that I was the one in the garment. It was undoubtedly the finest piece of clothing I had ever worn.

"It looks amazing! Thank you so much." I held out my hand to shake, but Vine pulled me into a warm hug.

"You are quite welcome." Vine pulled out of the hug into a smile. "Now you just need hair and makeup, and you'll be ready for the day."

The Petal from the day before was enlisted with this duty once more. In the end, I thought I looked really good, even if it didn't really feel like me.

While this was going on, I watched a young, twitchy girl talk to a nodding Grass. After the girl walked off, Grass came up to us.

"Pearl wants to see Pasin immediately."

Vine sighed with a flair of drama.

"You can't rush genius. But there's no choice I guess…" Vine threw her hands up in annoyance and stalked to the back of the room. "Here," she added, picking out a pair of shoes, "take these. Your other dresses will be brought to your room. Now go before Pearl bites my head off."

Grass shuttled me out of the room with an urgency that kind of stressed me out. Not to mention it's hard to put on shoes while hurrying through the halls.

We ended up back in the room with all of the rows from the day before. I nearly sighed with relief upon seeing they were empty. Pearl stood in the same area that I had stood for those painful hours the day before. She looked me over critically. Why was she frowning? I mean, I knew I wasn't Emerald, but I didn't look bad. Petal even hid my "heinous spots," which I'm sure was no small undertaking.

"This will work." That's all she said. I guess that's better than saying I looked terrible. But then she continued.

"Given the circumstances involved, I believe that you will..." Pearl stopped and narrowed her eyes slightly, just slightly. In my peripheral vision, I caught a glimpse of boy wearing a very amusing velvet hat.

Pearl abandoned her sentence and went over to the boy.

"Yes?" she asked.

The boy gestured for Pearl to lean over which she did, albeit grudgingly. His whispered message was silent to my ears, but it clearly agitated Pearl. She looked at me out of the corner of her eye, and I averted my gaze.

"Really?" her voice raised in incredulity. "He really...I mean, are you sure?" I could tell that Pearl was trying to keep her cool, but her reaction broke through the facade of indifference.

"Yes, madam. And please hurry." With that, the boy left.

Pearl turned back to me and just gazed for a moment, which did nothing for my nerves. Forbidden questions popped up in my mind.

"Grass, you are dismissed." Pearl ordered while keeping her eyes trained on me. When the door shut again, she addressed me.

"Come."

Pearl turned briskly around and walked with purpose out the door, I trailing in her wake.

#

Again, we strode through the swarm of people in the forest hallway. How many people scrambled through these halls anyway? Even without the mirrors, there would still be an immense number.

We entered the central hall and ascended the stairs on the left. The number of people significantly thinned out as we walked past the library and into the depths of the second story.

When we did stop, the reason was obvious. The door we stopped at was the only one in the corridor. It appeared to be a miniature of the throne room door, a mere one story tall instead of two.

Two guards stood watch, one on each side of the entrance. They nodded at Pearl when we approached and opened the door. Before I realized what was happening, I was thrust inside and by the time I turned around, the door had closed. I reached for the handle but never touched it because a sound grabbed my attention.

"You aren't good at remembering, are you?"

Oh pont. I had barely heard the voice before, but it was unmistakable. I whipped around, and my eyes trained on the figure standing there.

"Because this is the second time you have failed to bow."

Oramus' voice sounded as it had before, but this time it was amused, as if he were watching a kitten getting tangled up in a ball of yarn. His amusement disconcerted me for a moment. However, once my brain managed to function again, I hastened to bow before the king.

"I asked you a question." His voice hardened for a moment then waned back into softness. "Feel free to stand up and answer."

I did and managed to get a glimpse of my surroundings. It seemed a sitting room of sorts. It was covered in all sorts of regal trappings, but the only focus of the room was Oramus himself.

He stood in the center of the room of course, looking intimidating, dark and royal, all the things he seemed before. He smiled, still with amusement, I guess. His presence felt like a spark of electricity, making me acutely aware of every motion, automatically alert.

"I find my memory to be impaired when I am…thrown into unfamiliar situations." My mouth was dry. "Etiquette sometimes escapes me." Which means it's the first thing out the window when awkward situations come up. Normally I would stop talking and shut down, but that wasn't an option.

He cocked his head a bit to the side. "How distressed do you feel right now?"

Was this one of those times for polite lies? Well it didn't matter as I blurted out, "Quite."

"Quite? Not very or really?"

I pondered this for half a second and shook my head. "No, not really. Or very."

Oramus blinked and looked into my eyes thoughtfully. I realized I was trembling. Was it out of fear? I replayed the scene of me laughing at him. I kept waiting, waiting for him to mention the incident. The incident where I lost my mind yet somehow kept my head.

He said nothing. Without a word, he started to circle me, slowly. Hyperactively aware of his movements, I felt trapped in his gaze, unable to move a muscle while feeling each step he took.

He completed the circle and looked straight into my eyes. I couldn't decide whether to hold his gaze or look down, so instead, my head faced him while my eyes peered down. It didn't disturb Oramus, or at least, he didn't show that it disturbed him. He tilted his head to the side again and looked me up and down. My toes curled.

"You look much better than you did yesterday." Oramus' voice was still lofty, but this time it held traces of frankness. "Actually, you look beautiful."

That was unexpected. I looked up into his eyes. I saw a one-sided smile on his lips and felt a shy smile creeping onto my face. How embarrassing. I barely managed to reply.

"Th…thank you."

"Oh, you're welcome." Oramus didn't move or make any action to signify he was going to do anything, so I filled the silence before I could start laughing like an idiot again.

"How tall are you?" My voice cracked and rose.

Only then did Oramus' cocky grin split.

"Why in the world would you ask that?" he asked. Uhhh.

"I…I don't like silences," I replied. "They make me feel uncomfortable." I cursed myself internally for the lapse of propriety. I didn't think Spark could get me out of this one.

Oramus didn't smite me. Instead, it was his turn to laugh. It wasn't uproarious or unrestrained as mine had been. His short laughter resounded in the chamber. A nearby candle flickered from his breath.

"If you must know, I am six feet and one inch tall," the king remarked. The one-sided grin returned. "Any other questions?"

Well yes. Of course. I had hundreds of questions running about my muddled mind, but I couldn't ask them. No, I did the sensible thing and did not risk his wrath again. Surely his question was not meant in earnest.

I was about to give a polite no and opened my mouth to reply, but my stomach answered for me.

Oramus blinked. "Have you had lunch yet?"

"No, Your Majesty." My midsection agreed.

"Can't have that now, can we?" Oramus called to someone behind me. "Pearl!"

Had she been standing there the entire time? I turned around but was relieved to see that only then did the door open and did Pearl walk through.

"Yes, Your Majesty?" She seemed a little irritated as she curtsied.

"Nine."

"N–nine?" Pearl sputtered. "Sire, are you sure that…"

"Nine." Oramus' voice meant closure. He turned and walked to a nearby chair. "And feed her something. You are excused."

"Of course, Your Highness." Pearl curtsied again and I hastened to do the same. I didn't dare turn to look back as I exited my second encounter with the ruler of Falleon. Behind us, the two doors closed so quietly I barely heard them at all.

CHAPTER NINE

I was returned to my room, and Grass brought me lunch. Pearl left after saying my leveling ceremony would be held at sundown, whatever that meant. This left me with a good number of hours to do whatever.

I excused Grass and sat down at the desk where the Elemental lexicon had been placed. I wrote my first page of homework about Sparks. The writing only barely reached the page requirement, because the information in the book stretched from one page to another, and the second page was gone. It had to be the page Water tore out, but I couldn't figure out which Element it was about and there was no table of contents. I shook my head and finished writing about static-manipulating Sparks.

The other pages were written easily enough, and I did feel like I was learning. I did learn the temperature at which Ices lose their freezing abilities along with tidbits like how high Airs can fly compared to Gusts. When I finished my last page, I looked at the clock and saw that I still had time before this "leveling ceremony." I browsed through the book, reading more in depth when I felt like it, until I reached the "V" chapter. With a little trepidation, I turned to the entry on Voids and read:

"Void
Occurrence: Rare
Voids are one of those peculiar Elementals which cannot be directly attributed to any known force of nature. While most Elementals (like Rains or Lights) have a clear natural connection, Voids lack this reasoning within their existence.

The abilities of Voids are varied and range according to their personal power. The most common of these uncommon abilities is spatial reorientation, or the ability to draw objects to one's self. This is the limit of their physical capabilities. However, they also possess nonphysical abilities as well, primarily that of removal. This can range from removing a person's consciousness, producing a forced sleep, to removing a person's heart essence.

It is unknown how or why Voids exist, but—"

I heard the door handle turn, and by the time I turned around, Pearl had walked in. I stood up, casually flipping some pages over in the book as I did.

"Are you ready?" Pearl asked. Grass stood behind her.

"Yes," I replied, smoothing out some of the wrinkles in my dress.

"Then let's go."

This time, we descended the stairs to the ground floor and walked to a door at the back of the palace. We exited through it. We exited, and a forgotten excitement flooded my chest as the outside air rushed onto my face like the embrace of an old companion. I closed my eyes and took in a deep breath of autumn's perfume, a broad smile spreading across my face. I opened my eyes a moment later, but the smile remained.

We stood in a courtyard surrounded by stone walls covered in ivy, and fountains and benches dotted the path. I saw no one except for our trio, but I could definitely hear faint noises coming from beyond the walls.

Pearl turned to me. "You are to say nothing of your meeting with King Oramus. Understand?"

I nodded. Even I wasn't that dense.

Pearl led us through the door and my eyes widened.

Candles and drapes hung from trees and over bushes. Colored tongues of flame licked tree leaves without burning them, and cobblestone paths crisscrossed through the gardens. In the center of the courtyard stood a fountain of a lion roaring water.

The lion dominated the air space with its fierce expression, but what was much more terrifying was the gross amount of people mingling around it. So many people turning as the door opened and staring as we walked through it. I saw dozens of eyes slide over Pearl and come to rest on the stranger with the purple dress and terrified expression at her side.

"I present to you all Pasin. The official leveling ceremony will commence shortly." Pearl left, and I was left in front of a sea of people, most of whom continued to stare with odd expressions on their faces.

"What am I supposed to do now?" I whispered to

Grass.

"I believe it would be acceptable to talk to some people, Miss," she answered.

"Like, just go up to them?" What a terrifying thought.

Before I had to tackle the problem myself though, a puff of light green made its way toward me. That is, a beaming female in a light green flouncy dress wound her way through the crowd and ended up at my side, quietly followed by another girl. The first bobbed a quick curtsy, which I hastily copied, and then she burst into speech.

"Shining Solluna, I'm so glad to finally talk to you!" the female said, a wide smile showing off her ridiculously white teeth. "I'm Peridot, and I've been thinking about you, like, all day."

"Hello, Peridot," I replied, not sure where to look. "I'm Pasin," I said, for lack of anything better.

"As if I didn't know!" Peridot laughed, a clear laugh that hovered like a soap bubble, but then she lowered her voice conspiratorially, "Okay, do you remember yesterday, when we were all in that room giving suggestions and stuff?"

As if I could forget.

"Yes?"

"Well, my servant Smoke," she nodded at the girl who followed her. "She was standing near you during it. She told me the heart-shaped hole thing and I nearly died with laughter!" Peridot snickered in memory. I chuckled too, but more with apprehension.

"I wasn't trying to be rude or..." I started, but Peridot cut me off with a laugh and a wave of her hand.

"No, no, it's fine. Everyone knows my cousin can

be…difficult, don't worry." Peridot giggled into her hand. It did alleviate some of the worry that had nested in my heart since the day before.

"So, how've you liked it so far?" she asked.

"It's been interesting." Well that was pathetic. Peridot knew it too.

"Yes, I know that it's scary for the first few days. But I love it here and I know you will too." Peridot smiled and I smiled back.

"Now come on!" She grabbed my hand. "Let me introduce you to everyone."

Peridot gleefully led me through the lit trees and greenery and introduced me to the widest assortment of Elements I had ever met. From Garnets to Lights, I felt swallowed up by a sea of beautiful people. Most of them were nice, or at least polite. The only one to show open disdain was Emerald, but I avoided her. Even so, I felt so out of place, disconnected from the people surrounding me. My mouth was just beginning to hurt from the smile I had plastered on my face when a voice spoke from behind me.

"Pasin? Is that really you?"

That voice. That voice was a hook tugging at my memory. I turned and…

"Hex?"

My voice rang louder than I meant, and several heads turned. Even Peridot raised her eyebrows.

"I mean–Blaze?"

It really was Hex Blaze, that burn-maker, looking as arrogant as ever. He was taller, more mature, but not. He made that obvious just by the way he strutted over to us, followed distantly by another male in simple clothes looking just past me. But Hex was there, in the palace. What?

"You know him?" Peridot's eyes were wide, her smile incredulous. Kind of like the expression on my face except hers seemed pleased.

Hex answered for me.

"Oh yes, we go way back." Mischief lit his eyes. He followed this statement by casually brushing back the brown ginger almost-curls from his face. Ugh.

"What are you doing here Blaze?" I asked. Peridot raised her eyebrows even higher, presumably at the venom in my voice. The amount of disdain even surprised me. He smirked.

"King Oramus invited me. Family ties." So maybe he was related to King Dante the Victor after all.

"What's your excuse?" he asked in return. I just glared.

"I still have the scar you gave me." It felt like he had reopened my wound merely by his arrogant presence. That's why the anger rose in my chest. I wanted to lash out and fight back like I couldn't before.

Peridot tore her gaze away from our exchange.

"Look!" she said, pointing to the fountain where Pearl ascended a short platform. "Ooh, I wonder what level you'll be?" I turned my gaze away from Hex's infuriating smirk.

"I still don't understand that," I said. "What's this level or leveling ceremony about?"

"Oh, you don't know?" Peridot asked. "Well, I guess it's kind of like a rating system from one to ten. The higher the level, the better."

Is that what Oramus was talking about? But that would mean...

"What level are you?" I asked.

Peridot laughed, "Oh, I'm just a five. But that's

better than a two." She gave a small shudder.

"So ten is the best?"

"Yes," she began, but paused for a moment. "But no. Level ten is really for the older ladies; it's more of a prestige thing than anything. Level nine is the place to be. Those are Oramus' favorites–Emerald, Amethyst, you get the idea."

Hex snorted. "I wouldn't worry about that if I were you. Fledglings usually start out at two or three."

I glared again. "Well what level are you Blaze?"

This snort was pure scoffing. "You don't know anything do you? Gentlemen don't have levels."

I was about to give a scathing reply when Pearl's voice rang out across the garden.

"Attention!" she said, and it was given to her. She looked around the garden and any people still talking quieted themselves. "Attention! After careful consideration a verdict has been reached. Pasin has been placed at level…"

Why was I so nervous? All of the other faces around me were only vaguely interested.

"Nine."

The faces were more than just interested now. I heard a collective intake of breath. A few breaths were more like gasps, but they soon quieted.

"That is all. Enjoy the rest of the night."

I turned back to look at our group. Peridot was beaming again. Grass looked surprised; Hex looked shocked.

"Shining Solluna, that is so amazing!" Peridot gave a little squeal and did a little hop. "No fledgling has ever started out so high! Congratulations!"

"Really? That is amazing, I guess."

"You guess?" Peridot stopped hopping and

became momentarily serious. "That means that you get to sit at the highest tables at banquets and go on more outings with the higher levels. This is like one of the best things that can happen to a person!" She giggled and resumed her bouncing.

I did my best not to outright smirk at Hex then and there. The wandering eyes of those around us prevented this outburst of pettiness. I did give him a smile though.

He closed his gaping mouth and cleared his throat.

"Well, I didn't expect...but congratulations." He gave me a short bow. I managed to realize etiquette and gave a short curtsy. It was weird. His act of respect couldn't have been any more sincere than mine.

Now people took the initiative of coming up to me. Pleasantries were exchanged and compliments given. People congratulated and curtsied and bowed. At least ten different people invited me to their apartments. There were some people who were obviously mooching, obscenely nosy, and those that were merely curious. I didn't blame the last group. It made no sense at all, but I was okay with that for the moment.

With every introduction came the name of the person and their level. I recognized some people from the inspection chamber and came to know most of the other ladies on the ninth level. The one level nine person who did not come up to me was Emerald. The only welcome I got from her was a look of disdain.

Grass brought me a large glass of dark drink. The sight of the drink made me realize just how thirsty I was. I downed the drink though it didn't agree with me, but it didn't quench my thirst.

"Thank you," I said. "Can you get me another?" Grass nodded and disappeared into the crowd.

After what felt like the thousandth Gem coming up to me, I turned back to Peridot who had helped smooth the introductions so far.

"How many people are there?" Gobs of them it felt like.

"Well, there are fifty ladies of the court at one time. Five in each level."

She paused.

"Now that you're here, the lowest leveled one will have to go home, though."

Peridot cast a glance to a girl in light blue, morosely clutching her glass.

"Poor Mist," she said under her breath. She shook her head, then continued.

"I'm not sure about the number of gentlemen; they're mostly lords or people from connected families."

At this Hex nodded. He hadn't left our midst since Pearl gave the great announcement. He also added, "Most of us come from powerful or wealthy families."

"Great." Nice use of the first person plural to add yourself in that group.

Grass came back with another glass, which I downed as well despite the unpleasant taste. Peridot and Hex looked at me oddly, but neither explained their expressions.

#

Awhile later, Grass was off getting another glass, and the party seemed to be dying down. Peridot went off to do another something or other, so I walked over to a swing and sat on it, watching the scene. My head wasn't feeling that great, but I wasn't sure when I should leave. I saw Hex heading my way. I also noticed the person who had been following him all night.

"Who is this, Blaze?" I tilted my head. The teenage male had to be a servant, but he appeared far too thoughtful for the position.

"Him?" Hex jabbed his thumb in the man's direction. "That's just Air."

Air? Lucky. Air nodded and gave a bow.

"Hello," I said and smiled.

"Would you be interested in walking around the gardens with me?" Hex seemed agitated but extended his hand nonetheless. I didn't take it.

"Why would I want to do that?"

He furrowed his eyebrows. "I'm someone you won't have to explain yourself to. And I need to talk to you, privately."

"Fine," I replied. Why not?

I still avoided the hand and got up by myself.

"Wait." I stopped. "What about Grass?"

"Oh, forget her for now. Come on." Hex used the previously extended hand to wave Air away. Air obliged and watched from a distance as we walked deeper into the garden, alone but for the two of us.

It was darker here, farther away from the twinkling trees. The noises of the party faded into the background.

Hex leaned against one of the statues and crossed his arms.

"I heard there was supposed to be an Absent joining the ladies of the court," he started. "I thought of you first, but I didn't think it would really be you." He eyed me. Not suspiciously, but still with a sort of apprehension.

"Well, here I am." I spread out my arms and raised my eyebrows at him. He had definitely changed since his time at the school in Andor. He was leaner now, and though he was surely well fed, he had a hungry look in his eyes.

"What I'm curious about is how. No one else knows where you came from. All they know is that you're an ugly Absent that was somehow placed on level nine." The insult didn't hurt, but I did frown. Maybe he wasn't that different after all.

"Why would I tell you what happened?" I turned my gaze away from him, acting bored, and stroked the petals of a nearby rose.

"Why?" He straightened up and took a step toward me. "Because I do know where you are from. Though you might not tell anyone, I have no incentive not to." His smile was disgustingly cocky.

"What is that?" I asked. I left the rose and stood up to him. "Is that a threat? You're so pathetic!" Hex grimaced as I continued, "You're no different than you were then." I sneered and returned to the rose.

He didn't respond at first. He breathed in slowly before continuing in a controlled voice, "Okay, no, that's not what I meant." He let the breath out and continued, "And I am sorry that I burned you." I glanced up. He did look kind of sorry. "I happen to be very close to Oramus. It might be helpful for you to have me as an ally."

"No thanks." I plucked the rose from the bush and examined it closer. It was deep red, like a ladybug. Or like blood. Either or.

"Pasin…" Hex said, regaining his control and part of his cockiness. "Just think about it." He nodded and turned back to the party. I just stood still.

"Aren't you coming?" he asked.

"No. I think I'm going to walk around for a bit."

He seemed wary. "Don't do anything stupid."

I snorted. "Why don't you tell yourself that sometime?"

His eyebrows furrowed. "Suit yourself." And he walked off back to the light.

I went farther into the garden, into the darkness. Soon, there was no trace of the party or any kind of other humanity for that matter. Yes, I was sufficiently lost. But then something caught my eye.

I knew that this was not the way back to the party. But curiosity beckoned, and my foggy mind couldn't resist its call.

Through a break in the hedge wall, I spied a small wooden door. No one was around. The door made a hollow thud as I closed it behind me.

The small, unlit corridor stretched out to unknown lengths and I followed it, tickled by the whole adventure of the situation. I ignored my headache and opened the next door I came to. Beyond the door, I found myself in the central hall. The opening was set on one of the side walls near the grand staircase. I tiptoed slowly out, peeking about. There was no one to be seen. It had to be almost midnight.

My head felt fuzzy and light. The hall was so pretty. I giggled and hopped across the marble, piece to piece. The whoosh of up and down and the sheer feeling of gravity caused my laughter to grow. I reached the rose in my hand up to the sky and back down to the ground; I spun and stopped and went the opposite way. It was in this state that I ran along the wall, spinning and twirling, finally tumbling into a tall, dark man.

Oramus just stood there, looking down at me and me up at him. He must have been descending the stairs as I had acted the fool on the ground level. It was only a moment of terrified shock before my nose nearly led me to the floor, so low was my bow.

"I–I'm terribly sorry Your Highness...I didn't mean..." Any happy buzz in my head turned to the buzzes of hornets, the cloud of distraction. This was not a good time to have one's wits on vacation.

I felt a hand on my arm, helping me rise. Oramus was smiling, a bit bemused perhaps, but smiling.

"A simple curtsy is fine next time. Though I hope you don't plan on running into me again." Yes, definitely bemused, but there seemed to be kindness in his eyes.

"Of course not, Your Highness."

"Please, call me Oramus if we're just talking. I hear those titles often enough." He seemed rather nonchalant for having just been run into. "I see that you are quite the dancer."

"Oh!" That was unjustifiably kind. My dancing looked like a frantic squirrel in my opinion. "Thank you, but I'm not used to dancing in front of an audience. It's not really one of my strong points." At this I stopped because I heard something behind me. I turned my neck and saw a person open a door, freeze when he saw us, and quickly leave the way he came in.

"So," Oramus' voice brought me back to the scene at hand. "How do you like the palace?"

"It's beautiful," I replied immediately. "It's really

the most amazing thing I have ever seen."

"Ever?" He raised an eyebrow. "That's quite a long time."

There was a sensation coming from inside me, like a tugging of sorts, but that was probably just the headache and bit of dizziness I felt.

"Well, I have certainly never seen anything to equal it." I smiled. My insides relaxed too.

"Good." Satisfaction covered the single word. He looked at my hands.

"Did you get that from the gardens?" Oramus pointed at the rose.

"Oh, this?" It was then that I remembered that gardens are not meant for picking flowers. "Yes, I did, but I forgot–I didn't mean to…"

"Shh." He extended his hand toward the rose, and I placed it on his palm.

"Roses are one of my favorite flowers," he stated, examining the specimen. "Though I prefer white roses myself." He gave me back the rose. "What's your favorite flower?"

"Umm…the ignis flower I guess," I said. "Or poppies." Roses seemed pompous to me.

"Interesting." His gaze was on my face, and I could feel a blush come to it.

Oramus looked away and pulled something metallic out of his pocket. It was a pocket watch.

"It's getting late," he said. "You should probably go upstairs."

I could feel the fuzz in my head again. "I…I think that Grass is still in the garden," I replied. "She might even be looking for me…" I turned my head around as if I thought she might be standing behind me, somehow summoned by the mention of her name.

She wasn't there.

I felt a hand on my chin guide my head back toward the reality in the room. Oramus then lowered his hand and spoke.

"I'll send a messenger," he said. "But I think you should really go to bed."

I barely managed not to stumble when I went past Oramus and up the stairs. Remarkably, I found my way to the room without getting lost. I left Oramus behind, but the memory of his gaze followed me through the hallways, through the door, and into bed. It echoed in my fuzzy mind as I drifted off to sleep.

CHAPTER TEN

The next morning Spark woke me, and I complained about a raging headache. She mentioned taking it easy on the alcohol and that marked the end of the opening festivities.

The days after didn't rush by like a whirlwind of events. A storm of gossip erupted over my arrival. People whispered as I journeyed through the castle to dinners, to my studies, wherever. It was amazing and ridiculous all at once. As I left the first two days behind, I realized that that was the end of the beginning. Those days were the forward motion propelling me into a new stage of life.

Every morning, Spark woke me up with her combination of tenacity and friendliness. She was always quick to tell me about the castle, about the people, and, more importantly, about what other people thought about the people. As we talked about the affairs at the palace, a related personal story would almost always pop up, and so we learned more about each other with each conversation.

Spark might have been the one I had the deepest connection with, but I spent time with other people too. Peridot acted as my tour guide around the palace, introducing me to her friends and showing what ladies do in their spare time. Her kindness amazed me, especially compared to the looks of disgust I received from Emerald any time we happened to meet. Most of the other girls were nice I guess, but every once in a while, I would see an odd look aimed my way. To my relief, someone ordained that I should have etiquette lessons. So that ate up an hour or two every day and I did learn a few things–which dresses are appropriate for which events, how to make small talk, that kind of stuff. They never mentioned wandering off at parties and bumping into important people as a bad thing, but I guess that went without saying.

The lessons with Water were never quite as unusual as the first, though he did have a unique style of teaching. The next day he was prompt in telling me that my knowledge of modern history was atrocious, and he proceeded to give me about twenty pages of reading a night. The work tired me, but I found out a lot more about Oramus and how he had Falleon set up. The towns and provinces were all connected through roads and passages, some even used only for military use. There were maps and surveying notes, books on laws and Falleon's inhabitants, though some of the books assigned were ones I had read back in Andor.

Speaking of Oramus, I didn't really see him the few weeks following my arrival, which did not bother me at all. Fewer encounters meant fewer possibilities of embarrassment. I think I saw the back of his head a few times in the library, but nothing more. Anyway, no more encounters occurred during my first three weeks at the palace. Until one day after dinner, there was a knock at the door.

I looked up from my reading about flying laws as Grass went to open the door. A voice spoke.

"Message for Lady Pasin from the King." I saw a young courier with an expression of utmost decorum on his face. "Lady Pasin is invited to join King Oramus and the rest of his court at a banquet tomorrow night to celebrate the anniversary of his ascension to the throne."

The courier handed Grass a letter and left. She dutifully gave it to me and excused herself for some dinner. I must have read the letter seven or eight times, though it merely repeated what the courier said. My stomach tied into a furious knot of excitement and panic. Somehow, the chapter on flying laws did little to distract my attention away from the note. The slip of paper stayed at the edge of my memory the entire night, its golden lettering glinting as I closed my eyes to sleep.

#

"Good morning, Spark," I said.

"Hello, Pasin." She smiled again like she did every time we met. She was always awfully chipper for the early morning hours, and usually, it was borderline disgusting. However, that morning I woke up before she arrived.

"Sorry I'm late," Spark said as she sat down and pulled her feet up to cross her legs. So much for waking up before her. "King Oramus needed me, and

I wasn't about to tell him to wait."

"What did he need you for?" I asked. Spark shifted in her seat before answering.

"Sometimes he consults me about Elements."

"Doesn't Water do that?" I asked. "He said he was an Elemental expert."

"Yes," Spark answered, "We have different bases though, if that makes sense." She shifted again. "When I was young, I lived with my mother and the elves, and they taught all the kids about Elements. They study Elemental powers because elves don't have Elements. Understanding your neighbors, I guess." She gave a little chuckle, but it didn't reach her eyes. "Anyway, the elves have a long cultural memory and a large store of Elemental knowledge from their interactions with Elementals, so I'm able to give Oramus information that Water may not know."

"Oh, all right," I said. "Nice."

"Thanks," she replied. "So, are you excited about the banquet tonight?"

"How is it you always know what's going on this side of the palace?" Seriously, any time an event happened, Spark knew when it was, where it was, and what the main entree would be.

"My ears are pointed," she said seriously. "They hear everything." She stared at me gravely, then laughed, all pretense gone.

"Mine are too, kind of, but they don't have super hearing." I grabbed one of my ears and pulled at it. "Stupid dysfunctional ears."

She snorted. "Battling your ears doesn't answer my question. Are you excited?"

"Well yeah, I guess," I answered, dropping my

hands. "But I think I'm more nervous."

"Why?" Her voice was grossly nonchalant.

"Well, let's see. The first time I met Oramus, I laughed at his face. The second time I acted like a complete idiot, and last time I literally ran into him in a deserted room. Not the best track record."

Spark smiled. "You'll do fine," she said. "Just don't dance or laugh or talk this time."

I rolled my eyes. "Thanks. I don't know what I'd do without you." I grabbed a strand of hair and started playing with it, pulling it at it over and over again.

"That's right." She nodded. I sighed.

"So how is training going?" I asked.

"Just fine. We've got some new people that I get to introduce to swordplay." Her smile was mischievous. "I've got a feeling they'll remember this."

"Why is that?"

She smiled again with lit-up eyes. "Remind me to show you one day. Let's just say that sparring with me and my sword can be a bit…shocking."

I raised my eyebrows. She bade me farewell. Well, it was more like, "See you later," but farewell fit the surroundings better. Before she could leave though, I called out a question.

"Spark, do you know what a heart essence is?"

She stopped at the door and turned around.

"Yes," she said. "I do." She paused but continued before I had to ask her to elaborate. "A heart essence is something inside every person. It is involved in emotions and actions, and it determines a person's Element." She hesitated then continued again. "Basically, it connects a person's thoughts and actions. Most people don't know about it, and you don't really need to, because it functions just fine on its own. If it gets extracted though, then you'll have problems." She glanced at my hand, still playing with my hair.

"What are you doing?" she asked. I looked down.

"I'm nervous," I said.

"Well, stop that." She glared at my hand until I lowered it and she nodded. "That's better."

She placed her hand on the door handle.

"I need to go," she said. "Have fun at the banquet." She opened the door and slipped out before I could reply.

Later, while I was having my hair and face all done up, Peridot chatted excitedly at my side almost the entire time. I marveled at how she was able to gesticulate with her hands and still have people working on her eyebrows.

"So," she said, finally calming down a bit. "Aren't you excited to be sitting at the king's table?"

I almost choked on my spit.

"What?" I sputtered.

She tilted her head and then nodded. "Oh that's right, this is your first major feast! I keep forgetting that there hasn't been one in a month." She leaned over, while a servant Smoke simultaneously shifted a curling iron with the new position.

"Well, since you're a nine," she emphasized, giggling. "It's still hard for me to get used to that. You get to sit at the king's table with the other nines and tens. The room is set up so that…" She paused. "Well it's hard to explain; you'll see it when you get there."

For the next two hours, I couldn't get the image out of my head of me sitting with Emerald on my left, Pearl on my right, and Oramus staring at me without blinking. After getting ready, I looked ridiculously made up. Beautiful I guess, but nothing compared to Peridot or any of the other ladies, surely.

Instruction with Water was canceled for the day, so I spent the half-hour before the banquet alternating between reading about traffic laws and scribbling ideas down for my story, stowing them away in the desk next to the decrepit ignis flower.

Grass returned from her own dinner.

"If you are ready, Miss."

Ready might not have been the right word. Prepared? No. Eager? No. Apprehensive? Yes, that was it.

CHAPTER ELEVEN

The guards opened the doors to the royal dining room, and I took the scene in quickly. Five tables formed a "U" with the open part facing the entrance. The farthest table, bridging the distance between the other two lines of tables, sat several feet above the others and stretched twice as long. Each table had ten chairs at it, five on each side, except for the king's table, which held twenty-two. One chair was much larger than the others.

Grass directed me to the side and led me across the room. Both men and women lined the tables and whispered as I passed, some turning around in their seats to gawk. My ears burned, and their gazes were oppressive, but I stared straight ahead and imagined the open sky beyond the castle walls. It helped, but not quite enough.

Grass led me to a seat on the left side of the king's table, all the way at the end. To my great consternation, Emerald sat directly across from me. Her gaze felt as toxically green as her eyes.

People filed into the room in groups of twos and threes. Rarely was there a person who came in alone. I saw Peridot come in with some of her friends that I vaguely remembered from the leveling ceremony and the smattering of dinners we'd had together. She beamed at me, and I couldn't help but smile back. Emerald glowered.

After ten minutes or so, it appeared that every seat was filled except for three in the center of the king's table. I noticed Hex sitting on Emerald's side of the table, far to her left. I had avoided him since our encounter. His eyes never strayed my way either.

Pearl came next, looking stately as usual, and sat in the seat to the left of the center chair. After her came Corinth, quietly slipping in and sitting to the chair's right. The room quieted after Corinth sat, anticipation turning people's conversations to murmurs, waiting for the main member of the head table.

The doors opened again and at once, the room fell silent. Oramus entered, and everyone stood. He waited until everyone was up and then began to walk straight down the center of the hall. He looked to his left and right at the ladies and gentlemen that lined the tables. People met his gaze, but you could feel a tension as he stared down each member of the room. When he reached his seat, passing right behind me, I relaxed, realizing only then how rigid I had been. Emerald had a gleam in her eye.

Oramus stood in front of his chair and spoke.

"Sit," he said. We all did, and Oramus regarded us once again. He had a smile on his face that I couldn't read.

"Welcome to the opening celebration of the fourth anniversary of my reign as king. Today, four years ago, I began my journey to the throne, knowing well in my heart that this day would come, though I didn't expect it so soon. A moment of silence for the late King Gaeron."

We couldn't get any more silent, but Oramus bowed his head, and we mimicked him. I didn't know how Oramus became king, but I did have a vague memory of an announcement at school that King Gaeron had choked on some food and passed away. After a few seconds, Oramus spoke again, and we raised our heads.

"Your presence pleases me, and I am glad to know we will meet again as my reign continues." He looked up and down the tables again. "Let the feast begin!"

Cheers echoed up and down the hall, which I hastily joined. The double doors opened, and servants brought in large platters of food and delivered them to the tables. Oh, it looked delicious, with whole birds and ham and piles of delectable fruits and vegetables. The scent was overwhelming, and my tongue salivated at the sight. As the platters were set on the table in front of me (a heaping mound of fluffy potatoes sat right in my line of vision), I almost reached out to grab some, but I stopped myself just in time.

I looked around. Everyone else waited too and looked up to our table. I followed their gazes and ended up at Oramus. He ignored the collective stares. Instead, he reached with his fork and transferred some kind of fish filet from a platter to his plate. The silence bubbled into noise as everyone followed his lead. I happily put a large helping of potatoes on my plate. When I raised my head, I saw Emerald looking at me with disgust.

"No wonder your face looks like that," she scoffed. I paused for a moment, ready to come back with a sharp retort, but I managed to bite my tongue. The gentleman on Emerald's left looked at us with innocent curiosity but returned to his own food after accidentally meeting my eyes.

While the rest of the room engaged in spirited conversations, our table remained strangely silent. I wasn't about to break it. Instead, Oramus did.

"So Thorn," he said, looking at a man on the other end of the table. "How is Mandra doing? Have you heard from your father lately?" The man hastily swallowed his bite of fish before replying.

"Well, I've...a letter...don't know how...will..." The distance between his end of the table and mine made listening difficult; I only caught snippets of what he said. Instead of fruitlessly trying to follow a conversation I had no interest in, I returned to my plate and the vast array of delicacies before me. Winter watermelon, stuffed tomatoes, more meats than I could name. I was putting another slice of chicken on my plate when I heard my name, the only non-Element mentioned, drift down the table.

"And what about you Pasin? How are your parents?"

Oramus' question took me by surprise. I felt twenty-one pairs of eyes focus their attention on me as I put down my fork, trying to devise a polite answer. Blaze grinned impishly; I knew he would answer for me if I didn't respond quickly enough. Oramus looked genuinely interested, but Corinth's eyelids emoted vague annoyance as well as boredom.

"I'm...not sure how they are," I started. "I haven't heard from them in a long time." Emerald replied to this at once.

"What? Haven't you sent them a letter? Don't you keep in contact with your family?" She narrowed her eyes at me.

I shifted in my seat, realizing the inevitability of the truth.

"I grew up in an orphanage," I said finally, not looking at any one person. "I don't know who my parents are."

Noises of surprise filtered through the air, eyebrows rose, and I almost physically felt Emerald's smirk. One of the women further down the table had a different take though.

"What a delightful mystery!" she said, a broad smile on her face. "Your parents could be spies, or elves, or descendants of royalty!"

"Or filthy peasants," Emerald muttered underneath her court smile. I fought the fleeting urge to throw some potatoes in her face.

"I don't know if—" Hex began, struggle apparent on his face. His information meant nothing if I told it first.

"In any case," Oramus said, interrupting Hex to my great delight, "it is curious. We won't speak of that then. You've been here, what, a month? Are you still liking it?"

"It's wonderful," I said. "I feel very welcome in your court." I even took it one step further. "Thank you for granting me this honor."

Oramus smiled faintly at this. He looked from me to Emerald.

"How are your father and mother, Emerald?"

She answered quickly with her normal superior tone.

"Everything is marvelous as usual," she said, not even letting her body language hint that I might exist. "Father said our soldiers are more efficient than ever. The new regulations you implemented have really..."

I continued eating. I made Oramus smile without making a fool of myself, and just for that, the banquet was a success.

CHAPTER TWELVE

The rest of the banquet went off without a hitch. The food, conversation, and entertainment stretched the festivities late into the night, but it was worth it.

Somehow it only got better. I spent my early morning with Spark, late morning and afternoons with Water, and evenings with Peridot and the other ladies. Well, not everything was better though. Spark said Emerald was spreading rumors about me, something about a criminal background. While that wasn't entirely false, her version threw in some theft and arson. Nobody spoke of it to me, and Spark said that few, if any, people actually believed her, but the rumors still bothered me. Any time I passed Emerald, she either grimaced or refused to look at me.

Fall faded into winter, and the number of social events increased.

"It's a series of gatherings celebrating Oramus' path to becoming king," Peridot explained as we had dinner in her apartment. "The feast was for when he first came to the palace. There are some smaller get-togethers, but the feast is the big one. Oh, well," she laughed and shook her head, "and the gala of course. I can't believe I forgot that."

"What's that one for?" I asked.

"His coronation, I think. Oh you're going to love it," she continued, her eyes lighting up more than usual. "It's held in the throne room and the decorations are just over the top. Last year, there were live peacocks walking around!"

My mind wandered as I thought of the numerous ways that situation could have gone wrong. Also, it seemed odd that these events were for and about Oramus, but I hadn't seen him at any since the banquet.

"...and different nobility from around Falleon will be there," Peridot went on. "Really, it's one of the biggest events of the year. I'm hoping Ice will ask me to go with him. He's so cute."

"I guess," I replied, guilty for letting my thoughts drift, "I'm not really into red hai–oh pont." I stopped and groaned.

"What is it?" Peridot asked.

"I have a paper on trade regulations due tomorrow that I totally forgot about." It was the latest of a long series of paper about economics I'd had to write for Water.

"Ugh, that sounds terrible." Peridot shook her head. "Good luck with that."

"Thanks. I'm sorry to skip on you like this." I stood up and looked around, but Grass hadn't returned from her own dinner yet. "When Grass comes back, could you ask her to meet me in my room?"

"I will," she said. "See you later."

"Bye."

I left the room and started walking down the hallway. Even though Grass was nice, the absence of her nonintrusive yet persistent presence felt like a breath of fresh air.

Peridot's apartment was situated on the eastern wall instead of the northern one like mine. On the way to my room, I slowed down and stopped in front of an alcove consisting of little more than a carved wooden bench and a window. Unlike the windows on the northern wall, this one did not look down on the gardens and training fields of the palace. No, instead the view stretched out past the walls of the palace, and I could see the trees of the forest beyond.

An inexplicable ache of nostalgia sank into me. Of almost…sadness. That didn't make sense though. When had my life been any better than it was at that moment? For the first time, I felt care, kindness. Maybe even acceptance. Not from everyone of course, but more than I had ever felt before. Even so, my hand lifted and settled itself onto the cross-hatched window, the cold from outside seeping into my fingertips. I stood there and regarded the mountains, inscrutable thoughts darting through my mind but failing to come to rest. After a period of unknown time, I removed my hand from the glass and turned away from the view. I exited the alcove and started walking again, leaving the window and thoughts behind me.

CHAPTER THIRTEEN

A day later I found myself on my way to another event.

"So what is this exactly?" I whispered to Peridot as we walked through the castle.

"There's no official name for it really," she answered. "It's kind of like the banquet, but a lot more informal. We just sit around at tables, eat from the spread, mingle." Even after over a month at the palace, the thought of mingling made me uneasy.

"How informal is it?" I asked.

"Semi-formal," she said. My eyes widened in dismay at the ambiguity of the word. Peridot looked at me and giggled.

"It's like the level ceremony, but indoors. Technically we don't need to sit with the same levels, but that's how it ends up usually. It's a come-and-go as you please kind of thing."

"Okay, thanks." At least I wouldn't be the center of attention.

It turned out to be quite informal after all. Well,

informal as far as palace events went. I ate finger food and actually managed to mingle with some people before the doors reopened, and the room stiffened.

Oramus and Corinth entered with a nonchalance in direct opposition to the room's new atmosphere. Conversation continued as before, but the whole mood of the room changed. Oramus migrated from group to group until he found his way over to ours.

"How are you doing, Peridot?" he asked coolly. She giggled, blushed, and pushed a lock of hair away from her face before answering.

"Oh, I'm all right," she answered.

"And you, Pasin?" he asked, looking right at me.

"Oh, I'm all…right." Idiot! She just said that. I smiled and grimaced simultaneously. Oramus raised half of his mouth in what was either a smile of amusement or his own grimace.

"I'm not staying long," he said to everyone and no one in particular. "I'm merely stopping here for a few minutes before meeting with the peace council about possible unrest in the Andor Sector."

"Did you say the Andor Sector, sire?" I heard Hex Blaze's voice before I saw him. He trotted toward us from a good distance (had he been listening to our conversation?) and shimmied his way into our group.

"I lived there once you know!" he said, looking at Oramus like a dog seeking approval. "In fact, I know everything there is to know about the place. Ask me anything, I…"

"Excuse me," I murmured and slipped away from the group. I was not in the mood to listen to that slimy windbag speak, and I didn't want to slip up in front of Oramus again.

I was making my way toward another table

occupied by people I knew, but someone accosted me before I reached them.

"Pasin! How are you? I haven't seen you around in like, forever!" Emerald of all people spoke these words and sauntered up to me in her typical fabulous manner.

"Oh! Hi, Emerald." I smiled in response to her smile, but dozens of questions bubbled up in my mind. Why was she being nice? Was she sick? Was it because Oramus was there? She must have sensed my unease.

"Look, I know I wasn't the nicest person when you first came, but I'm really not like that." She frowned as she continued, "I guess I just felt threatened by having another girl here, and...can we just start over? I'm sorry, and I feel like we could be great friends if you gave me a second chance."

It still didn't make sense. She seemed genuine enough with her big green eyes, but her sincerity had yet to be tested.

"Sure—I mean, if that's what you want to do that would be...great..."

"Great!" she exclaimed, her eyes wide and lit up. "Oh shining, you're the best!" She giggled and hugged me before I could get out of the way. Once we separated, I pointed to her neck.

"That's a beautiful necklace," I said, nodding at the ruby and emerald-encrusted gold piece.

"Oh, thank you! It's a family heirloom. It's been handed down in my family for over a hundred years." She fingered the jewelry lavishly as she said this.

"Oh, wow." Her family must be loaded.

"Hey!" she said, bringing me back to the present. "I know how I can make it up to you! Can I get you a drink?"

"Sure," I replied. "No wine though, or any alcohol," I added. I did not need a repeat of the level ceremony.

"You got it! I'll be right back." She hurried away to the drink table, and I took the time to look around. Peridot was right—nearly everyone sat with their respective levels. I saw Blaze still bending Oramus' ear about who knows what. Oramus seemed interested, but Corinth looked bored out of his mind as usual.

"Here you go!" Emerald returned and handed me a glass.

"Thank you," I said and accepted her token of friendship. She raised her own glass.

"To King Oramus," she said. I felt surprise at this but followed suit.

"To King Oramus." We clinked our glasses together and drank.

As I lowered my cup, I saw her glance at Oramus with a small smile, and as she turned to me, the smile widened, showing off her pearly white teeth. Yes, it was a smile, but it immediately unsettled me. I smiled a little in return and shifted where I stood. I could feel a headache building in my left temple, probably from all the prolonged human interaction.

"So, what have you been doing? I asked her. She said nothing but kept smiling her toothy smile.

"Um, Emerald, are you oka—"

"I'm doing fine," she answered. She blinked several times and redid her grip on her glass. "And what about you? How are you?"

"The same as usual, I guess." I didn't quite know what to say, but she didn't reply to this, so I continued in an attempt to fill our silence. "How do you like the food? I think the salad is really—"

"Why are you still talking?" she asked through her toothy, clenched-teeth smile. Her eyes widened as she said this.

"E—Excuse me? I don't know what you…"

"Why are you still standing?" Her face was still smiling, but her gaze turned manic. I still had no idea what she was talking about.

"I…"

"I put the whole-dricking-bottle in there!" Her voice rose, and I saw a dozen people turn their heads toward us. My headache intensified, and her hands were clenched, shaking.

"Why…how…?" Her smile melted off of her face, was replaced by sheer fury. I started to back up.

"What are you—"

"Why aren't you dead?" she shrieked. Everyone in the room turned, some gasped. I stumbled backward away from the girl whose visage reeked of hatred. She threw down her drink, let it smash against the floor, and scrabbled at her necklace. Oramus began to stride over to us.

"Guards!" he shouted. Two men appeared from the wings of the room and descended upon Emerald. She tried to fight them off, but it was no use.

"I used the whole bottle! The best gold could buy!" She kicked and flailed, hair coming undone, powder streaking with the effort. She caught sight of me standing there, not sure what to do with myself.

"Something's wrong with her! She should be writhing, foaming, dead! Dead!" The men dragged the shrieking girl out of the room, and my headache reached a painful, new high.

"Ah!" The pain made me cry out and nearly fall to my knees. I heard feet rush toward me, and an unknown, cool hand pressed against my temple.

"She's feverish," a voice said. Oramus? I faded out of consciousness as voices surrounded me, lifted me, and took me to who knows where.

#

When I came to, I felt the familiar warmth of my blankets. *I must be in my room*, I thought. As I opened my eyes, I was taken aback by the number of people around the bed. Three unknown people, Grass, Peridot, and…oh wait, another unknown.

"She's awake!" I heard Peridot say. One unknown nodded at a smaller, younger unknown and the latter scurried out of the room. The former unknown, an older man, came up to me and placed his hand on my forehead.

"The fever's gone down," he said. "How do you feel?"

It took me a moment to realize he was talking to me.

"Fine, I guess. Tired." How long had I been out? I felt more tired than I was at the gathering. "What happened?"

"Emerald slipped a poison into your drink. Cyanase," the healer answered. He took my wrist and placed two fingers on the artery there. I saw Peridot fidgeting from the corner of my eye, but she didn't look directly at my face.

"Normally cyanase causes seizures within the first thirty seconds of contact," the man continued. "Death usually occurs within five minutes." He stopped. I waited, but no one said anything else.

"Well then, why aren't I...?" I couldn't finish the question. The healers looked at each other. Another one answered.

"We don't know, Miss," he said. "When we found the poison residue in Emerald's necklace, we administered the right antidote immediately, but you should have been...too far gone by then." Another silence fell. How did that make any sense? How could something like that just happen?

Peridot glanced around, then came to my bedside.

"I am so, so sorry Pasin," she said, grasping my hand. "I knew Eliane didn't...like you, but I never thought she would..."

"It's okay," I said. But, no, it wasn't. But I didn't know what else to say. Peridot started to cry, and I felt confused, so confused...

"She's awake?" The doors opened, and a familiar voice asked this question. Peridot quickly stepped away from the bedside, and Oramus took her place.

"Are you all right?" he asked, looking down on me in concern. I felt so awkward and uncouth with the gaggle of people around me, especially him.

"I'm fine," I said. He crouched to my level.

"Emerald is in the dungeon," he said. "She can't hurt you. She's not coming out for a long time." I saw Peridot three feet behind him. She bit her lip, mouth quivering, and her eyes were even shinier than usual.

Oramus turned to the healers.

"Is she going to be all right?" he asked.

"Yes, Your Majesty," one said. "Her temperature and breathing are normal, and the pulse has come down as well. We would suggest rest for the next few days and a plain diet, but little more."

"Good," he said. "You all may go. You," he said gesturing to Grass. "Wait outside until I leave." They all gave their myriad bows and left. And then I was alone. With Oramus. Again.

He grabbed the chair from my desk and pulled it to my bedside.

"I didn't think anyone in this palace was capable of murder," he said, shaking his head. I had no idea what to say, so I said nothing.

"While I was talking to Blaze, he mentioned something I didn't know. He said you two went to school together in the Andor Sector."

Ugh, Hex.

"Yeah, but he only went there for a year before he moved. I went there since I was five."

"So you've lived in Andor your entire life?" He shifted closer in his chair.

"Mhm," I answered, not caring about the lack of words in my reply.

"I didn't realize you lived so close to Falleon City," he said. "What was it like living there?"

I looked at him with mild, sleepy surprise.

"Well, it wasn't great, but it wasn't terrible," I started. He nodded, and I continued, reassured. "I mean it was never easy, being the only Absent there, but the walk every day to school was so beautiful, with the trees and the breeze and the view of the palace across the field…"

I kept talking; I felt like I was rambling, but Oramus kept listening, looking absorbed in my words, asking questions and giving comments at the right moments, keeping the conversation going. I told him whatever came to mind–the brick walls of the orphanage; the hours I spent writing in my room; the way Slate, Brock, and others treated me at school; how lonely I felt among all of those people. An hour passed before I knew it. My throat started to itch, and it broke at one point.

"Oh," he said when he heard this crack. "I shouldn't have made you talk so long when you're recovering."

"It's okay," I rasped. "Thank you for listening." He smiled.

"I'm happy to get to know you better. The other girls here—they all have the same background, but not you. Very intriguing." He stood up and replaced the chair.

"I'll have your servant fetch you some water. Get well soon." He smiled at me one more time and left. I drank the water greedily when it came and fell asleep again soon afterward. My sleep was dreamless, but that was better than nightmares.

CHAPTER FOURTEEN

It only took two days for me to feel better, but those two days were packed with visitors. Peridot visited at least three times, and the three remaining nines all came at once with their well-wishes. Oramus even came once for a few minutes to check up on me. I was most excited when I woke up the next morning and saw Spark sitting in my desk chair.

"Spark!"

"Looks like someone's been busy, hasn't she?" Spark picked up the chair and dragged it over next to my bed, much like Oramus had done. "How are you feeling?"

"I feel just fine," I said. "I wish people would stop asking me–it's like they don't have anything else to talk to me about."

Spark laughed.

"Well, it's not every day that someone gets poisoned and lives. I heard it was cyanase–is that true?"

I shifted against my pillows.

"I think so," I said. "That's what the healer said."
She snorted, laughed in near disbelief.

"That's ridiculous. Do you know anything about cyanase?"

"Not really. They said it gives people seizures, and it's supposed to be deadly."

"'And it's supposed to be deadly'," Spark mimicked. "It's one of the deadliest poisons known. I've never heard of anyone surviving it. Nothing to kid about."

"Do you know anything else about it?" I asked. I wanted to look it up in the library, but I wasn't allowed out of my bed except to use the lavatory.

"Yeah, let's see…the elves call it the minute nightmare because of how it kills both quickly and painfully. It comes from a rare mushroom found only in the deepest parts of the mountains. I'm guessing Emerald paid a whole bunch of gold to get it." Spark fiddled with her sleeve as she spoke about the poison and the poisoner so nonchalantly.

"The healer said they don't know how I survived it," I said, looking at her face. Spark looked up, and I noticed she was chewing the inside of her cheek.

"That is odd," she replied. "Good, of course, but still strange."

We were both silent for a moment. I could even hear the activity taking place in the courtyard outside my window.

"I need to get back to the training area soon," Spark said, standing up and replacing the chair. "I just wanted to stop by and see how you were doing."

"Well, thanks for visiting." I smiled at her and she smiled back. "Could you do me a favor before you leave?"

"It depends on what it is," she replied.

"Could you hand me some paper and a pencil from the desk?" I asked. If I was going to be stuck in bed, I might as well use the time to get some writing done.

"Sure," she said and retrieved the requested items.

"Thanks, Spark," I said as she handed them to me.

"You're welcome," she replied and walked toward the door. She stopped before exiting it though.

"If you want," she said, rubbing the back of her neck, "you can call me Erise instead of Spark. I mean, I feel comfortable with it. You don't have to, but—"

"No!" I interjected, then shook my head, "I mean, yes, I would like to call you Erise; thank you." Something warmed inside me, a bubbling happiness that Spark felt confident enough in our friendship to offer her first name. I wanted to do the same, though I knew it was impossible.

She put her hand on the handle.

"See you later, Pasin," she said.

"Bye, Erise."

#

I was able to return to my normal activities the next day. It actually felt nice to get back to tutoring; it made me feel like a lost routine had been reestablished. This routine was thoroughly disturbed, however, the day after my return when Oramus walked into the library halfway through our lesson.

"I need to talk to Pasin," he said as he walked up to us, boots thumping on the wood floor, cape rippling behind him. I started at the sound of his voice, unexpected as it was in the normally quiet library. Oramus walked up to the table, stood right beside me, and continued, "I hope you don't mind if I borrow her for a minute?"

"Of course not, Your Majesty," Water replied, bowing his head in deference. Oramus lifted one side of his mouth into an almost-smile, then turned to me.

"I am having a private lunch today," he said, speaking above me so I had to tilt my head up to see his face. "I would be delighted if you would join me." He leaned to the side and looked down on me as he awaited my response.

"I...yes!" I answered hurriedly, not wanting to make him wait. "I mean, I would be honored to dine with you." I did feel honored, but I knew that even if I had wanted to, I couldn't exactly refuse. Oramus nodded his head.

"Water," he said, turning his gaze to the old man. "Finish up what you're doing and send Pasin along."

"Of course, Your Majesty," Water answered. Oramus nodded again and looked at me once more.

"See you in a while," he said and walked off before I could reply.

Water exhaled and looked at the pages scattered on his desk.

"I won't be able to finish this in the time frame King Oramus desires," he said. "You can go ahead but be sure to do the reading I assigned."

"Yes, sir," I replied and took the book he held out. As I turned, I saw him close his eyes and move his hands to his temples. As I left, I vaguely heard a mutter about "silly socials" before the doors closed behind me.

\#

Grass and I walked back to my apartment where I dropped off the book and took a few minutes to double-check myself in the lavatory mirror. After I was sure I still looked respectable, Grass led me down the stairs, through the central hall, through the forest hallway, and to a plain, unguarded door on the first floor. She opened the door for me; I entered and heard the door close behind me.

I expected a small group of ladies and gentlemen to fill the space, but only Oramus sat at the table in the room, and only one other seat accompanied his. He stood up and walked to me.

"Come, sit," he said and led me to the other chair. He sat as well and spoke again.

"I don't usually dine here," he said, "but it's nice to get away from the others sometimes."

I nodded, though my preferred getaway would have more sky showing. Two servants entered, presented our dishes to us, bowed, and left.

"What I want to do," Oramus said when they left, "is just talk. I enjoyed our talk the other day. I want to do that again, but in a more relaxed environment, not when you're sick in bed." He smiled and chuckled, and I laughed a bit too, though at the moment I couldn't say sitting alone with Oramus was relaxing.

Oramus looked at me expectantly, but I didn't know what to say. After a couple of seconds, he began again.

"So, Pasin," he started, digging his fork into a stack of greenery, "You said you liked seeing the palace across that field back in Andor, right?" I nodded. "Why is that?"

"Well, it was the only place I could really see the

sky stretch if you know what I mean," I began. Oramus nodded, but I wasn't sure about its authenticity. I continued.

"I especially liked it during autumn though, with the leaves framing it with their colors." I began to cut a piece of fish, but I added at the last moment, "What's your favorite season?"

"Oh, winter of course," he replied. "It makes hunting more challenging. And when the snow level is just right, not too much or too little, I enjoy horseback riding with the winter wind in my face." He took a drink of his beverage and continued, "Do you enjoy riding?"

"I've never been."

"I guess you'll have to come with me next time," he said, putting his glass down and looking at me expectantly.

"I would love to," I replied and smiled, not just a polite smile, but a genuine one at the prospect of being outside again beyond the palace walls. Oramus smiled too and broached another topic.

As the meal went on, I did start to relax in his company. At some point, the conversation wandered back to my experiences at Andor. I talked to Erise about Andor too, occasionally, but while Erise merely listened, Oramus kept asking questions, so that our conversation stretched past dessert.

"And this...Slate, was it?" he asked, raising an eyebrow. I nodded and took another sip of tea. "He purposely treated you worse than the others?" I grunted and lowered the cup from my mouth.

"Definitely. The way he stretched out my name every single time, mangled it, ahh." I shook my head at the memory, but Oramus' eyebrows furrowed over set eyes. After a moment, he looked back up at me.

"Why? I don't see why someone would treat you like that." My chest warmed at Oramus' concern, and I answered easily.

"Because I'm an Absent," I replied and half-shrugged. I moved the teacup from hand to hand a few times before continuing. "It wasn't just him; it was everyone." As soon as the words spilled from my mouth, I shook my head. "Okay, not everyone, but it felt…" My voice trailed off without finishing the sentence, and I dropped my head, shying away from his gaze. However, as I looked at my hand-enfolded teacup, another hand wrapped around mine.

"Even so," Oramus said, staring straight into my eyes when I raised my head, "that shouldn't have happened to you." I shrugged again, but Oramus shook his head.

"I mean it," he said, "it shouldn't." I looked back into my tea.

"He'd do it again," I mumbled. Anyone outside the castle would, and so would many inside. Oramus' hands lifted mine off the cup and enveloped them. I looked back up into his face.

"Show me," he said.

#

The next day I walked down a path I should have walked over a month ago, wearing clothes I hadn't touched since I put on that first velvet palace dress. I had ridden on a horse next to Oramus to the path out of the Andor sector, but now I walked alone toward the schoolhouse I thought had been relegated to my past.

Even as the wind blew through my thin clothes, I enjoyed the relative freedom of the moment in the open air. The familiarity of the scene did nothing for me, however. I marveled at how quickly the palace had become so familiar. It felt strange to return to a place I had lived for sixteen years, only to feel out of place and misfit. Then again, I had never fit in to begin with.

I clutched a paper in my hands, detailing Dante the Victor's identification legislation, which started the tradition of identification coins. I stayed up late the night before to write it. Oramus had questioned me about the paper when he saw it, but he shrugged after my explanation and didn't mention it again. I couldn't see or hear them, but I knew that Oramus and Corinth weren't far behind. I also had the letter Oramus had given me for Slate, supposedly from the Andor prison.

Focus, Pasin, I thought, and shook my head.

The schoolhouse appeared around the bend. It hadn't changed one bit—same drooping roof, same sad stone exterior, same repulsion I felt upon seeing it. No, nothing changed in this place at all.

The morning wasn't even halfway done, so there were no children outside to deal with. I looked behind me at an empty road, took a deep breath, and stepped inside and made my way to my classroom.

The initial noise that greeted me quickly collapsed into silence, then whispers. The faces were so familiar; their stares were so uncomfortable. A class of thirty all staring at me, sixty eyeballs wide under raised eyebrows. Well, sixty-two if you included the man at the front of the room.

"What are you doing here?"

Slate attempted to hide his surprise under his well-practiced sneer. His eyes traveled up and down as if checking to see if I had grown extra appendages during my absence.

"Well," I started, and all whispers from the class stopped. "I was being held in prison, and they just let me out this morning." My eyes darted around nervously, seeing all of the wary faces around me. The lie seemed so stupid after saying it out loud.

"I have a note," I added and handed Slate the paper Oramus had given me. Slate kept eyeing me for a moment, and then took the paper with an air of disbelief. As he read, he pursed his lips. He reeked of stale alcohol.

"I see," he said finally, and then tossed the paper on the desk. He turned to the class.

"Copper–it was your friend who prompted Pasin's arrest, correct?"

Brock smirked. "Yes, sir."

Slate smiled back. "Good for him."

He turned back to me and opened his mouth as if to say something, but instead, his hand shot to his forehead. He took in a quick breath but then shook his head and returned his sight to me.

"I'm guessing you failed to write that paper I assigned you then, hmm?" He smirked again.

"Actually," I said, reaching out with my other papers, "I have it right here."

Slate's smile soured, and he grabbed the papers from my hand. He grunted as he read the first few lines. Not ten seconds later, he looked up again.

"Pasin," he said, drawing out the word, savoring the indignity of it.

"Pasin," he repeated, lifting the essay as he said my

name. "This is complete trash. This is nothing more than complete garbage." And with that, he snarled a smile again and threw my work into the wastebasket. My heart burned for a moment, and I looked him in the face, steeling myself for the abuse I knew was coming.

"Pasin," he said, coming closer to me, "that paper was just like you. Worthless."

Why did I even come back here? Why?

"And good only as trash," he ended with triumph on his skinny face. Even as he leered though, something clicked in my mind.

"Stop," I whispered, barely, through clenched teeth.

"You will never," he said.

"Stop," I repeated louder.

"Ever—"

"Stop!"

"Ever amount to anything."

"Enough!"

It wasn't me. The order came from the man who walked through the doorway, the man with ice-cold rage burning in his eyes. Gasps fluttered through the room as Oramus, in all his regal glory, walked to stand in front of me and stared down the man now cowering like a beaten dog.

"What did you say to her?" Oramus asked, his eyes flashing and fingers toying with his belt.

Slate sank like a rock to the ground.

"Your Highness," he gasped, face to the ground in a bow. "Please…"

"How dare you insult her," Oramus said, stepping forward, "you dirty piece of filth." Oramus stopped with his feet right next to Slate's head.

"I'm sorry," Slate sobbed, "Forgive me, please…forgiveness."

His voice broke as Oramus moved his foot to the side and pressed down on Slate's hand. Slate cried out, but Oramus' gaze didn't change. He stared down coldly at the whimpering man beneath him. His right hand moved away from his belt, and I saw a knife glint in his hand. Oramus turned his gaze to me.

"I can get rid of him if you'd like."

I looked at Oramus, his expression serious and steady, and then at Slate, tears now running down his face. So many times had I wanted to make him hurt as I did, but those tears, that terror…

"No," I said, looking away from Slate.

"Are you sure?" Oramus asked, eyebrows raised.

"…yes."

Oramus lifted his foot and stepped back from Slate, a sobbing heap on the floor. Oramus turned to the silent group of children, barely four years younger than he, while still brandishing his knife.

"If I ever," he said, staring down each individual, "if I ever hear anyone speak in such a manner about this lady, the consequences will be severe." He looked at Brock as he said the next line, "But for Pasin's decision, this man would be dead."

Oramus turned from the students, looked at me, and smiled.

"Are you ready to leave?"

"Yes," I replied, not wanting to see the looks on the faces of my previous peers.

"Then let's," he said, sweeping out of the room. I hurried to follow but gave one last look at my former teacher.

Slate, the bane of my previous existence, stared at

me, stared with the most fearful face I had ever seen. The face stayed in my mind as I joined Oramus by his horse.

"I would have done it, you know," he said, taking my hand in his. Corinth finished brushing off Oramus' horse's saddle and stood next to him.

"Corinth searched the minds of the people inside while you were in there," he said. "He told me what that man was thinking...terrible things. And I couldn't let that continue." His grip tightened around my hand.

He looked into my eyes with an almost gentle smile and then asked, "Are you ready to go back?"

"Home? I mean, to the palace? Yes." I blushed a little at my blunder.

Oramus smiled wider.

"I'm happy that you think of it as home," he said and helped me mount my waiting horse.

"I'm still not quite sure about this whole horse-riding thing," I said, looking at the faraway ground unsteadily.

"Don't worry," Oramus replied. "I'll make sure you're safe."

He clicked his tongue at his horse, and it began to trot down the road, stopping for a moment for me to catch up. I rode a bit behind on Oramus' right and Corinth rode even farther behind on the left.

The view was radically different five feet in the air. The ground moved swiftly beneath us as the horses beat the dirt road. Just over the tips of the trees, I could see the towers of the palace. Somehow, that distant silhouette had become my home.

The view was even stranger in Andor. The same shops lined the streets, but no matter which way I turned, no faces looked back. Everyone was prostrate, bowing in front of the king as he passed by without giving anyone or anything a second glance. Still, all the sights were the same, and my mind raced with memories. I saw the bookshop I was thrown out of, the stand where I first met Corinth, and the watch store.

"Oramus?" I asked tentatively, pushing the horse a bit to catch up. "Could we stop for a minute?" He paused before answering.

"All right," he said and halted his horse. He dismounted and helped me do the same.

"Wherever you like," he said. I started toward the watch store with Oramus not too far behind and Corinth trailing the both of us. I entered first and was engulfed by the sound of a thousand clocks ticking just like before.

"Now what's all the commotion outside?" I heard a crotchety voice call. The old man walked in and stopped short when he saw me.

"Oh, it's you," he said. "What's going on outside then?"

"Uh…the king is going through," I answered, avoiding the man's gaze and moving toward one of the glass cases. He huffed and cackled back.

"And what would the king be doing in Andor?" he asked. "Now see here," he continued, "If you don't plan on buying anything, then I suggest you get to leaving…"

The man stopped short as the door opened.

"Is there something here that you wanted?" Oramus asked me, entirely ignoring the wide-eyed man quivering behind the counter.

"Well," I said as Oramus walked up beside me.

"You'll probably think it's silly, but I've always wanted a pocket watch." Wow, I felt even sillier than I thought I would by saying that.

"Is there one in particular you like?" he asked, now scrutinizing the watches under the counter.

I looked down. The row of pocket watches flashed, each watch attempting to catch my attention with its charms. Several were obviously made for influential clientele, encrusted with semi-precious stones and flaunting hefty price tags. The one that pulled me in did not, however.

"That silver one, behind the two gold-rimmed ones." The watch was smaller, a logical size that could actually fit in one's pocket. It was of smooth silver, with only a little scrolling on the edges. Simple, but beautiful.

"That one?" Oramus considered it but then nodded with approval. "Yes, that will do. You," he said, addressing the man behind the counter. "Fetch me that one." The man's hands trembled as he unlocked the glass case and removed the watch. He managed to hand it to Oramus without dropping it.

Oramus held the pocket watch with the tips of his fingers.

"Yes," he said. "That will do just fine." He handed me the watch and folded my fingers around it. It fit perfectly in the palm of my hand.

"Thank you." My gaze met his, and time seemed to stop despite the ticking of dozens of timepieces.

"Is that all?" he asked.

"Yes."

We emerged outside where the horses waited and the crowd stood still as before. The most peculiar feeling settled at the bottom of my stomach as we left

Andor. Not loss, not sadness, nor happiness. Maybe closing. Maybe that's what it was.

It wasn't until we were outside of Andor that I realized something important.

"Oh."

"What is it Pasin?" Oramus automatically turned to look at me.

"We...I...the watch was never paid for." And it cost what? Eighteen gold pieces the sign said?

"Oh, that." Oramus waved his hand in dismissal. "I rule the land; I own everything in it. Nothing to worry yourself over."

I must have seen unconvinced for he continued, "And besides," he said. "Imagine how much business our visit will give him. He'll come ahead in the long run."

Corinth rode up to Oramus' right, and they talked in low tones as I thought back to the offer Oramus had made me, the offer about Slate.

I didn't understand why, but I wasn't supposed to ask why, right? I shoved the questions aside, shoved the internal heaviness aside, and looked again at the man ahead of me. Straight and tall, precise and powerful he sat, but when he looked at me, the gentleness in his eyes soothed the tempest inside, stalled the storm of emotions for that much longer.

When we returned to the palace, I took my leave of Oramus and went back to my room to do the homework I had put off the night before. I took a pencil out from the drawer, pausing to examine the ignis flower once more. I touched a petal, and the tip I brushed immediately crumbled.

"No more contact, I guess," I muttered to myself. I closed the drawer and began my work.

CHAPTER FIFTEEN

"King Oramus was not the first ruler to take a census," Water said as I took notes the next day. The rain pattered a dreary tune against the windows and cast an unusual pall on the room's interior. "Dante the Victor began the practice during his third year as king, but Gaeron Zinc ended it in order to cut government expenditures."

My quill quivered as I stifled a yawn. I had been up way too late the night before; for once, Erise came in the evening instead of morning. She said she just wanted to ask how the outing with Oramus had been, but we ended up talking for nearly three hours. It felt so easy to talk to her, especially compared to the other court members, even Oramus. My laughter could flow freely around her, and she did the same.

"King Oramus reinstated the census almost immediately after his coronation. He likewise reinstated the identification piece program with a new addition in order to–are you even trying?"

My head jerked at the abrupt change in Water's tone. He frowned at me and gestured toward my paper. When I looked down, I saw that my notes had devolved into little more than scribbles.

"I…I'm sorry sir," I stuttered, mortified. Oh shining, almost half the page was like that. "I didn't mean to—"

"Is there a reason for this?" he asked. I looked at him again and felt my cheeks redden as I answered.

"I stayed up too late last night," I replied, embarrassed at my own response. The rain continued steadily in the background, like a never-ending line of soldiers moving forward. Water took off his glasses and pinched the bridge of his nose with his fingers, closing his eyes as if he were in pain.

"Pasin, I understand that this is not the most interesting topic for a young woman, but please pay attention." He let out a deep breath, then put his glasses back on and looked at me again.

"This is information that affects policy right now," he continued. "This affects you."

"I'm sorry, sir," I repeated. I didn't know what else to say. Water sighed.

"You are dismissed for the day," he said. "Next time, come ready to focus." He picked up his ever-present notebook, turned around in his chair, and said nothing else.

I just sat there for a moment in stunned silence. Ears burning under my hair, I gathered my things and walked toward the door, away from Water's turned back.

I left the library with Water's words fading in my mind, settling next to the headache building in the middle of my forehead. I turned right to follow the normal route back to my room, but the back of Hex's head stopped me in my tracks. Hex stood with two of the other men and their servants. I was not in the mood to interact with him. Only Hex's servant Air turned his head as I abruptly changed my course to the opposite direction.

I had never been into this section of the palace, or at least, not that I could remember. I followed the hallway through its turns, but nothing revealed familiarity. A couple of minutes into this I considered turning back, but something stopped me.

Two familiar, muffled voices buzzed in the air and to my horror, I saw a doorknob jostle and slowly open. The hall held no hiding places, so I did the stupid thing and instead of calmly walking on, I turned to the nearest door. I twisted the knob frantically and when the door opened, I ducked inside the dark room before I could be spotted. My heart raced as I leaned against the door, barely letting myself breathe while the voices passed.

"Is there anything else I can do, sire?" Corinth asked, voice as clear as if he stood next to my ear.

"No," Oramus replied, "nothing large at least. Everything is working well. All I need you to do is double-check those sources…" Their voices trailed off as they rounded the corner. Only when their murmurings could no longer be heard did I breathe openly again.

I decided to wait for a few minutes, just to make sure the two were well on the way to whatever destination they were going. Once my heart rate returned to normal, I took a moment to look around the room, or tried to at least. Unlike the hallways, this room had no lamps hanging on the walls. Instead my eyes were drawn to a flickering light on the opposite wall.

This light didn't appear as one source. Instead, it leaked out of the edges of what appeared to be a large cabinet or armoire. The cabinet dominated the wall, but from what I could tell, it looked rather plain. The rest of the small space held a few odds and ends–a broom, a pile of rags, a bucket. The only remarkable feature in the room was the soft blue, pulsing light flickering through the cracks of the cabinet. The way the light moved in the air captivated me. Most of the light issued through the crack between the two front doors of the cabinet. I reached for the door and noted how the right door was slightly ajar. Someone must not have closed it properly.

The doors parted at my pull, and an ethereal brightness issued from the uncovered space. It flooded the room, forcing me to shield my eyes after the previous darkness. The light flickered and convulsed in the air, creating dynamic, constantly shifting shadows on the walls. After my eyes adjusted, I took a better look at the actual contents.

Behind the wooden doors stood five, six shelves lined with small, glass bottles. Each shelf had at least fifteen jars spanning its length and an unknown number of bottles lined up behind. The light itself came from inside these jars. Each jar held an individual ball of light, some darker or larger or more spastic than others. The ball of light sat inside each bottle, remaining in one spot while little tendrils of energy constantly dashed around it.

I leaned forward to look at the bottles, too afraid to actually touch them. I had seen nothing like the light before, but something seemed wrong about it, though I couldn't say exactly what. Despite the darkness of the rest of the room, the light from inside the bottles illuminated the jars just enough to read the labels. I scanned the middle shelf and read things such as STN, GRS, GST, DRK. Each bottle had three letters on it, and the jars were lined up in no apparent order. Despite my curiosity, I still refrained from touching them.

I finally regained sense long enough to realize the hallway should be clear. I closed the cabinet doors, and I heard a definitive click as what must have been a locking device reset. I listened at the door for a moment and heard no one. I exited the room and began to retrace my steps back to the library hallway.

The questions in my mind both intensified and weakened as I made my way back, head looking at the ground in an attempt to concentrate. Part of me wanted to ask Erise about this while another part didn't want to admit to snooping around the castle. As I turned into the hallway before the library's hallway, I decided on the latter course of action. I nodded to myself and looked up, promptly meeting the displeased gaze of Corinth.

"What are you doing here?" he asked.

"I got lost," I replied with only a little hesitation. It was the truth, kind of. Corinth raised his eyebrows.

"You have no reason to be in this wing beyond the library," he said. "Stay where you belong."

I expected further berating, but Corinth was finished.

"Yes, sir," I replied and hurried off, Corinth's gaze following me. I didn't come close to turning around.

#

I spent much more time with Oramus after our outing, having at least one meal with him every day. Water wasn't pleased by the interruptions while Peridot listened breathlessly to each new experience I shared with her. Erise expressed interest as well, but not the gossip kind of interest Peridot displayed.

One day as we finished lunch, Oramus took my hands in his.

"I have a surprise for you," he said, "out in the garden. Would you like to see it?"

CHAPTER SIXTEEN

Once we reached the doors leading to the gardens, Oramus covered my eyes with his hands and carefully led me across stone paths to the unknown destination. A light breeze picked up, and I smiled at its touch. After a minute or two, we stopped.

"You said your favorite flowers are ignis flowers, correct?" Oramus asked.

"Yes, there used to be a big bunch of them in the garden outside my window," I said. It was one of the few enjoyable memories of the orphanage.

"Well, we didn't have any in the gardens, so I had this done..." He removed his hand, and a massive grin overtook my face.

Thirty, forty, fifty ignis bushes filled a nook to overflowing, their deep, deep red a sharp contrast to the other plants fading for winter. In the center of the patch stood a stone statue trying to mimic the beauty of the plants behind it. Oramus squeezed my hand.

"It's all for you," he said.

"Thank you so, so much!" I wanted to hug him,

but it didn't seem quite right.

"You like it?"

"I love it." I moved to one of the bushes and plucked a flower. Its color radiated against my pale skin, making me realize how much I missed live ignis flowers. I turned to Oramus.

"Would you like one?" I asked. To my surprise, he shook his head.

"I don't like ignis flowers myself," he answered. He must have seen the slump on my face, for he continued, "When I was younger, about eleven, my father…" He shook his head. "My father was a blacksmith, and I was his apprentice. I never did well enough for him, and he burned me once for it." My eyes widened.

"I'm so sorry…"

"Don't be," he said. "He was never a loving man anyway. Used to use his sword as a cane…" Oramus shook his head again.

I did it. I dared to ask, "What happened to him? Is he still a blacksmith?"

"He died," Oramus said without looking at me. "He died right after I became king."

All was silent for a moment. Then Oramus spoke again.

"Anyway, that's why I don't like those fire flowers–or fire in general, really."

I smiled a bit.

"You know," I said, "I was burned when I was younger too, about eight I think." Oramus looked up with raised eyebrows. "Yes, right on my shoulder. You know Blaze?"

"Yes…"

"We fought a lot when we went to school together.

We got into an argument, and he hit me with a fireball. He told the teacher he just meant to light my hair on fire, but I never believed that."

Aah. A small wave of pain pulsed against my head. Not another headache...

Oramus frowned.

"Blaze did say he knew you from before, but he failed to mention that," he said as we began walking again.

"He's always been a show-off," I said, still holding the flower in my hand. "I remember one time when he—" The strength evaporated from my legs and I collapsed, but Oramus caught me just before my head could hit the ground.

"What happened?" he asked, worry in his voice, on his brow.

"I–I don't know...I–aah!" Another wave of pain pulsed in my head, threefold the pain of before.

"What is it? What's wrong?"

"My head," I choked out. Burning tears formed and fell down my cheek. Oramus' face swam in my vision. In one motion, he swept me into his arms and walked, jogged, ran back to the entrance of the garden.

"Corinth!" he called to the man waiting just inside. "Get Herb now!"

Corinth ran off, and Oramus set me down on a couch. I shivered and sobbed, trying to choke back tears flooding my face.

"Now tell me," he murmured, kneeling to my level. "What hurts?"

"My head," I repeated. "It's pounding and–and it's burning. And my legs, my arms–they feel so weak. I can't...I can't move my legs..." Terror mingled with tears; pain and panic set my heart racing. I reached for something, anything, and Oramus took my hand once more. It felt like ice on mine.

"Here, sire," a strange voice called as an unfamiliar man entered the room and walked over to us.

"What seems to be the problem?" he asked.

Oramus repeated what I had told him. The healer stood over me, put his hand on my head, and frowned.

"What Element is she?"

"She's an Absent," Oramus replied with a certain strength in his voice. Herb *hmmed* at this.

"What were you doing?" he asked while simultaneously pressing on my neck.

"We were walking outside in the garden when she collapsed and said her head was hurting her."

It was good that Oramus spoke for me, because I doubted my own ability at that point. Herb kept squeezing down my shoulder and arm until he stopped at my forearm. I couldn't see his expression for all the tears in my eyes, but I heard his voice, low and urgent.

"I think I know what's wrong," he said. "I need to speak to you privately, sir." Some kind of eye contact must have been exchanged, because Oramus pressed my hand again and whispered, "I'll be right back. You're going to be fine." And then the hand was gone.

I could see the blurred shape of Corinth against the wall, but that was it. I heard the murmured voices of Oramus and Herb, but I could only distinguish a little bit.

"How long has she—" Herb started.

"A month and a half," Oramus replied.

How long what? A month and a half…how long I'd been at the palace? What? But the pain fogged my mind and refused to let go.

A minute later, the air moved and Oramus took my hand again.

"Pasin," he said urgently, "Herb has to prepare a medicine, but it's going to take some time. I can make you fall asleep so that you're not in pain while he makes it."

The pain escalated, racing closer to the breaking point.

"How long…will it take…"

"At least thirty minutes–and you have to be unconscious when it's administered." My vision began to blacken at the edges…

"We have to hurry, Miss," Herb interjected.

"Okay, okay. Just do it." Sweat beaded on my brow.

"I'll be right here," Oramus said. Then he surprised me. Oramus leaned over and kissed my forehead. "Are you ready?"

"Y–yes."

And the pain faded.

#

The sleep wasn't natural. That much was clear. Floating in nothing, seeing nothing, feeling nothing but a slight pressure on my right hand. Then the pressure left, and I was entirely adrift in the darkness. But then–but then a weight was lifted, a weight I never recognized before–it was gone, and I arched my back and burned, and the darkness was on fire.

#

Consciousness returned like a tide, coming in higher and stronger with each pass. Touch arrived first–I felt softness all around me, which triggered the desire for more sleep. Taste and smell returned hand in hand, but they didn't do much. Next was hearing, but that yielded similar results. I heard breathing, but little else. Finally, I opened my eyes.

I lay in a bed, my bed, covered by a mound of blankets. Before much more observation could be made, a voice spoke from beside me.

"Pasin? Are you awake?"

I turned my head to face the voice, and Oramus sat there, smiling gently. I nodded.

"Does anything hurt?" he asked. I did a quick check.

"No," I replied, voice creaking. "I just feel weak…my arms and legs…" Moving my hand against the blankets felt like trying to lift a cow.

"So what did Herb say?" I asked. "What's wrong with me?"

"You had an allergic reaction," Oramus said. "The ignis flower–Herb said your body started to shut down because of it."

The ignis flower?

"But…I grew up with it…how?"

"I told him what you told me, and he said that encountering the flower after so long of an absence triggered the reaction. He said it's residual–that it builds up over time until the reaction happens. Also, the larger quantity made it that much worse."

I thought of the flower in the desk five feet away. I saw it every time I opened the drawer to grab a pencil.

"I…" he started and placed a hand on top of the blanket. "I am just glad that it happened here. If not…" He seemed lost for words and then settled. "Well, that didn't happen. And that's what's important."

But the flower…it didn't make sense.

"How long 'til I recover?" I asked.

"I'm not sure," Oramus replied. "I'll send someone to fetch Herb in a moment. But hopefully you'll be better soon."

I nodded, but he wasn't finished.

"Pasin," he started again, "Corinth brought me some news today. Important news." I looked at him blankly, and he continued.

"I had Corinth find out about your parents."

My body jolted to attention. I sat up, pulling my arms out from under the blankets, and turned to the man beside me.

"What did he say? What did he find out?"

Oramus said nothing for a moment. Instead, he bundled up my hands with his.

"Pasin," he said, quietly, gently, "Your parents are dead."

His words slapped with the force of a gale. I blinked quickly, over and over again as the implications set in. Not that I expected, but I had hoped…I said nothing, but Oramus added more to his story.

"We found out about them though. Your father's name was Triet Water and your mother was Lanelle Light. They lived in the Wessen Sector in Falleon City, Water as a carpenter and Light as a healer. They died two years after your birth during the influenza outbreak."

Oramus' words washed over me, gave me context, and more importantly, time to regain control of my emotions.

"Are there...any surviving relatives?" I asked meekly. Oramus shook his head.

"We couldn't find any," he said. He squeezed his hands on mine. Tears crept at the edge of my vision. He sighed.

"Pasin, I am so sorry," he said. "I can't begin to think how hard this is to hear." The tears flooded my eyes and began to leak down my face. Oramus lifted a hand and wiped one away from my face. "At least you're here now," he whispered, "With me."

I looked at him; he looked at me. Sadness and gratitude collided in my chest. We leaned forward together, and I wept in his arms until I had no tears left.

CHAPTER SEVENTEEN

Oramus left shortly after his announcement, talking about a meeting or something. I saw no one but Grass for the rest of the day, and that was fine. I didn't want to talk; I didn't want to interact with anyone. I just lay in my bed until night came and felt relief when I could surrender to sleep.

Erise visited the morning after the incident.

"You need to stop getting into trouble," she said, face flushed with more concern than I would have expected.

"Oramus said Herb said it was an allergic reaction," I mumbled from my prostrate position on the bed, "I can't help that."

"Even so," she said as she pulled the desk chair up to my bedside. "You don't need to be getting sick all the time." She sat on the chair, cross-legged as usual. "So how do you feel today?"

I tilted my head toward her. My eyes still stung from the previous day's news. I grabbed a strand of hair and started stroking it.

"I'm all right," I answered. "I can't really move, but I'm all right." Erise peered at me, but I didn't feel like meeting her eyes. For once, I wanted to be alone instead of with her. She frowned.

"You can move enough to mess with your hair," she said and smiled, but I didn't reply.

"Are you sure you're all right?" she asked. She lowered her shoulders and voice with the next question. "Did something else happen?"

I turned my head away from her and felt tears stinging at the corners of my eyes.

"Erise," I started, willing my voice not to shake too much, "I was left at the orphanage as a newborn. Yesterday, Oramus told me my parents are dead." I couldn't stop my quivering jaw or the water leaking down my cheek. Erise didn't react immediately; she gave me time to calm most of the shaking before she spoke.

"I'm sorry to hear that," she said. When I looked at her, her face revealed none of its normal cheerfulness. No, it held a solemnity more than mere seriousness. "I really mean it. I'm sorry you found that out."

Neither of us spoke. I wiped the tears from my eyes, but Erise sat completely still until she spoke again.

"Can I tell you something?" she asked. I nodded.

"I told you that I grew up with the elves, right?" I nodded again. Erise shifted in her seat and continued, "My mother was the elven half of my parents, and I grew up with her and the other elves until I was ten. I didn't know anything about my father until he sent a message, requesting I join him at the palace. Apparently, he was the brother of some nobleman...I don't know." She waved her hand in the air at the thought before returning it to her lap.

"My mother wanted me to go. I didn't really understand at the time, but now I realize how different I was, having an Element among the elves. I think she wanted me to go somewhere where I might fit in. So I left her and came to the palace as my father's servant.

"My father was an Earth, and he was kind to me most of the time, except when he had too much to drink. Six months into my time with him, he got into a brawl with King Gaeron's son and almost buried the man alive." Erise's hands tightened in her lap. She looked down and continued, "I knew it was just the alcohol, but Gaeron took it as an assassination attempt. My father was executed the next day." I inhaled sharply at the news.

"Oh, Erise, I'm so sorry." I reached out and patted her knee, but she didn't move or respond to me.

"I was released from the palace, but when I got back to the forest, I couldn't find the elf community. I walked the base of that mountain at least three times, but I couldn't find them." Her muscles tightened. "I couldn't find my mother."

I opened my mouth to offer condolences once more, but I closed it again. I could see the veins bulging in her arms.

"But I made it," she continued. "I did what I needed to. I assisted; I worked; I stole. I managed to keep going, even when my father's brother refused to help me. One day when I was assisting a merchant, we were attacked on the road. I grabbed one of his swords and found an ability beyond my Element. After a lot of training and a change in monarchs, I made it back to the palace to where I currently am."

"That's amazing," I murmured, wondering if I could ever muster that much determination. After a couple of seconds, Erise's muscles relaxed some, though not all the way.

"What I'm trying to say," she said, looking up at me, "is that yes, it is absolutely terrible to lose parents, and you should have plenty of time to grieve. But after that, after taking that kind of a blow, you still need to get up and keep going with what you have left."

A small, small smile lifted the very edges of her mouth.

"I'm here for you," she said. "You know that, right?"

I nodded and smiled back.

"Good." Erise nodded and shifted in her seat again. "Now let's talk about something else."

I closed my eyes and let out a little snort, but I knew where she was coming from.

"Sure," I replied.

#

Oramus came by about an hour after Erise left, and he returned every day to sit with me and eat dinner with me. Halfway through the second day, I was able to sit up and engage in actual conversation, but the activity ended there. I couldn't walk until day three and that was only to go to the bathroom without help. Peridot dropped in as well, going on about how I had to get better before the gala and the preparations that were being made for it. The way she described it sounded impressive indeed, what with ice sculptures being made and purportedly thousands of candles, but I didn't know if I believed that one.

A week after the incident, I sat at my desk trying to catch up with my homework when Oramus entered.

"What are you writing about this time?" he asked. I put down my pen and looked up at him.

"I'm doing a compare and contrast bit on the local governments of Morrit and Daven," I said. Oramus' upper lip curled as if in revulsion.

"I don't like it either," I said. Oramus leaned against the desk and pushed the paper away with one hand.

"I wanted to ask you something important," he said. I expected him to continue, but he paused for longer than I expected before doing so.

"Pasin," he said, his gaze meeting mine, "will you accept the honor of accompanying me to the gala tomorrow night?" He pulled his other hand from behind his back and offered me a white rose. I looked down to the flower and back up to his eyes.

"I would love to," I replied with a shy smile. He smiled back and placed it in my hand.

"We didn't have any poppies in the garden," he said as I peered at the flower. "so I gave you a favorite of mine."

"Thank you," I answered, stroking the petals. "It's beautiful."

"Just like the recipient," he replied promptly. My ears burned under my hair at the compliment. He put his hand on mine, covering it and the rose.

"I have business to attend to in the different sectors of the city," he said, "so I won't see you until tomorrow night, probably right before we enter the gala." His face relaxed, and one side of his mouth bent up. "Now don't get into any more trouble while I'm gone, okay?" I grinned and chuckled again.

"I won't," I replied. He gave my hands a light squeeze and left.

I opened my hand and regarded the rose again. The petals felt so smooth, caressing my fingers like silky, supple skin. Twisting the rose stem between my fingers, I opened the desk drawer that still contained the remains of Arina's ignis flower gift. I had not touched the object since the reaction, but nothing had happened when I opened the drawer to retrieve writing utensils.

After looking at it for a few seconds, I reached into the drawer and gingerly picked up the dead bloom. Half of it collapsed into powder as I lifted it. I placed it on a sheet of paper, crumpled the paper, and tossed it into the wastebasket.

Oramus' white rose filled the vacated space nicely. I smiled to myself as I closed the drawer again, half in gratitude at the gesture and half in anticipation for the coming night.

CHAPTER EIGHTEEN

I sat in one of the chamber chairs, trying hard not to fidget while Grass stood nearby. She said Pearl had told her to bring me there to wait, but I didn't know what we were waiting for. The gala was going to start soon; maybe it had already started. I couldn't even play with my fingers. For once, Vine made a short-sleeved dress, but she included a set of near elbow-length gloves. Yes, the silver dress and glove combination made me giggle with glee when I first saw it, but by this point, I wanted to peel the gloves off to let my hands breath. Before I could however, the door opened.

"You look absolutely beautiful," Oramus said. I turned toward him, smiling at the sound of his voice.

"Thank you," I said. "So do you. I mean—you look handsome." My ears burned at the misstep, but Oramus took it in stride. He smiled as well and took one of my hands in his.

"Are you ready?" he asked. The momentary confusion I felt in the nondescript room vanished when our gazes met.

"Yes," I replied.

Oramus escorted me through another door, where a servant waited on the other side by a set of double doors. Oramus nodded to the servant, and the doors were thrown open.

Applause erupted from the unveiled room. We stood in the throne room at the top of the throne's platform, maybe twenty feet in the air. Scores of people packed the room like a rippling sea of satin and jewels wedged between the forest-covered walls. The candles on the wall ledges burned softly, but the combined force of hundreds of wicks lit the walls and the people between them just enough to leave shadows. These shadows danced as the applause continued, the disturbed air tugging the tongues of flame with it.

Oramus and I stood in front of the throne, and Oramus let the applause carry on for a fair amount of time before lifting his arms for silence.

"This is a momentous occasion," he began. "Four years ago on this day, I officially became your king."

The crowd below burst into applause again at his words, and I clapped too, though I didn't quite remember the event.

"Look around," he said, "See how Falleon has changed, has changed for the better these past four years. This is not just an anniversary of my own rule, but of the betterment of the entire kingdom!" Cheers rose again while Oramus stood straight up and down, a broad grin spread across his face. He held his arms out, hands facing up, as the cheers subsided.

"Let the celebration begin!" he called.

A last round of applause roared in the air, the

movements tearing some of the flames from their wicks. A band started, and Oramus, still smiling, reached out for my hand. We descended the stairs on the left to the floor below as couples began lining up.

"Will you dance?" he asked me, the candlelight gleaming in his eyes.

"Of course," I responded, and he swept me into the whirl of people.

He led me easily, like a second nature, and I followed his lead across the floor. As time wore on, candles blended into half-lit faces. I had glimpses of others, of Hex's scowl, of Peridot's smile and the ginger-haired man next to her, but my attention kept returning to the man holding my hands and guiding my steps. His face remained constant in my vision, filling me with warmth, and his touch sent heat to the tips of my toes.

Nearly an hour passed in this manner before I extracted myself from the revelry.

"I have to get a drink," I said, half panting. "I need to sit down."

"Are you feeling all right?" Oramus asked, his easy manner gone and his brow suddenly heavy.

"Yes, I'm fine," I reassured him. "I just need to sit…for a bit. Nothing's wrong, I promise."

Oramus led me to a side table where I sat, relieved to get off my feet. A nearby servant brought me a glass of water, and Oramus watched me drink in silence. Through the glass, I saw Corinth approach our table, lean toward Oramus, and tap him on the shoulder.

"Not now," Oramus said to him, but Corinth insisted.

"Sir, I have what you were asking for earlier."

Oramus sat in silence for just a moment before standing.

"All right then." Oramus squeezed my hand quickly. "I'll be right back."

"Okay," I answered. He gave me a peck on the cheek and disappeared.

I finished my drink, and as I turned to watch the rest of the room, I heard someone whisper my name.

"Pasin."

I looked around. Was that Erise? She beckoned with her hand from behind a pillar. I looked around again. Oramus stood at the other end of the room, talking with Corinth, and almost everyone else was dancing.

"Pasin, come here," Erise whispered more urgently. I put down my cup and joined her behind the column.

"What is it?" I asked, anxious to sit down again.

"I need to tell you something, come on." Before I could reply, Erise scurried to a side door that led into the hallway to the lavatories. She pushed the door open and motioned for me to follow. After a last glance, I did. She walked a bit further, and we turned the corner to reveal–Air? Hex's servant?

"Pasin, this is Air," Erise said, gesturing to the blond male.

"We've met," I replied, looking him over. Air seemed out of place, maybe even a bit embarrassed.

"Hello," he said, but didn't continue. The three of us just stood there, Erise and Air's eyes still on me.

"Well, what is it?" I asked, impatience and embarrassment flaring inside of me. My feet moaned under the weight of my body. "What do you want to tell me? I want to sit back down." They didn't say anything. Air's gaze flicked to Erise, but she stood still except for her chewing the inside of her cheek.

"I'm going," I said, turning and wondering if Oramus had noticed my absence.

"Wait," Erise said and grabbed my shoulder.

"What?" I let the word drop heavily, hoping it resonated with the impatience and growing annoyance I felt. She took a quick breath before answering.

"You asked me a question before that I couldn't answer," Erise said quickly. "You asked me about the bracelets on your arm."

The bracelets. I glanced down at the gloved area where the bangles wrapped around my wrist. I hadn't thought about them in so long—they just were, like the always-lit hallways and the always-warm air. It didn't make sense. It just was.

"Those bracelets neutralize Elemental power," she said, looking me dead in the eyes. "That's what they're made for. One can stop a Blaze from shooting fire. Two can kill an Earth."

I looked over at Air. He didn't meet my gaze. This news didn't make sense either.

"Then why—" I began.

"There is an Element," Erise continued, "that does not appear naturally over time. It has to be...awoken by some sort of dramatic event. Emotions have to be so supercharged that the Elemental power literally bursts out of its inhabitant. This is supposed to be incredibly violent, but afterward the person has immense powers."

Something was forming in my mind, like a long-forgotten dream, but that couldn't be possible, it just couldn't...

"That Element has the power of a Star, fire and air combined. Pasin, you're not an Absent. You're a—"

"No," I said. Don't you dare say that Erise, I repeated in my mind. Don't do that to me.

"That's not possible," I continued. "I can't...I can't..."

"I know it's hard to believe," she said, trying to recapture my gaze, "But it's true, I promise you."

The pieces fit together. My arrest; the anger, no, the fury I felt...but it couldn't. Not after all this...

"What makes you think that? How can you be so sure?" I asked.

"Corinth told me about your arrest. The way he described it–the fact that you showed no significant physical difference after those bands were put on you, how you got sick when they were on for so long–that's what made you sick," she continued. "The pent-up energy was eating away at you from the inside. It was killing you," she emphasized. I said nothing. She kept talking.

"The only reason you fainted when you were arrested is because your powers were just coming in. Otherwise, that first bracelet would have done nothing. And when that healer healed you? All he did was take off the bands to let out the energy. If he didn't, you would be dead by now."

Dead. Puh, I thought I would be dead the moment I walked into the palace. Then again, I thought back to the ignis flower I had stored in my desk for so long, how it hadn't seemed to affect me despite Oramus' explanation.

"But, but..." I stuttered. Erise opened her mouth to speak, but I stopped her. "No, wait."

I leaned against the wall, paneling smooth under

my fingers and shoes pinching my feet. I closed my eyes and thought. It made sense. It all seemed to fit, and this was Erise talking, the Element expert. My chest rose–but hope? Hope? It was far too late for that.

"So what…what is he doing here?" I asked, gesturing toward Air. "Why is he here, why are you…why are telling me this Erise?" I turned and looked her in the eyes once more.

"Air and I are part of a group," she said, "a group focused on exposing Oramus' plans. We were going to tell you at some point, soon, but we found out—" She peered at Air who nodded, "—that we're running out of time. We have to tell you now."

Ice gripped my chest.

"Tell me what?" What else? What else could there be?

Erise glanced at Air again.

"Oramus knew about your Element, because I told him," she said. My mouth dropped, and questions rose in my throat, but she continued, "He would have killed you otherwise for what you did in the throne room." Erise took a breath. "He's the one who ordered for the Element nullifying bands to stay on you. He made sure you didn't find out about it. And he's the one manipulating you so you'll trust him."

"But that–why?" I asked. "Why bother?" Even though I didn't quite believe her, my insecurities flooded back in with her words.

"As Erise said," Air spoke finally, soft but precise, "you have immense power, currently untapped. Oramus wants to use it to achieve his ends."

"Like what?" I asked. Exasperation lit up in me again and mixed with surprise, fear to create a sickening anxiety in my stomach. My feet sent shock waves up my legs. Oramus would have noticed my absence by now.

"He wants to use your power of flight to go over the mountains and spread his empire," Air said.

...what?

"That's ridiculous," I spat out. "Absolutely ridiculous," I repeated, partly for myself.

"We were going to tell you," Erise said, pleaded. "We would've done it at a better time, but Corinth was informed that there are spies in the castle. We'll be mind searched; we'll be found out if we stay." Her eyebrows were furrowed, and nerves strained in her forehead and arms. "Come with us Pasin," she said, pleaded. "We'll keep you safe from Oramus, we'll find someone to get those bracelets off, prepare for battle—"

"Battle?" My voice rose. Against Oramus?

"He'll have you, one way or another. Either you do what he says willingly, or he'll take out your heart essence–he'll be able to control you and your powers."

"No! Oramus loves me!" My voice rose even more, but I shook her words from my ears and strengthened my posture. "And I love him too."

"It's not real," Erise answered, shaking her head. "He doesn't love anyone but himself. If anything, he loves you for your powers. Nothing more."

"Well, what do you want me for then?" I asked, once again looking from Erise to Air. "What makes you two any different?"

"I'm your friend," Erise said. "And you're my friend. I don't want him to do that to you, please."

But I was shaking my head, the thoughts crashing

into one another even as she spoke.

"No." I faced her head on. All of the confusion hardened in my chest. "No. Erise, you're the one doing this to me. I can't believe you, I can't..." I gnashed my teeth together; I tightened my face. But the tears came.

"I was happy!" I choked, letting the words hang in the air. "You can't do that to me–I'm finally happy! Why are you doing this?" I tried to stifle the sobs, but they racked my chest all the same.

"Because I care!" she answered, heat flaring in her voice. "I had to tell you before it's too late!"

I didn't reply, and Erise fell silent though her chest rose and fell rapidly after her last statement. Air looked up and down the hallway, but I didn't care. I just didn't care anymore.

"No," I repeated, wiping my eyes with the back of my hand. "This is my life now. I can't just give it up on, on someone's words. I trust Oramus." I looked up and met Erise's gaze. Any desperation I had seen in her eyes evaporated, leaving them blank. She opened her mouth, closed it, then opened it again.

"That's your final word?" she asked.

"...Yes."

And with one word, I closed the door on the possibilities bubbling in me and ended the inner dialogue. Erise's expression didn't change, but I saw her chew her bottom lip once again.

"Then I guess that's that." Erise turned away from me toward the long hallway. "We have to leave now," she added quietly.

My voice lowered too.

"Permanently?"

I looked after Erise, but she didn't turn back

around toward me.

"Yes," Air answered. "Corinth will figure out we're the spies soon enough. We have to get out as soon as possible."

"So this is goodbye," Erise ended. She waited as Air walked to her side. She nodded at him and, after a moment, at me, and they both started to set off down the passage. Though my eyes still stung from my earlier tears, I stood dumbstruck for a moment before calling out to their fleeing backs.

"We're still friends!" I said, feeling new tears rise to my eyes. "I won't tell it was you or anything."

Neither replied, but Erise did give one look back. I stood there, watching them leave, the largest knot of emotions welling up in my stomach. Anger, frustration…loss.

No. I pushed the feelings aside. Not today. Not tonight.

"Pasin?" And then Oramus was there, enveloping my vision with his presence. "Why are you out here?"

"I…I was getting some fresh air," I said, willing the new tears to dry where they sat. "I just…needed a break."

"Tell me next time," Oramus answered, standing wonderfully, awfully close. "Don't scare me like that, please."

I nodded. Oramus wrapped his arms around me and pressed me to his chest. His warmth erased the doubt. Erased…disguised? I thrust the thought aside.

"Let's go back to the dance. I need to make an announcement." He took my hand and we reentered the throne room.

"Attention!" Oramus called, one hand raised, the other with mine. The instruments stopped; the dancers stopped; only Oramus and I moved. He stepped forward and guided me to join him.

"Four years ago, on this day, I ascended to the throne as king." Cheers filtered through the air again; Oramus nodded and continued, "Four years ago, I achieved one of my dreams, to become ruler of this, the great land of Falleon. Tonight, I am going to achieve another dream." He nodded at a young boy, who raced off on some silent mission.

"Pasin," Oramus said, turning to me, smiling gently at me. "Pasin came here only two months ago," he said, addressing the assembly still. "Two months, and it feels as if I have known her for a lifetime."

Hundreds of gazes seemed to crawl over me, but Oramus' face filled my sight.

"When we first met, Pasin was here, in this room, and she laughed. She is the one and only person who has dared laugh like that, and I'm glad she did." He paused.

"Pasin has taught me…how to find joy," he said. "I have found my joy in her."

The boy came back with a large, flat box in hand. Oramus took it.

"Pasin," he said, looking me straight in the eyes. "I want to spend every day of the rest of my life with you." He opened the box, and something glinted inside. The breath caught in my throat.

"Pasin," he repeated, "Will you marry me?"

A collective intake of breath echoed around the room before collapsing into anticipatory silence. All was silent except for the sound of my own beating heart pounding in my ears.

I stared at him, mouth open. His words, Erise's words, my thoughts and questions, confusions, and misunderstandings collided. His question marked the turning point. No turning back.

"Yes," I whispered. "Yes!" I exclaimed with the broadest smile on my face.

Oramus' own smile spread softly across his lips at my words. He lifted the glinting object from the box, a silver necklace with a nest of silver circles as a pendant. A beautiful maelstrom. The chain seemed light and smooth, but the ends were black.

He held the necklace up and moved the ends around my neck. The chain draped across my neck and with a quiet click, the ends connected, never to separate again.

Applause and cheers thundered through the air around us. Oramus buried me in his embrace, and I cried in his arms. Tears of happiness?

Oramus released me and wiped a tear away from my face. His hands stroked with gentleness, and gentleness beamed from the eyes above his smile.

"May I have this dance?" he asked. I nodded and managed a new smile. Oramus raised his hand, and the instruments started a deep, mysterious melody.

"I had this made," he said, taking one of my hands and resting his other on my waist. "Just for you," he added.

"Especially for me?"

"Yes," he answered, whispering into my ear. "Everything."

In that moment, I chose to forget. I chose to ignore the words still echoing in my mind, ignore how Erise bit her lip, like she does when she's worried. I chose to ignore the terrible, terrible sense it all made. Oblivion. Just wait until the end of the song, I reasoned.

And what glorious oblivion it was.

Oramus pulled me into him, practically supported all of my weight and pressed his skin into mine. The strings guided our motions together, apart, but always reuniting as we twirled and spun around the open space. Happiness seized every surface, reflecting my own joy from every candle, face, and depthless shadow. The strings kept us together and refused to weaken, escalating, escalating, escalating and urging faster, faster, faster, faster forward, together apart but back again in the sweeping motion of a new day's sky, a new night's dreams, and the light in between.

With each note, the finale marched closer; each count drew us closer to the inevitable ending. Fitful and violent, I poured every feeling into him, pressed my body against his, and let him pull me in with each cherished new note.

The music vaulted into a crescendo then stopped, though the music echoed for a couple seconds afterward. We pulled together one final time, and how the people cheered as we stood together, sweat beading on my forehead and my breath catching.

"You are amazing," Oramus murmured into my ear. So soft his voice made me. But the song was over. I could will it to play forever, but even I knew it shouldn't and wouldn't.

"Oramus, can I talk to you alone?" I whispered. My gaze met his. Something veiled appeared in his eyes, but his words were as open as the sky.

"Of course," he said, as the other couples began to dance to a new tune. "I know the perfect place." He grasped my hand securely. "This way."

He led me through the throne room, graciously waving away well-wishers, and we walked through the hallway where Erise had spoken to me and into a room I had never seen before. Nothing was inside but for an enormous tapestry, entirely covering one wall. Even compared to the other trappings of the palace, I felt awed at its workmanship, though my mind was on other things.

"Beautiful isn't it?" Oramus asked. He gazed at the tapestry with satisfaction, his right hand still entwined with my left.

"Yes," I replied. Despite my urgency, the vibrant colors and intricate scenes drew me in, but I stopped when I realized the violence it portrayed. Elementals battled each other in brilliant detail, woven flames flickering against fields of threaded stone. I turned toward Oramus, but he stared at the tapestry with lit-up eyes.

"This room is very special to me," he said still looking at the piece. Oramus let go of my hand and took a step toward the tapestry.

"This tapestry belonged to several rulers before me. When I look at it," he paused as in thoughtfulness, "When I look at this, I see beautiful, terrible things. I see possibilities. It makes me think that my rule over Falleon might lead to greater things. Greater things because of me. And…"

He turned and looked at me with a small smile.

"And I'm happy that I will be able to do it with you."

My heart nearly broke in two at the sureness in his voice, and my heart seemed to bubble with the tenderness I felt for him. An inkling of shame crept in as I thought about how I had doubted him and could not echo his certainty.

"Oramus," I began, but stopped. He stepped away

from the tapestry, shaking his head.

"You wanted to say something, right. My apologies." He came close once again and took my hands in his. They felt so right together.

"I heard some things," I said, looking down at our hands. "And I want to know if they're true."

"What is it?" he asked, tilting his head down over me. I took a moment before answering.

"I heard that...that I'm not an Absent." I looked up into his eyes, seeking a reaction. "I heard that I'm actually a powerful Elemental. Something called a Star."

Oramus' face didn't change or move in any way. I widened my eyes at his blue irises, willing to see something, but his gaze revealed nothing. If anything, it misted over. I continued, desperate for a reaction.

"And I heard that you knew."

The mist left his eyes, and something in them seemed to harden. I kept my sights on him, and he opened his mouth delicately, then closed it and opened it again.

"Who told you?" he asked, looking down at our hands, slowly tightening his grip. My mouth and heart dropped with his words.

"What? You really—"

"Who told you?" he repeated steadily, looking up at my face, calculation tinting his eyes. I pulled my hands away from his.

"I'm not telling you," I said. His eyes flashed, but the gleam disappeared as soon as it appeared.

"I need to know who—"

"Why didn't you?" I asked, voice rising. I trembled where I stood, some part of me still expecting a reasonable explanation. "Why didn't you tell me?" I asked again, the sting of betrayal cutting my voice. Fire burned in my throat, at my wrists, and my breath came ragged. "Why didn't you—"

"Pasin." He drew out my name slowly once more in that soothing voice. "There is still a lot to figure out. So much we—"

"But why?" I asked, stepping back. Hot tears pooled at the corners of my eyes. "Why not?"

"I was going to," he said, stepping forward. "It was for your own good." He reached out as if to take my hand, but I jerked it away.

"Really?" I tore the glove off my hand and lifted my arm. The silver bangles shone in the light.

"So you put these on me?" I asked. Oramus' eyes widened. "I know they almost killed me," I said. I paused, then finished, hoping against hope that what I said was a lie, "I know you just want me to cross the mountains, for whatever power these are holding back."

I looked up at him, and he looked back, but his warmth was gone. His calm was gone as well, leaving nothing but a grimace on his face. He said nothing, and something inside me broke, like a glass figurine against a stone floor.

A twitch shook his jaw, and Oramus strode over to the still-open door.

"Guard!" he called. "Get Corinth!"

As he spoke, my breath shortened even more, quickening every second. Blood howled in my ears and pulsed in my wrists. The bracelets burned with invisible fire, and my throat was as dry as his eyes.

He came back in and closed the door behind him. He advanced toward me, and before I could react, he grabbed my wrists with a strength I hadn't felt before.

I tried to break free, but I could feel him pulling me from inside, pulling me closer.

"Pasin," he said again, "You need to calm down."

Hot, steady tears ran down my face despite his words, because of his words.

"You don't, you don't—" I tried to say, but his grip tightened.

"Pasin, what you need is to get some rest, to go upstairs, and go to bed."

The tears increased, and my chest heaved. I could barely choke out the words.

"You don't...care about me."

"Of course I do," he said angrily, shaking his head. He took one hand and used it to tilt up my chin so our gazes met.

"I need you," he said. "I love you." His eyes softened.

I wanted to believe him. I wanted to trust him so badly. And yet...

"No...n–no. You don't love me." I couldn't see a thing through my tears. The burning on my wrist and in my throat was unbearable but escalating still.

"Yes I..."

"You don't love me!"

The screamed words echoed a thousand times inside my head. My vision went red, and unimaginable heat pounded through my limbs, tore at my skin.

"You don't care at all!"

The pain and rage within me burst. Everything burned red. Oramus' grasp left my body, and I heard him gasp in pain. My own arm burned, hot metal on skin. Heat flowed through every vein in my body, and every tear I had evaporated.

I didn't see at first. I felt. I could feel Oramus

falling back, hand over his face. I could feel the guards patrolling the halls and the dancers frolicking in the ballroom. I could feel everything happening, like insects crawling over my consciousness. My fingertips tingled with power, with possibility.

My heart was bursting, desperate for escape. My legs moved automatically, to flee the scene, to flee the betrayer. I heard a metallic thud as the bangles dropped from my wrist. The last thing I saw was Oramus crouching in front of the burning tapestry, malice burning even hotter in his eyes.

CHAPTER NINETEEN

"Guards!" Oramus shouted as he struggled to stand. "Guards! After her! The flame is lit!"

The people crawled; they crawled and itched and scratched over my consciousness. What I saw rushed by, all the drapes and tiles and candles, flashflashing by, but this new awareness...it was like a map felt but not seen. I ran up a flight of stairs then swerved right without knowing why, and behind me, a man barged through a hidden door, the heat of him pulsating in my mind. I had sensed him, felt him...panic rose higher in my chest, and I ran faster faster faster down the corridors.

I heaved with invisible tears, sobbed as the heat screamed through my body. My feet pounded a path away from the beacons of heat swirling below.

"The flame is lit!"

The words rattled in my mind, over and over and over again. A candle, a cannon, glorious and fatal had been lit, and the spark burned closer and closer to the end of its wick.

The farther I ran, the more pain each new breath caused. No escape, no escape, no escape. The next level up was the roof, and there would be nowhere to go from there. They'd capture me; they'd take me back down to that dungeon of his hands and the illusion of warmth. The illusion lay broken before me, shattered like a stained-glass window struck by a stone.

But it didn't matter. There was no escape. The thought clawed at my mind. Blood boiled in my ears louder and louder and louder.

I threw open the door to the roof, and guards rushed toward me from a nearby turret. Automatically, I ran once more, away from the guards, their dots of heat burning in my consciousness.

I sprinted across the gray, gray stone I barely let my feet touch, too much behind me to dare stop. The edge came closer, but beyond that, I saw the palace wall and beyond that, the thrilling, dire expanse of the star-spotted sky and a too-large moon dangling over my head.

Some memory of a revelation flared within me. Air's words pulsed in my mind, and against the dark outline of the distant mountains, I made the snap decision.

I jumped. Shouts echoed behind me as I sailed through the air, as I started to fall.

"No!" I shrieked as the wind whipped in my ears. "NO!"

I spread my arms wide and let the wind rip through my dress, quicksilver in the darkness. An eternal moment passed, but then the wind in my ears subsided.

The ground leered at me, a good fifty feet down. But it didn't come any closer.

Spectators gathered on the ground far below, pointing and yelling, all little red dots on my consciousness. They looked and felt so far away, not coming closer despite my location. I was still. So that meant…

I was flying! I flew! For the briefest moment, a giddy smile erupted on my face, broke through the memories of the past hour. I gave a whoop and tried to rise higher. Concentration and force combined, and I rose and descended, moved left and right through the air. Ecstasy vibrated through my body. Until I felt something tug at my deepest part.

And he was there on the nearest turret, his heat barely registering, hand raised, concentration gnashing his teeth. And I began to slide back.

"No!"

I struggled, pushed harder and harder against his pull, lashed out against the ties trying to bind me once more.

The fear and rage inside me combusted. I threw a hand out toward Oramus, and a flash of fire shot toward him. The pull released. I fled into the sky, crossed the palace border, and refused to look back.

#

So what next? I had no idea.

I couldn't fly forever. The second time I dropped altitude when my mind wandered, I decided it was time to land.

I touched down in an alley in an unlit part of the city. For a moment, it felt normal; there were no points of heat clouding my mind. But the comfort I felt from the blankness didn't last. All around me were charred, broken buildings, their skeletons making black silhouettes against the night sky. I swayed on my feet, exhaustion pounding at my skull, and collapsed. I cried.

Who knows how long later, I felt the tiniest pinpoint of heat creep into the desolate area. I bolted from my spot and hid in some nearby wreckage. The point moved lightly, softly across the ground. The heat it emitted wasn't strong, but it didn't waver.

"Pasin?" a voice murmured. Was it really? I stepped out from the wreckage.

"Air?"

Air, the one who had told me not two hours before who I really was, stood in the exposed walkway, his hair nearly white in the moonlight.

"Pasin!" He turned my way and did a double take for some reason. He shook his head and rushed to where I stood. "Are you okay?"

"Yeah," I said. "At least, I…I think so."

"How did you—" Air began, then cut himself short. "No, we need to get to Erise." He took my shaking hand and the similarity between this action and what had happened back in the ballroom temporarily drowned me. My body itched to collapse again, to take the pain away from my feet and heart.

"Can't we just…fly to wherever we need to go…Air?" The words fell from my mouth like pieces of lead.

"Flying is outlawed within the city," Air said. "It would draw too much attention, and we can't risk that."

"Oh."

"By the way," Air added. "You can call me Leyes. Yes," he added in almost a tired tone, "like not telling the truth."

Guess he heard too many questions about that. Lies, Leyes then.

"Would you like me to call you Star?" he asked.

"No," I answered immediately. I could not face that yet. We didn't say anything for a moment, but I had to ask…

"How did you find me?"

"I had some loose ends to tie up at the palace," Leyes began. "I was in the courtyard on the way out when you escaped. I followed you with some other Air guards, but they gave up once you got out of sight. You're pretty fast for a first timer. After that it was mostly luck."

We hurried through the devastated streets, shoes crunching over shattered glass. Leyes wore a pair of leather quasi-boots while I still had my dress shoes on.

"Where are we?" I asked. Literally, we were the only humans within blocks.

"There was a fire here," Leyes replied. "An arson, I think. It's a restricted zone, so we'll have to be careful getting out."

We reached the border between the lights and darkness. Three pinpricks of heat marked the guards along the border.

"There's someone there," I whispered, pointing to a building unremarkable in every way, except for the glow I could feel emanating from inside it.

"Why do you say that?" Leyes asked.

"I…I can feel it…" I answered, realizing how ridiculous I sounded. "Like, I think what I'm sensing is the person's body heat. Does that make sense?"

"I don't know. But I don't mind."

We crept around the edges of the wreckage, out of the view from the windows. On this side of the border, people were scattered on the streets. Smoke curled from stoves and cats called from alleys.

We walked steadily, tried not to catch any person's eye. After the third person openly stared at us, Leyes quickened his pace.

"We need to get you out of here," he muttered from the side of his mouth. "You're too noticeable."

I thought about how I looked–silver gown, hair up, heels. Like an iridescent duck on a pond.

"Where are we going?" I asked.

"A tavern near the middle of the city. Erise and I agreed to meet there."

So we stuck to the shadowed edges and dark corners of the streets. As we walked deeper and deeper into the heart of the city, the dots of heat multiplied and swarmed, itched and crawled. My focus split among the dots, pulling my attention this way and that. Concentration waned, and my vision swam before me. Each step became a struggle, and at one point, my "real" vision let out and I stopped, putting one knee to the ground.

"Are you okay?" Leyes asked, kneeling at my side.

"There's too many...I can't..." All of the people, the burning dots...

Leyes glanced around, then led me to a dark corner.

"Wait here," he said. "The tavern's right there. I'll get Erise." And he was gone.

I curled into a ball against the wall. The wind ripped through my dress and the temperature of the wall contrasted violently with my skin, but I didn't feel the cold. Not on the outside, at least. I sat there, alone, sniffing back tears, water pooling in my eyes. It wasn't physically painful, but mentally, like my mind was being pulled in a thousand different directions. There were just too many people nearby, moving through the buildings, level on top of level, each dot moving without end.

Soon enough, I saw Erise and Leyes coming my way.

Erise stopped for a moment, looked at me as Leyes had. Why?

"Pasin, what's wrong?" she whispered, crouching down next to me.

"There's too many..." Each word was a fight to say. "Too many people...and they're all moving..." I lost focus again, and words failed me.

"Do you know what she's talking about?" Erise asked Leyes. I sensed her turn her head to look at him.

He whispered back, and Erise gently took my upper arm.

"Let's get out of here and go somewhere with fewer people."

And off we went again through the city.

I heard them speak in low tones as we walked. After a while, the dots lessened, and I was able to think and speak again.

"Erise—"

She turned to me.

"Are you okay now, Pasin?"

"Better," I replied. "Where are we going?"

"We want to get as far away from the palace as possible," Erise said. "But we need to get some sleep.

You look like you need it."

"What time is it?" I asked.

"Around two in the morning."

No wonder I felt so exhausted.

"Can you tell me what happened?" Erise continued.

I explained everything that happened after she left. Fewer and fewer people appeared on the streets, and my mind cleared. Even so, the heat from Erise and Leyes struck me every once in a while, fogging my mind once more.

A mile or so past the city limits, a rickety, wooden building came into view. A faded sign read, "Edge Inn—Last Stop, Cheapest Rates." Cheapest made sense–the place appeared ready to fall apart.

"Let's stop here for the night," Erise said. "It looks like they won't ask too many questions.

"Act oblivious," she added. Before I could get clarification, though, she led me into the inn.

The smell was borderline wretched, a mixture of goat and moldy straw. The hovel looked like it used to house livestock.

Erise strode forward and rang the bell on the wooden counter. Almost a whole minute passed before we heard shuffling feet come from the back.

"Mighty late comin' in, eh?" the man grumbled without looking up. "'Ow many?"

"Three," Erise said. "One room."

"All I 'ave is a one-bed room. I reckon you can either draw lots or get well-acquainted. Names?"

"Brare Earth," Leyes said.

"Mina Bronze and Kagar Rain," Erise added.

"Can the other lass no' speak fo' 'erself?" The man looked up and his grizzled face was taken aback. I tried not to react, adopting a vacant look.

"Mighty nice for a Rain," he said, dabbing his lower lip with the tip of his tongue. "Wha's wrong with 'er?"

"Too much to drink," Erise said quickly, taking out a coin purse from her pocket.

"I reckon I can take 'er off yer hands fer a tidy sum," he said, wringing his hands together and smiling.

Was he suggesting...? It was all I could do to keep a blank face.

"She's also my fiancé," Leyes said curtly, nodding toward the necklace around my neck.

The man shrugged his shoulders.

"Wouldn't stop some," he said bluntly, "The right price can change many a man's mind. But so's your decision, lad. One room will be three bronzes."

Erise passed the pieces over into the man's grubby hands. He counted them out, twice, before nodding.

"Ah' right then, to your room." He led us up the stairs, three rooms down the right side.

"The offer still stands, lad. Otherwise it looks like Bronze'll be stuck on the ground." The man laughed like a braying donkey, then retreated down the stairs.

The room held a bed, a window, and a chamber pot, nothing more. Despite the stench, I collapsed onto the bed, ecstatic to finally be able to relieve the pain in my feet. The mattress was filled with straw, smelly straw at that, but it was a horizontal blessing.

The crawly, super conscious feeling was still present, but the twenty or so people in the inn slept soundly, except for the pair in the room beside us. Even the old man sat sedately in his chair downstairs, hands folded across his chest.

Leyes sat on the other end of the bed with a hard look on his face.

"What's wrong?" I asked sluggishly. The time was catching up to me.

"That man," he said, disgust on his face. "Trying to...to buy you."

"Why would he do...do that?" The bed beckoned. The thin, filthy bed beckoned.

"Pasin, when your Star nature came through, it changed things about you. Flying for one, but appearances too," Erise said. "You've heard of shining, right? The strength of it depends on the strength of the Element."

I turned to the window, and my jaw dropped. It was still me, but my face was clear, my features sharper. It might have been the time or the warp of the window, but I thought my face even glowed a bit.

"It's not permanent," Erise added. I nodded slowly, but I couldn't take my eyes off my reflection. I wanted to take it in while I could.

"You said something earlier," she continued, "about when you escaped. You said the bracelets broke?"

I nodded again, still staring at myself. I seemed unable to take my eyes off my reflection.

"Wo-ow." A broad, goofy smile broke across her face. "That...that is exciting news."

I finally looked away.

"Why?" I asked.

"That means you have massive untapped power. We can definitely work with that. But," Erise paused, pushed a lock of hair behind her ear. "Not tonight. We need to sleep, so we can get going in the morning. Feel free to take the bed."

"Yes," Leyes chimed in. "You've had a long day."

"Thank you." I leaned back but stopped short.

"Where are we going after this?" I asked.

"Fenicks," Erise answered, sitting on the floor. "We need to meet up with a few people there."

Okay. Sure.

"Good night."

#

I slept for a while. Even in my sleep, ghosts of red dots haunted the edges of my mind. As such, I was rudely awakened when the couple next door started vigorously…wrestling. Let's go with that.

Thirty minutes of activity later, I considered waking up Erise just to have something different to think about. But then something changed downstairs. Two mounted horses rode up to the inn, and two warm dots dismounted from their steeds. Something about them…something about them felt terribly familiar.

I stood up and walked over to the window. The human shapes of the two warmths became more defined as I got closer.

Two men walked up the stone path to the entrance. As they passed below the window, my heart stopped.

"Erise!" I scrambled over to the figure lying in the corner. "Erise!"

"What is it?" she mumbled, head still down.

"Oramus and Corinth are downstairs!" I shout-whispered, seethed. I felt Corinth shake the old man awake, felt Oramus stand over him.

"What? Are you sleep-walking?"

I sensed the old man nod, lift his hand, point at the ceiling, straight to where we were sitting.

"No! They're downstairs, we have to–ah!"

Something jabbed at my mind. Erise clutched her head, and Leyes stirred in another corner. Below, Corinth turned to Oramus and nodded. Oramus raised his head, turned our way, and—

Blackness.

#

The sleep wasn't natural. That much was clear. Floating in nothing, seeing nothing…but I felt. I could still feel the warm pinpoints of people, the men downstairs, Erise and Leyes in the room. I felt Erise and Leyes get up, felt Leyes open the window, felt Erise lean toward his ear and then disappear through the window. At the same time, Oramus pounded up the stairs, Corinth in tow. In the darkness I was in, I felt something more–a sensation of being dragged across the floor, Oramus' hook in my chest, pulling me closer to the door.

I felt him push the door aside, bend down toward me, hand outstretched…

The darkness dissipated, my vision returned, and Leyes grabbed my hand, pulled me up, and we sprinted toward the open window. Behind us, Oramus shoved aside the door Leyes had blown into his face. We jumped out and started to fly away, but I felt that hook of Oramus' power again. I fought, I raged against the string pulling me back and jerked Leyes back with the struggle.

"It's him!" I shouted. Leyes looked at me and understood, pulling even harder.

"Come…on!" Leyes yelled in frustration. We strained together, suspended in the air not eight feet out from the window. Oramus, hand outstretched, similarly strained behind us. Behind him, Corinth slipped something from his sleeve and threw it our way.

"Aah!" The dart pierced my right calf, breaking my concentration just enough that Leyes and I were pulled back within a foot of Oramus' grasp.

"No!" I gave an end-all push and we broke free. Oramus stuck his head out of the window, venom on his face.

"You can't run forever!" he roared. "I will find you!"

I didn't give him a second look, though I heard his voice continue.

"You idiot, Corinth!" his muffled voice rang out behind us. "What the shriking were you thinking?"

Leyes let go of my hand, and we soared into the night, the longest night of my life.

CHAPTER TWENTY

Somehow, we managed to evade Oramus and Corinth. I don't know if we outstripped them or if they let us go for the night. Either way, we didn't stop to rest until streaks of dawn appeared over the eastern trees. The moment my body was on flat ground again I fell asleep, too exhausted to dream.

It felt like no time had passed before a cool hand on my arm shook me awake.

"Pasin," Erise whispered, shaking me harder when I didn't respond. "Wake up–we need to get moving."

"Unn…" I tried to move my limbs, but stiffness made the effort horrendous. I managed to sit up. "I–ahhhh…"

I held this flat note as I looked around. A dense forest of trees surrounded us. Leyes messed with his stuff next to the extinct fire, and Erise stood over me, looking worried with large bags under her eyes. But I could sense both of them before I saw them, like little pinpoints on the sphere of my consciousness once again.

"What's wrong?" she asked.

"I…" I paused, took a deep breath, began again. "That really happened, didn't it?" It wasn't a dream or a delusion. I didn't wake up in the palace; I didn't even wake up in the orphanage. But with the realization that this was, in fact, reality, came the realization of the pain dealt to me the night before.

Erise half-grimaced.

"Yeah," she said. "It did."

I looked around again. Nothing had changed. I turned back to Erise, opened my mouth to speak, closed it. Then just as quickly I turned back away from her, suddenly aware of a raging pain in my throat, like someone had rubbed it with sandpaper. The burning intensified and without warning, tears began to leak from the corners of my eyes. Before I could even try to contain myself, a choked sob came out of my throat. Then another and another surged forth as my shoulders shook and my throat burned. I felt Leyes pause and then continue his work, but Erise reached forward with her hand as if to pat me on the shoulder. It hovered for a few seconds, but the moment she started to lower it I spoke.

"Don't," I said. My body wanted it desperately, a reassuring touch, but not from her. Her hand paused in mid-air. My voice spoke with more resolve the second time. "Do not touch me," I said.

Erise removed her hand from my airspace and placed it in her lap. The hard exterior only lasted for the moment it was needed. I began quivering and crying in as hushed of tones as I could manage for a while longer before I was able to look at Erise again.

"Erise?" I said.

"Yes?" she replied, her pitch rising.

I paused again, mouth open, but the words found their way out.

"Erise," I repeated. Then with eyes still wet from my tears, I asked her, "How can I trust you?"

Before she could reply, I turned to Leyes, still fiddling with his things.

"The same goes for you," I called out. He lifted his head and looked with a blank expression. "How can I trust either of you when you both knew what was going on?" I looked at Erise again and gave in to the pain I felt inside.

"Why didn't you tell me?" I demanded. "That first time we talked–why didn't you tell me then? You could have prevented all of this, ALL of this!" The last sentence peaked in a voice that didn't sound like me. Erise looked like she had been slapped in the face.

"Would you have believed me?" she fired back. Her eyes were bloodshot and exhaustion etched lines in her face. "Would you? A total stranger telling you this, really?"

"You could have tried!" I replied. "Sometime in the two months we talked you could have tried!"

"But then what?" she asked. "We didn't have a plan on how to get you out or take off the nullifiers. What if Corinth searched your mind again? You'd have your heart essence taken out for sure, and we," she said, pointing to herself and Leyes, "would be dead!"

"Well, what about this?" I yelled. I grabbed the engagement pendant from around my neck and thrust it out in her direction. "How do you plan to get this off?" I let the question hang in the air for a moment. Even as I said it, I choked up, because I knew the answer. I would carry that reminder with me until the day I died.

Something flickered in Erise's eyes.

"We didn't know about that," she said finally in a low, slow voice. Another moment of silence passed before she continued, "We were following what we thought was the best course of action. It wasn't supposed to happen like that."

I frowned and turned away again. The anger I felt did not fully abate, but I could see the point she was making. It didn't make the reality of the situation any easier.

I didn't say anything and neither did Erise. Leyes was the first to speak.

"We really need to go," he said, "We need to reach Fenicks as soon as possible."

"Now wait," I interjected. I stood up and turned to him this time. "Why should I go with you? And why Fenicks?"

"There's more than what we told you last night," Leyes replied. He glanced at Erise, but she didn't react. He looked back at me. "The western center of our group is headquartered in Fenicks. It would probably be best to have Water explain the rest of it to you."

"Which Water?" Erise asked from her kneeling position.

"Both," he answered.

"Water?" I asked, thinking back to the pensive man at the palace. "Like my tutor, or—"

"No," Leyes said, "these Waters are the western leaders in our group, and they live in Fenicks. That's why we need to go there." Silence again as I thought about what he said.

"It's a two-day walk," Erise said, finally looking at me once more. "Please, just come with us and hear the whole story there. I can tell you more about the Star Element along the way."

I didn't answer. After a moment though, she continued, "And if you don't come with us, where will you go?"

Even before she voiced the question, it had been darting around in my mind. I couldn't go back to the orphanage; I couldn't go back to the palace. I had ties to nowhere, nothing. Even if my heart hadn't yet forgiven her, Erise was the closest thing to…anything I had left.

"Fine." I crossed my arms and looked down at myself. I still wore the silver dress from the night before, albeit with a few singe marks. Despite the light fabric and chill morning air, I didn't feel cold. Even so, I knew it wouldn't be the best outfit for traveling undercover.

"Do you have something I can wear?" I mumbled to Erise. Her face held masked relief as she stood to her full height.

"Yes," she replied, "Yes, I'm sure we can put something together."

A couple of minutes later we started walking, I in a pair of Leyes' shoes and one of his shirts (Erise's blouses being far too small for my waist) and a pair of Erise's drawstring pants.

"Why do you wear such large pants?" I asked her after putting them on. The legs were wide, but the bottoms cinched around my calves due to our height difference.

"I keep my scabbard there," she answered, simultaneously pulling out her sword from the left leg of her pants. "I don't carry it openly. It would draw too much attention."

"Hm." I could see why. Not many people wandered around with a sword on their hip. "You said you would tell me about the Star Element," I added. I still couldn't quite say "my" element. The idea was too foreign to my mind.

"Yes, I did," she said, and she launched into an explanation of the various skills of the Star. Flight and fire generation were the two major abilities of the Element, but she continued with a list of secondary powers that came with the combination of these two powers.

"Higher body temperature is a big one," she said. "And apparently heat sensing of some sort," she added with a small smile on her face, "along with a greater resistance to poison."

"What do you mean?" I asked. A light breeze picked up as we walked down the deserted dirt road.

"This is just my theory," she started again, "I don't remember anything like this from the elves; these are just ideas I've had after seeing you and hearing you talk about stuff. When Emerald poisoned you—" My mind flashed back to that night and the female's toothy, too-large smile.

"Yes?"

"I think that the energy inside of you kind of…burned away the toxin." She looked at me and shrugged her shoulders. "I can't say anything for sure, but with the two bangles keeping that much heat within you, I guess it counteracted, or at least lessened the impact of the poison."

"So, are you saying the nullifiers saved my life?"

"Maybe. But at the same time, they would have

killed you if you wore them for too long." Erise shifted the pack on her back and spoke again. "Still, this is all new information for me. There is so little known about Stars, and the Elemental Nullifiers are only, what, three or four years old?" She looked at Leyes who shrugged. "It's a lot of new information," she repeated.

"So how do you know all this anyway?" I asked.

"I learned a lot with the elves," she said. "They can't manipulate Elements, so I guess that's how they compensate. It was part of my education there."

We fell silent again. I mulled over the information she had shared. Now that my curiosity was for the most part sated, a part of me remembered my anger towards Erise.

I didn't speak again for most of the day, though Erise and Leyes talked back and forth for a while about what to do next. They kept throwing out names and places I didn't know, so I turned my attention to the surroundings instead.

I had never been this far outside of Falleon City before. It wasn't that different, really, but the sky kept drawing my gaze, even more than before. Before, it had been just an unreachable dream. At that point, it was suddenly an attainable destination.

Through the day, soldiers passed along the paths, but I could sense them soon enough that we had time to take cover in the trees. That night, Leyes spent some time showing me proper flight techniques, but it wasn't that hard. It felt right, like my body had merely been waiting for the correct time to show off its talents. It felt right, the cool night air swirling across my hot skin.

I didn't try to do any fire manipulation though.

Even if I still felt anger toward Erise and Leyes, I didn't want them to be scarred like I was, and starting a forest fire would be a give-away for the soldiers looking for us.

That night, Leyes woke me up to keep watch sometime between midnight and morning. About an hour into my watch, I realized that the fire had gone out. I looked over at Erise's pack where the flint was, but I didn't quite know how to use it and I didn't want to wake Erise up.

I looked around. Erise and Leyes seemed comfortable enough with their coverings. I shifted my gaze up and watched the stars until they faded into the morning light.

CHAPTER TWENTY-ONE

The next day was just more of the same, but as the sun drifted across the sky, the landscape shifted from forest to plains to scrub. The sun had long set behind the distant western range when we passed over a hill and Leyes lifted his hand.

"This is Fenicks," he said.

An assortment of low-slung buildings rose up from the half-sand, half-dirt desert before us. In the near distance, an outcropping of rocks stood and scraped the sky, but beyond that, the desert stretched on and on. On the skyline, the distant peaks of the Caeltactus Mountains peeked at the small, moonlit town.

"It's too late to have you meet Water tonight," Leyes said, even more subdued than usual. "Let's rest for the night."

For the first time, Leyes took the lead and led us down into the town. He slowed down as we approached a certain house. Leyes stopped for a moment and stared at the windows glowing in the fading light. Without turning to us, he walked forward, opened the door, and entered without a word.

"Does he know these people?" I whispered to Erise.

"I think this is Leyes' home," she answered.

We heard a shriek echo inside the house and rushed in. The first thing I saw was a short, bosomy woman wrapping Leyes in the largest bear hug I had ever seen.

"Oh, Leyes!" The woman's voice broke as she said his name. "You terrible son!" She promptly released him and smacked him on the arm.

"Eight months!" she said as she smacked him again. "No visit, no letters. Eight months! I thought you were dead!" She grabbed him around the middle and gave him another hug. "I'm so glad you're home."

"Hello, Mother," Leyes replied, hugging her back.

"What's the racket?" another voice called from inside the house. A man, old enough to have some gray beginning to show, stepped out from behind the staircase.

"Hello, Father," Leyes answered quietly. The man stopped in his tracks and stared at Leyes. His face held obvious strain, but his jaw twitched only once.

"So you came back, I see," the man said. "You staying?"

"Not for long," Leyes replied. "Just to get Filio. Then we'll be going."

The man's eyes flickered toward me and Erise, barely registering our presence.

"And who are these ladies?" Leyes' mother asked. She turned and smiled at me.

"Hello dear," she said taking my hand. "I'm Gaille

Sand, Leyes' mother." She shook Erise's hand too.

"Nice to meet you," I said, smiling back at her bubbling energy.

"This is Erise Spark," Leyes said, pointing at Erise who waved. He then pointed at me.

"And this is Pasin Star."

The room paused for a moment, but Gaille took it in stride.

"Nice to meet you too," she said to me with another smile. "This is Duran Sand, my husband."

Duran nodded, but I knew I wouldn't be calling him by his first name any time soon.

"So how long will you be here?" Gaille asked Leyes.

"Two, maybe three nights," he answered.

"All right then!" Gaille clapped her hands and turned back to Erise and me. "We need to set you two up with some beds! If you will follow me…"

I started to walk toward her, but then I heard the door open once more behind me and a new warmth enter the room.

"Hey hey hey!" I turned to look at the newcomer, and my jaw dropped.

"Guess who just scored thirty silvers playing cards against the Granite brothers? Me that's—who are you?"

Leyes stared at us from the doorway, eyebrows raised, and his hands left in the air from his half-finished boast. But it wasn't Leyes—Leyes stood next to his mother, annoyance clearly visible. The Leyes in the doorway didn't look quite right though; his skin was tanner and he stood a little bit taller.

I turned back to the Leyes next to Gaille.

"You have a twin?"

196

"Hey, Leyes!" The imposter spotted his brother and punched him in the shoulder. "What are you doing here, man? Back for more of your crazy conspiracy activities, hmm?"

Without waiting for an answer, the look-alike faced Erise and me.

"Why, hello there," he said, extending his hand. "I am Seyel Sand, but people call me Seyel. They also call me the most powerful Sand in the Hadestian Desert, but that's beside the point."

Erise shook his hand gingerly.

"Spark," she said.

"Nice! Feisty," he said with what he must have thought was a dashing smile. He turned to me.

I extended my hand and started, "I'm S—"

"Wait." Seyel's expression turned serious, and he backed up a step. "Are you two part of Leyes' conspiracy freak show?"

Erise and I looked at each other, but Duran spoke before we could.

"Looks like it," he grumbled.

Seyel groaned and rolled his eyes.

"Seriously? Did he drug you or something?" Seyel looked at his brother. "What did you do to the girls, man?"

"I did nothing," Leyes said sharply. His gaze flickered around the room, avoiding anyone else's eyes. Duran's jaw stiffened.

"Yeah, sure." Seyel brushed the hair out of his eyes and turned to me.

"So you're really with the whole overthrow-the-government thing? I heard about that Star girl running away from the palace. I guess you had something to do with that?"

News travelled fast. I expected Gaille or Duran to answer, but neither did.

"A bit," Leyes finally said, a ghost of a smile appearing on his face.

"What was her name again?" Seyel asked. "Walkin'…Runnin'…?"

"It's Pasin," I said. As if I hadn't heard that before.

"Pasin," he snorted. "What a stupid name."

I saw red at the edges of my eyes again, but I ground my teeth to stop myself from lashing out.

"I'm sure she didn't choose her name," I said through clenched teeth. Behind him, Erise held her hand to her face, but I could still feel the smile she was attempting to cover.

"Like it matters," Seyel said dismissively. "Speaking of names, what's yours again? S…?"

I smiled a clenched-tooth smile.

"Smoke," I said, somehow managing to shake his hand. "I'm Smoke."

#

Gaille showed us around the house.

"We built it ourselves, you know," she said. "Duran and I. Solidified sand, one of the best in Fenicks. We even made the windows with one of our Blaze neighbors.

"I can't tell you how much of a surprise it was when we found out Leyes was an Air," Gaille continued. "First one in the family. We had to move his room to the top floor."

She looked at me apologetically.

"I hear you're part Air too, but the only open room we have is in the basement. Sorry about that."

"It's fine," I said. Even so, my skin itched at the thought of being underground, so far from the sky.

The room held two beds with hand-knit quilts and a pallet of glass windows.

"We use this as a guest room and storeroom," Gaille explained. "Is there anything I can get you?"

Erise looked at me, and I shook my head.

"We're fine," Erise said.

"Well, if you need anything, just say. The lavatory's in the back and the kitchen's always open." And with that, she left.

I settled into the bed and looked out the sliver of a window. The light of the moon fell through the opening and glinted off of the pallets of glass. The space wasn't large enough to get through if needed, but at least we weren't entirely contained.

The glowing dots of Leyes' family settled too, each to their respective resting places. Seyel's warmth faded quickly as he slept as did Erise's warmth, but Duran and Gaille took longer to fall asleep.

I closed my eyes and waited for sleep to come. It danced on the corners of my mind, mocked from the darkness I wanted to sink myself into, but something stopped me.

Leyes paced in his room, back and forth, back and forth. His red dot was like a circling gnat. After at least fifteen minutes of incessant movement, I got up and slipped out of the room.

I paused at his door and then knocked. Leyes stopped his pacing, raised his head, and answered my knock after a few seconds.

"Pasin!" He had bags under his eyes, but surprise filtered through his exhaustion. Dim moonlight barely illuminated his room, and I could just barely distinguish a row of shelves whose objects cast odd shadows on the far wall. "What...what are you doing here?" he continued. "I mean—"

"Sorry to disturb you," I said, immediately regretting getting out of bed. "I just, I just felt you pacing back and forth up here and–and I wanted to check if everything is all right."

Leyes paused again, his eyebrows darting up for a moment.

"Yes," he said finally, nodded the slightest bit. "I was just..." His mouth remained open, but he didn't finish the thought. "Nothing's wrong though," he said.

I nodded, though I didn't quite believe him. Thinking of how I had felt him acting before, I wanted to offer something to cool the heat I could sense in him. I opened my mouth, but I didn't know what to say.

"Good," I said. I looked away, not sure what to do next.

"Well, good night," I added.

"Good night," he replied after a moment.

My ears burned on the way back downstairs for bothering him when his nighttime wanderings were none of my business. Leyes' dot went to his bed and stayed there, but his warmth didn't cool before I fell into the darkness of sleep.

CHAPTER TWENTY-TWO

I woke to a room empty but for the beam of sunshine coming through the tiny window. Erise's bed was made and cool; she must have left it more than an hour ago. I glanced at my reflection in one of the windows, but whatever glow I had achieved after my shining transformation had vanished. Shaking my head, I changed and then went upstairs. Gaille greeted me once I reached the kitchen.

"Good morning, dear," she said brightly. "Would you like some oatmeal?"

"Yes, thank you," I replied.

"It's quite chilly today, you need to have some warmth in your belly," she said as she ladled me a heaping bowl of oats.

"Leyes and Erise went to talk to Filio," she continued. "They said to tell you to meet them at his house after you eat. Here, sit at the table while I get some more wood for the fire." And Gaille bustled away, but I wasn't alone.

Duran sat at the other end of the table, reading a

logbook of some sort without looking up. I said nothing and tried to focus on my meal. He broke the silence.

"Star," he started, putting his book down on the table. "Though I do not entirely agree with Oramus and his policies, I equally disagree with what Leyes and Filio are doing. While you are staying in my house, any conversations about such matters should not occur in my presence. Understood?"

"Yes, sir," I replied with a nod. He nodded back and returned to his book. I returned to my breakfast and sped up my eating.

"Looks like we need to chop some more wood," Gaille said as she reentered the kitchen. "This is one of the last pieces. Are you almost done dear?"

I swallowed my last bite.

"Yes ma'am." Thank Solluna.

"Right, now Filio's house is just past the city center. Take this road to the well and turn right. It's the one with the goats."

Wondering at just how many goats one house must have to be known for it, I followed her instructions and started down the dirt road. Judging by the sun, it was still morning, though perhaps later than I had hoped to awaken. The everyday life of Fenicks people swirled around me, from dogs barking and the blacksmith doing his pounding to children screaming up and down the street. I received a few curious looks, but the town was small after all. The well seemed to be the literal center of the town–I saw a line of at least seven women waiting to get water.

The only house to the right of the well with goats was larger than the rest of the townspeople's. It was also made of both sand and glass. Not just windows;

some walls were partially constructed with thick glass.

I walked up to the door and after a moment of steeling myself, I knocked. An older man opened the door.

"Are you the friend of Air?" he asked. He held his head high but leaned against the doorframe.

"Yes, sir," I answered.

"Come in." The man stepped out of the doorway with a slight hitch in his step, then waved me in. After closing the door, he turned to me and smiled.

"It is an honor to have you here, Star," he said. "I am Water, mayor of Fenicks and Filio's father. I would have greeted you properly sooner, but not all of the townspeople approve of your platform."

Something twisted in my stomach. My platform? It was still a bit early for that.

"Filio and the others are outside," he said, gesturing toward another door. "Will you have dinner with us tonight so we can discuss our plans?"

Was this what Erise meant when she talked about the Water in Fenicks?

"Sure," I replied. "I mean, yes. Sir."

Water nodded again, and I ducked past him, not sure what to make of this new development.

The moment I stepped outside, I was swarmed by a mob of goats.

"Ah!" I yelped. Their beady eyes peered from everywhere and their bulging bodies pressed up against me, creating a bleating wall around me.

"Really?" a weary voice asked from beyond the goat horde. "You're afraid of goats?"

I flew above the mob and touched down by Erise, Leyes, and a new person, a dust-haired male my height with a quaint nose and dark eyebrows simultaneously raised and furrowed. I scowled.

"Last time I saw a goat, it tried to eat my shirt," I replied. I looked at the third member and he looked at me. Filio looked so serious, and Erise said we were the same age? He gave his head a little shake, then spoke again.

"My name is Filio. My assigned Element is Water, but I would rather you call me Filio."

I nodded.

"I'm Pasin St—"

"I know," he said, cutting me off. "You don't need to state the obvious."

I raised my eyebrows. Rude, yes? Leyes must have thought the same thing.

"She's just being polite," he murmured. Filio didn't reply.

"I'd like to test your abilities," he said. I waited for more, but he said nothing else.

"I haven't really practiced," I said after a moment's hesitation. "I don't really know how to—"

"Then this will be fun," he replied, and his mouth curled into a minute smile. Was that a glint in his eye? Really?

Erise and Leyes sat on the fence separating us from the cacophonous goat herd while Filio and I squared off twenty feet apart. Filio struck a beginning stance, and I saw the goats' water stir in the trough. I shifted on my feet, not sure what to do with them or any part of my body really. The only practice I had was with flying.

"I'll let you go first." he said, smile still on his face.

I looked at him, tried to figure out what I was supposed to do. I looked at my hand, flexed my fingers a few times, but I still had no idea. Whatever anger-fueled power I had used before refused to show itself again.

I brought my hands together, focused my energy, and peeked up. Filio almost looked wary. With a dramatic throw of my hands, I pushed out at him with all I had.

Nothing.

Filio chuckled under his breath.

"My turn."

I saw him twist his hands, and that was the last that I saw. Tears spilled from my tear ducts and clouded my vision. Could he control even that minutely? I could still feel his warmth though, so the point was moot.

"Some great Element," he said. I felt heat rise to my cheeks.

"What is this?" I called out.

"Ability," he replied and lashed out his hand again. I felt it move and leapt up into the air before his jet of water could touch me.

"Hmm," he mumbled this time.

He lashed out again, over and over and over. I just kept dodging each attack. I saw where it started and could tell where it would go. It was rather easy, actually. I settled back onto the ground.

"If you'd wait a second, I could…"

Before I finished, he lunged forward again, but with his body, not just a water attack. I sidestepped at the last moment.

"Just wait, and I'd—"

He didn't let up; he sent another shot of water my way. I didn't register the movement until it was too late. I turned, but the edge of it slapped me in the face.

"Stop it!" My words snapped in the air as my face stung. I turned to him and punched my hand toward him again.

A jet of flame issued straight toward the taunter. He barely sidestepped the flame, and it hit a fence post instead.

The mist fell from my eyes as Filio rushed toward the water trough and channeled the water from the trough to the burning post. For a brief moment, the goats even stopped bleating. The post was barely alight for five seconds before he put it out. I lowered myself to the ground, cheeks burning again.

"Sorry," I said. I felt sorry for the post, not necessarily sorry that I didn't at least singe his eyebrows. He turned back to me.

"At least you can do something," he said finally. He pursed his lips and spoke again. "How did you avoid my attacks?"

I twitched my lips, happy to have one up on him.

"I could sense your movements." His face was blank, so I continued. "I can sense heat, body heat."

He looked at Erise and Leyes and back at me.

"I guess we have more to talk about than I thought."

Erise spoke for the most part, explaining the Star mythology to Filio and what had been going on at the palace. I punctuated her narrative a couple of times with my own experiences as well as the story of our escape. He listened intently, his bright eyes focused on whomever spoke. He leaned against the wooden fence of the goat pen, arms crossed, never smiling. I didn't know what to make of him.

Our conversation was beginning to wind down when a distinctly non-goat presence appeared among us.

"Mlah!" the goats cried as a furry, black beast rushed through the herd, scattering the creatures around their enclosure.

"Motsy!" Another creature dashed through the goat pen. The second caught the first; a flustered girl wrapped her arms around the struggling dog and nearly wrestled it to the ground.

"Motsy, you bad boy!" The girl cupped the dog's face in her hands and frowned significantly at it. "Why are you scaring the goats?" Motsy barked once and licked her face.

"That's why you don't leave the gate open, Rora." Filio's words sounded stern, but his face relaxed. He smiled as the girl dragged the dog out of the goat pen. He turned back to Erise and me.

"This is my little sister, Sorora Rain," he said. Sorora walked to stand behind him. "Rora, this is Erise Spark and Pasin Star." I was surprised he told her my real name. She couldn't have been any older than nine.

"Star?" Her voice reflected the surprise on her upturned face. The dog capitalized on the girl's concentration lapse and escaped, running to sniff Erise and me. "Is that even an Element?"

"Apparently," Filio replied before I could say anything.

"So what is that?" Sorora continued, still looking at me. "What can you do?"

What was with this family?

"It's a mixture," I said, trying to remember what Erise had said. "It combines Fire and Air," I ended lamely, not knowing what else to say.

"Hmm." Sorora squinted her eyes at me. "If you're

a fire person, then I could beat you. Okay!" She gave me a beaming smile.

"I don't know about that," Filio said. Sorora turned back to look at him, confused, and he continued. "You're going to have to beat me first, and for that you need more practice…Drizzle." A mischievous smile spread across his face at the last word. The girl's face turned from confusion to outrage.

"Don't call me that!" she yelled. She moved to hit Filio's arm, but he dodged it. "I'm a Rain!" she yelled as she chased him around the yard. "A Rain!"

Sorora failed to catch him and in desperation, she looked around. Her eyes lit up at the sight of the goat water trough. Her hands shot up, concentration flooded her face, and in a second's breadth, she sent a whip of water at Filio. Filio saw it coming; another smile on his face, he took control of the water as she released it and stood with a levitating ball of water when she was done.

"That was better," Filio said as he played with the water suspended between his hands, "but I know you can do even better than that, Sprinkle."

Sorora opened her mouth to retort, but she stopped when we heard a door open and a middle-aged woman call, "Sorora! Come help with dinner please!"

"Yes, Mama!" she called back. "Oh, that's right!" Sorora looked at the four of us. "Dinner should be ready in an hour. Just so you know." And with that, she flounced away, Motsy trailing behind her. Filio watched her go, then returned the water to its place and turned to us.

"I need to get some things in order before dinner.

See you in an hour?" The question sounded odd with his voice, too relaxed, but he seemed fine with his different manner. No, I did not understand this person.

"Yeah," Erise replied, "I wouldn't mind cleaning up before the big meeting.

"See you in a while then," Filio ended cordially. "Leyes, can I talk to you for a minute?"

We left them to talk and returned to Leyes' home. The hour passed quickly as Erise and I talked about the encounter with Filio.

"He seemed angry that I was there," I said halfway through the conversation, fiddling with my hair. "Did you see him? Seemed like he disliked me from the moment he saw me."

"I don't know Pasin," Erise replied as she washed her face. "I don't know him personally, but Leyes told me a lot about him. He's supposed to be great with tactics, and he is one of the leaders of this movement with his father."

Her eyes darted to my fingers, but instead of the eye roll I expected, she burst out laughing.

"What?" I asked.

"You—" Erise looked away for a moment like she was trying to collect herself. "You're straightening your hair."

I looked at the strand of hair I'd been playing with, and yes, the curl had been smoothed out.

"What? How?"

Erise stepped forward and grabbed my hand.

"You're hot," she said and let go. "That's what did it. Are you nervous?"

"Maybe."

"It'll be fine," she said. "Don't worry."

I snorted.

"Well, it wouldn't kill Filio to be more polite," I said.

"At least wait until after dinner," Erise requested. "Hear his side–well, our side really," she amended. "Hear the plan explained properly before you judge him."

That was some consolation. At least I'd be getting some answers soon.

I mumbled an answer and spent the next twenty minutes preparing myself for the conversation ahead.

CHAPTER TWENTY-THREE

After we knocked on the door, a woman who introduced herself as Ice let us in. I saw the family resemblance immediately with Filio's nose and Sorora's hair. She led us into a side room with a large circular table laden with all sorts of dishes. Water rose from his place at our arrival, a cane leaning against the table beside him. Filio sat to his right, and Leyes sat next to Filio. Ice sat at Water's left with Sorora on her left.

"Thank you for coming," Water said. "Please sit down." We did and he continued, "Before we begin with business, let's enjoy the meal my wife made for us." He turned to the woman on his left.

"Thank you, dear," he said, then pecked her on the cheek. The rest of us said thanks as well.

"Oh, you're welcome," she said. "Sorora, can you fill the cups please?"

Sorora nodded and moved her arm toward the water-filled basin in the middle. She manipulated the water into each of our glasses. I took a sip, and coolness washed through my mouth. On second glance, I noticed the basin shimmering like glass.

About an hour passed full of light conversation, tasty food, and a lovely atmosphere. As we passed plates around, I glanced at the cactus pieces with suspicion, but Leyes and Filio's family seemed to enjoy it. I took a bite and decided to leave the dish to the locals.

Yes, I participated in the conversation, but my eyes kept moving away from Water to Filio, Sorora, and Ice. Each time I saw Filio speak to his sister, a smile lit his face and Sorora laughed at his words. And even while Ice spoke to Erise, her own eyes darted to her children and her own mouth curled gently at the edges. My throat threatened to tighten, and I averted my gaze.

When the meal was over, Ice told Sorora it was time to go upstairs.

"But Mama, why?" she asked, looking up to her mother.

"It would be better if you didn't hear," she answered, "Just in case."

Sorora pouted a bit but stood up and left. Ice started walking in the same direction but then stopped and turned to Water.

"I'm going to go upstairs too," she said. "For the same reasons." Water nodded.

"See you in a while," he replied. His face looked toward the sound of her retreating steps and only turned back to us once the footsteps faded.

"Star," he began. I nodded at the title, though more out of etiquette than recognition. "Thank you for meeting with us here. We appreciate it greatly." He and Filio nodded at me as well. "And of course, thanks to Air and Spark for bringing you here." More nods all around.

"Spark and Air explained to me the extent of Oramus' plans that they told you," Water said. "That he plans to use your powers to leave Falleon."

"Yeah, something like that," I replied, trying not to squirm.

"Well, that is only part of something much bigger," Water said. My mind went blank.

"Like what?" I asked.

"Did they tell you how he planned to force you to use your powers?" he asked.

"Something about my 'heart essence'," I said. "But I don't really know what that means." I turned to look at Erise. "When I asked you about them at the palace, you didn't say much."

"It was the wrong time," Erise responded with a miniscule shrug, like an almost twitch. "And at the banquet we didn't have time either. We had to get out of there." Leyes nodded.

"Spark," Water began again, "could you explain heart essences to Star?"

"Yes," Erise replied and shifted in her chair to look straight at me. "Each person has a heart essence, which acts as a connection between their mind and movement, especially their Elemental ability. One of Oramus' Void powers is to separate heart essences from their owners."

"So what does that mean?" I asked.

"The people become unable to rebel against others," she continued, looking down at this point, "They hardly have personalities, nearly unable to do little more than care for their basic needs and follow simple orders once their heart essence is unconnected to a person."

"You are sixteen, right?" Water interjected, "You had your level test?"

"Yes, I'm sixteen" I replied, "but I never completed the level test. I got arrested before that happened." Water raised his eyebrows, but he continued speaking.

"Ever since Oramus implemented the level test, sixteen-year-olds have been leaving their towns," Water continued. "Or rather, low-leveled Elementals are being invited to the palace."

"All right. And?" That sounded like a step up for a lot of people. I wouldn't have turned that down when I thought I was an Absent.

"We have reason to believe," he said, "that Oramus is removing the heart essences of extremely low-leveled Elementals in order to use them at the palace, mainly as servants."

I stared at him for a moment.

"What? How do you know that? How—"

"Fenicks has lost two young people to Oramus. And I've spoken to other leaders across Falleon who've reported the same."

"But how do you know he's doing that?" I asked again. "The heart essence thing?"

"I saw it," Leyes interjected, finally speaking, "not the actual procedure, but the aftermath. I went to the palace to look into the rumors. A girl who used to live here, I met her at the palace. She used to be really energetic, but Grass was like...nothing when I saw her there."

"Wait," I stopped him. "Grass? Grass as in—"

"Yes," Erise said, "your servant." Filio furrowed his brow at this piece of information. "And there are others, mostly in the kitchens or serving the other higher-ups.

"I noticed it too," Erise continued, "with some of the other servants. I'd learned about this part of his Void power, but I wasn't sure until I met Air and he told me about the before and after with Grass."

I stretched my memory and imagination, but I could not see Grass as energetic or anything besides her...dull self, to be frank.

"Why didn't you tell me about this part? At the palace?" I asked, looking from Erise to Leyes.

"Probably thought you'd react quicker to a personal threat," Filio answered immediately.

"We didn't have much time," Erise said as I shot Filio a scowl. "And really, I didn't think I could explain it well enough."

"We had to get you out of Falleon City as quickly as possible," Leyes added.

Silence fell, and I was glad for it. A little space and time to think in to process the information. But another question popped up.

"So...where do I come into this?" I finally asked, looking around the table. Leyes was busy with something in his hands, but now both Filio and Water were looking at me intently, twin sets of gray eyes staring at me. Erise looked at me as well, but her gaze flickered from me to the two Waters at the table.

"We have reason to believe Oramus planned to remove your heart essence in order to control you and your powers," Water said.

"We think he would have done more than just remove the essence," Erise added. "Instead of just removing it, Voids can transfer the essence to a small containment device to be kept on his or her person.

When the Void or whoever else maintains contact with the container, the de-essenced person is completely under the wearer's physical control."

My throat constricted as she finished. Complete control? Complete control under Oramus...my throat clenched even more, and my skin burned against the cool necklace around my neck.

"And how do you know this?" I asked. Erise answered easily.

"Partly from growing up with the elves and partly from one of Oramus' personal servants," she said. "He said he saw it once, when Oramus served under King Gaeron, and his description matched what I learned."

"Okay, and he wants me to—"

"Go over the mountains," Erise continued. "He talked about wanting to do it before you came, and I mentioned...I mentioned the possibility that a Star could do it."

I felt my face fall ever so slightly at this new piece of knowledge. Erise must have seen it.

"I didn't want him to change another person," she said, "so I did what I thought I had to do." I tightened my lips in response, but I asked another question.

"Why? Why does he want to cross the mountains?"

"He never said," Erise replied.

"Yes," Water continued, "I don't think anyone knows his full plans, except maybe Corinth. In any case, he should not be in power."

Water's fists clenched as he spoke. He closed his eyes, took a deep breath, then spoke again.

"I am the northern leader of a group with similar

goals," Water said, crossing his hands on the table. "We want to remove Oramus from power and end this chain of failed monarchies. Instead of a monarchy, we want to institute a government where three leaders representing a separate part of Falleon would come together to rule."

"Who?" I asked.

"The southern leader, the eastern leader, and I," Water replied.

"So what am I here for?"

Water took a deep breath and then continued.

"We hope you will join our efforts. Your story would convince more people to ally with us. Yes," he said with a smile, no doubt in response to my raised eyebrows, "I'm sure most of the citizens of Falleon have heard about the palace's escapee, but not the reason behind her actions. You could tell them why with your information and ours, and we hope our swelling numbers will force Oramus to abdicate. And if not, well then—" Water paused a moment. "—You can use your power to help us defeat him."

My jaw dropped.

"No, I can't," I replied, "I don't know how to fight at all." Just because I wanted to didn't mean I could. Dodging and fleeing were one sort of thing, but offensive attacks were quite another; the spar with Filio had shown that much.

"We can find someone to train you," Water answered. "Our network stretches across Falleon. I know some Blazes and Gusts can be found."

I looked away from him, away from the other people at the table. Yes, my lack of fighting experience concerned me, but that wasn't the real problem.

"What we're hoping," Water continued, "is to have a representative for our cause, but one who isn't doing it for power. I mean..." He drummed his fingers on the table, "I'm not doing this for power; I'm doing it to prevent Oramus from abusing his subjects. But if it was just me and the others leading it, it would seem like nothing more than a grab for power. That's the problem we were looking at until you came. That's why we need you."

"And if I say no?" The words spilled out quickly, but I managed to keep a straight face.

"What?"

Filio raised his arm and planted his elbow on the table, pointing his finger at me.

"Why? These are real people whose lives are in danger! Why wouldn't you help if—"

"Filio," Water interrupted. Filio, mouth still open to continue, looked at his father then closed his mouth. His hand lowered, but his elbow remained on the table.

"We sincerely hope you choose to join our cause," Water continued, looking at me again. "Your assistance would be greatly valued. However, if you choose to abstain, we will happily offer you a place to stay here." Filio glanced at Water out of the corner of his eye, and I saw Water's interlaced fingers tighten. I took a moment before answering, surprised by the offer.

"That's very kind of you," I replied, "but..." I trailed off without saying more, but I knew what I meant. I didn't want to stay alone with total strangers, no matter how welcome they seemed. That didn't work out for me last time.

"'No' is not an option," Filio said, looking me in

the eyes with his chin tilted up. "We can't afford to have you captured. If you don't come with us, you're staying here." I raised my eyebrows.

"Or what?" I asked.

"Not an option," Filio repeated.

"If you think you can make her stay," Erise interjected, "then good luck with that." Filio turned his head toward her and she smiled. "She escaped from the palace—do you really think you could force her?"

Filio opened his mouth, but Water cut him off.

"It won't come to that," he said to Erise, and continued to me, "but if you do choose not to join us, then it would be best for you to stay here. For your safety."

"If I do agree…" I replied in a slower voice, "If," I reiterated, "What would happen next?"

"The next step would be moving throuhout Falleon and organizing our separate groups into a unified whole," Water answered. "You four will need to find the southern and eastern leaders in order to truly unify our groups for the inevitable confrontation."

"Us four?" I asked. "You aren't coming?"

"Unfortunately," he started with a grimace, "I have a condition that prevents extended travel. My son will be going in my place."

I looked at Filio again, but he didn't look back at me. He gazed at his father, his back straight and his expression somber. I looked at Erise and Leyes.

"So you would be coming too?" I asked. Erise nodded.

"We don't exactly have jobs anymore," she answered, a smile returning to her lips. Leyes nodded.

"Still," I said to Water again. "I would like some time to think about this."

"Of course," he replied. "And when can we expect your response?"

"Tomorrow morning," I said. Water smiled.

"Wonderful," he said. "We look forward to your response."

#

I spent the rest of the evening wandering around the surrounding desert, away from the others, away from the lanterns of the city, under the stars clustered in the night sky.

Could I do it? As seen with the spar with Filio, I had no idea how to actually engage someone in battle. All I could do was sense or fly away. Or catch things on fire, apparently, but would that even count if I couldn't control it?

What else was there to do? Where could I go? I had no home. The orphanage wouldn't take me back, and the palace would be far too happy to do so. I had no money, no possessions. Even if Water's family took me in, that could only last for so long. No matter the homey atmosphere, it still wouldn't be a home. Then again, a trip across Falleon wouldn't be a home either, would it? And then after...

Did I even want to do it? Yes. After what Oramus did to me, to the other people—yes. But again, could I do it?

I lay spread-eagle on the sand and stared up at the sky. No mist, no clouds, nothing to obscure the emptiness. Just thousands of spots in the dark, little tongues of light in the night. I wanted to stay there, in that spot, that moment, forever.

I lifted myself onto my elbows, still looking up. The night didn't change, but at some point, I did stand and begin the walk back to town.

#

When I returned to Leyes' house, the only warmths I felt in the kitchen were Filio and Leyes himself. I opened the front door, ready to hear the tail bit of whatever serious conversation they were having.

"No, I will not play cards with you!" Filio said as I entered, his eyes protruding from his face more than usual as he shoved a deck of cards away from him.

"Hey, if you're gonna be in my house, you gotta pay up somehow, man."

The other person grabbed the deck and shuffled it, then looked toward the open doorway.

"Oh hey," Seyel said, "your girl's back."

I shook my head. Ach, I could sense shapes, but if they were identical shapes…

Filio sighed when he saw me.

"Thank Solluna," he said and rubbed his eyes.

"I said I would tell you tomorrow," I said.

"I know," Filio replied, "I just wanted to make sure you came back." He stood up and made to leave.

"Ooh," Seyel intoned, wiggling his eyebrows. "Do I sense some relationship troubles?"

"No," Filio replied flatly, not even looking at him.

"Ooh," Seyel repeated. "So you're open?" he asked me.

"No," I said, passing Filio in the opposite direction.

"Good night," he said as I passed.

"Night."

"Shining, you people are boring," Seyel said, looking from Filio to me and back again. "Maybe the zinger girl will be up for some fun."

I laughed as I descended the stairs into the basement. After checking my warmth sense a little more closely, it turned out Leyes, Duran, and Gaille were all upstairs while Erise lay on her bed below.

"What are you laughing about?" she mumbled from the bed.

"Seyel thinks he has a chance with you," I replied. Erise snorted.

"No wonder you were laughing," she said. "Anyway, welcome back."

"Thanks," I said and got ready to change.

"Is Filio gone?" she asked.

"Yeah." I slipped into a nightgown loaned by Gaille. "He really didn't need to be there."

"I was up there with him for a bit," Erise said. "He's really committed to this."

"He said he wanted to make sure I came back. What did he think, that I'd run off or something?"

"No, I think he thought you might get captured," she said. She held her hand out over her head, playing with a thin string of electricity between her fingers. "I wasn't worried though."

"Well, thank you," I replied. I sat on the bed across from her. "Also, thanks for earlier." She looked at me and I continued. "The similar thing with Filio at the dinner."

"Oh." The electricity dissipated from Erise's fingers and she sat up. "Well it's true. As if they could keep you here, puh." She grinned at me.

"Still, thanks."

"No problem."

I lay down. I expected Erise to ask about my decision, but she didn't. I mentally thanked her for that as well. I closed my eyes, ready for sleep.

"Pasin?"

"Yeah?"

She didn't answer for a while. Finally, I opened my eyes and leaned on my elbow. Her gaze met mine.

"I really am sorry for not telling you sooner," she said, "about your Element. It just...it just didn't go how I hoped. At all."

"I understand," I replied. "Now. I guess. Yeah, I do." I shook my head, but sleep beckoned. Erise grinned again.

"Good."

Before sleep could entirely overcome me, I remembered something.

"Water mentioned Oramus possibly stepping down as leader," I said. "At the palace, you went straight to battling him."

"Ah," she replied, with a half-grimace, half-smile. "I don't think Oramus would give up power willingly." She paused, then continued. "No matter what your response is tomorrow, how about I give you some lessons in self-defense? You know, just in case."

I nodded.

"That would probably be a good idea. Yeah."

"Yeah," Erise echoed. She yawned and leaned toward the candle as if to blow it out.

"Good night?"

I lay down again and closed my eyes.

"Good night."

Erise let out a breath, and the flame extinguished, and the darkness settled into deeper darkness still.

CHAPTER TWENTY-FOUR

The winter sun's weak rays followed me as I walked alone to Filio's house. I had taken my time at Leyes' house that morning, so Leyes and Erise had already gone ahead.

Everyone was in the living room, from Leyes sitting neatly by the window to Filio standing near the door, shifting back and forth on his feet. As I entered, I saw him open his mouth then shut it, twice, before Water spoke.

"Have you had enough time to make your decision?" he asked.

"Yes," I said.

Everyone in the room seemed to lean forward.

"And yes," I continued, "I want to join your efforts."

A collective breath released, and the room was lined with smiles from Erise's broad grin to Leyes' simple upturned corners of his mouth. But even Erise's smile was nothing compared to Filio's enormous smile, face beaming in a way I hadn't thought possible.

"Yes," he said, almost skipping over to me. "That's absolutely great. Fantastic." He shook my hand and patted my shoulder, still beaming. Water smiled behind him and shook my hand next.

"That is wonderful to hear, Star," he said. "Thank you."

"You're welcome," I replied. The happiness was infectious; a grin of my own lit my face.

"So," Erise said, standing up, "when do we leave?"

Water and Filio looked at each other.

"Tomorrow," Filio replied. "We have the preliminaries done; we just need to finalize the route and some peripherals. You can come and look."

"Actually," Erise said, "if it's the same to you, I promised Star a defense class today."

Filio nodded. "Good idea. Feel free to look later."

He, Water, and Leyes began to walk toward the stairs, but Erise grabbed Leyes' sleeve.

"I need to borrow you for a minute," she said. Leyes looked at Filio who shrugged.

"Come on," Erise said, and herded me and Leyes outside.

#

"We need to work on your training if you're going to be any good with combat," Erise said, unsheathing her sword. I looked nervously at the uncovered blade.

"Am I going to get a sword too?" I asked. The metal thing looked menacing as it glinted under the desert sun.

"Nope," she said simply. "You need to learn to deflect weapons using just your Air abilities. Leyes, can you show her how to make an air blast?"

"Sure," he replied. Ten minutes later I managed to do three consecutive air blasts without doing nothing, or worse, falling backwards. He went back inside, and Erise walked twenty paces away from me.

"Are you ready?" Erise asked. I nodded, though apprehension gnawed at my insides.

"Are you really going to use your sword?" I asked.

"Yes," she said. "But I'll use the blunt side so it won't actually cut you." A smile spread across her face. "You haven't seen this sword in action before, have you?"

I shook my head, and her smile turned scary.

"Now on the count of three," she continued, "I'm going to run at you with this, and you need to try to push me to the side. Understand?"

I nodded again.

"All right. One, two, three!"

Erise charged, sword over her head like she was out for blood, and I tried and tried to make a wind gust, but it just wouldn't come.

"Come on, come on!" The last attempt failed, and I tried to jump and fly, but Erise beat me to it.

"Ya!" The blunt edge of the sword hit me on the left calf, but instead of just the pain of impact, a current of electricity zapped me.

"Ahh!" I fell out of the air and on my back. My hair stood on end.

"What—the pont—was that?!" I panted from the encounter, but Erise almost beamed with glee.

"That is my signature move," she said. She offered the hilt of the sword to me; I saw the entire thing was made of metal.

"I had this sword made because I can send

electricity through it. Once I contact skin–ZAP!" She giggled.

"Is that really necessary?" My calf muscles twitched.

"Yes. You need to learn to fight under pressure. I hope this will give you a reason to try harder," she said. "Again. And don't try to fly away this time."

I looked at her in disbelief.

"Really?"

"One, two—"

It took four shock treatments before I finally managed to knock her off her feet. When she stood up again, she looked genuinely proud.

"Good job!" she said, smiling while I panted with the effort and strain. "See, it worked!"

I looked at her and realized that this would only be the first of who knew how many more sessions to come.

"I hate this already," I said. She smiled again and sighed with glee.

"Man, I love training. Now get back on your mark."

I knew I had a long day ahead of me.

#

We stopped at lunch, and Filio and Water gave us a summary of what they had been doing. Our first destination was friends of Filio's family whose cottage Erise, Leyes, and I had passed on our way to Fenicks.

"They have a press," Filio said, "so we'll get some flyers made to be distributed, saying what we're trying to do and everything. The flyers will tell the people what's happening and show Oramus that people are on to him."

Erise insisted we keep practicing after lunch, and we moved to Leyes' larger backyard. After Leyes' initial guidance, air manipulation came easily, or at least easier than I thought it would. I even managed to focus and knock just the sword out of Erise's hands. Other times, I wasn't quite so lucky.

"Ah!" I didn't see her sword until it was too late. That blow pushed me to the ground.

"Shining, Erise," I said, feeling myself to ensure nothing was broken. "Try to kill me, why don't you?"

Erise didn't apologize; she stood there grinning at her triumph. After a moment, though, she reached out her hand and helped me up.

"I think that's enough for now," she said. "We'll do more tomorrow."

"Great," I replied. "Maybe tomorrow I'll have seven bruises instead of three." I looked at where she hit with the blunt edge of the sword. It was already changing color.

"Sounds good to me!" she said brightly. I glared at her and she flashed another toothy smile.

"I'm getting some water," I said, flying away before she could reply.

The back door to Leyes' house stood wide open. I landed on the stone that acted as the stoop, but before I could take a step, I heard a voice within.

"I'm just not sure," Leyes said. I sensed inside and felt him sitting at the kitchen table with someone else. "I think it's there, but I haven't let myself think about that since…"

"I know honey," Gaille replied. "It's going to be hard, I know." They sat in silence for a moment; I almost took a step in when Leyes continued.

"How is she?" he asked. I stopped and tilted my head toward the door.

"They left," his mother answered. "About two weeks after you did. I think they went to Lainsford." Leyes groaned.

"I never apologized," he said. "How can I make it right if I can't even…"

"Shh. Let's not talk about it right now." At this point, I realized how far forward I was leaning trying to understand a conversation I had no business listening to. Guilt heated my face. I turned to leave, but Gaille spoke again.

"Now what about the other?" she asked. "What does Filio think?"

Leyes let out an almost spiteful laugh.

"You know Filio," he said. "I can't talk to him about this, he…"

I stepped off the stone step and on to the gravelly sand. Crunching it beneath my feet, I stepped back on the stone stoop, knocked on the door, and called with resonating, "Hello!"

"Oh, come in dear," Gaille replied. I walked into the kitchen where she sat at the table. Leyes had vacated his position and was rummaging through the cabinet.

"Could I get some water?" I directed at Gaille. She stood up immediately.

"Of course," she said, and directed me to a water jug. "I'm sorry it's not chilled; we don't have any Ices in the family so that's out of our hands."

"Oh no, that's fine," I said.

"Leyes!" Gaille turned to her son, still rummaging. "Fetch Pasin a cup, please." Leyes did as she asked and handed me the earthenware mug.

"Thank you," I said.

"You're welcome," he mumbled.

I poured myself a drink, and we stood around silently as I drank. Leyes was the first to break the silence.

"I'm going back to Filio's," he said. He turned to leave when his mother spoke at his retreating figure.

"Why don't you talk to him while you're there, okay?"

Leyes didn't look at Gaille, but he did answer.

"Sure." And then he flew away.

#

We left early the next day. Gaille held Leyes tightly, though Duran only nodded at his son. When Leyes walked away though, I saw Duran's brow line soften and fall. Seyel had his bit to say too.

"I wish it could have been different between us," he told Erise. She let out a snort and turned away. He looked at me with a waggle on his eyebrows, and I resisted the urge to do more than roll my eyes.

Filio was in the process of finishing up his goodbyes when we reached our meeting point outside of town. He let go of his mother and kneeled in front of his sister. She threw her arms around his neck and buried her face in his shoulder.

"Come back soon," she said, her words muffled by his shirt.

"I will," he answered quietly. After a moment longer, Filio gently moved her away from him and stood up.

"And when I get back," he continued with a smile, "I expect to see some fancy new water manipulation,

Rain." Her face lit up.

"That's right! You won't know what hit you!" Sorora beamed, then skipped back to her mother. Filio adjusted his pack and walked to us.

"Ready to go?" he asked. We all nodded, and he nodded as well.

"Good." He turned to look at his family.

"See you in a while," he said and waved.

"May Solluna light your path," Water replied. He, Ice, and Sorora waved as we took our first steps forward toward the rest of Falleon and whatever might be waiting for us there.

CHAPTER TWENTY-FIVE

Our first stop was the couple with the printing press. In a small cottage whose insides nearly burst with tottering piles of paper, I told my story to the Mud and Earth. The husband and wife's eager eyes put me off at first, but the room we sat in calmed me, the papers surrounding us like birds out of their pens instead of being bound to bookshelves as at the palace or even the school library.

After hearing my story, they spoke with Filio about designs, slogans, and other things I didn't really care about. Erise and I went outside where she bestowed some more bruises upon me. By the time we returned for dinner, a spread of posters covered the table, the ink still glistening on the page. A flaming star blazed from the center of each paper.

"We'll talk to your father," Mud said to Filio, "about getting all the local Airs to take these around Falleon."

"Our Air can take them to Fenicks," Filo said. He turned to Leyes. "Can you get to Fenicks and back tonight?"

"Sure," Leyes said.

"I can go," I said. Filio turned his head to me and raised his eyebrows. "I mean, I am faster," I added.

"No," he said without hesitation. "You can't just go traipsing around on your own when there are more soldiers on the road."

"I can sense the soldiers, you know," I said, hand curling around the edge of the paper-laden table. I had been the one to alert our group when we almost walked into a large group of people travelling in formation earlier that day. From the cover of some roadside trees, I grimaced at their black tunics bearing Oramus' seal.

"No," Filio repeated. "Air knows the way better, and, unlike you, he isn't being chased by Oramus' forces." He turned back to Leyes and started a stream of brisk instructions. I opened my mouth to reply, but Erise touched my shoulder and I dropped the subject.

Leyes' eyes were bloodshot the next morning when we left the cottage before the sun came up. Filio said Morrit, our next main stop, was only three days away, but we had plenty of smaller villages to visit before we reached Morrit. That is, Filio, Erise, and Leyes had plenty of stops. Filio insisted I remain outside these villages the first time we approached one and found soldiers patrolling a paltry forty-person group of buildings.

When we weren't stopped, we walked. Filio wouldn't let Leyes or I fly during the day because it would be too suspicious, he said. Every once in a while, we saw an Air soldier patrolling the sky, enforcing what Filio said were civilian "no-fly" zones. A rush of jealousy shot through me at the sight.

A different rush coursed through me the first time we passed a message post and saw a flaming star poster dominating the space.

"Great," Filio said, nodding with upturned lips. "That's great," he repeated as the smile widened.

Every night, we would set up camp when the sun had disappeared behind the western mountains but remnants of its light lingered in the sky. It felt great to lose the weights of the bags at the end of the day. Then we would have some training time in our separate areas. Erise and Leyes switched off with me–Erise teaching swordplay and general Elemental tricks she knew, while Leyes focused on my Air abilities.

At Filio's prompting, I tried to light the campfire the first night and succeeded in catching a nearby bush on fire.

"Sorry," I said after Filio extinguished my mishap. "I guess I was just...warming up?"

After a collective groan from the others, we mutually decided to wait on the fire training, though not without some berating from Filio.

After training, we had dinner, decided who would take which watch during the night, then split up to our various nighttime occupations. Erise tended to her things, sharpened her sword and whatnot while Leyes spent a lot of time alone by the fire. I wrote in a notebook Mud had given me before we left. Filio though...he spent almost all of his free time after dinner playing with a squirt of water. He would bend it, twist it, and do other Water stuff with it, but it never pleased him. The concentration on his face was only magnified by the accompanying frown.

At night, though, the nightmares interrupted the relative peace I had. Images flash flash flashing by–

Oramus' hands on mine, the burning tapestry.

Halfway through the morning of the fifth day, we made it to our destination.

"This is Morrit," Filio said, pointing to the mass at the other side of the clearing we stood in. An enormous stone wall reached high enough to obscure the forest behind it. I focused, stretching my consciousness, and felt the teeming of a city within. I withdrew my focus; the number of people reminded me of the first night in Falleon City, their warmths scurrying back and forth behind the wall. Guards paced on top of the wall's battlements.

"Our objective is to find two people, as well as restock our food supply." Filio looked at me, and closed his eyes, as if in pain. "Pasin, you need to come. As proof."

My head jerked toward him, and a smile almost bloomed across my face before I caught myself and attempted a nonchalant scratch of my neck instead. Filio raised his eyebrows and frowned.

"You're going to have to turn that thing around," he said. He waved his hand at my neck where the engagement necklace still sat. "Or something. Just in case."

That did make sense. I did as he asked and felt the coolness move to the back of my neck.

We waited until another group approached the gates and joined the small crowd. I tried not to let my back stiffen as the guards' eyes slipped over us, but I still felt my body relax once they let us pass. As we walked through the gates, though, I tightened once more and tried, unsuccessfully, not to think of the walls surrounding us from every side.

CHAPTER TWENTY-SIX

We entered a marketplace of sorts, stalls and carts jumbled together across a wide cobblestone space teeming with scurrying people. A wooden platform stood in the middle of the area, but beyond the square, all of the city's buildings were made of stone. Only the multi-hued banners of merchants' stalls broke the internal grayness of the city. Even the sky was mostly covered in clouds.

I reopened my consciousness a little then immediately withdrew with a quick intake of breath at the number of warmths around us. It felt as if a dozen chickens were pecking at my mind. Leyes looked at me.

"Is something wrong?" he asked.

"No, I'm fine," I said, shaking my head. Filio glanced back.

"What happened?" he asked with a scowl.

"Nothing. I'm fine," I repeated through gritted teeth. It was much harder to block the warmths out when he gave me that look.

"What are we looking for?" Erise asked.

"Baker's Alley," Filio said. He looked across the plaza and jerked his head. "This way."

We wound our way through the crowded square until we reached an alley entryway over which hung a wooden sign displaying a poorly painted loaf of bread. Filio muttered a number under his breath and ducked into the alleyway. Erise, Leyes, and I followed him into the shop four doors down.

The scents of yeast, barley, and flour assaulted my nose when we walked into the crowded shop. Filio waited his turn at the counter and asked the harried girl behind it where to find a Smoke. She gestured toward the back room before turning her attention to the man squawking about too many seeds in his rolls.

A man stood rolling dough at a table, patches of rogue flour contrasting against his golden-brown skin.

"Excuse me," Filio said, "Are you Smoke?"

"Yes," the man said, continuing his work. "And who are you?"

"I'm Water," Filio said, "from Fenicks." Smoke's eyebrows lifted.

"Ah," Smoke said, lowering his roller, eyes darting between the four of us. "Good to see you. All of you," he added. "This way."

We followed him through another door farther back in the store and entered a small storeroom crammed with sacks of goods dimly lit by the peripheral sunlight coming through the window. Even so, the city walls, visible over the tops of neighboring houses, blocked most of the light.

"Do you have any more of those posters?" Smoke asked, wiping his floury hands on his apron.

"Yes," Filio said. He pulled out some papers from

his pack, gently unwrapping them. "Did you not get enough, or—?"

"All the ones we put up were taken down," Smoke said. "Now, who are you?" he asked, pointing at Leyes, Erise, and me.

"Air."

"Spark."

A split second of hesitation.

"Star."

He smiled. "Nice to meet you all." He turned to me. "And thank you for joining us, Star. Glad to see the ball rolling."

"I...you're welcome," I said. Feeling like I should say more, I continued. "It's terrible what Oramus is doing."

Smoke's mouth lifted into a small smile, but his eyes didn't change.

"My nephew was taken after his level test," he said. "I haven't seen him since." He set the new posters aside. "But we have to keep going, you know?"

No one said anything; the only sound was the crowd outside, feet on stone and the shouts of stall keepers. Filio broke the silence.

"We were told there were two leaders here," Filio said, "Is there an Earth?"

"Yes," Smoke said. "I saw him last night, but not yet today." He peered out the window at the bustling street. "He was supposed to be here by now. I know he wants to be here for the meeting," he said.

Filio scrunched his lips.

"We need to pick up some supplies," he said. "But we'll be back in an hour or two."

"Works for me," Smoke said. He picked up a bag of flour and started to head back.

"Star is staying here, though," Filio added. I snapped my head toward him.

"Why?" I asked.

"You're here for the meeting," he said. "Nothing else. No need to take unnecessary risks."

I opened my mouth to retort, but the thought crossed my mind that if I stayed behind, I wouldn't have to be around Filio.

"Fine," I said.

"Is it alright if she stays here?" he asked Smoke.

"No problem," Smoke answered. He nodded at me. "Make yourself comfortable."

As the others left, I sat down at the table and pulled out my notebook. The room darkened and I glanced out the window and watched as a cloud obscured the thin stretch of sky over the wall.

#

An hour and a half later, I still sat at the table, munching on a flaxseed roll, when one voice, significantly louder than the others, rumbled from the front of the store.

"Everyone out!" it said. "To the square, town meeting!"

Footsteps shuffled from the front of the store, and I sat there, unsure of what to do, when someone shoved the door aside. A man wearing a black tunic with Oramus' silver seal entered.

"Are you deaf?" the soldier asked. "Outside with you!"

I clutched my notebook to my side and ducked my head as I passed the man, but he did nothing more than grumble under his breath as I left the building.

The alley was nearly deserted when I entered it. Another soldier directed me and some other stragglers to the left, to the main plaza. Smoke was nowhere to be found, so I followed the directions mutely, trying to quell the panic rising in my throat.

If the plaza was busy before, it was nothing compared to the horde of people currently flooding the space. Though I tried to focus on myself, the seemingly innumerable warmths of bodies rippled across my consciousness, scratched over my mind.

"Hey!" a familiar voice called out from not too far away. A hand touched my shoulder.

"Hey," Erise repeated and stood by my side. "Are you all right?"

"Yeah," I said. "Do you know why we're here?"

"They've closed the gate," another voice said. Filio came up to us, followed by Leyes. Filio's face was nearly white. "They're not letting anyone through. I don't know for how long."

"Couldn't we spend the night with Smoke?" I asked. "If we had to?"

"Yes, I'm sure we could," he snapped with a scowl, "but the gates are being shut for a reason. Why would they close them in the middle of the day?"

"It probably has to do with that," Erise said.

She pointed at the wooden platform in the center of the square. While it had been empty before, now three gallows stood erect, three dark silhouettes against the clouded sky. My heart jumped.

"Is there another way out?" I asked.

"Nothing inconspicuous," Filio said.

"Keep moving!" another soldier shouted. More people pressed in from behind us, and the surge swept Erise and Filio forward. I almost pushed forward to follow, but Leyes' fingers plucked at my sleeve.

"We'll find them," he said, though in the noise of the crowd his voice sounded barely louder than a whisper. "Look," he said, glancing up again at the platform.

A line of shackled people, two men and a woman, stood in a row on the platform. Even in the dim light from the clouded sky, I saw the glint of Elemental Nullifiers circling their wrists.

The crowd of black-clad soldiers parted as one man, vaguely short and fairly fat, ascended the platform. By the fineness of his clothes and the smirk he gave the prisoners, I took him to be the person in charge.

He held his arms out for silence. The crowd complied, and I glanced around. Even in the crowded space, people avoided the soldiers, creating bubbles of emptiness with black centers through the square. Soldiers still walked along the city walls.

"Greetings, citizens!" The man's voice rang with a bit of phlegm. "We have gathered here today to remind ourselves of the nobility of loyalty and the joy of citizenship. These scum," he spat, throwing the word at the prisoners, "are what you would call subversive. These filth," he spat again "are plotters, schemers, trying to undermine the great society upon which we rely. All have been accused and convicted of attempting to join the resistance and rebel against the king himself.

"Verit Grass, Hoss Earth, and Indra Cloud," the man said, gesturing to each person in turn, "are all traitors." My eyes widened at the second one.

"Is that the one Smoke…" I began.

"And are hereby sentenced to death," the man continued.

"I think so," Leyes said.

My heart pounded in my chest. My throat constricted.

"Treachery is wrongdoing. And wrongdoing must be punished." With this, a soldier dragged the first man up to the waiting noose. His body stiffened, but his face was unwavering stone, eyes set on something past the walls of the city.

A scream tore through the crowd.

"Daddy!" A little girl of maybe five or six ran up to the platform. A mother tried to restrain the child but could not stop the shrieks.

The father looked at his child but was gagged before he could say a word. The soldiers around the platform laughed.

"No!" she howled. "Daddy!" Two soldiers came forward and pushed her aside from the stage. She fell hard onto the ground. The noose was placed around the man's neck.

"This!" cried the speaker, "This is the punishment for those who dare defy King Oramus!"

A lever was pulled. The man fell hard, just like his daughter. Hushed gasps rippled through the crowd. His uncovered face turned blue, eyes bulging, hands scrabbling at his bonds, useless against the taut rope. The girl was screaming, the soldiers were laughing, and I thought my heart would burst right there.

The child on the ground wailed. The soldiers swarmed upon her, heavy boots pounding on the ground. They kept laughing, guffawing, and blood pounded in my ears. My ears were hot, burning under my hair.

"This fate will fall on anyone," the fat man shouted, "who tries to join the resistance."

"Shut up," I whispered through clenched teeth. "Shut up." I could feel Leyes' warning hand on my shoulder.

"Because those who resist deserve nothing but death!" He spat these words into the face of the girl, now sobbing.

"Shut up!" I screeched. The words flew from my mouth and a sea of heads rippled, a thousand faces turned to look me. Up ahead, I saw Erise and Filio; Erise's eyes widened while Filio's expression stormed, eyes like lightning flashes. Total silence rang through the air.

"Seize her!" the man on the platform shouted with a vicious, malicious smile. "Make her next for the gallows."

The people closest to me dissipated into the greater crowd as soldiers shoved their way through the throng. I leapt up, dodged the projectiles shot my way, and easily dispatched the soldiers with wind gusts that sent them crashing into the stone buildings surrounding the square. My real fury, though, was directed at the man still pointing in my direction even as the smile dripped off his face and his hand went limp.

A roar echoed out of my mouth and a jet of flame burst from my hand toward the man's fat, terrified face. His own hands barely came up in time to shield his face. The flames coursed around him, licking him like a pack of hellhounds from Nox.

"No, please!" His eyes watered; his mouth blubbered; gasps racked his chest. "Please don't! Mercy, mercy…"

The man fell to his knees and rocked back and forth clutching his singed hands to his breast.

"Mercy?" I spat right back at him. "Is that what you felt when you called these people scum? When you killed that man?"

I don't know if the crowd made any noise. All I could hear were the man's pleas and the pounding of my heart.

"Mercy, mercy," he cried, again and again, like a charm to keep away a nightmare's curse. I curled my lip.

"Save your breath." I shot him straight in the face with a wind gust, snapping his head back so it hit the wooden platform. He fell hard, like the girl, like the man he had just killed, but he wasn't dead. I was not yet as ragingly cold as that.

While the man lay limp at my feet, a few of the soldiers I had knocked down earlier were rising to their feet. I turned toward them, stood erect and strong, then pointed at the remaining prisoners.

"Release them," I said. "And take off the nullifiers."

A tense moment passed, but I knew how it would end and so did they. I, the interloper, had bested their leader. Until someone bested me, I took his place. It was the one rule of Falleon that didn't change.

One of the black-clad men stepped forward and uncuffed Earth, then held a silvery key to the nullifier, creating a seam, which he pulled apart to remove the bangle. Another soldier did the same for Cloud.

Whispers filtered through the crowd, and I turned my gaze to them. A thousand faces looked back at me, a thousand faces crowded with fear, confusion, maybe even some hope? At that moment, though, I realized what I had just done.

"People of," I started, but stopped, took a deep breath, and started again. "People of Morrit," I shouted as I jumped to hover thirty feet above the ground and seized the fire burning within. "I am Pasin Star."

The whispers swelled and grew in volume, but I continued even louder.

"I am not here to kill your rulers or take your city," I said, "but I cannot and will not stand by as innocent people die for speaking the truth about Oramus' tyranny." The words poured from my mouth and echoed across the plaza, and the people quieted as I spoke. "Our movement is not one of force, but of right. We are here to right the wrongs our king—" This time I spat the word. "—Is inflicting upon us."

I might have heard a shout. The crowd might have cheered, might have clapped, but I was caught up in my own words.

I turned to the remaining gallows. Harnessing the fire still burning within, I set them alight. The crowd's cheer swelled into a roar as the flames grew higher, and a smile played on my lips.

I turned back to them, and my eyes swept the people surrounding me, the thousand faces a flurry of joy. But my gaze stopped on one.

The little girl from before sat at the foot of the stage, body quaking from cries lost in the uproar. I landed next to her to kneel at her side, but her words stopped me.

"Why," she sobbed, looking me straight in the eyes "Why didn't you save my daddy?"

The world stopped for a moment and drowned, drowned in her tears and her straight-forward eyes,

eyes that accused but understood and seemed to hate me all the more for understanding.

The cheering continued, but it faded in my ears where my blood boiled and balked at the acknowledgement of my failure. One step, two steps, three steps back, and I couldn't take it anymore. I fled, like a fox from a hunter, over the crowd singing my praises, over the unconscious bodies of the speaker and the hanged man, through the smoke rising from the burning gallows. Chaos pounded at my temples and I drowned in the sky. I flew over the stone walls. The noise from the city followed me into the wilderness and into my head, a noise that paled in comparison to that one girl's question.

#

I fled to the woods, constantly alert for the warmths of pursuers, but no one followed me; the only warmths I felt were the occasional bird or rabbit. I didn't know what to do, where to go. We had never planned for this, what to do if one of us got separated from the group.

My limbs shook. I tried, I tried so hard to forget, but the girl's face kept resurging in my mind, her face and eyes red from the tears that rocked her body.

I looked down at my trembling hands. The fire had sprung to my palm so easily, and my hand had been so quick to lash out at the speaker. The right side of my mouth curled. Too bad he had blocked the shot…

I walked to a nearby stream and tried to summon the fire again, but I stopped. It didn't feel right, and I didn't want to screw up. I could feel the power in my palms, but without the anger, it didn't seem like it would work right.

Hours passed. When the sun had almost entirely disappeared over the mountains, I decided to start heading back to Fenicks, back to Filio's family. They would know what to do. I tried not to imagine the disappointment I would inevitably see on Water's face. I had failed.

Five minutes of flying later, three familiar warmths crept into my consciousness. I could barely believe it, but when I looked from afar, I saw Erise, Filio, and Leyes walking down the dirt road.

I landed right in front of them with a thud, and Erise whipped out her sword before recognition dawned.

"Pasin!" Erise darted forward to me, sheathing her sword. "Are you all right?"

"Yeah, I'm fine," I replied.

As I looked at the others, Leyes gave me a small smile, but Filio's wide eyes and set jaw were overshadowed by the tone of his voice.

"What do you think you were doing back there?" he asked. It was almost a sneer, the way his words bit in the winter night. A glow of heat lit my cheeks.

"I couldn't just stand by," I said. "Not when I could do something."

"Do you…" The word faded, and Filio closed his eyes, took a breath, then stared at me again. "Do you realize what could have happened?"

"I—"

His words felt like a slap in the face, his expression a demeaning force.

"I saved their lives!" I said. "They would have died if I hadn't done something!"

His eyes bulged.

"People die every day!" Filio's voice rose, rang out on the deserted road. "They knew that! If you'd been captured, that man would have died for nothing! Nothing! At least let him die for something!"

I gnashed my teeth together; clenched my fists; felt burning in my ears, neck, and hands; but couldn't say anything. Filio continued.

"You know why we're here? We had to get Earth and Cloud out. They couldn't stay there after, you know that, right? We almost got caught three times, three!" He stuck three fingers in the air, waved them in my face. "And what would have happened then?"

I opened my mouth, but he flung his hand down, then brought both fists to the side of his head.

"You think just because you're this amazing Element, you can go off and play hero?" His volume lowered, but disgust muddied the tone, enraging me more than his anger ever could.

"No!" I said, heat pouring into my words. I could hear my voice echoing through the woods, but I didn't care. "You don't even…"

"It takes more than your dricking title to even get close! You pull a stunt like that and you cheapen everything we've worked for!"

"You don't have a clue!" I shot back. His words stunned me, not with guilt but with rage. My body shook. "You don't even…GAH!"

My last word was a wild cry of emotion. I took off once more, flew away from the intense rage I wanted to lash out at the man who didn't know…didn't know I still felt like the Absent I was in Andor. The girl people still made decisions for.

A hundred feet or so away, I finally landed. I reached out with my senses and felt a nearby warmth.

A small rabbit–a sniffling, squintering little creature hopped cautiously into the small clearing. It must not have noticed me due to its unabashed advances. I looked at it with cynical, disgusted eyes. So cute, so stupid.

Disinterested, still seething underneath, I raised my hand and set a spot of dead grass on fire next to the beast. It leapt away, tried to dart in the opposite direction, but I threw another lick of flame toward it.

The creature scurried and hurried, terror on its sad, stupid face as I cut off its escape routes one by one. Finally, it stood quivering in the middle of a circle of flame, panic leaking from its eyes, its heart throbbing.

My fingers flexed hard as they directed this fiery symphony. I snarled, I smiled at the control I held. The pathetic little beast was mine, completely and totally.

All of the heat poured out of my fingertips and I could feel its heart beat faster and faster and faster—

"Pasin."

I whipped around at the human voice. The flames fell into embers without my focus, and the rabbit sped off into the dark forest. Leyes rushed forward and stomped on the embers, extinguishing them. When he turned to look at me, disappointment clouded his eyes.

"Leyes, I—"

"Pasin…" he said, walking toward me. "I'm not—" He stopped, took a breath, licked his lip. "Can we walk back? Do you think you're ready?"

"Yeah, sure." We walked in the direction of the others, stiffly and carefully side by side.

"I'm not saying it's easy," he began, "but maybe it would help to just think of something else. At least until the emotions die down."

A surge of shame flared up as I remembered what I did to that rabbit.

"I'll try," I said finally.

"Thank you," Leyes said. Remnants of acorns and fall leaves crunched under our feet as we walked back. He continued, "Filio is strong in his opinions and doesn't react well when people disagree with him. I can understand where both you and he are coming from. But he's the one who planned all of this, and not for personal gain, either."

Though I still felt anger pulsing in my chest, a drop of softness toward Filio mixed in with the emotion, maybe, possibly. A lump of resistance remained, though.

"He doesn't know what it was like growing up as an Absent. He can't just...assume things about me or my Element."

"Filio has always been touchy about the Elemental Classification System. At the end, he lashed out against it, I think, not you." Leyes paused then continued, "That's why he's trying to freeze water every night. To prove them wrong."

We continued in silence. I could feel the two warmths of Erise and Filio up ahead. Leyes said one more thing.

"From...personal experience," he said. "I can tell you that sometimes it's best to let it go. Find forgiveness from yourself, others, if possible...and let it go."

I couldn't go back and apologize to the rabbit. But maybe, maybe I could forgive myself.

We found Filio and Erise again. They parted from their conversation, and Filio took a step my way.

"I don't regret what I said," he said. "But I could have said it differently." He looked at me, the smallest bite of apology on his face. I quelled the resurgence of emotions and looked at him steadily in the face.

"I don't regret what I did," I said. "But I will try to…focus more on the bigger picture." I turned my gaze away, felt my muscles twitch beneath my skin.

"Thank you," he said finally. After a moment, he added, "I appreciate that." More silence and awkwardness seeped through the air until Erise spoke.

"Okay, now that that's done with, what's the plan for tomorrow?"

Filio instantly transformed back into his leader self.

"We need to set up camp," he said. "And based on what we found out in Morrit, we need to contact a Wood in Lainsford. She might know the Light that Fire mentioned."

We each nodded and separated to our different planes of nighttime activities. As I took out my notebook, I stole a furtive glance in Filio's direction.

He sat in his corner, away from the fire, concentration creating sweat that glistened on his forehead. The small glob of water remained liquid, no matter how hard he tried.

I took out my pencil and drew triangle icicles on the top of the page, but I knew Filio didn't want those.

CHAPTER TWENTY-SEVEN

Along the way to Lainsford, a growing number of travelers cluttered the roads despite the harsh weather, despite the increasing number of soldiers. We soon discovered why.

"There's a festival going on in Lainsford," Filio said after asking a passing group. "Right when we're supposed to be there." These claims were verified as posters for the event began to crop up at signposts and on the trees along the way. Filio only let me approach the poster at the signpost once the other travelers had continued on their way. His paranoia perturbed me, but I understood. As I walked up to the board, I saw myself staring back from an even larger poster.

"WANTED," it read, "Pasin Star–Fugitive of the Kingdom. Information to her whereabouts will be rewarded. Harborers will be swiftly and severely punished." The picture was the weirdest part–myself–but the head in the picture was at least twice as large as my real one. Ach.

"They even have the necklace," Leyes pointed out, gesturing to the drawn pendant as large as a fist. I fingered at the real thing pulled behind my neck. No matter how warm my skin got, the coldness in it remained. Even more astounding than the attention to detail was the reward offer listed beneath my name.

"Wow." Erise's eyebrows raised, and she looked at me. "I could really cash in if I changed my mind."

"Don't even joke about that," Filio interrupted with weariness in his voice. But I saw the smile on Erise's face. I grinned back. Filio shook his head and tore down the wanted poster. He rummaged through his bag, took out one of our posters, and tacked it to the post in its stead.

"But think," Erise continued, pointing at the other sign. "The festival is tomorrow. We can't delay until afterwards; our food supply is running low."

The next half-hour of walking rang with Filio and Erise's back-and-forth, back-and-forth. Statement, interruption, annoyance, counterstatement, snort of derision, etc. After this verbal battle, Filio conceded to going to Lainsford during the festival.

"Besides," Erise said, unable to keep all of the gloat out of her voice, "with that many people it'll be easier to blend in."

"Yeah, I heard you the first time," Filio replied. The pause hung in the air like wet laundry, and I considered moving in. I had been silent about the proposition thus far, but I did want to know…

"With that in mind," I ventured, "I was wondering if I could join …"

"Seriously?" Filio asked, turning to look at me, eyebrows arched. "You're asking that?"

"Yes," I said. It had been four days since Morrit. I

knew I was over it.

"No," Filio replied. "Absolutely not."

"But there'll be a lot of people—"

"No."

"With costumes, the sign said…"

"Did you see the bounty on your head? That's enough to feed a family for a year!"

"The other travelers said there would be thousands of people there! I could wear a disguise and…"

"No no no no no no no NO!" Filio almost shouted in agitation. "What part of 'no' do you not understand?"

Leyes and Erise remained silent through this entire exchange, and I fell silent at his last words. But my blood boiled inside, and I flexed my fingers, worked my jaw, but the anger was building. And it needed a release.

"I don't care what you say," I said, "I'm going to the festival."

Filio stopped; he literally stopped and turned to me with incredulity. But incredulity fell away to disbelief.

"You wouldn't," he sneered, taunted. A moment of pause, and then—

"Yes, I would. And you can't stop me." I looked him in the eyes; he glowered in return. I didn't back down, but I was the first to turn away. I walked straight past him and continued down the road, the slightest strut in my step. I took the lead and kept it. Well, for a little while at least.

\#

After a few minutes, Erise caught up with me. I

felt Leyes and Filio stay behind.

"What are you doing, Pasin?" she asked wearily. I didn't answer; I didn't want to dwell on the negatives creeping at the edge of my buoyant spirit. "Why do you keep pushing him like that?"

"I'm tired of being treated like a child!" I felt my body heat rise with my words. "He doesn't believe or trust me! At all!" I paused, tried to stop, but I couldn't.

"How does he expect me to do anything if I can't do anything? I feel…I feel I might just go if…if…" I did stop here, but because I understood the slightest, slightest bit and I felt selfish. Terrible, terrible feeling, this want with that guilt.

"Forgive my cliché, but it is better to be safe than sorry. And all that."

More grumbling, reluctant understanding, and a stiff apology to Filio later, we came to an understanding. I could go…but I had to stay with him.

#

Filio and Leyes went ahead and brought back a small variety of disguise items–cheap masks, wigs, little trappings that we divided among us. Erise and I donned masks covering the tops of our faces, and I choked back a snort when Filio put on a crazy white wig. He jammed it on his head and pulled one more thing out of the bag.

"You need a scarf," he said, and tossed it my way. I snatched it mid-flight and looked it over. The beige wool felt nice against my skin, but I could tell it was going to be hot.

I sighed a little bit on the inside but donned the soon-to-be-stifling thing nonetheless.

#

A thousand-fold of people swarmed through the wood and stone structures of Lainsford—three thousand-fold of lanterns hung from lines across the sky and brightened it, making day out of night. We stood on top of the closest hill and looked over the brightly lit city.

"Erise," Filio started. "Can you check up on the other lead Fire gave us?"

"Yup."

"You know where you're going Leyes?" he asked. Leyes nodded.

"And it looks like we're together," Filio muttered. "Well then, we're ready. Meet back on the left of the entrance in two hours. Understood?" Each person nodded, and we were off, each to his or her own. Well, except for me and Filio.

We wound our way through the crowds. All around us, people danced to loud music, ate weird-looking food, and even showed off their Elemental abilities. A man in striped pantaloons juggled fire while balancing on top of another person. I even saw two people coax a plant to grow between the cracks in the flagstones despite the chill weather.

Voices screamed through the air, and Filio dashed on, almost getting lost in the crowd. I tore my focus away from the sights and did my best to keep up. Every once in a while, Filio stopped and asked a bystander a question. What that was, I couldn't tell; the other voices drowned out his words. As we walked on, crossing a massive stone bridge festooned with ribbons and banners, we passed the largest concentration of festival goers and the sound died down, or lessened at least.

As Filio searched for our contact, Wood, I followed him like a trained dog. I decided to seize the opportunity to try to learn more about him.

"Hey, Water—" I hoped he would recognize my attempt at security and respect by the use of his Elemental Classification.

"What?" His tone didn't acknowledge my stealthy communication.

"How did you and Air get to know each other?"

He shot a quizzical glance in my direction but kept going.

"We grew up together," he said. "We've been friends since we were kids. We went to the same school until he had to leave Fenicks."

I paused for a moment, then—

"What do you mean Air had to leave Fenicks?"

This time Filio physically stopped and turned to me.

"You don't know?" For once, his question wasn't accusatory. "I thought Erise would have told you by now."

"Told me what?"

But Filio didn't reply. Instead, he twitched his mouth, furrowed his eyebrows, but then he finally spoke.

"What do you know about Air's past?" he asked.

"Well, I…" I didn't really know. "I assumed he went to the palace for the sake of this movement. Of his own choice," I added. Filio took a few seconds to answer.

"He did choose to go to the palace for us," he said. "But he didn't choose to leave Fenicks." Filio continued walking, but he did slow down. He said nothing after this. I didn't want to push him, but…

"Can you…elaborate, please?" I asked. I could see his mouth twitching even from the side of his face. After a few moments, he sighed.

"Air and Sand are twins–you know that, right?"

"Yes," I said. I tried not to roll my eyes.

"Well they used to act alike, not just look alike," he said. I thought back to Seyel Sand and grimaced.

"There was a period when we were in school where Leyes spent a lot of time with Seyel–a rebellious phase I guess, I don't know. I tried to snap him out of it, but he just kept on doing idiotic stuff with Seyel."

"What kind of stuff?" I asked.

"Oh, skipping school, setting snakes loose in the market, you know, not illegal, but not good stuff. They used to go drinking at the end of the day too."

I tried to imagine Leyes as a drinker. The picture didn't quite work in my head.

"Also, they were both…" Filio sighed, sounded exasperated, like he didn't want to have this conversation. "Womanizers, I guess."

I raised my eyebrows.

"Really," Filio added, "I'm not making this up. Seyel was always like that, still is, but Leyes went along with it for almost a year."

He paused again, but this time his aggravation showed through.

"Anyway, Leyes ended up blinding a girl in one eye. Got drunk one night and made a mistake." Filio didn't look at me anytime during this exchange, and I was glad for that. I didn't know how to compose my face in reaction to this revelation, let alone think of how to respond. Filio sighed again.

"The girl lived, but Leyes' father couldn't stand it. He'd always dealt with Seyel, but Seyel never actually hurt someone. He told him to leave. Leyes…the whole thing changed him. Did a total turn around. He decided to try to do something with a purpose and chose to go to the palace to help with the resistance. He's been there ever since. Until you showed up at least."

Silence again. I guess he didn't feel like saying any more.

"I…I didn't know," I finally said. Filio rolled his eyes at this.

"As if that's news." He stopped, and then a half-grin flashed across his face. "For a Star, you're not very bright." He continued walking before I managed to reply.

"That was just bad," I said finally. "That's something I would say."

Filio's face blanked at this.

"Great, it's wearing off on me."

#

When we reached Wood's house, Filio told me to wait outside while he verified this was the correct Wood, as in Wood, the southern leader of the movement instead of Wood, random person with twenty cats or something. One of the dangers of more common Elements, I guess.

"Don't go anywhere. Don't touch anything. Don't act suspicious," he told me before turning to enter the dwelling.

"Your confidence astounds me," I said. The only acknowledgement I got was a 'whatever' wave in my direction.

So I sat down in front of the building, watched life go by, pondered. Dozens of people passed–not as many as the main square, but a good amount nonetheless. Each one wore some sort of accessory– mask, glasses, hoods, wigs. As time moved by, they began to seem like puppets, like shadows of real people, but not real themselves. This delicious feeling of anonymity stole over me as I looked at people and they looked at me. I didn't know who they were; they didn't know me, and we didn't care! Any of those people could be guards, Oramus supporters, or even Oramus himself. At the same time, any of those could be Pasin-supporters. If I wanted them to be, then they were. In my mind at least. We could enjoy the surroundings regardless of who our fellow revelers were–lords, ladies, townsmen, women, priests, fugitives. It just didn't matter.

A smile found its way across my lips despite my past, despite the conflict with Filio, despite the metal chain around my neck. For the first time in a long time, my heart rested softly in my chest, felt light in the midst of the thousand lanterns equally lighting the sky.

Soon enough, Filio exited the building.

"We have it!" he said, the lanterns casting conflicting shadows on his face. He lowered his voice, but continued, "Ignatio Light. Daven. It sounds like we can make our headquarters there." He looked almost giddy. Wow.

"Wood would like to meet you," he continued,

"but only for a minute. We need to go back to the others."

We went inside for a quick exchange with a tall woman, maybe thirty years old, with curly black hair and a scar cutting across her neck. She wished us the best of luck, pushed some food into Filio's hands, and sent us on our way.

Filio lead again, through the strange crowd of who-knows-whos and I-don't-cares. When we drew nearer to the river, however, the people absolutely swarmed. I noticed the lights dimming. What happened to the lanterns?

"Let's try another bridge," Filio said. But before we could maneuver around the masses, a woman with a bundle in her hands accosted us.

"Where are you going?" she nearly yelled over the jostling crowd. "The river's this way."

"We're trying to go home, actually—" Filio began, but the woman interrupted him.

"Where are your boats?" she asked. Before a word crossed our lips, she grabbed two of the objects dangling in her hands and pushed them into ours, almost making Filio drop the bread rolls.

"Come on, I'll show you," she said, handing the bundle to someone else and grabbing my hand. "You go down there, and I'll take her." She shooed Filio away, but before he turned away, he mouthed, *Same place*, and I nodded.

"What is this?" I yell-asked the lady who genially, politely, but still forcibly dragged me toward the river.

"This is the Endwish Ceremony," she replied. She slowed down and turned to me. "Is this your first time?"

I nodded.

"All right," she continued, "I'll explain. But first, what's your Element?"

"Smoke," I answered. Her eyes lit up.

"Interesting," she said, and not facetiously either. "And lucky too. I'm a Grass, so I had to buy this packet from a stall." She pulled out a small bag of dirt and seeds.

"The Endwish Ceremony isn't as formal as it sounds," Grass said, moving us closer to the riverbank. If anything the crowd thickened, and we moved much slower. "The festival celebrates the past year and the year ahead. People use the lanterns from the festival to hold their wishes in. You put some form of your Element in, make a wish, and send it down the river."

We finally made it to the edge of the river. The person ahead of me stepped aside, and I stepped forward. Grass opened her packet of dirt and seeds and poured it into her lantern boat thing. Focus knitted her brow, and then from beneath her fingers, tendrils grew until the entire bottom of the boat was green. She closed her eyes and smiled, then softly placed the vessel on the slow-moving water. It joined a hundred others dotting the river; I saw the products of Vines, Fires, Lights, and even an Ice or two.

I turned to my own creation. First things first, I set the rim of the basket on fire, letting it dance pleasantly while I considered how to add the Air part of it all. I focused on my hands, created a small ball of whirling air, and placed it in the middle of the fiery ring. The spinning air disrupted the fire but didn't blow it out. Instead, the fire was pulled in and stretched with the wind. As I pushed the little vessel out to sea, I remembered the wish part of Endwish. I whispered it under my breath and looked up across the boats on the water to where people mimicked the ceremony on the other side. I don't know why I raised my head, but I did, and on the far side of the divide a familiar warmth stood out.

Leyes kneeled on the edge of the water and set his own boat adrift. He kept his head down a moment more before lifting it. His entire countenance spoke of solemnity before his own eyes rose up. I lifted my hand, caught his attention with the motion. His eyes met mine and he smiled, the fire from the various floats reflecting in his far-off eyes. I smiled back and felt a stronger warmth in my cheeks than normal.

He stood up, pushed the hair out his eyes, and waved back. I moved first, gave one last smile, and turned to leave. I thanked the helpful Grass and swam through the crowds, feeling lighter than ever despite the growing darkness.

#

We got back together again and left the town. Erise came back with the same name, Ignatio Light. Filio consulted the map and plotted our course for the morrow. We all broke into our nighttime activities–Leyes checked our supplies, Filio played with his glob of water, but Erise asked me a question.

"Did you do the Endwish ceremony?"

"Yeah, did you?"

"No, not this time, but I've done it before. I got this instead."

Erise held out what appeared to be a whip of sorts, but completely made of metal.

"So," she led with her words, "what did you wish

for?"

My turn to pause. I thought back to the moment, but...

"I don't remember," I replied. Erise tutted but smiled simultaneously.

"Well that just means it's going to come true," she said. "Or it's already happened."

I thought back again, but all I remembered were the lights. Light, lights everywhere.

"Great," I said, smiling too. "That's something at least."

CHAPTER TWENTY-EIGHT

After four days of travelling, the trees cleared, and we were confronted by the most enormous sky I had ever seen. The expanse of grayish blue stretched far ahead of us, past where the land ended, all the way to a blurry line. The ground far beyond us rippled, trembled. I squinted, unsure of what I saw.

Filio stopped in his tracks.

"How," he began, lips barely moving with his set jaw, "how did we reach the ocean?"

I looked out again. The ocean…so that must mean that line was the horizon, that fabled boundary I had never seen before because of the trees and mountains. An enormous smile stretched across my face.

But in front of the horizon swarmed the gray mass of water, the stuff of nightmares and ghost stories. No one, no one ever sailed across it and returned. As far as I knew, only a handful of people had tried.

Out of the corner of my eyes, I saw Filio grab the map from his bag and trace our path with one finger. Erise pointed over his shoulder.

"There," she said, tapping a crossroad. "Wasn't there a blockade there and we went around?"

Filio glared at the map then groaned.

"Right," he said. He twitched his mouth and looked back at the map.

"Well it's straight north from here," he said. "Come on."

He put the map away and turned left.

We followed the cliffs up the coast, the ocean and sky stretching endlessly to our right. Over and over again, it drew my gaze, out to where sea and sky met and disappeared into the unknown.

#

The nightmares returned that night. I fell and flailed in the burning darkness, unable to catch myself or my breath.

I gasped as I awoke. The night air blew cool against my fevered skin as I sat up. Slowly, eventually, my heart rate slowed, and my breathing returned to normal. I looked around. Filio and Erise were lumps under their respective blankets. Great. I fell asleep on my watch.

I relit the fire and watched it dance in the darkness. Filio snored in his sleep and Erise rustled around. I frowned and looked once more. Filio, Erise, but no Leyes—his area was flat. No Leyes sleeping there.

I felt around for his warmth. His familiar outline appeared about fifty feet from the camp, near the edge between ground and air. The cliffs.

I left the campsite and crept toward where Leyes stood on the edge. He didn't move, but stood, head raised to the sky. I watched him from behind a tree. I began to feel creepy, standing there and watching him, but then he moved.

Leyes took a deep breath, in out, up down. He turned his head parallel to the horizon and paused. Then he jumped.

I almost sprang out from my hiding place to grab him, but before I could react, Leyes caught himself in the air and soared above the edge of the cliff, far out from the actual ground. I heard him laugh unrestrained and unashamed, felt the smile spread across his face. His eyes stayed closed while he spun and looped through the air, but we both knew he wouldn't hit anything.

I crept back to the campsite and left him to his moment. Everyone deserves a moment.

CHAPTER TWENTY-NINE

It took another two days to reach Daven. Filio made me wait outside the city in the deepening twilight as he, Leyes, and Erise went ahead to ascertain that Ignatio Light was, in fact, on our side. I wrote in my notebook for almost an hour before Leyes descended from the sky with news.

"He's good," Leyes said, landing neatly on his feet before walking over to me. "And it turns out he's the governor of Daven."

"Wow." Impressive. He was the first government official we had encountered other than Filio's father who was actually for us.

We made the short flight over to the main gate, and in the air, I noted the setup of the town. Like Morrit, a wall surrounded the city. However, the governor's house (or really fortress—it was that big) stood at the front of the city, right behind the gate instead of sequestered in the middle or back of the city. After a moment of introduction, we passed the guards and entered the manor.

Erise and Filio sat at a rough, wooden dining table with two strangers, a brown-haired, bearded man in his middle ages and a woman with long auburn hair and a sour look on her face. Around them, rich woods made up the floors, walls, and furniture. A roaring fire lit up the room from the fireplace on the left wall and illuminated several faded tapestries covering the walls. Upon our entrance, the man stood up.

"You must be Star," he began, walking over to us. "My name is Ignatio Light. It is an honor to meet you. Welcome to Daven." He extended his hand and I shook it, noting the strength behind his handshake.

"Thank you," I said. "Yes, I am Pasin Star." It still felt odd to say that.

"This is my wife, Roxanne Fire." He gestured toward the woman at the table.

"Fire," she said. She nodded at me, but her expression remained the same.

"Come, sit down." Light motioned toward the table again, and I sat next to Erise, Leyes on my other side. Light sat next to his wife.

"As I was telling Water and Spark," Light said, "I am the northern leader of the resistance." He looked at Filio and nodded. "It's good to finally meet my western counterpart." Filio's nodded back.

"Likewise," he said. "Though technically, that is my father."

"Even so," Light said. Filio's mouth tilted into a smile. I glanced between them.

"So you two have never met?" I asked.

"No," Light said. "And we never communicated."

"It was for security," Filio added. "Because of Spark," he said, tilting his head towards Erise, "we knew about Corinth's mind-reading abilities, and if one of us got caught, this would lower the possibility of exposing the entire organization. That's why we had to go to Morrit and Lainsford—to know who to find in the east."

"So today marks a momentous occasion," Light said, opening his arms to gesture to us all. "This meeting marks the beginning of the end. Our goal is in sight."

I glanced at his wife. Fire didn't look at anyone at the table; instead, she stared at the candle on the table, arms crossed and jaw set.

"How prepared do you feel your people are?" Filio asked.

"Very well prepared," Light replied, his bright eyes glinting. "We have the largest training ground outside of the palace."

"Oh right!" Erise cut in. "I heard some…several," she amended, "of the soldiers I trained talking about another training field, but they wouldn't talk about it in front of me."

"Well, of course not," Filio said. "If I remember right, relations between Daven and Falleon City have been strained." He looked at Light. "Is that true?"

"Yes," Light answered. "That's probably why they wouldn't talk of Daven in front of you, Spark."

Right. Erise was regarded as a higher-up in Oramus' military system, wasn't she? I looked at the girl on my left. She seemed so strong, so sure of herself, so…grown-up, though a year younger than me. Filio too, though at least we were the same age. But still. How did this happen to people? How did they become like this?

"So," Leyes said, "why do Daven and Falleon City

have such a strained relationship?"

"Ah yes," Light smiled and scratched his beard. "It's more that Oramus has a problem with us." He looked at Fire, who snorted. Light looked back at us.

"Oramus grew up here," he said.

Eyes widened around the table.

"What?" Erise asked.

"Really?" Filio continued.

"Yes, he and his family lived here before he became king," Light said. "A pretty nondescript family, really."

"What do you remember of them?" Filio asked.

"Not as much as I would like," Light said. "They didn't stand out much. I was…thirty-five, I believe, when Oramus' Void powers emerged. That was big news, the first Void in Daven, but his father didn't want that. If I remember right, he was a blacksmith, a Silver, yes."

"Are they still here?" Erise asked. Light shook his head.

"Oramus told me his father died after he became king," I said. Everyone looked at me, and I stifled the urge to squirm. "At least, he said that. I mean—"

"No, you're right," Light said. "We don't know about his mother, but his father is dead, yes. Oramus killed him."

My eyes widened again. Oramus hadn't mentioned that.

"When Oramus first became king," Light said, "representatives from each city went to the palace. I couldn't go because Fire was about to give birth, so I sent a Gust in my stead."

Across the table, Fire's jaw tightened.

"When she came back, Gust said she'd been sitting

with Oramus when Corinth came in with a gray-haired man in fine but worn-out clothes, not what you would expect from a city's representative.

"The man limped forward, leaning on a sword, and started babbling about how great it was, how proud he was, how they would regain what they had."

Light paused and clasped his hands in front of him.

"Now, Gust had no idea who this was. She said Oramus took the man to a back room, but when he came back, he was alone. Gust only told me this because Oramus sent her away right after, without even discussing tax expectations."

"So how did you know it was his father?" Filio asked.

"Silver always had a sword with him," Light said. "When he injured his leg, he used it as a cane.

"But what Gust reported the man saying was just as important. Oramus' family used to be well off, but Oramus' grandfather squandered most of their money. I don't think Silver ever got over that. I think he saw Oramus as his way back to fortune.

"Silver never returned to Daven," Light continued. "The smithy burned down a few months later."

We sat in silence for a few moments. The flame of the candle on the table danced in the air, perturbed only by our breathing. When I really thought about it, Oramus' actions didn't surprise me.

"It's getting late," Fire said, standing up. Light nodded.

"Right. I can show you to your rooms."

As Filio, Erise, Leyes, and I stood, Fire left the room at a clipped pace.

Light led us through the hallways, pausing to stop

at the room for Leyes and Filio, then led me and Erise on.

As I looked around, I saw none of the trappings of a child-rearing household, with which I was well acquainted, having lived in one my entire life until recently.

"Where's your child?" I asked.

Light kept walking.

"He didn't make it," he said. Before I could answer, he gestured to a door.

"Here's your room," he said to Erise and me. "Sleep well." He nodded and headed back up the corridor without another word.

#

Erise and I prepared for bed, but right before actually climbing into it, I realized something important.

"I need to use the lavatory," I said. I glanced at Erise. "They're downstairs, right?"

"I think so," she replied, laying her travelling clothes next to her sword. "Go down together?"

"Sure," I said, and we left the room. I could feel Leyes and Filio in the room next to us as well as a couple servants in the halls finishing their tasks for the night. Farther down at the other end of the hall glowed the warmths of Light and Fire, the latter's significantly more pronounced than the former's.

"Oh!" Erise stopped short and twisted her mouth into a grimace. "Hold on, let me go back. I forgot my sword." She started jogging back in the direction of the room. I looked after her, nonplussed.

"But we're in a fortress!" I called out.

"Hey," she said, stopping to turn and give me a serious look. "You can never be too sure." She turned again and continued as I realized the urgency of my situation.

"I'm going ahead," I said to her and carried on down the hall with haste in my step.

As I walked farther down the corridor, I heard the voices of Light and Fire. It started as a buzzing sound and escalated, louder and louder as I walked forward, desperate to reach the stairs by their door as quickly as possible. Of course the only staircase I knew of had to be in the least suitable position at the moment. I was almost there when the voices became distinct.

"—not our battle!" Fire's exclaimed, her voice carrying through the hallway. "Why can't you leave it and—" The door to their quarters opened just as I tried to slip by it. Fire's eyes widened and she scowled, almost snarling at me with a curved upper lip. I opened my mouth in preparation of apologies, but she let out a snort of air, turned on her heel, and strode down the hall I had just traversed, leaving the distinct scent of smoke in her wake.

I looked and sensed around, but Light was in the depths of his chambers and no one else was around to have witnessed the moment. I shook my head and continued on my mission. A minute later, I sensed Erise's arrival as well, so I waited until she was done in order to walk back together.

"What did you do to tick off Fire like that?" she asked, eyebrows raised.

"I didn't do anything!" I protested as we walked to the stairs. "I was just walking by." I sought Fire's pinpoint of heat. Well, it was more like a boiling outline of a human, but yes, I found her. She stood in

Filio and Leyes' room. Hmm.

"In any case, something has her bothered…" Erise's voice trailed off as I motioned for her to be quiet when we reached the top of the stairs. I felt Fire nod and exit the males' room. She looked up and down the hall, and we stopped walking when she spotted us.

"Star," she began as she walked toward us, "You need to be at the training ground tomorrow at seven, understand?"

"Yes—yes, ma'am," I answered. She nodded.

"Good. Good night Star, Spark," she added, giving Erise a nod as well. Before either of us could answer, she swept away back to her quarters.

We stood there for a moment as the sound of her footsteps became muffled. I gave Erise a look and went to Leyes and Filio's door. I knocked three brisk strikes on their door.

"Who is it?" Filio asked from beyond the door.

"It's us," I said quietly. I heard grumbling from the other side and in a moment Filio opened the door, looking annoyed. Big surprise.

"'It's us' is not even close to an acceptable response; you know that, right?"

He shifted his weight on to his right and crossed his arms, his eyebrows furrowed. "You could have said 'tomato' or 'pig slop' and it would have revealed just as much."

"The point," I replied, "was that you would recognize me by my voice." Beyond Filio, I could see the back of Leyes as he pulled off his outer shirt.

"And what if someone was making you talk to gain entrance, hmm? What then?" Filio asked. Leyes chuckled from behind him.

"Can we talk about this later?" Erise asked as Filio and I glared at each other. She nudged me out of the way and talked to Filio. "What did Fire want?"

Filio relaxed his stature and looked at Erise.

"She asked about Pasin's training," he replied. This news made me pause.

"What did you say?" I asked.

"That Leyes is helping with Air training and Erise is doing more general battle tactics. That's it."

"Did she say why she wanted to know this?"

"No," Filio said. "She didn't." We stood there in silence for a moment. Erise shrugged.

"I'm sure you'll find out tomorrow," she said, looking at me. "Speaking of which, you need to go to bed if you're waking up that early." I groaned.

"Yeah, you're right." I turned back to the doorway. "Good night, Leyes!" I called over Filio's shoulder. Leyes looked at me and smiled.

"Good night," he replied. I looked at the male standing in between us.

"Good night, Filio," I said much less enthusiastically.

"Night," he murmured, mirroring my level of excitement.

"I'll be there in a minute," Erise said. I nodded and went back to our room.

I lay on top of the majority of the blankets with only one thin bedspread covering my middle and legs. Tilting my head to the left, I could just see the edge of the moon through the window. The moon was waning if I remembered correctly–shrinking into a curve of what it once was. I smiled back and buried my head in my pillow, feigning sleep when Erise entered. True sleep followed soon after.

#

I woke the next morning before the sun came out. I groaned internally at the earliness of it all but managed to drag myself downstairs for some breakfast before going outside to the training ground. Erise came too, far too cheery for such an early start.

The training ground was really just a very large field. Most of it was open space, but a couple of structures stood around the area–ledges and towers and quite a few sparring dummies. Only a couple of people populated the space; in the foreground stood two of them, a man and a woman both decked out in leather armor. They were the only ones not actively training, so we made our way toward them.

"Are you Star?" the male asked as we approached. He had tan skin and cropped black hair with eyebrows that didn't quite have the bushiness one would expect coupled with the texture of the hair on his head. He appeared to be in his twenties or so.

"Yes," I said. The man extended his hand and I shook it, feeling the roughness of work on his skin.

"I'm Blaze," he continued, letting go of the handshake.

"As am I," the woman on his left added, shaking my hand as well. She had a narrow face with arching eyebrows that did seem to go well with her light brown hair pulled up into a short ponytail. She seemed roughly the same age as the male Blaze. The female Blaze looked at Erise.

"And you?" she inquired, putting out her hand again.

"I'm Spark," Erise replied genially, shaking both of

the Blazes' hands in turn. "I've been training Star in general defense and maneuvering. Feel free not to go easy on her." She flashed a grin in my direction. The Blazes chuckled, and Erise shifted on her feet and bumped me with her hip.

"Good luck," she said and took off toward a group of sparring soldiers.

"Well," the male Blaze started, clapping his hands together. "Let's get started then." He looked at the female Blaze and she nodded.

"How much practice have you had using your fire abilities?" the woman asked.

"Not much," I replied, "Nothing formal."

The woman nodded.

"A clean slate then, good." She looked at Blaze who nodded in agreement.

"Yeah, better than that Fire from Gimmerton," he answered. They both shuddered, and I couldn't help but smile.

"So before we get started on the practical side of fire handling," the male Blaze continued, "we need to go over the concept of it."

He stepped back about ten feet and turned so he was in profile, the morning sun casting shadows across his face.

"Fire handling is all about control," he began, "much, much more so than other elements." He extended his right hand and took a deep breath. "The creation is the easy part–once you get it, you've got it." He breathed out, and a tiny tongue of flame appeared in his hand. He turned his head to look at me.

"Have you learned how to generate a flame?" he asked.

"I've made fire before," I answered, "but I've never tried just holding it like that. It's always been directed at something." The male Blaze let the flame go out and looked at the female Blaze. She raised her eyebrows and looked at me.

"Was this during times of high emotion?" she asked.

"Yes," I replied without hesitation.

"That's going to be your problem," she said, tucking a stray lock of hair behind her ear. "While you certainly can manipulate fire with the power of emotion, you won't have the control—" She tilted her head toward the other Blaze. "—in order to use it properly. Raw strength can be a formidable force, but it's more likely to do more damage than good."

"Yes," the male Blaze said. "It takes longer than you'd think to regrow eyebrows."

The female Blaze chuckled. He smirked at her and continued, "Remember—being a fire handler does not make you fireproof." Female Blaze hummed in agreement then spoke again.

"Put out your hand," she said, and I did. "Now focus on your palm. Let the feeling of heat center there."

I did as she said, and in a couple of seconds a small tongue of flame manifested itself.

"Good," she urged. "Now keep it that size."

The smile that appeared on my face at the emergence of the flame melted into dismay as, despite my effort, the fire grew larger and larger in my hand. My heart raced and the fire grew larger, faster.

"Rain!" the male Blaze yelled. A nearby boy with a bucket raced toward us and motioned the water over the fireball in my hand, easily dousing it.

"You let yourself panic," the male Blaze said. "It feeds on that sort of emotion, and if it gets hold of a fuel source outside of you, then you can't stop it. With enough self-control you can lower the flames substantially, but even then you can't make the heat energy disappear completely."

"Well, some people can't," the female Blaze said. The male Blaze sighed.

"I have no idea how you can do that," he said, shaking his head and then looking at me again. "Either way, let's assume you can't for now to avoid any complications."

"Not a bad first effort though," the female Blaze added. I smiled at the encouragement and initially, she smiled back. After a moment, she raised her eyebrows and motioned to my hand. "Again."

It took at least eight tries before I could hold a steady flame in my hand for more than a couple of seconds. Two or three times I lost my nerve and threw the ball of flame away from me. I felt bad for the Rain boy who had to keep running back and forth to extinguish my mistakes.

We worked on this technique for the rest of the morning. Erise spent the morning there as well, sparring with some of Light's fighters on the other side of the training area. Filio and Leyes appeared for a while too, but no one bothered our group. After two hours, the sweat was positively pouring off me, partly from the fires and partly from the leather armor they had me wear. It was in this sweaty, disheveled state that Light's wife found me.

I was focusing on my palm for the fiftieth time that morning, making the ball grow and shrink at my prompting, when I heard her voice behind me.

"How is she doing?"

The sudden close voice startled me, and I dropped the fire before either Blaze could answer. Rain rushed over and, with almost an air of weariness about him, doused the fire.

"Better than that," the female Blaze answered with humor. "No," she continued more seriously, "she's been progressing well enough for just one morning."

"Hmm." Fire didn't sound amused. "Go again," she told me, her dark brown eyes peering somberly from behind her bangs.

I did, and though it wasn't my best attempt, I managed to maintain a steady ball of flame and extinguish it without Rain's assistance.

"Fair," she said when I was finished. "I expect better tomorrow though." She looked at the Blazes as she said this.

"Yes, ma'am," they replied quickly.

"Have you worked on combat techniques yet?"

"No, ma'am."

"Well get on it," she said, then turned and departed.

As she left, the male Blaze took a deep breath, almost a sigh, then launched into a speech about sparring tactics. After trying out some of the techniques on a dummy, we broke for lunch. Afterwards he had the female Blaze and I face off.

"Focus on the Fire techniques," he said. "Don't use any Air or Star stuff—I can't critique you on that. Now go!"

Roughly three seconds later, I was flat on my back and Blaze had a fireball next to my neck.

"Hmm." Male Blaze scrunched his mouth around as female Blaze extinguished the fire and helped me up. "Try again," he instructed.

We did, and this time it took seven seconds for Blaze to overwhelm me.

"You're…you're not…" the male Blaze started and stopped, conflict on his face. "You're not being offensive enough," he finally settled on. "You're staying on the defense instead of going for it."

"I don't want to hurt her," I grumbled. This statement seemed laughable, considering how quickly and thoroughly she had beaten me.

"I'll be fine," she said. "Even if you shoot at me by mistake, I can redirect it."

"But—" All I could think of was the burning tapestry room back at the palace.

"Just try," she said.

For the next half hour, I did try, but after several near misses (I must have singed part of her hair with the second), I semi-consciously pulled back. Either way, she beat me every time.

"That's enough for the day," male Blaze said when the sun had passed the sky's midpoint. "Meet us here tomorrow and we'll practice some more."

I nodded at his dismissal, removed the leather armor, and shuffled over to the other side of the field where Erise was busy thrashing an Earth type.

"Ya!" She ducked under his barrage of dirt clods and cut up with her metallic whip. He jerked and fell backward; as he fell, Erise whipped out her sword and moved its tip to the man's throat. She held it there for just a few seconds before pulling it away, a satisfied smile touching her lips.

"Good match," she said as she helped him up. He mumbled something in return and quickly took his leave.

"How did you get so good?" I asked as I walked up to her.

"Practice," she said simply. She sheathed her sword and looked at me.

"You like my new toy?" Erise asked, moving the whip so I could better see it. The whip seemed to be entirely metal, like her sword, yet lithe and supple. She nonchalantly coiled it.

"Want to try it out?" she asked with an eyebrow waggle. "Go for a round?"

"Not really," I replied, eyeing the new object.

"How did your lesson go?" she asked. I sighed, twitched my mouth.

"Not well," I replied. "Actually...no it went pretty badly. I don't know how many times Blaze pinned me." Erise grimaced sympathetically.

"Yeah, I saw that." We began the walk back to the manor. "Did you get her at least once, or..." Her voice trailed off and faded as I twitched my head back and forth, like a horse being bothered by a gnat.

"It's not going to come automatically," she said after a moment.

"I get that, but I thought I'd be better than this. Didn't you say Stars are supposed to be super powerful?"

"Yes, but power doesn't equal skill."

I grunted at her words.

"So I've heard."

We entered the manor and made our way into the main common room. Filio, surrounded by piles of paper, sat at the table while Leyes read a book by the fireplace. Filio looked up when we came in.

"Light's going to be gone for a few days," he said. Erise and I looked at each other.

"Where did he go?" Erise asked.

"He's visiting the leader in Mint Leaf Bay, getting the eastern group organized." Filio took a breath and let it out with his eyes closed. "We're staying here for a while," he added. "This might be the last place before the confrontation."

Silence followed his statement. I didn't want to think about what he was saying, so I was happy when Erise spoke.

"So what do we do until then?" she asked, taking a seat on the other side of the table. Filio pushed some of the papers around and took out a clean sheet.

"I was thinking we should try to connect with the elves." He grabbed a pen and looked at Erise expectantly. She snorted and raised her eyebrows.

"How do you plan on doing that?" she asked. Filio arched one eyebrow in response.

"I thought you would lead that expedition," he replied. "If you think they would be hostile, then—"

"It's not that," Erise interjected. "You won't find them. And if you did, you have to signal them with some sort of ceremony to get in. If you don't, they'll either ignore you or shoot you."

"Didn't you live there?" I asked. "Don't you know this ceremony?"

"I was a kid!" she exclaimed. "And I never entered by myself. The only time I went, my mother did whatever it is. I haven't been there since." She crossed her arms across her chest. Filio looked at Erise through squinted eyes.

"Are you sure?" he asked, flicking his pen against the table.

"Yes, I'm sure," she answered, voice acidic. "Why can't you just believe what I say? You're always questioning, shining." She snorted again and picked up one of the books on his table. Something in her tone made even Leyes glance up for a moment before returning his focus to his book.

"I wasn't questioning you," Filio replied. "I just wanted to make sure."

"Either way, you aren't going to find them," Erise said. "You don't think I haven't tried?"

At the sound of the edge to Erise's voice, I sidled away from their discussion. I walked over to Leyes and asked, "So, what are you reading?"

"A report comparing and contrasting different Air types," he answered. I grimaced.

"That sounds terribly boring."

"That's because it is," he said with a slight smile, "but Filio needed someone to see which jobs suit Airs compared to Gusts compared to Smokes, what have you, so I volunteered."

"I could have done it," I said, placing myself in the chair across the side table from his.

"You have more important things to do," he said. I looked at him, nonplussed, and he continued. "Fire handling?"

"Right." That mess.

"I'm not really a fighter anyway, so my time is better spent doing something useful." He looked down and gave a low chuckle. "No matter how slowly."

"Still." I picked up one of the books on the side table. "I'm not practicing now. Is there something I can help you with?"

Leyes lifted his eyes and tapped his bottom lip with his pen.

"Sure," he said finally. "Find and write down the

qualities unique to Smokes. If you want, add how they differ from purely Air or Fire types." He offered me a pen and a sheet of paper.

"All right." I accepted his gift and got to work.

After a while, Erise and Filio left, both saying how the library would clearly reveal the other to be mistaken, leaving Leyes and me by the fireplace with our respective tomes and papers. After twenty minutes, which felt like an hour, I spoke.

"This doesn't make sense," I said, putting down the pen and looking at Leyes.

"What?"

"One of the articles about Smokes referenced another one comparing Fires and Blazes," I replied, searching the page for the right section, "and...yes, here: 'The primary differentiation between Fires and Blazes lies in their relative power levels. However, each has abilities unique to their form of the general fire type.'" I skimmed ahead and shook my head. "And then it goes into how Fires can extinguish their flames while Blazes can't. The female Blaze training me has no problem putting out her fires."

"Maybe she was miscategorized," Leyes answered. "It's kind of the same with Airs and Gusts. I think it comes down to power level, like the book says."

"But she's just as powerful as the male Blaze," I protested. "I mean, at least from what I can tell. And he can't put down his flame at all."

Leyes tapped his pen against his bottom lip again.

"I don't know," he finally said. "You should talk to Erise about that. Or Filio. He's a lot more interested in that kind of stuff."

"Hmm." The thought of voluntarily starting a conversation with Filio didn't thrill me.

We both returned to our work, but after only a couple of minutes, Leyes let out a sigh and dropped his pen on the side table.

"What is it?" I asked.

Leyes breathed in, out and twisted his mouth into a smile.

"This isn't how I like spending my afternoon," he said. He looked at the papers and rolled his eyes. I laughed.

"Well, how do you like to spend your afternoons then?" I asked.

Leyes took one last glance at the papers and then looked away.

"It's not necessarily an afternoon activity," he said, "but I like creating things."

"What do you mean?"

Leyes twisted his head the other way, and a sheepish smile lurked on his lips.

"I like making metal figurines," he said finally. "People out of wire." Leyes reached into his pocket and drew something out, a copper model of a person sitting, one knee curled up to its chest, head bowed. The other leg merely jutted out from the base, still a work in progress.

"Oh, wow," I said, peering at the creation.

"I make stories for them, too," he added, passing the piece to me. I took the miniature and held it up to my face to better see it.

"What's this one's story?" I asked, placing it back in Leyes' palm.

"I'm not sure yet," he replied. "Sometimes I figure it out before I'm done, sometimes after. I'm waiting until I finish to decide with this one."

"Sounds good to me." I shifted in my seat, then

continued.

"I like to make stories too," I said. I looked up at Leyes' face for a moment but then looked away again.

"What kind?" he asked.

"Writing," I said, still not looking at him. "I have a book in the works."

"Is that what you do after dinner? In that notebook?"

I paused.

"Maybe."

Leyes chuckled.

"I always wondered what you were doing over there," he said.

"Same here," I said and gestured toward the wire piece. "Is that what you do?"

"Maybe."

He smiled, and I opened my mouth to reply when Filio reentered the room.

"We haven't found anything yet," he said to us, mouth set in a firm line across his face. "But there has to be something. How's the research coming?"

"Working on it," Leyes said, pointing at his notes.

"Keep at it," Filio said and walked back to the table covered in papers. He sat down and added after a moment, "Please."

Leyes and I exchanged glances and a smile played on my lips, but I lowered my head and returned to the task at hand.

CHAPTER THIRTY

Another two fruitless days of fire handling training passed, and the bruises accumulated on my arms and legs while the female Blaze's remained clear. I winced as I sat down for our post-dinner talk.

"We need to get support from the elves," Filio said, pacing once more. He still hadn't dropped the subject. "They can't be happy with Oramus' policies, what with the rumors of his interference in the forest."

"Is there someone we can ask?" Leyes threw out. "An expert outside of the elves?"

"The last Elemental to gain access to their area was Dage Snow," Erise answered from the armchair in the corner, one arm draped over her face. "But he died over thirty years ago."

"Dage Snow," I repeated slowly. "Dage...Snow." Filio shot me a glance and Erise lifted her head, but I put up one finger, head tilted in concentration.

"Dage...Sow? Sow!" Yes, that was it! "Did Dage Snow write a book about elves?"

"Probably," Erise said. "It'd be over sixty years old, though."

"Yeah, but I think…I read his book! Secrets of the Woods, or Forests, or something like that." I sat there beaming to myself about my memory. Filio strode over to me.

"Well?" he asked. "Do you remember what it said? About the ceremony?"

The light faded from my face.

"No," I replied. "I can't remember." Filio groaned, Leyes sighed, and Erise twisted her face into a frown. I replied, flustered, "That was forever ago–I was only eight!"

"How did you remember the guy's name then?" Erise asked.

"We had these really old books in Andor. I saw this book, but the 'n' had rubbed off his name, so I wondered how someone could have a pig Element."

They all looked at me with inscrutable expressions. I tried to clarify.

"Like…sow. Snow, sow."

"We got it the first time," Filio said with wide eyes.

"I just can't believe you would make that connection," Erise added.

We sat in odd silence for a moment.

"Anyway," I said, shaking the oddness off. "The book is at Andor orphanage." I stopped for a moment and verbally crept up, "I could just go and pick it up—"

"No." Filio's answer came quick and sharp. "You can't go back to Falleon City; that's stupid."

"We need the book, don't we?" Challenge bullied into my voice.

"Yes," he replied testily. "But Leyes can go; Erise

can go; I can go–we can't afford to send you—"

"But I'm the fastest!" I interrupted. "I can get there and back in a day, and I know exactly where it is."

"Why don't we see if Light has the book?" Leyes asked. "Now that we know the author?" His ridiculously sensible suggestion halted the charged exchange Filio and my eyes were having in the air.

It turns out Light did not have the book, nor did any bookstore in Daven. One bookseller told Erise that it had been out of print for half a century–any person who did own it should consider him or herself lucky. I smiled to myself as the alternatives slipped away from Filio. After another day of arguments and wheedling we finally reached a decision.

I left for Andor a little past dinner, ready to fly for five or six hours, pick up the book while the matrons and orphans slept, and spend another six hours flying back.

When I finally arrived at the orphanage, the sun had long been nothing but a memory in the western sky. No lights emitted from the dark, brick building. I flew over the gate, the cage of my past, easily.

I did a scan and felt no warmths moving within the building. I tried the doors and windows one by one, but it wasn't until I flew up to the third floor that I found an unlocked window. The room held no occupants, for which I was thankful; I had no desire to see a boy in his underwear.

I crept down the stone stairs staying light on my feet. No noise interrupted the quiet of the building except for the occasional snore. Familiarity oozed from the place despite the darkness. I went to the bookcase. Using my newly honed ability, I held a small ball of flame in my hands and scanned the titles, but instead of the familiar, worn bindings of my youth, I spied new books with which I was unfamiliar. I went through the bookcase three times, but I didn't recognize a single title.

In my bewildered state of mind, I didn't sense the warmth moving down the stairs until it was too late. The door creaked open. My fire extinguished, and I shoved myself into a dark corner. A girl stumbled sleepily into the room and headed toward the kitchen. I heard the rummaging noise of earthenware cups as I tried to identify the person's identity.

As she exited the kitchen, a thought flashed through my mind, and I swooped down upon her, placing my hand over her mouth.

"Arina," I whispered. "This is Pasin." Even as I spoke, I could hear Filio's voice roaring at me for taking this risk. "I need your help. If I let you go, do you promise not to scream?" Arina nodded from under my hand, and I let go.

"Pasin." She took a step back, and in the moonlight creeping through the window, I saw her eyes widen. "Is it true?" she asked. "Are you really the Star everyone's talking about?"

I nodded, but I didn't think she saw it.

"Yes."

"So you do have an Element?"

I nodded again, but then I shook my head.

"Wait," I said, "this is stupid."

I focused for a moment and conjured a small lick of flame in my palm. The fire's reflection danced in Arina's eyes

"Yes," I replied, feeling the corners of my mouth tilt up. "That's right."

"So you were engaged to King Oramus? You ran away from the palace?"

My smile faded, and I put out the fire.

"Yes."

"That's amazing!" she said, voice rising in the darkness. "When you didn't come back, a bunch of people thought you were dead or something." Oh. "But with the posters and stories—"

"So you've seen them?" I asked.

"Yes," she said. "I think soldiers keep taking them down, but they keep getting put up often enough that I'm sure everyone's seen them."

"What do people think?"

Arina shifted where she stood.

"I think a lot of people don't know what to think," she said. "We can't really talk about it at school, but I've heard the matrons whisper about it, saying stuff about some of the other kids here who've been taken to the palace. Matron Water thinks you're lying, though."

She paused, then continued.

"For the record, I didn't think you were lying." My smile returned.

"Thanks."

A comfortable silence hung in the air for a moment before I turned back to the bookshelf.

"Do you know where the old books went?" I asked. "I'm looking for the one about elves."

"The books?" Arina shook her head. "Some people gave us these new ones and took the others away."

"Do you know where they took them?"

"No."

My heart fell. My hand darted to my hair, playing

with it in the way that drove Erise insane.

"Why do you need it?" Arina asked.

"It's for this thing we need…a ceremony…" What was with that word anyway? Ceremony. It made me think of all the ridiculous goings-on at the palace…I pulled in a sharp intake of breath.

"That's it!"

"What?" Arina asked.

"I know where to find another copy of the book!" Excitement bubbled in my chest, and I resisted the urge to do a little dance.

"Where?"

"At the palace! In the library." I had passed that shelf every time I went to tutoring with Water.

"So you're going to break into the palace?" The excitement in Arina's words brought me back to reality.

"I…don't know." Filio's voice resounded in my ears. *Stupid–stupid–stupid.*

"Well…do you really need this book?" she asked.

"Yes," I said. We had agreed on that in Daven, hadn't we?

"Really?" she repeated. A surge of heat rose in my chest.

"Yes!"

"Well then you need to get it," she said. She made it seem so cut and dry. But we did need it…

"But how am I going to get in?"

Arina said nothing. My hand went back to my hair.

"I could try to contact Water," I said, talking mostly to myself, "and have him send it. No, but that's dangerous, anyone could read that—" I twiddled with my hair even faster, and I felt it heat beneath my fingers.

"Maybe I could get in through the servants' entrance," I mused, still pacing. Arina shifted where she stood. I'm sure she was tired; I could feel exhaustion itching at my eyes. "But how could I disguise myself?"

"What are you doing with your hair?" Obviously Arina's eyes had adjusted to the renewed darkness.

"I do this when I'm nervous," I said. I looked at the lock of hair. "See, it's straightening now." Arina raised her eyebrows.

"What if you straighten all your hair?"

I stopped twiddling and managed not to smack myself in the forehead.

"That…is a good idea," I said finally. I shook my head. "That means I'll have to go in the morning though." Arina shifted again.

"I don't have a roommate right now," she said. "You can sleep in there."

I spent that night in my old room on the same worn bed sheets I had months before. I woke at the edge of dawn and spent an hour and a half heat-straightening my hair. Not fun. Some of my old clothes were still in the dresser, so I changed into the cleanest outfit I could find. I placed my travelling clothes in my old school bag.

I looked in the mirror. So much happens between mirror visits after all. I barely recognized myself with straight hair, but that was the point, looking different. And really, who's going to be looking for a fugitive in the place she fled from? At the last moment, I moved the necklace pendant to the back of my neck. It wouldn't do to leave that hanging out.

I left before the rest of the orphanage woke. Arina bade me goodbye and I thanked her for her help. I stood in the window and waved before leaping from the sill and flying off toward the palace's silhouette in the distance.

#

It took half an hour to reach the inner city due to the fact that I couldn't fly past the city's edge. It wasn't hard at all to find the palace, the dominant feature of the skyline. It took a while to find the servants' entrance, but all I had to do was follow the similarly dressed people. Cooks, stable boys, and minor servants followed a narrow path leading to a small door on the side of the palace wall.

Each person looked like they had a purpose. I replicated this purpose with a good helping of humility. I kept my head down, and the guard didn't even give me a second glance.

From the wall I followed other servants to the kitchens and eventually to the hall of perpetual forest. It hit me.

Oh shining. I was in the palace.

CHAPTER THIRTY-ONE

The halls whispered remnants of memories as I walked through, head down and feet measuring a clipped pace. I wove my way through the forest hallway, vaguely familiar faces flickering past as I tried not to get lost in the crowd, in the memories.

I climbed the stairs and walked calmly past the guards in front of the throne room door. The people thinned out, and the hallway to the library was surprisingly empty. I slowed down, donned a look of belonging and purpose, and opened one of the library doors.

Water's desk stood empty but for the stacks of haphazard papers scattered about it. My eyes saw no one and my ears heard nothing. I sensed over the floor level, but...

A noise. I didn't feel the man standing on the ladder one row over until it was too late.

"Star?" Water asked as he looked over the bookcase. "It's you, isn't it?" He chuckled. "I knew you would come back someday."

My mind raced as he descended. Fight or flight? But I had to get the book; there was no other choice. I tensed my muscles, ready.

He appeared from around the bookcase and ambled over to sit at his desk. He seemed to have no problem with his back turned to me and didn't shout or send a signal of any sort. When he turned to look at me, he appraised me with what seemed like fondness. I eyed him back warily.

"Judging by your dress," he started. "I am inclined to believe this visit is not because of any permanent return."

I shook my head, and he smiled.

"I didn't think so," he said. "So if you aren't here to stay, then why are you here?" He reached across his desk and grabbed his notebook and quill, dipping the quill into an inkpot and looking up in anticipation as well as expectation.

"I'm here to get a book," I said slowly. He nodded.

"Is this book of vital importance?" he asked. I nodded.

"And so you have sneaked back into the lion's den in order to get it, risking health and freedom…" He laughed. "How like you, Star." He chuckled again. "That is so you."

Waters annoyed me. Greatly.

I struggled for a moment with the inclination to tell him what for but then turned on my heel down another row instead. Water didn't call out or follow me, so I walked down the aisle in boiling peace.

It took me almost ten minutes to find the book. During that time, Water didn't move from his seat; he spent the entire time writing in his notebook. I grabbed the cracked leather tome from the shelf and headed for the exit.

"You're not taking that book, are you?"

I turned and saw Water looking with amusement over his spectacles at me. "You wouldn't dare actually steal something," he said.

I wanted to smack his half-cocked head so badly…

"People change, sir," I said as evenly as possible.

Water's smile lessened.

"Yes," he said. "I suppose they do."

I turned again to leave, but Water called after me.

"Wait!" he said, standing up. "I have something to show you."

Now that my annoyance had settled, the sheer riskiness of my situation reasserted itself.

"I shouldn't be here," I said. "I have to leave…"

"It will only take a minute," he replied. "No one comes through here except for the king, and he's off looking for you."

I didn't move.

Water grunted and rose. "See?" he asked, "now I've had to stand up for you. Come over here; this is important." The impatience in his voice made me believe him. I returned to his desk.

"Here," he said, pushing something into my hand. I looked down and my eyebrows rose.

"Your notebook?"

"Yes," he said with a shadow of a smile. "Now open it already. At the bookmark."

I did as he asked, and a paper fell out. As I bent to pick it up, I noticed one of its sides was jagged as if it had been torn out of a book. When I turned back to the notebook, I first saw a line of black, and underneath were written these words:

"I can't believe it. All these years, with all these

Elementals...I almost don't dare to believe it. The answers, the attitude, the stories I've heard around the castle...this young man in front of me must be the first Star in centuries..."

"You knew?" I asked, unable to keep the hurt out of my voice. Blindsided again.

"Yes," he replied with his shiny, shiny eyes alight.

"And you didn't tell me?" Comparisons formed in my mind—Oramus, Erise, Leyes. At least the last two bothered to mention it at some point.

"Well," he said, "if I had told you, then I would have been arrested, and you would have lost your heart essence months ago. No, instead I set out to teach you anything you might need once you did know: war theory, history—even Oramus' history, the untold one that isn't taught anywhere outside this room."

I kept my face blank. Water continued.

"I did what I could," he said, "without putting either of us in danger. And besides, I knew someone would tell you eventually."

I looked at the paper I picked up from the floor, unfolded it, and read:

Star

Occurrence: Most Rare

Notable Persons: Jusste Star

A Star is one of, if not the, rarest Elementals known to mankind. Stars have the immense power of Fire and Air combined and possess talents such as heat detection and the ability to fly to extraordinary heights.

Unfortunately, little is known about the Star Element. The only record of such an Elemental is from the year 200 in the story of Jusste Star. His story chronicles a young man's fight against captivity by others and Falleon itself. The end of his life is shrouded in mystery. Some say he eventually found a way to leave Falleon over the mountains. However, modern people who know the story regard it as a myth, and the rest don't even know of its existence.

According the story of Jusste Star, he never experienced any Elemental properties until the age of nineteen, when he saw a man mugging a girl. He wrote that "Rage, unequal to the Heat of the Sun / Burst from my Heart, and the Power came."

If one must really experience moments beyond the glow of celestial bodies, then it is no wonder that no other Stars have been seen throughout history. Perhaps there are others, maybe dozens of people under the guise of unprovable Elements walking the streets, who really are Stars without knowing it.

I looked up from the paper. It didn't tell me everything I wanted to know, but it was a start.

"Do you have this story?" I asked Water. "The one about Jusste Star?"

"In fact I do," he said, and pulled a thin volume out from his desk drawer. He handed it over, and I clutched it, pressing the leather binding into my fingertips as if I could soak in the words.

"Now this book is one of the few remaining copies, so take care of it."

"I will," I said. A goofy smile crept onto my face. I wanted to get out of the palace, yes, but for more than one reason now. Something nagged at me though.

"So, you thought I was a boy?"

Water chuckled.

"Yes," he said. "At first I did. Forgive me, but I had never encountered such fervor in any of the other royal ladies. I apologize for that assumption."

"It's fine," I said, and shifted the books in my hands. "I should go now." Water nodded.

"Yes, you should." He straightened, arms straight at his sides, then tilted forward from his waist in a motion I had only seen others do toward Oramus.

"May Solluna light your path," he said.

A little bubble of warmth settled in my chest and clouded my mind as I opened the library door. However, it burst when I turned the corner and promptly ran into a man I noticed too late.

We collided, and the books fell out of my hands. I mumbled apologies out of the corner of my mouth and picked up the book about elves. I reached for the Star book, but a foot pinned it to the ground.

"What are you doing here?" a familiar voice asked. My heart froze.

"I asked you a question," Corinth said, voice rising. "Answer me, servant."

"I—I'm sorry, sir." My voice trembled as I squeaked a falsetto. "I was sent to fetch a book, one of the ladies sent me…"

Corinth snorted.

"I doubt it," he said. "Stand up."

I kept my head lowered as I stood, and Corinth bent over and picked up the book.

"Jusste Star," he said. "Who would…"

Before I could move, his hand shot to my neck and lifted my chin. His eyes met mine, and they widened.

"You," he snarled, pressing into my throat. "Miserable, wretched…"

I kicked, hard as I could, right between the legs. He cried out and let go of my neck just enough for me to wrench myself away. The Star book was still in his other hand, and he rose before I could recover it.

"Guards!" he bellowed. I shot a gust of wind that hurled him against the wall. I focused heat in my hand, ready to attack again, but I saw men advancing from the doorway behind Corinth. I ran the other way.

"Guards!" Corinth shrieked from the ground. "Close the gates! Capture her!" His voice rose higher and higher.

Voices echoed around me. "Close the gates! Close the gates! It's Star!" As I ran and flew and pushed surprised people out of the way, the words surrounded me.

"Hall 22, Hall 23, Corridor 15!" Most of the warmths I felt running in the castle were coming down from the upper levels. Chances were, these were the people to avoid.

I barely got through "Corridor 7!" before I burst into the forest hallway. Very large, very muscled men appeared at each end of the hallway. Drick. And I could sense more soldiers behind this door, that door, that door...double drick.

I shoved more people out of the way and went through the only door without burly men on the other side. The morning light streamed through stained glass windows and sent rainbows tumbling across the floor. I shot to the door on the other side of the room, but it was locked, and guards started to pour through the door I had just entered.

"Surrender!" one shouted. I flew higher, crowding the ceiling, thirty feet high. The man sent a blast of fire my way that I barely managed to avoid. Another man shoved the first.

"Remember orders!" he yelled. "Shoot to disable!

Ices, on your mark!"

What was I, target practice? I shot my own fireballs back, but my efforts were weak with the book in my hands. In formation, a line of guards shot ice at me. I singed and destroyed all but one, which glanced off my shoulder and crashed through a window. An idea flashed through my mind as the glass dropped to the floor. I shot another punch of flame and the rest of the glass shattered.

"The air!" someone shouted as I squeezed through the opening. I flew over the courtyard, and a barrage of rocks, flames, and wind gusts came at me, but I just climbed higher. The walls and shouts of the palace fell behind me, and I rushed over Falleon City to the safety of the forest, book still in hand.

#

The return trip exhausted me. My hair eventually lost its straightness as effort and sweat cloaked it. Around the fourth hour of flying, I stopped for a break. My stomach rumbled like a miniscule earthquake, but I had nothing to eat. I drank from the river instead.

I sat down and enjoyed the water as well as I could on an empty stomach. I opened the book and read two pages before I heard horse hooves.

I grabbed the book and took cover in a tree. Ground to foliage, two seconds flat. However, I chanced a peek beyond the leaves. I was in the middle of the woods; who else would be here?

A flash of black and purple answered my question. Oramus on horseback, riding through the trees, grim determination twisting his face. It was only a glimpse stolen through the leaves, but it was enough for me. I had had enough surprise encounters in the last twenty-four hours to last a lifetime.

#

By the time I reached Daven, the sun was on the edge of the horizon. I touched ground a hundred feet or so before the walls and walked forward. The moment I cleared the trees, I heard a voice.

"Pasin!" Leyes' voice called from somewhere high above me. He descended quickly from one of the towers.

"Hey, Leyes."

"Are you all right?" he asked. "No wait," he amended. "Let's go inside." He nodded at the guards, and we flew over the gate together.

On the walk to the door, Leyes asked again. "Really, are you all right?"

"Yes, I'm fine. I just had a few difficulties." Just a few. "Everything's fine."

Leyes frowned a bit as if he didn't believe me but left it at that. Filio however, did not.

"Where were you?" The words pummeled me the moment I stepped into the room. "You were supposed to be back yesterday! I thought you were captured or dead, shining."

Erise on the other hand, came up to me and squeezed my arm. "Did you get the book?" she asked.

"Yes, it's right here." I handed the book to her, and her gaze darted to my shoulder.

"What's that?" Erise pointed at the cut in the cloth and the deep scratch that the Ice gave me. "Were you in a fight?" She raised her eyebrows, delight shining from her eyes. I shifted on my feet.

"Well," I said. "I need to tell you something." Filio turned back toward me and Leyes took a seat.

"What?" Filio asked, eyes flashing. I avoided his gaze and took a seat next to Leyes.

"I didn't exactly get the book from the orphanage." I sensed Filio stiffen even more, but I didn't look at him. "They didn't have it anymore."

I peered up.

"So I had to go to the other place that I knew had it…"

"No." Filio closed his eyes and shook his head, as if trying to destroy the thoughts. "You did not."

Heat rose to my cheeks.

"We agreed this was crucial! So I went to the palace library."

"Shining Solluna," Erise said, smiling broadly, impishly. "Nice."

"Shining Solluna is right!" Filio said. He walked toward me now. "Of all the stupid things to do—"

"We agreed it was important!"

"Important enough to risk your capture? This entire effort?"

Filio and I glared at each other. I imagined steam emitting from the middle of our locked gaze.

"Hey, what's important is that you're fine, and we have the book," Leyes interjected. He reached out, pushed Filio with his foot, and Filio, fuming, took a seat.

Erise poked me in the knee.

"So how did you do it?" she asked. "How'd you get in?"

I gave them the whole story, from Arina to the disguise. I had just finished explaining about Jusste

Star when Filio interrupted.

"So why is there only one book here?"

"Well," I started.

"Great," Filio muttered. "Another well."

I shot him a look.

"After I left the library, I ran into Corinth…"

"What?" Filio jumped from his seat.

"Oh, shut it," Erise said, waving her hand in his direction. "It's just getting good."

"You are going to be the death of me, Pasin," Filio added, covering his face with one hand. "Gads."

I shot him another look, but Filio didn't look back.

"I dropped the books and picked up this one," I continued, tapping the book in Erise's lap. "Corinth got the other one and recognized me before I could do anything about it."

"So…" Leyes started.

"Corinth has the book," I finished.

"Which means Oramus has it," Filio added. He paced a moment then asked, "You said it was the legend of a Star, right? So it's about him?"

"Yes."

"If it gives any descriptions," Filio continued, though muttering only to himself at this point. "Any descriptions of his powers–of course it will, it's a legend–then that means…" He stopped and turned to us again.

"That means Oramus will know more about your abilities than you."

His face clouded, but his meaning was clear and grim. An uneasy silence filled the room. Erise bounced her foot, and Leyes frowned on one side of his mouth, then the other.

My stomach rumbled. I looked down in

embarrassment.

"I'm going to get some food." I said.

"Here, I'll come too," Erise said, standing up.

"Me too," Leyes said.

"While you are all eating," Filio said, walking over to us. "I will be reading this book. Or, in other words, I will be doing something actually useful." He snatched the book away from Erise and sat down once more by the fire. Erise then attempted to take it back and a mini-war ensued. I chose to stay out of it and walked toward the kitchen, Leyes in step next to me.

After a minute of silence, I pondered out loud.

"Something I don't understand," I said, turning my head to Leyes. "is how scared Corinth's voice was when he yelled for help. Was he afraid I would attack him, or…?"

"No," Leyes said with a shake of his head. "No, I don't think so. I think," he said, "I think Corinth was scared you would escape."

"Why though?" I asked. "It's not like I was already captured…he had no idea I'd be there."

"Maybe not. But imagine explaining that to Oramus. 'Pasin was here in the palace and I ran into here, but she still got away.' He's not going to be happy about that."

"Good point."

"And besides," Leyes added. "I think Corinth is scared of you–scared you'll take his place as Oramus' favorite."

My jaw lowered. I opened my mouth, about to reply.

"Pasin! Wait up!" I turned and saw Erise jogging to catch us.

"I'll see you in there," Leyes said, and continued toward the kitchen.

"Hey," Erise said once she reached me. "You never explained how you got that cut." She pointed at my shoulder once more.

"Oh, right. Some Ice pelted me with his dricking projectiles, and one hit my shoulder."

"Fair enough." She paused and added, "And I thought our day was exciting. Oramus showed up here today."

"Whoa, really?"

"Yeah. He came to the gate and demanded a reception, but Light refused him."

"Shining...what happened?"

"We all came to the outside tower, and Oramus yelled that he knew Light was sheltering us. He gave Light the option of giving you up or going to battle and Light said...oh what was it? 'Better to fight and to fall than stand alongside you.'"

"Wow." Silence for a moment. "So that means this is really happening? This battle?"

"Yes, so we have to find the elves as soon as possible, or we won't have time to convince them to help us."

It felt like my feet had turned to lead. It was really going to happen, this confrontation. A battle.

"But about something else," Erise said, returning to her normal upbeat tone. "We were really worried about you, so don't do that again, all right?" She grinned as we reached the door to the kitchen. "Leyes spent the last day on top of that tower waiting for you."

Erise opened the door and my nose filled with the scents of sage and sweetness. I smiled to myself and let the moment envelop me whole.

CHAPTER THIRTY-TWO

That night, Light made an announcement to the people of Daven, telling them of my presence and story, of Oramus' actions, and of his own intentions to actively help lead the resistance. He gave them the choice to stay and stand by us to face the consequences of his choice, or to leave the city with some funds from his own coffers. A couple of families arrived at the manor to pick up the travelling funds, but most of the citizens chose to stay.

I returned to training the next day. Fire strode over to our part of the training ground just as the female Blaze felled me for the fifth time that morning. Fire grimaced.

"Again," she said.

I stood up, rubbing my shoulder where the Ice had cut me. It had been sore ever since. Female Blaze assumed her position.

"When you're ready," she said.

I took a breath, willing concentration to flow through me despite Fire's heated presence. I exhaled and punched toward Blaze.

A fist-sized fireball whistled through the air between us and I chased behind it, but Blaze stood still. Right before it hit her, she lifted her arms and redirected the shot around her back and back at me.

I twisted to avoid the jet of flame, but as I did, Blaze darted forward, swung her leg under me and knocked me to the ground. My head hit the floor, and Blaze held a ball of flame to my neck. I couldn't tell if the heat on my face was from the lick of flame or embarrassment. Probably both.

Fire marched over to us.

"Why didn't you blow the flame away?" she asked. Her voice rose with each word, punctuating the training ground air. "You know how to do that, don't you?"

"Yes," I said as I stood up, rubbing my shoulder again. "Yes, ma'am," I amended.

"So why didn't you?"

I peered at the male Blaze.

"I was told not to use my Air abilities during fire-training."

Fire snorted.

"Who told you that?"

"I did," the male Blaze said, stepping forward. He glanced down but then brought his gaze back up to meet Fire's piercing stare. "I can't evaluate any non-fire activity."

"Then get someone who can!"

Fire's warmth flared in my consciousness, and her voice rose even higher.

"You!" she said, pointing at the Rain boy with his bucket of water. "Go get Gust." She turned back to us as he scurried off.

"And you," she said, pointing at me. "Use everything you have, you understand me? Fire, Air, Star, whatever it takes. I'll check in again later."

She turned on her heel and muttered as she walked away.

"If we're doing this, let's do it right."

#

The rest of the day's training came much easier. I combined Gust's instructions with Blaze's and overtook Blaze after two tries. The only thing that really stopped me from getting it the first time was the pain in my shoulder. When Fire returned, she nodded in a way that might be taken as pleasure. I left for dinner with a spring in my step.

When I entered the hall, Filio was talking to Light about our plans for the next day.

"Air and I are going to Gimmerton," he said, "to meet with our people there. Star and Spark are traveling west to meet with the elves. We should all be back by the week's end."

"Be careful in Gimmerton," Light said. "Wave, the lord there, would not want to be connected to us."

"Why not?" I asked as I took a seat next to Erise. "Hasn't he heard of what's going on?"

"I'm sure he has," Light said, reaching for a roll.

"But then why?"

Light took a bite of the bread and swallowed before sighing.

"He has a daughter at the palace," he said.

"So?"

Light looked up at me and raised his eyebrows.

"Would you want your child around Oramus after

pledging to overthrow him?"

I grimaced. Well no duh, Pasin.

"That's the case with most of the people at the palace," Light continued. "They're sons and daughters of influential families across Falleon. Even if they disagree with Oramus, they say nothing because of what might happen to their children.

"Of course there are other reasons as well," he said as he picked up a knife to butter his roll. "Greed, ignorance, fear for their own lives. But this is just another way Oramus keeps his hold over Falleon. Does he really have any interest in those boys and girls and their palace squabbles?" He stabbed the knife into the butter and took out a chunk. "He keeps them there as leverage, hostages in return for their parents' loyalty. And it's considered an honor to be chosen."

Light didn't look at us as he spread the butter.

"I didn't choose to not have children," he said, "but I am overjoyed that Oramus has nothing over my head to sway my actions.

"Anyway," he said, putting down the knife, "be careful in Gimmerton. May Solluna light your path."

#

Later that night though, something caught my eye through the window.

Fire stood in the courtyard, twisting her hands this way and that. I stared as delicate tendrils of flame issued from her fingertips, wove themselves together creating a bouquet of burning flowers.

Even from the window, even in the darkness, I could see the care she took with each flower,

315

concentration etched on her face.

I paused and watched as Fire continued her creating, making more and more and more...

Until she stopped.

The flowers of flame burned in the night, illuminated her downcast face. I continued my walk, but I could still feel her and the heat of her flowers. Her warmth remained outside long after the heat from her creations dissipated.

#

The four of us left together the next day. We decided to travel north together to Tright before heading our separate ways.

Light gave us a handful of coins on our way out, apologizing over the kitchen's lack of food ready for our expedition. Filio, Leyes, and I stopped at a food stall on the way out as Erise idly read a nearby message board. Other early morning shoppers kept sliding odd looks our way and once again I wondered if I really looked that obvious. I fingered the chain of the engagement necklace, searching for a groove I would never find.

"Filio!" Erise called out from the board. Filio turned, and Erise motioned him over.

"Buy these for me, will you?" He dumped a variety of food into my arms and left to join Erise. I snorted, but I found Leyes and we bought the supplies.

After putting Erise and my shares into my bag, I began walking over to where Erise and Filio seemed to be in a heated discussion. As I got closer, Erise looked up, cut Filio off with a wave of her hand, and trotted over to me.

"Come on, let's go," she said, steering me toward the gates.

"What was that about?" I asked.

"Oh, Oramus just raised the award money for you," she replied quickly. "I thought I should tell Filio."

"Ugh." My mind teemed with the possibilities. "He's going to be even more paranoid now. Do you think he'll let me go into Tright?" An even worse thought crossed my mind. "You don't think he'll make me stay in Daven, do you?"

Erise grinned at the panic in my voice but shook her head.

"I don't think so," she replied. "He knows we need two people to speak to the elves and I don't think he thinks he could make you stay after promising you could go."

I gave a little laugh at this and relaxed.

"I have been pretty stubborn, haven't I?"

Erise's smile widened.

"Almost as stubborn as him."

#

Tright was only a day's walk away, and we decided ahead of time to spend the night in the surrounding area before splitting up the next day. We didn't meet any other people on the road we travelled. The only time we abandoned the path was when I sensed a guard posting just around the bend. Other than that, the day passed uneventfully. Hence, we were bored out of our minds by twilight.

"We're almost there," Filio reassured us as the sun disappeared behind the trees. I had long abandoned walking, and I hovered barely half a foot above the ground instead, keeping pace with the group. I attempted to shake the lethargy and looked around, searching for any change in the scenery.

"Oh, hey." I lifted my arm and pointed to a spot up the road. "There's a message pole. Maybe there's something new to look at."

I felt Erise's body momentarily stiffen at my words, but this tension didn't reach her voice.

"Oh, thank Solluna," she said. "I'll go ahead and see if there's anything interesting." She ran ahead while Filio. Leyes, and I kept up our slower pace. I felt curious too, but I had no idea where she found the energy to run like that just for a post.

Filio seemed to be going even slower, though that might have just been my imagination. The trees cast shadows over the majority of the road, and I realized how long it had been since we had traveled like this every day. How quickly I had forgotten how annoying it was.

Erise reached the message board and disappeared to its other side. We couldn't see her, but I felt her moving, doing something, I didn't know what. After a bit, she reappeared and called out to us.

"Nothing new," she said.

"That's good then, right?" Leyes answered as we reached her.

"Yeah," she replied.

I glanced at the board as we passed it. Another picture of myself looked out at me, its edge curling from the breeze. I searched for the new gold amount, but the same number was displayed as before. I guess the post manager hadn't received the new poster.

We walked over one more hill and a tiny little city

stood sprawled before us. We all looked at it for a moment.

"Yeah," Filio said, pausing for effect. "That's Tright. Not much. Let's set up for the night."

#

We easily fell into our old routine as we unpacked. I set up the fire and my single blanket quickly, then looked around for something else to do. Leyes and Filio worked in their edges of the camp. Erise took out her blankets and as she did, a crumpled piece of paper fell out of her pack. I opened my mouth to tell her, but a draft of wind picked the paper up and took it out of her vicinity and into mine. I grabbed it before the wind could make any more mischief and just held it in my hands for a moment. Something, something about how she was acting didn't sit well in my mind. I glanced to ensure she was still busy, then opened the paper and read:

"STAR." The letters sprawled across the entire top of the page. "This is Destin Snow." A picture beneath my name showed a man in his late twenties, early thirties. "He was found guilty of assembling anarchist forces in your name.

"This," the notice continued, "is Chasity Darkness. She was found spreading anti-government literature under your banner." Another picture showed a woman in her middle ages with thick eyebrows and a determined frown on her face.

More pictures and descriptions followed, creating a row of people stretching from one side of the page to the other. Under each picture were written three numbers separated by dots, a date for each person.

Each date was seven days from the last.

"Star," the sign repeated under the row of pictures, "For each week you remain in hiding, one person will be executed." I felt the breath catch in my throat. I looked around, but no one seemed to have heard.

"Either come to your senses and return, or meet me in battle. Until then, their deaths are on your head." At the very end of the sign, a stamp with Oramus' crest and initials glittered like an insect: O.V. I tore this edge off and let the paper smolder between my fingers.

"Erise?" It took all I had to keep my voice even as I said her name.

"What is it, Pa…sin." The words faded as she turned and saw me with the crumpled paper in my hands. Her voice did seem out of place, and Leyes and Filio likewise turned to see the source of the concern. Filio's eyes widened, and he snarled when he saw the paper.

"You let her see it?" he called over to Erise. Erise opened her mouth to reply, but I beat her to it.

"*You let her see it?*" I mimicked, clenching my fist around the paper. "Why did you keep this from me?"

"Because we knew you'd act like this!" Filio answered, standing to face me. "You can't let Oramus get to you so easily—"

"Get to me? Filio, these are people's lives!" I thought of the date under the first man's picture. "That Snow only has three more days to live! We have to move the plan up!" The wind blew through the campsite, the same that had delivered the evidence of treachery to me. It lifted the hair from my face, so the loose curls fluttered out behind me.

"No!" Filio moved closer to me, narrowing the gap

between us. "We can't afford to hurry and risk mistakes! We have to follow the plan and do it right."

Erise and Leyes sat frozen, Erise looking guilty and Leyes with a face of neutral concentration and concern. But I focused on the man in front of me.

"Is a plan worth letting people die for? How…how can you live with yourself knowing people died because of you?" The wind subsided for a moment and the curls came to rest on my shoulders. The fury in my heart didn't quell though.

"What do you think's going to happen at the battle?" Filio replied. The breath caught in my throat, but he continued. "And besides, how do you know if these people are even real? How do you know this isn't a bluff Oramus is using to lure you out?"

He paused and upon hearing my silence, continued once more, "Pasin, I'm in charge of the majority of our operations, and I haven't heard of any of these people. Wenton Smoke, listed as head of Mint Leaf Bay activities? The leader there is a Gust."

Doubt flickered at the edge of my mind, but still…

Erise, perhaps sensing a break in my anger, started to speak.

"I'm sorry Pasin, I—"

"And you!" All the rage flooded back into me as I turned to my friend. "You lied to me!" The wind came back nearly twice as strong as before, a gale sweeping through the campsite. "I trusted you Erise! If these people died and I didn't even know—"

"They're probably not even real, Pasin," Erise interrupted. "Like Filio said, Oramus—"

"But what if you're wrong?" My words hardly made it through the din of the gale. I felt fury in my blood, and I couldn't tell if it was the weather or me controlling the wind. "What if he's not bluffing and these are real people? Real people, real lives, families—"

Tears flooded my eyes, but they evaporated just as suddenly as they appeared, leaving salty residue behind. I looked from Erise to Filio and back again, and disgust poured into me and mixed with my anger. With a strangled cry, I broke off eye contact, spun around, and ran in the opposite direction. I had only just made it into a dead grass field when the dam inside me broke. The anger and betrayal I felt inside rushed out of me through my fingertips.

With a ragged yell and a push, I let everything out. I released the inner fury and for once, I didn't hold back. Flames danced all around me, flashed like a dome building as it raced away before dissipating after a good distance.

Once the flames disappeared, I realized the true power of what I had just done. A perfect circle of burnt grass surrounded me, maybe a fifty-foot diameter of destroyed nature. The odor of singed hair drifted on the breeze of a much slower wind, and I noticed several parts of my shirt and pants had scorch marks like I'd been too close to a blacksmith's fire.

I stood there for a moment, then lowered into a crouch. I felt Erise, Filio, and Leyes come closer, though not within the burn border. I didn't care. Even then, even then...I couldn't fix what was wrong. Something, someone always stood in my way. And all my yelling and temper tantrums? Nothing, they accomplished nothing.

Leyes was the first to cross the border. He came up to me and lightly placed a hand on my shoulder.

"Maybe we can talk about—" he started, but I cut

him off.

"No," I replied, standing up. "I'm done talking with them." I shook his hand off my shoulder, shot up into the air, and flew back to camp.

I was already under my blanket when the others made it back.

"I'll take the second shift," I said from beneath my blanket, turned away from the others. No one said anything, and I was perfectly fine with that.

CHAPTER THIRTY-THREE

Hours of sweet darkness later, I was awakened by Erise.

"It's your turn," she said, nudging me with her shoe.

"Nnnn."

"Get up," she said, exhaustion clear in her voice. "I need sleep."

Once I rose, Erise quickly sank into sleep while I paced back and forth in front of the flickering fire.

I hated how he made me question myself. I hated his devotion to a plan at any cost. And her...this was the second time Erise withheld information from me, vital information. My fists clenched, and I felt the fire rise higher. I looked around at the sleeping bodies and snorted.

Dragging my finger through the dirt, I wrote a message.

"Going for a walk," it said. I could keep part of my mind focused on the area, and besides, who else would be walking through the forest on a dark, icy, winter night?

Instead of rambling through the forest however, I cut a path towards town. I flew until the trees no longer covered me. A town, a village, people—not what I wanted exactly, but it was away, away from the others. A town was a sign that there was life outside of all this.

Hardly any people were about. Cool dots of warmths lay still in houses. It had to be one or two in the morning after all. Darkness cloaked the entire town; only the stars cast any light, except for the occasional torch. I strolled into the town with purpose, confidence and ease echoing in each step I took. Foggy breath billowed out of my scowling mouth as I tried to settle down, but peace wouldn't come. I didn't even care enough to charade with the trappings of cold weather clothing. Rolling up my sleeves to let the freezing air dance across my skin, I continued to walk in the dark, deserted streets with anger heating my body and curling my extremities.

I turned left and right without care or consideration. After one such turn, I realized the lane I walked was actually a narrow, dank alley that the Absent me would have avoided, even in daylight. I curled my lip at the thought of my old self and walked on.

About a quarter of the way in I recognized body heat registering halfway into the corridor. Some man, medium-tall and burly, crouched behind a stack of crates in front of a door. I walked on, loudening my footsteps, *clapclapclap* on the ground, taunting him.

Come on, I thought. *I dare you.*

He must have heard my thoughts; he must have, it went so easily. As I passed his hiding place, the man jumped out, grabbed my arms with one hand, and placed a knife to my throat with the other. The cold metal almost sizzled as it touched my skin, and his breath felt chill as he spoke into my ear.

"Scream," he whispered, "and I'll slit your throat."

"I'm not going to scream," I said back evenly. His whole countenance momentarily paused; I guess he didn't get many coherent victims.

"In here," he said, roughly pushing us through the nearby door into a filthy room, its soaring ceiling filled with darkness. "Now give me all your valuables," he continued, breath rank like the room, "and there won't be any problems."

"I don't have anything," I said still evenly in spite of the blade against my throat. "No gold, no silver, nothing." He pushed me up against the wall and slid the tip of the knife between the engagement necklace and my neck.

"It won't come off," I said, as he tried tugging the chain off. My fingers and the heat within begged to be released, to come out and play, but I waited. It had to be just right. He grunted but gave up after a moment.

"No money, huh?" He looked me over, but I had no bags, no bulging pockets. "I guess we'll have to find some other way of payment then." He looked me up, down again, this time periodically dabbing his lower lip with his tongue.

"Now what's a girl like you doing out this late at night?" he asked, moving closer to me. I stared straight back into his eyes made black in the darkness. I let the heat blossom inside of me, hardening and bursting silently within. He apparently didn't expect a reply for he continued, "You sure picked a bad night to be out alone."

"No," I said. "You did." I let the heat inside release; he gasped and fell backwards from the force of it. The knife fell from his hands, from my neck, and I watched the steel edge ooze liquid on the floor.

"Don't even th-think about it!" he said striking some ridiculous battle stance. "I am Stone, and you have no idea—"

"Ha!" I laughed at this, hard and spiteful. "I have no idea? You idiot."

Stone tried to begin the fight, but I shot out a wind gust and slammed him against the wall. As he stumbled to rise, I lazily flickered a fire to life in front of the door, his only escape route. I soared into the air to look down on the self-proclaimed fighting champion now quivering in his stance.

"You have no idea!" I roared at him. "You're just like him, thinking you can control me!" The heat pulsed against the pendant around my neck. "It's my turn now!"

The man tried to raise a stone barrier, but I obliterated it easily with a fireball. I knocked him to the ground with another gust of wind, and then I set fire to a small pile of rubble next to him. It grew, and Stone scrambled up to avoid it. I set the flame loose, and it followed him around the room, and I smiled, wide and broad, flashing my teeth in the growing light of the blaze. Finally, he was encircled by the flames, pinned against the wall. The whole room burned, and I flew above, and I liked it. I loved the overwhelming heat, its sheer, unadulterated power.

"Please!" the man sobbed. Sweat poured off his face. "Please! I'm sorry! I'll never hurt anyone ever again! Please!"

I said nothing but reveled in the sight of the pathetic creature cowering in the circle of fire. The absolute control–delicious, delicious power.

As the man whimpered and begged, I remembered another circle of fire. That stupid rabbit, the one Leyes had–Leyes! I zoomed my focus out and on to the campfire and there they were; Filio and Erise remained asleep, but I felt Leyes walking around the fire.

Different emotions flooded the rage in my chest, leaving nothing but shameful, overwhelming self-loathing in its place. The fires in the room died down except for the one encircling Stone. It burned on, but the heat lowered. Stone rose from his knees and stared at me, but I couldn't look at him. I slowly descended until my feet touched the floor.

"What's your full name?" I finally asked. He still couldn't get out of the circle, but he wasn't about to be burned alive anymore.

"Bander Stone," he said, eyes darting around the room.

"Bander Stone, I am so, so sorry." My head dropped, but my hands balled into fists. I was no better than the man I hated. I let his circle of flame lower until it was little more than embers.

"Go," I mumbled, head still down. He didn't bolt like I thought he would; he glanced at the embers, as if expecting them to flare up again.

"GO!" I shrieked, flame momentarily circling me this time. He jumped and ran past me and out the door, leaving me alone in the crackling room with tears burning as they slid down my face.

#

I finally exited a few minutes later. It took all I had not to immediately take to the skies after getting out of the black room, but I managed to leave the city before flying back to the campsite. I landed around twenty feet before the circle. Leyes was still awake, this time on his hands and knees dragging his finger through the dirt with broad sweeping motions. As I entered the campsite, he destroyed his creation and turned to me.

"Hey," he said. "Is everything all right?"

I twitched my mouth before answering.

"It will be," I said. I looked around for my note, but it was erased as well. A moment or two passed before I broke the silence.

"Leyes, why are you so nice to me?" I asked. Odd question, stupid question, I know. I was tired, and frankly, his kindness astounded me. After the night's proceedings, the thought seemed impossible. He let a moment or two pass before answering.

"I don't know," he said, sitting down in front of the fire, "I just…I—"

He paused again.

"I feel these ways sometimes, and I want to do something that might help someone else. If I…can't feel the way I want to, then maybe how I act will at least do something good…for someone else." He didn't look finished with the thought. I hesitated and then sat down next to him, though four feet away.

"What do you mean?" I asked. "When you say, 'these ways'?"

Leyes looked at the campfire. Its reflection crackled in his eyes.

"There are times," he said, "when I feel like I'm

splintering into a thousand pieces. There are times when I hear everyday words, but I don't understand them. There are nights when I feel the glare of the moon outshines the sun."

I shuffled where I sat. "How do you resolve that?"

"I don't," he said, still staring at the fire. "I just think about something else."

I thought of the story Filio had told me. People make mistakes; does that make them bad? It was hard to imagine that the boy in the story was the same man sitting four feet away.

A thought crossed my mind and I vocalized it before I thought it through.

"Do you ever wish you could leave Falleon?" I asked.

"Not really," he said. After a moment's pause he turned his head to me. "Do you?"

"Yes," I replied instantly, "Ever since I was little. I wanted to leave and find a place where I…where I wouldn't be the outsider." I lowered my eyes and took my turn looking into the fire. Leyes hesitated and then asked another question.

"What about now?" he asked. "Now that you know you have powers, I mean."

"It's still there," I said, looking back up, over the fire and the dark forest beyond it, up to the sky. "The thought of just leaving still has its appeal. To not have all these commitments and expectations, I guess."

Silence dominated the scene for the next minute, broken only by the sounds of insects and the crackling flames. Leyes said nothing in response to my last statement, but he was the first to speak again.

"I can cover the rest of your shift tonight," he

said.

"You don't have to—"

"I can't sleep anyway," he replied. "You look tired; you should rest." I considered arguing with him but sleep beckoned.

"Thank you," I said, looking at him.

"You're welcome," he replied, looking back at me. Our eyes met until I turned away.

"Good night," I said.

"Good night."

I left him and returned to my sleeping bag away from the fire. He sat directly in front of the flames, and my perspective gave the impression that his silhouette was burning away the night around him.

CHAPTER THIRTY-FOUR

We split up the next day. It only took a day to reach the forest, but it took another day to find the correct part of it. Erise ran through the trees, seeming to intuitively know where to step, when to duck, when to spring. I, on the other hand, kept running into tree branches and getting scratched. The trees were too tall to fly over while keeping within earshot of Erise, and the branches were too thick to fly through, so I was stuck with walking.

"It's up here!" Erise's voice echoed through the forest, stilling some of the birds singing in the evergreen trees. I stopped, put my hands on my knees, panted. After only three seconds, Erise called again.

"Pasin? Did you hear me?" Her head poked through the branches, and I grimaced at her.

"You're sure? It's been four hours. I might die if we have to go another four."

"That's what all that flying gets you," she replied. "You keep doing that and you'll lose the ability to walk." She pranced on ahead.

"Come on. It's right there. Promise."

"You said that an hour ago!" I yelled.

"Come on!" she yelled back.

I sighed, picked myself up, and followed her.

When I caught up to where she had stopped, I looked around for some telltale sign, but this patch of the forest looked like any other.

"This is it?" I asked. She nodded.

"The markers line up," she said. She pointed. "See? Rock, tree, mountain."

I followed her finger to where a boulder stood in front of a forked tree. The boulder looked like a miniature of the vast mountain behind the forest, the mountain's snowy peak perfectly centered between the forked tree branches, just like in the book.

"You ready?" I asked, but Erise was already at work, scouring the ground for the implement prescribed by the book. She found a rock, picked it up, and threw it through the branches.

We waited, breath bated, and…nothing.

Erise bent over, grabbed another stone, and threw it through the gap. A few more seconds and still nothing. I shifted on my feet as Erise reached down for another.

"Maybe it's somewhere else—"

She pitched the stone like a vandal trying to break a window. It sailed through the air, and her eyes followed its descent, breath ragged. Nothing. I walked over to her.

"I don't think—"

"Who calls?" a voice whispered through the leaves. I started at the sound, strengthened my heat detecting, but I could sense nothing besides me and

Erise.

"Visitors," Erise answered, standing up straight, still panting a bit. "Travelers who seek the honor and aid of y-your people."

Despite the slip, Erise remained straight up and down, unmoving, but I glanced around. I sought the voice's owner, but felt nothing, and yet—

"Welcome," the voice said. A dark, lithe being appeared from amidst the foliage, seemed to melt into being from the trees. "Pardon me for the late reply; we haven't had outside visitors for a long time." The elf was slim, short, and clothed in wrappings simultaneously tight and loose. "I am Feil. What are your names?" He looked at me first.

"Pasin Star," I said.

"Erise Spark," Erise said.

"Erise...yes, I have heard of you," the boy answered. Erise's eyes grew large, and I felt a slight electric current run through the air.

"I'm sure Saphin and Lostrano will want to see you," Feil continued. "I can take you to them."

He turned and began to walk away. Erise and I looked at each other, and Erise was the first to bound after Feil. I followed less enthusiastically.

He led us through the dormant trees and evergreens. Finally, he stopped and turned back to us.

"I need you to close your eyes," he said. We looked at each other again, eyebrows raised. This wasn't in the book.

"You can't come in otherwise." He paused then continued. "It's not much farther."

"All right," Erise said. "Let's get it done with." She refused to look at me, and instead closed her eyes. Feil walked forward and fastened a blindfold around her head. She stood perfectly still, and when he was done, he turned to me.

"Your turn," he said. Mischievously? I couldn't tell. I conceded and closed my own eyes. Cloth blanked out the rest of the light. A light hand, whose body I still couldn't sense, rested on my wrist and led us forward.

Only a minute passed before the cloth was pulled away. I could still feel nothing, except for a couple of animals, but when my sight returned, I drew in a breath of surprise.

At least thirty people stood in the clearing, holding pots, speaking in groups, working looms. However, their occupations were set aside as they noticed us, one by one. I could almost feel their eyes crawling over us with questions.

Erise looked merely excited on the outside, but I could tell by her warmth register and the extra static in her hair that she was ecstatic. I realized that this was her hometown.

I don't know what I had expected, but I was surprised by how seamlessly the buildings blended into the forest. At a quick glance, one might think that the center of their establishment was just another patch of forest. But on closer inspection, I could see doors outlined in the trees and smoke from fires winding their way through the air.

"This way," Feil said, ignoring the stares from the onlookers. He led us through the camp and up to the largest building around. We stopped at the entrance. Feil stood right outside the door and called in.

"Sir? Ma'am? We have two visitors here to see you." Silence ruled the air as we waited for a reply.

"Visitors?" The question slithered through the air

and settled uncomfortably around us. "What a lovely surprise. Send them in."

Feil opened the door and ushered us in. Once inside though, he left and shut the door behind him. I turned from the door and looked at the two elves in front of us. A man and a woman sat cross-legged on two cushions. Each wore what seemed like a seamless blending of fall leaves; this curious fabric draped across their auburn skin, barely covering even half of their bodies. Even I would feel uncomfortable wearing that little clothing in this cold weather.

"Greetings, travelers," the woman began. "Welcome to our tribe."

"We hope your journey was easy," the man said.

"I am Saphin," said the woman.

"I am Lostrano," said the man.

"And who are you?" they said together.

Erise and I looked at each other, not sure who should go first.

"I am Erise Spark," Erise said.

"And I am Pasin Star," I said.

"Erise," Saphin said "As the first speaker, you will be the spokesperson of your delegation. Please join me in Lostrano's position."

Lostrano stood, vacated his spot, and Erise silently took it.

"Pasin," Lostrano said. "As the secondary speaker, you will have no sway over what happens here. Stay where you are, and I will join you." He took Erise's spot and sat.

"Sit, please," he asked. I did. Saphin began to speak to Erise, but I couldn't hear what their low voices said.

"Now," Lostrano continued. "We may talk, but it

will have no bearings on their proceedings." He paused, but I had no idea what to say. What would a diplomat say?

"May I ask you some questions about your culture?" I asked. He smiled.

"You may."

"Thank you." I paused and asked the first question that came to mind. "Aren't you cold?" The question had to be asked. He chuckled again.

"My kind has a much lower body temperature than humans. We do not heat or cool in response to the weather; we move with it, letting us better adapt to the seasons." He paused, then asked, "You know little about elves, am I correct?"

"Yes, sir," I answered sheepishly.

"Hmm," he looked away then back. "I would have thought Erise would tell you more about us. She did leave early though, I suppose."

"You know her?" I asked.

"Yes, I do," he replied and smiled. But he said nothing else on the matter.

"Elves," he said, "are very similar to humans, which is why mating is possible, though improbable." He glanced at Erise again. "Pure elves cannot manipulate the world like Elementals; our abilities lie in understanding nature, not changing it. Perhaps due to this difference, our weapon-making abilities are far superior to Elementals'." Was that a threat? Or was he merely just stating a fact?

"Why are you here instead of…well…"

"Instead of with the Elementals?" Lostrano finished. I nodded.

"When the great migration happened," he said, "hundreds of years ago, we were allies, the Elementals and the elves. We fled from the threat, but after he…" Lostrano stopped. I had no idea what he was talking about.

"You don't know, do you?" he asked, leaning in a little bit. "You don't even know your own history?"

I opened my mouth though I didn't know what to say, but he cut me off.

"No, I forget, I forget. My apologies." He smiled at me, but his words did little to comfort me.

"Here," Lostrano said, shifting in his position. "My turn for questions. I am familiar with much of Elemental culture. Your second name is your 'Element,' yes?"

"That's right," I answered.

"So if you are Pasin Star, then your Element is a Star?"

I nodded.

"Interesting." He dabbed his lip with his tongue. "If memory serves me right, Stars are some of the more powerful Elements in your world, correct?"

"Correct."

"How do you use these powers? For what purpose?" He leaned in a bit more. I resisted the urge to lean backwards.

"Actually, that's what they're talking about," I said, gesturing towards Erise and Saphin. "We are part of a large group attempting to overturn the current dictator in Falleon." Something sparked in Lostrano's eyes, but he said nothing. "I normally don't use the majority of my abilities, but I will when we fight him."

"I see," he replied thoughtfully. "And as one of the most powerful, I suppose you are one of the leaders?"

I looked at Erise. I wasn't sure if I should disclose too much, but Erise was deep in conversation with Saphin.

"Of a sort," I said finally.

"Interesting." Lostrano tipped back, looked away for a moment, then moved in again, even closer.

"Now tell me," he said, nearly whispering. "How do you plan on leading your group to victory if you don't have the courage to speak first?" My eyes widened; my jaw dropped. He raised his eyebrows, his gaze piercing.

"I…"

"Lostrano," Saphin called. "It is time for the verdict." Lostrano rose, maintaining eye contact, and only turned his head once he was back at full height. He and Erise switched places. I looked at her, but she didn't look like her normal confident self.

"While we appreciate the length of your journey and value the esteem you place on our forces," Saphin said, "we cannot join you in your endeavors." I breathed in quickly at her words. Erise didn't look at me.

"We hope," Lostrano continued, "that this will not damage any diplomatic ties between us, but that is our decision. You may spend the night if you need to, but we ask that you leave by morning's end."

"Thank you for the hospitality," Erise said. "But our business is finished here. We won't burden you any longer." Though her words were polite, I could sense an edge under them that was unlike the speaker.

We exited the building, and Erise turned to Feil who stood next to the door.

"We are ready to leave," she told him.

"Wait." I rested my hand on her shoulder and

whispered in her ear, "Are you ready? Really?" She looked back at me without her usual warmth and nodded curtly.

The blindfolds came back on and within five minutes, we stood alone in front of the forked tree.

"Erise," I started quietly, "did something happen?" She didn't look at me. She glared into the foliage and spoke.

"She's gone," Erise said. "She left, and no one knows where she went."

I could think of no response to this. But that did mean her mother might still be alive.

"Erise…" I started again, but she shook her head.

"I don't want to talk about it."

I fell silent. A lone breeze picked up, making the dead tree branches rattle against each other.

"Do you want to split up?" I asked. Her gaze wouldn't even come close to mine. "You run, I'll fly, and we'll meet up by that town we passed?"

She paused, chewed on her bottom lip.

"Sure," she said.

She stood up and ran off before I could say another word.

I took to the skies and watched as the pale winter sun sent shadows over the brooding forest. The mountains stretched to the clouds on my left, the majority of their peaks hidden by the gray. I kicked my internal heat up a notch as the temperature dropped with the sun. Speeding forward, I looked up at the mountain range beside me. Such monstrously large things. Could I really fly over them?

A cold, bitter wind blew from their tops. I guess I'd find that out some other day.

CHAPTER THIRTY-FIVE

We met again at the edge of Beren several hours later and began the trip back to Daven in silence. It took one night and day of traveling before we arrived, and it took another day for Filio and Leyes to return. I told them and Light about the elves' refusal, much to Filio's discontent.

"That could have been it," he said, pacing once again, "the extra edge we need…"

"Well we don't have it," I fired back. "Let's just drop it and focus on getting moving, all right?"

Things had cooled between me and Filio since the argument. We decided to continue with the plan as formulated, but two weeks of recruiting and training time had been cut. It still left time to gather our forces but gave us something of a time crunch. Light readily agreed to the plan with the revised timeline. Leyes helped convince Filio, though Filio was never entirely on board. Erise sat this one out, preferring to spend the majority of her time alone in our room or training.

That's why I wanted Filio to shut up about the elves. Erise became so withdrawn and I really had no idea how or if I could help. I did know that his incessant yapping wasn't going to help matters any.

Filio and Light's days were almost entirely filled with work to do organizing our forces. Each day it seemed like more people roamed through the city streets outside our window. I, however, could do little more than keep practicing with the other soldiers. My fire skills were improving but using the Star abilities definitely helped. Some days Leyes joined me and we would spar. I felt bad by beating him, but he said he didn't mind.

"I'd rather be a messenger," he said after my apologies.

Finally, after almost a week of waiting, Filio and Light agreed it was time. I stood in the courtyard with the others and watched as Light attached a letter to a bird's leg and let it go. The bird sprang out of his hand and into the sky, carrying a note setting the date for our confrontation.

Oramus' reply was quick. The next day the bird returned carrying his decision.

Next Friday it is. Be at Clashing Field an hour past dawn and meet your destruction.
—O.V.

A wax seal acted as his signature. The familiar O.V. made my blood boil, and yet my mind chilled at the other words on the page. Clashing Field, the battle site, the only battle site in Falleon, where hundreds, thousands of people had died in the past for whatever cause. A field drenched in history and blood. That was where we were going.

"So a week," I said. Seven days until the end.

"We need to leave tomorrow," Filio replied and then turned to Light. "The notices have to be sent out tonight. How many Air types do you have?"

"Only two," Light replied, but Leyes shook his head.

"You have three," he said, then looked at Filio. "I can do a lot more doing this than sitting at Clashing Field."

"You're right," Filio agreed. "So you and the two others can each take a third of our centers. Do you want to take Fenicks?"

"Yes," Leyes answered quickly. "I would."

"All right." Filio put the reply aside and turned to a nearby map. "So if you're going to the southwest area, then you need to stop by Morrit and Mint Leaf Bay as well. If you fly straight there and back, you'll reach Clashing Field on Wednesday…"

"Wait," I said. "There's a massive no-fly zone through the middle of that, right? Isn't that dangerous?"

Filio simultaneously raised and furrowed his eyebrows.

"Yes," he said. "The same no-fly zone you didn't have a problem with two weeks ago." I felt my ears burn, but not with the normal anger.

"Well I…I mean—" I cast around in my mind, searching for something, something to reply with. "I can fly faster than him, so I thought…" I trailed off lamely. Filio rolled his eyes and turned back to Light.

"Shall we write the notice together then?"

"Yes," Light replied, an amused smile lurking on his lips. "Let's."

#

Leyes and two Gusts left an hour later. I was the last one to return inside, choosing instead to watch their dots disappear into the twilight.

It took us three days to reach Clashing Field. Light and Fire remained in Daven, but Light assured us he would follow as soon as he could. There were already a few tents scattered on our side of the field. We knew it was our side because halfway across the battlefield stood a sign reading, "Any rebels found past this point forfeit their lives."

"Of course," Filio muttered, glowering at the sign. "Oramus wants the better side; he's got those outcroppings…" He pointed to a few boulders scattered here and there on the other side of the battlefield. "No matter; we can create our own when more people arrive."

And yes, more people came. Every day, dozens of people joined our ranks, and Filio knew exactly what to do with them. He tasked Erise and me with recording each new group–their number, Elements, and hometowns. During the day, he met with each of the leaders and at night, he took our lists and worked on battle plans with the different coordinators.

The first two days were nice; I enjoyed being able to finally do something and working with Erise kept my mind off of Friday. However, this illusion of safety evaporated every time Filio came up to our table and said, "Star, there are some new people I'd like you to meet." At this point I lowered my hood, removed my scarf, and braced myself for the whispers and pointed fingers as realization dawned on row after row of faces. It was incredibly uncomfortable, really, but Filio insisted on me showing my face.

"They really need a person to rally behind," he explained for the umpteenth time, deliberately walking slowly through the campsites. "Once you add a face to an idea, the force behind that idea is that much stronger."

"Why can't that be you?" I asked, returning the wave of one particularly courageous group. "You're the one who's actually putting this together."

"They don't want me," he replied instantly, though not bitterly. "They want you."

I let out a huff of disbelief, and Filio stopped.

"Are you really that dense?" He began to count on his fingers. "One, you have ridiculous powers. Two, you have a story. Three, you've faced and escaped Oramus before. That's like...the exact requirements for a movement's representative."

"You make me sound way more interesting than I am," I replied, ears burning beneath my hair. Filio nodded.

"Yes," he said, then continued, "Well, maybe. Anyway, I wouldn't want to fill the role myself. I'd rather stick to planning."

"And what if I'd rather be behind the scenes as well?" I asked, miffed. Who was he to say where my place was? Filio laughed.

"You like attention; don't try to deny it." He smirked at me and continued, "And yet, you run away from conflict. Sounds like your Fire and Air sides can't come to an agreement."

I felt stunned by this revelation. I felt stunned for a variety of reasons but pursued the most intriguing one.

"I thought you were above that," I said. Filio's head turned my way at this statement.

"Above what?" He sounded perplexed, annoyed. Exactly how I wanted him.

"Above judging people's personalities based on their Element." I glanced at his face, pleased to see it nonplussed. "I thought that was your thing, proving the classification system wrong."

"It is," he said, shaking his head. "That's what I'm doing after this Oramus thing is over. But it's different when the person acts just like their Element, like you," Filio continued. "But what about me? If the universe knew what kind of person I'd be, I'd be a Fire. But that's the way it is, isn't it?"

Before I could answer, Filio was introducing me to another of a long line of various resistance leaders and coordinators. On Monday, it was the Falleon City coordinators, one from each sector. The Andor sector representative greeted me warmly, but I couldn't quite return the enthusiasm.

Tuesday brought Diriga Wood from Lainsford, as well as Light and his group from Daven. Leyes joined us on Wednesday with a small delegation from Fenicks, but Filio kept me so busy talking to people and training that I didn't have the chance to say any more than a quick hello. Filio's face was stonier than normal that day; his father hadn't come with Leyes. We all knew it was because of his ill health, but I guess Filio hadn't thought it was that bad.

Meanwhile, different groups of Earth types were shaping our side of the battlefield to accommodate the strategies being devised in tents across the site. All different types of Stones, Grounds, and Flora constructed blockades, fortifications, and defenses across the dead, winter plain. Groups of Elementals dueled in a set-aside place, and other people were gathering healing items for the inevitable damages. I tried to ignore it, but the unavoidable future was blatant around me.

On Thursday, Filio assigned me and Leyes the duty of telling the entire encampment that there would be a meeting at sundown. We picked our way through the tents and campfires and spread the news to each person we encountered.

"You know," I said after an hour or so, "it would probably be faster if we split up." I smiled as I said this, trying to show Leyes my appreciation for his company. I sure didn't want to talk to all of these people alone. One Snow, remarkably displeased with the conditions of the camp, nearly got into a fight with Leyes when he couldn't tell him where to find a place to buy food.

"Yes," Leyes replied, "but that would be boring." He smiled back, but the smile didn't reach his eyes. Everywhere people showed signs of stress over the upcoming battle. I tried not to think about it, but it was hard not to with Filio and Erise. True, Filio's behavior was same-old, same-old, but Erise had become increasingly detached and withdrawn since our trip to the forest.

Leyes and I spread the word to all the people in the tents and moved toward the training area. Two representatives from Falleon City had replaced Erise and I at the sign-in table, so Erise now spent most of her time sparring with other people. This time though, she was alone.

"Can you tell the rest of them?" I asked Leyes, jerking my head toward the groups of fighters. "I need to talk to Erise."

"Sure," he replied, and walked off to the closest sparring partners. I wound my way through the clearing to where Erise was swinging her sword around and slicing a gravely lacerated tree.

"Nice," I said, walking up to her. "You sure showed that tree who's boss."

Erise looked at me and lowered her sword.

"Hey."

I scrunched my mouth around, then approached the striped tree and gave it a good look.

"I can imagine it now," I said and adopted a squeaky tree voice. "'Leaf me alone! I'll root for you tomorrow, promise!'" Erise snorted and smirked but didn't look at me as I walked back to her.

"The root one was pushing it," she said, still staring at the hilt of her sword.

"Yeah, I know–I just couldn't think of anything better." I came to stand by her side, and still she didn't look at me. I took a deep breath, turned to her, and spoke.

"What's wrong?" I asked, searching for her gaze. "Whatever it is, you need to talk about it. You can't hold it in like this."

Erise pursed her lips but said nothing. The gathering shadows of twilight darkened her face and made her seem older, harder. I didn't drop my gaze, and finally, she inhaled deeply and spoke.

"I thought," she said, now looking at the horizon of trees opposite her. "I thought that going back to the elves would fix everything. I'd finally fit in somewhere. I'd find my mom."

Neither of us spoke. At our edge of the training field, we heard birds twittering above the sound of far-off steel on steel.

"Erise," I began, softening my voice. "I'm really sorry that it didn't work out. But they said...they said she left, right?"

Erise grunted in response. She folded her hands on the hilt of her sword and rested her head atop them.

"You might not have succeeded today, but there's always the future, right?"

Erise still said nothing. Her eyes looked out across the field, but they continued past the duelers, past the trees.

"Erise," I said again, feeling a sort of desperation I didn't expect, "You still have the possibility...that you'll see your mother again. Don't let that possibility slip away because of setbacks." I paused, reorganized my thoughts, and began again.

"You are the strongest person I know." A level of sincerity I hadn't felt for some time came out through my voice. "Physically and emotionally. You can finish this."

Still Erise said nothing. And yet, something changed in her eyes, something I couldn't name. I took this as encouragement and continued.

"If you want," I said cautiously, "we could go looking together. When this is all over. You don't have to do it alone."

"No." Erise rose from her thoughtful pose and looked me in the eyes. "You're right—I have to keep going. But this is something I need to do alone."

Her gaze softened.

"But thank you," she added. Erise leaned forward and we embraced. She was smiling when we separated, and I smiled back.

"By the way," I said in a lighter tone, "Filio called a meeting for sundown." I looked to the west where only a few rays of light lit the mountainous horizon. "I think we better go."

"Yes, it wouldn't do for the guest of honor to be late now, would it?" Erise flashed her familiar grin at me and ran in the direction of the campsite. I flew after her and managed to sit with Wood, Filio, and Light before the meeting began.

We sat at a rough table in front of the whole of our assembly, about four hundred strong, scattered in groups in the field in front of us, their murmurs, whispers, and the odd bark of laughter rumbling through the air.

"About time," Filio muttered as I took my seat to the right of Light. Filio leaned forward to address me from Light's left.

"We're each going to talk," he said, pointing at himself, Light, and Wood on his left. "But not for too long. Individual groups will have meetings later."

"Do I need to say anything?" I asked. I looked back at the gathered crowd. Far too many eyes looked up to meet mine.

"You don't need to," Filio said. "It would be great if you want—"

"No, I'm fine." I leaned back in my seat and let out a breath I didn't know I held.

"Are you all ready?" Wood asked Filio and Light. At their nods, she stood and raised her hands.

"Friends," she called out, and the crowd's chatter faded. "Today is the last day. The last day before our confrontation, yes, but more importantly, the last day of Oramus' tyranny."

Cheers roared through the crowd, ascended into

the twilight.

"You've heard the stories. You've seen the people. But now, you, I, we are here to take a stand, to stop the one who's done this to us."

Cheers erupted once more, and Wood sat down as Filio stood.

"Some tears cannot be mended," he said. "Some pains cannot be healed. Sons and daughters, sisters and brothers. Friends." With the last word, he glanced at me with solemn eyes. "When he hurts one of us, he hurts all of us. This cannot and will not stand."

The whole audience sat silent, and I felt something bubble up within me at the sight of their enthrallment. I leaned over to Light.

"Can I say something after you?" I whispered.

"We've come to put an end to that," Filio continued, then sat down. As Light stood, he nodded at me.

"Tonight is the beginning of the end," he said. Oh, how long it felt since he had said that back in Daven! "But tomorrow is the end. Tomorrow is victory."

Even more cheers rose as he sat, and Filio was about to stand, but I beat him to it. I glanced at him, but he paused and lowered himself back down. His eyes widened, but he nodded. I turned to the crowd.

"Thank you," I said, "for standing with us. Thank you so, so much for your willingness to take this risk, not just for yourselves, but for everyone." I looked out at the crowd, eyes gleaming as they stared back at me. "Not just for family and friends, but for those you don't even know."

I flung my words out into the empty air, into the waiting ears.

"I don't know many of you, and yet you came here to join me, to join us, to fight our common enemy, to defeat him. Thank you."

Those two words didn't feel like enough to encapsulate the gratitude swelling within me, but they were truth holding its own power.

"Together, we can do it," I cried out. "And tomorrow, we will do it."

Cheers roared from the crowd before us; hundreds of hands pounded an avalanche of applause as Filio then Light and Wood stood up, clapping too. I smiled and bowed my head to the audience and the people beside me before sitting again, face undoubtedly red. Eventually, everyone quieted and sat down except for Filio.

"You have each been assigned your respective formations," he called to the crowd. "Now, please meet with your formation leaders to go over your specific plans for tomorrow."

Yammering voices shattered the quiet, and Wood and Light moved out to join their smaller groups. Filio came up to me, though.

"That was good," he said, patting me on the shoulder. "Great."

He began to walk away, but three steps out, he turned back once more.

"Seriously," he said, lowering his head and raising his eyebrows. "Good job."

He smiled and walked away.

#

Two hours later, Erise, Filio, Leyes, and I sat in our circle, a memory of the past month and a half.

The rest of the assembled forces sat in their own circles nearby, but the gap between them and us spread wide enough to create the facade of aloneness, if you chose to think of it that way.

No one from outside our circle ventured near us. I don't know if they were scared or intimidated, but I didn't care. The time or two I looked to the outside circles, I saw heads swivel away, their faces momentarily warmer as they turned.

Erise sharpened her sword, Leyes fiddled with a piece of wire in his hands, and Filio toiled over his nightly work with the water. I sat and drew plans on the ground, drew attacks. I practiced on a miniature scale some of the attacks I had learned over the past month. Flame, heat, wind. All of it.

Erise finished tending to her weapon. She laid it on her lap, the blade glinting across her knees, reflecting the fire. I looked up and saw her staring at the fire, eyebrows knit.

"What's wrong?" I asked.

She stirred herself from the fire-gazing and turned, slowly, to my direction.

"It's…it's nothing. I mean…" She opened her mouth, then closed it, opened then closed it again.

"What is it?" I asked. Leyes lifted his head and watched our exchange.

Erise's mouth twitched and she spoke.

"I like what you said to the others," she started. "It was…inspirational, I guess. But something bothers me about tomorrow." She stopped. I felt irritation and the faintest bit of apprehension. I pushed the second aside and continued.

"What is it, Erise?" I repeated, revealing a bite of my annoyance. She sighed and met my eyes.

"What are you going to do with Oramus?" she asked. I just looked at her, and she continued, "Have you ever killed someone before?"

Heat rushed to my face. My head twitched a shake and I came right back at her.

"Have you?"

"No," she answered, glancing at her sword before looking back up. "Not yet.

"You know what's expected," she continued. I looked away. "What else did you mean by 'defeat' him?"

I said nothing. I could feel her gaze though I kept my eyes averted.

"Pasin," she said, leaning forward. "Pasin, are you going to be able to kill him?"

"I…"

"I did it!"

Our three heads swiveled to Filio sitting in his corner.

"Yes!" he shouted, pumping his fist in the air. "Take that! Yeah!" In his other hand, something glinted, white and opaque.

"Is that ice?" I asked, craning my head over the fire.

"No, it's a mushroom," Filio sneered. "Of course it's ice; why else would I be excited?" But the disparagement fell from his face as he turned to his creation, love and pride emanating from his visage.

Erise and Leyes walked over to Filio with congratulations. I wiped the diagrams away and turned to follow them.

"Not you, Miss Firepants," Filio said, holding the icicle away from me. He twitched his lips and amended his words. "I don't want it…just stay over there, okay?"

I smiled a half-mouth smile and looked beyond our circle again. Five or six people watched Filio as he danced around with his icicle. I glared at them, and when one noticed, he whispered to the others and the odd looks stopped. Filio kept on prancing. He deserved a moment for himself.

#

After five minutes of continuous refreezing, Filio recognized that his creation would never last this close to the fire, not to mention his own body heat.

We formed a mini processional–Filio in the front with his icicle held out in front of him, Leyes one step behind him, Erise three steps, and me hovering about ten feet behind. Just in case.

We left the campground behind and walked maybe fifty feet from our site. Filio stopped in the middle of a small clearing shaded by some ancient trees with frost in their branches. A small creek wound its way past in the background.

No one said anything. Filio held the icicle up to his face, and I thought he was going to kiss it. He laid the icicle on the ground. We all watched in silence, the unmoving little streak of ice on the ground. After thirty seconds or so, Filio finally turned away.

"Let's go," he said. "We've got a big day tomorrow."

"That's for sure," Erise added. The two of them turned and left, but I stood a moment more and watched the icicle. It was already melting. All of his hard work and practice was already fading back into the grass.

Leyes walked up to my side as I turned to leave too.

"Tomorrow is a big day," he said.

"That's for sure," I echoed Erise. We walked in silence again until Leyes spoke again.

"You never answered Erise's question," he said.

"I know," I said. Leyes let out a small chuckle.

"I'm guessing you knew that, but you still don't know the answer?"

I looked at him; he looked at me. I kept walking.

"That's for sure."

CHAPTER THIRTY-SIX

The next morning, I woke up early with anxiety clawing in my stomach and rain falling on my face. Not quite rain, but drizzle fell from the clouds and created a semi-permeable fog. Filio was already up and out of his mind with worry.

"Are you going to be able to fight?" he asked me. The drizzle stuck to his hair and made him look like a wet porcupine.

"I can still use my fire and wind," I replied. "But my heat sensing is kind of fuzzy." I could still sense where people were, but their outlines faded in and out with the fog.

"Great," he murmured under his breath. "But we can't do anything about that…how about you Erise?"

"I hate rain," she replied deadpan. She sure did look miserable curled up under a tree. I almost laughed at the sight until I remembered what was coming.

Filio did the last preparations with our assembled troops. I looked out at all of the people who had the choice and came. Groups of twos and threes dotted the field with their own earnest looks of steeliness and anxiety. A sea of faces gathered in front of our camp as we finished the last of the preparations. A sea of faces watched Filio as he took the spotlight for the final time before the battle.

"We came here to fight for freedom. And freedom is worth any price. Some of us may not come back, but you know what? It's worth it!" Conviction lit up his face. "It's worth it!" he repeated. "Now who's with me?"

The field of people cheered, wholeheartedly even, but I felt a chill in my heart as I looked at the people committed to this goal. Who knew how many would return?

"Failure is not an option!" Filio shouted. I and countless others nodded. "So let's go out there and finish it!"

As per Filio's announcement, we each got into groups and lined up for battle. Filio led our third as we marched through the woods and the fog toward Clashing Field. I soared above the first line and another twenty or so Airs and Gusts came behind me. Leyes was among this number; Erise was somewhere below.

"Star!" It was Filio's call. I swooped down to where he walked at the front of the line.

"We're almost there," he said. "Can you sense them?"

I tried despite the fog.

"Yes," I said finally. He must have noticed the apprehension in my voice.

"How many?"

I tried to estimate, but I couldn't.

"A lot." He twitched his mouth but didn't crack.

"Pasin, your job is to find Oramus," he said. "Don't get caught up in trying to save everyone else. You have to find him and you have to be the one to finish him, do you understand?" I nodded even as a wave of conflicting emotions boiled within me.

"The battle will not be over until you defeat him." His eyes peered straight into mine. "Now go and do it," he said, paused, then continued, "because I know you can." He let the smallest smile appear on his face and I reciprocated it. Without another word, he turned back around and continued the march. I resumed my position in the sky as we moved forward.

I felt the lines of Oramus' troops before I saw them. Row upon row upon row...I couldn't tell where it ended. Our forces reached the clearing and made our own lines. Through the fog I saw each soldier clad in the same purple and gray uniform. In front of them all stood Oramus in the flesh, unprotected and even more menacing because of it. He stood too far away for me to see his eyes, but I saw his face briefly turn my way before looking away again. Each side stood silently as our full force arrived.

The only sound across the field was the pitter-patter of rain on the frosted grass. We squared off on the edges of the plain, maybe two hundred paces apart, waiting for someone to make the first move. Oramus obliged.

"You are all about to die," he yelled, his voice echoing across the field. "If not on the battlefield, then in my dungeons, painfully and slowly. For treason." He paused but continued before we could reply.

"Give me Star," he said, "and I will spare you all. One life in exchange for the many." I felt and saw a hundred heads take a glance in my direction, but no one answered.

"We will not," replied Filio. "One more life lost to you is one too many." Oramus didn't respond at first. He stood there, hair glossed back from the drizzle, but my mind replied for him. So be it.

He glanced up at the sky again.

"Each of these lost lives is on your head, Star," he called out.

The first words were done. It was Oramus' turn to carry on the tradition as countless others had in the past.

"One!" he yelled. The voice of the challenged.

"Two!" Filio shouted. The cry of the challenger.

"Three!" The entire battlefield took one mighty breath.

"Charge!"

The two armies surged forward into the mist and war cries flew through the fog. Filio rushed on the front line, but Oramus didn't move. His advancing troops swallowed him up, and I lost sight of him before I knew it.

Elements flashed through the air as purple met motley and soldier met rogue. Ice, rock, fire, and wind burst through the air as I navigated my way to where Oramus should be. Each time I glanced below, a new obstacle tried to blast me out of the sky. A small boulder just barely nicked my shoulder, right where the Ice had hit weeks before, and sent me careening. I looked around and saw that I was one of the few still airborne. A floating target, really.

I alighted in a relatively clear area. Pairs of people

stood here and there facing off with swords and hands, knives and blows. I ran through the masses, avoiding the largest clumps, searching searching for the man I was responsible for.

Only three minutes into it, bodies began to dot the ground, the warmth in them fading fast. I have to get there, I thought. This can't go on, not because of me. When I find him, it will be over.

While thinking this, my attention dropped for a moment and in that moment, stone encased my feet. I almost fell over with abrupt cancellation of motion, and I saw the Stone dart forward to finish his prey. I found the presence of mind to shatter the rock, jump in the air, and turn to the assailant. His surprise deepened as he saw my face. Instead of trying to fight though, he turned and ran off.

I shook my head and refocused on the warmth sensing. Normal register in the immediate area, but beyond the nearest horde an abnormally cool man watched. And waited.

I made my way to this darkest warmth in the area. A ring of soldiers surrounded him. Once again, when they saw my face, they did nothing. They looked at each other, and some moved aside leaving a path for me. I rejected the opening and instead flew over their heads and paused, twenty feet above the ground and fifteen feet away from him. A smile played across his lips when he saw me, but his arms were folded across his chest. The rain by this time had stopped, but (was it my imagination?) the air felt colder.

"Hello, Pasin," Oramus said, still smiling without revealing his teeth. "It's nice to see you again." I said nothing but waited.

"There are many people fighting," he continued,

barely gesturing his head to the greater conflict. "You are responsible for each one who dies. You know that, right? Not to mention Snow, Darkness…" The superior glint in his eyes, in his tone–the way he casually mentioned his victims–a rage, a fury was building inside of me.

"They're your subjects," I answered, though his words still cut deep. "You're the one slaughtering your own people."

He paused, but not for long.

"They're traitors," he said. "Weak. They don't deserve to live if they won't live peacefully."

Spurts of flame lit the sky, and shouts echoed from beyond the ring of soldiers. We didn't have time for this; each minute passing could be another life lost.

"I'm done talking," I said. Before he could reply, I shot him with the strongest gust of wind I could summon. Oramus flew back forty feet with the force of the blow, skidding across the ground, and finally rolling to a stop. He only stayed down for a moment; he was back up and in a fighting stance within the second, but this time his eyes actually revealed something. Apprehension. Possibly…fear.

But I was on him again. I soared above and shot down a stream of fire; it surrounded him, pinned him within the confines of a burning cage. The fear leaked onto his face as I pulled my arm back, readying the final blow.

When the comparison struck me. He looked like the would-be mugger from Tright. He looked like that rabbit from so long ago. The only difference between these fears was the packaging and the ferocity on his face despite the fear. Filio's words crashed in my ears, but I...I couldn't...I...

The fireball in my hand melted into another wind gust. I thrust it toward him and blew him against the ground, making even the fire go out. But I couldn't kill him.

He looked at me as he raised his head. Incredulity. Realization. Calculation.

This time, before I could react, his hand jerked to his belt, grabbed the first of his three knives, and threw it in my direction. The steel sliced through the air and I dodged it, barely, the wake of its closeness chilling my skin. The knife buried itself safely into the ground, and I had the time to sense, but not see Oramus raise his other hand above his head.

An invisible, intangible hook burrowed into my chest, and snatched me out of the air. Caught off guard, I could do nothing as Oramus' Void power drew me out of the sky and slammed me against the ground, knocking the breath out of me.

"Now!" he yelled.

Still dazed, I tried to sense whatever it was he called, but nothing changed. Despite that, a blurred vision of brown-skinned, lithe bodies swam before my eyes. I sensed nothing, but there they were, these visible specters. Before I could jump up or move, their hands reached out to my body, and two, three, four cold, metallic bands were strapped around my limbs.

The sudden absence of power, the instant between before and after the Element Nullifiers were strapped on felt like I'd been punched in the stomach. All sensation fled from my body, all my strength poured out of my limbs, and coldness took its place.

Before I could catch my breath, the phantoms

flipped me over, so my front faced the sky, my underbelly exposed like a beaten dog. Eight limbs held me down, and Oramus said with a hovering voice like a demon of Nox.

"One, two…"

Three came and went, and the nullifiers went with it. The briefest, briefest moment of warmth appeared, but it just as quickly vanished. For after that millisecond, Oramus' hand pressed against my chest and then released. With his hand, an invisible string pulled taut between his palm and my chest. He pulled and he pulled, and a pain, stronger than any injury, fiercer than the sun, exuded from his touch. His hand pulled back and it took something with it. I screamed; I writhed; I raged against my constraints, but my power wouldn't come to me. A thousand knives carved their way out of my chest and I shrieked, I screeched, and it echoed a thousand-fold in my ears, but the pain would not let go.

Through tears, I saw a white, ethereal ball convulsing beneath Oramus' fingers. The edges of my vision began to go black, and through my eyelashes I saw him channel it into a silver locket, the silver glinting in the coldcoldcold winter air. No warmth, no heat, just–pain.

Oramus spoke, but I didn't hear him. The pain overwhelmed me, and I fell into nothingness.

#

When consciousness returned, it came quickly. Voices, shouts filtered through the air, unintelligible words echoing through the cold. And the cold, the cold! With the returned consciousness, I trembled, shook violently with the bone-aching chill. I tried to warm myself with the Star heat, but nothing happened. I felt cloth beneath, and confused, I opened my eyes.

Four people surrounded me, holding me up on some sort of stretcher. These were the dark-skinned phantoms, and I realized why I couldn't sense them at the time. These phantoms were elves–I could tell by their look, their ears and clothing. No wonder Saphin wouldn't commit to us. They had already made their choice.

A hand lay on top of my head, and the hand was warm. I turned my head to look at the hand and the hand's owner. Oramus. But I couldn't move, could barely shift my head to see him.

"It's over," he said, calling to unseen persons, just beyond the edge of the cot. I focused, pulled myself together enough to lift my head and see his audience. My heart broke as I saw Filio, Light, Wood, and Erise standing there. Erise, Wood, and Light stood stunned, but Filio...his hands were balled up at his sides, clenched, turning white at the knuckles. Another figure appeared.

"Pasin!" Leyes rushed up from behind Erise and Filio. "Pasin!" he cried out, anguish on his tongue. He tried to run forward, but a score of purple and gray-clad men blocked his way.

"What did he do to you?" The hopelessness in his voice doused me with the blatant realization. We lost. We lost...and it was entirely my fault.

"Don't answer him," Oramus said quickly. Any words that might have been forming died in my throat. Oramus continued, this time to the quintet.

"It is over," he repeated. "Star is under my

control. If I wanted it, I could have her kill you. Right now."

The pain still ached in my chest. I could barely keep my head up as it was.

"Surrender now or die where you stand," he said. They looked at each other, looked at me, but the pain, the pain blurred my vision and the cold froze my face.

One of the guards went first to Wood. She looked at him, tilted her chin up, let out a breath.

"I surrender." The words sounded terrible, terrible coming out of her mouth. The man roughly grabbed her arms and handcuffed her. He then placed an Element Nullifier on her left wrist. She took a sharp intake of breath, but otherwise stood still as this happened.

"I surrender," Light said. The smuggest smile spread across Oramus' face as a guard placed the chains on Light's arms. Light didn't look at Oramus; instead, his eyes faced east, where his wife surely waited for news about the battle.

I managed to glance at Leyes' face, but instead of betrayal or blame, I saw worry. As if he didn't care about his own imprisonment, but instead—

"It's your turn," Oramus said, flashing a grin in Filio's direction, canines glinting in the dim light. Filio clenched his jaw like his hands. He opened his mouth, closed it, then opened it again.

"You didn't even fight, did you?" he asked. "You couldn't even fight your own battle, could you?" Oramus' smile remained, but it hardened.

"'Cuff him," he snapped at the guard while maintaining eye contact with Filio. The guard did what he was told. Filio didn't move, neither fighting nor giving in. The guard pulled his arms behind his back and set the shackles on; meanwhile, Filio continued.

"First Corinth, then the elves, and next Star. You would be nothing without other people, would you?"

Oramus' smile melted into a twisted grimace. The guard tried to attach the Nullifier, but Filio twisted his hand and I saw the man stop, rub his eyes, trying to get rid of the fog now there. In three beaten and handcuffed steps, Filio leapt up to Oramus, got in his face.

"Coward."

I saw the spit hit Oramus' face, and I saw his hand reach to his belt once more. Before I could shout, Oramus buried his knife into Filio's chest.

"Filio!" The cry came from three mouths. He drew a shuddering intake of breath, but he didn't seem surprised. The light shook in his eyes.

Oramus shoved Filio, who fell like a lightning-struck tree. He landed on his back, and Oramus put his foot on Filio's front.

"Whatever you believe," he hissed. "I still won."

Oramus raised his foot and stamped it down on the end of the knife. Filio gasped this time, and I watched the lights extinguish. And he was gone.

Tears flooded my eyes, and I tried, I tried to sit up.

"How c-could you!" It was supposed to be a shout, but it came out a ragged whisper. I saw Leyes nearly bent double before some guards cuffed him and began to drag him away. Oramus turned to me, his hand on my hair once more.

"I didn't mean for you to see that, darling." He stroked the top of my head, and I neither had the ability nor the warmth to get away.

"You k-k-killed him," I sobbed, reviled at his touch, but unable to escape. Filio's body laid on the ground only a pace away.

"We need to get you home," Oramus said. He physically moved my face, so I faced the sky, not the body.

"You k-killed him," I said feebly, but he cut me off.

"Shh. Save your strength. Don't talk until we reach the palace."

I fell silent staring at the sky and the rain returned. But it wasn't rain–it was soft, white, and falling far too gently compared to what just occurred.

The snowflakes danced across the sky, danced across my vision, and my strength evaporated with the onset of grief. My vision faded to black as exhaustion overwhelmed me, and the last thing I saw was the hushed sky of white.

CHAPTER THIRTY-SEVEN

The first sensation I experienced upon waking was a goosebump-inducing coldness. In the dark of closed-eye consciousness, I explored my surroundings with sensations. I felt weight upon me—soft, yet heavy weight. My body reclined on a similarly soft surface. I heard little besides my own breathing and the rustle of my chest against what had to be blankets. Blankets, and yet this chill I couldn't shake. And my body—so tired, so sore. I tried to flex a muscle, but this soreness held me back. And the cold!

Something moved beyond my left elbow. Ceramic clinked, and a warm hand supported my neck while a cool spoon slid the most amazing liquid into my mouth and down my throat. I had no concern for taste, but the warmth it gave me! Then the liquid ran out and I waited eagerly, impatient for it to come again. The specter hands didn't disappoint. As I finished drinking the broth, I tilted my head to the side and opened my eyes, eager to show my gratitude to the giver of warmth.

"I see you're finally awake."

Any remnant of blessed oblivion was obliterated by the sight and sound of the man beside me. Oramus looked at me, smiling (smiling!) and continued.

"How are you feeling?"

The memories crashed back into my mind. The battle, the fight, Erise, Leyes, Filio, Filio! All because of this vile, wretched...

"You..." My voice cracked with its first utterances in who knew how long. I attempted to leap out of bed, but the blankets, the soreness, and his warm hand on my chest stopped me.

"You shouldn't strain yourself," he said. "It takes a few days to recover from the procedure. You need to rest."

"Where are Leyes and Erise?" I asked, still trying to sit up.

"Oh, not dead," he replied. "Not yet. There could still be some use left in them."

He sighed lightly, almost playfully.

"I'm sorry I killed that Water so soon," he continued. "I could have thought of something more special for him, but it's my own fault for letting anger get the best of me."

He looked down at his hand on my chest and twisted a cord from my dress around his finger, dreamy smile haunting his lips.

"I mean, really," he had the gall to continue, "what's a Star like you doing with a bunch of common Elementals like that? I can almost see a Spark, but Air? Water?" He pulled the string taut. "They aren't even good enough to execute personally."

He looked up and frowned.

"No crying," he said. The flow of tears stopped, but the water remained on my eyes. Panic pounded in my chest.

"How—?" I began, voice rising, but Oramus interrupted.

"Quiet," he said. "Relax." Somehow, my muscles loosened and my voice lowered, but not because I decided to do so.

"What's happening?" I asked at a normal volume, completely opposite of the surging emotions inside. Oramus sighed.

"What happened," Oramus replied, finally taking his hand off my chest, "is due to this." He reached through the neck of his shirt and pulled out an ornate silver locket.

"I had it made just for you," he said. "I placed your heart essence inside, and as long as I wear it, I decide what you do. Your heart's connection to your physical body is now mine. If you try to disobey, you will feel such immense, intolerable pain that your body will do whatever it takes to relieve it." The rage and hatred still burning in my chest began to cool and transformed into the beginnings of fear. My mind flashed with the memory of a cabinet in a dark room, flickering light contained in rows of glass bottles.

"Now, I can't have you do anything, but I ask that you not disobey. The last person who did that ended up killing himself. On that note, no suicide, all right?" His smile returned, and my fear melted and hardened into horror. He did that to people? How many others…he must have seen it on my face, for he sighed again.

"Don't look at me like that," he said. My facial features rearranged before I realized his meaning.

"Better." He continued to inspect me, like an insect under glass. "I'm sorry it had to come to this, but you did make your own decision, dear."

He moved his hand to touch my face, but I jerked away.

"Ah, ah, ah, don't turn from me." He placed his warm hand under my chin and turned my face toward his. Powerless, I averted my eyes as he stroked my cheek.

"I knew you would be worth something, but I didn't expect this."

His smile seemed so genuine, so warm, but it chilled me in a way I couldn't shake off.

"We'll see how your other powers perform after you recover," Oramus continued. "We have to get you ready for our wedding and departure; they're only a month and a half away."

My heart jumped in my chest.

"I will never marry you," I said with a spite that defied my frail body. His smile faded a bit, but his arrogance didn't change. If anything, it intensified.

"Don't say that," he replied, putting the heart essence locket back under his shirt. "You don't have a choice." He stood up and walked to the door.

"Get well soon," he said. But I didn't see him anymore; the unshed tears flooded my eyes, and I only knew he left by the sound of the door shutting.

#

A week later I was deemed recovered by Herb. The first thing Oramus did was have Corinth search my mind. I couldn't stop his needling presence; I didn't want to think of all the secrets he would share with Oramus. Tears soaked my face when he finished.

A banquet was held in my honor, but this time I, not Pearl, sat on Oramus' left. Oramus acted as if no time had elapsed between our engagement and my return; he acted like nothing had happened at all. I was reinstated as a lady of the court, this time as a level ten. I wore fine dresses, resumed tutoring, and acted as before except now people referred to me as "Your Highness."

Of course that didn't mean things were the same. I had a different tutor, a Sand who mumbled and never looked me in the eye. I never saw Water in the library, and no one would answer when I asked where he went. While I could ask, that is. Once Oramus found out, he forbade such questions.

This was only one of the changes. I could not visit any of the ladies, and dinners were normally only between Oramus and myself. The few times I saw Peridot in the halls, I couldn't even say hello for Oramus' commands held me tight. Every day was the same; wake up, go to tutoring, eat lunch, go to training, do homework, go to dinner, attend meetings about either the wedding or after, and then go to my room and try to sleep.

The training was more testing than anything. Oramus had me jump through hoops proving myself to him. He made me shoot fire as far as I could, sense as far out as I could, and test my limits in every possible way.

"Wonderful," he said more than once. He smiled at me, but his gaze moved north to where the mountains lurked over the forest, where we would be going far too soon.

Through the entire time, no matter what Oramus ordered me to do, I remained downcast, depressed, dark. Unable to mourn, unable to escape, my inner spirit slugged along, despite the smiles Oramus spoke on to my face. For nearly every time he spoke to me, it was another order, another to do or not to do. His words loaded my heart; with each new command I could feel the chains of oppression pull tighter as I lost my remaining freedom bit by bit.

And he was happy. Oramus was in the brightest spirits I had ever seen him in the weeks following my enslavement. His whole being shone with joy and it showed. I could tell from the other ladies and gentlemen; they noticed his change. The only person who seemed disgruntled with this was Corinth. He sulked even more now, not that I even saw him but three times in three weeks, practicing with his throwing darts on the training grounds. When he saw our approach, he flung one last glint of steel into the center of the target, then vacated the field.

One night when Oramus was away from the palace, I ventured outside to the garden. I tried to ignore the guards trailing me and focus instead on my surroundings.

But no direction brought peace. Winter had killed the flowerbeds; snow covered gray bark and dormant branches. I bundled my fur-lined cape closer.

I followed the paths without an end in mind, but I knew my destination when I saw it. I saw the stone ignis flower statue but nothing else. Every flower, every bush was torn out, the ground still rough from the demolition.

I lifted my eyes, and the gray of the walls met the gray of the cloudy sky, a sky I could no longer reach. I looked down, unwilling to face it. Instead, I walked to the statue and sat at its base, not even bothering to brush the snow aside.

I sat there in silence until a guard touched my

shoulder.

"It's time to move on, Your Highness," he said. He shifted where he stood. "Don't want you to get sick."

I stood and walked back inside, choosing not to look back, choosing not to look up. Just return.

CHAPTER THIRTY-EIGHT

A couple of days later, the cold stung my face as Oramus and I stood outside in the training ground. Well, it was Oramus, me, and about five other people standing at a respectful distance.

"Today," Oramus said, "we are going to test your flying abilities."

My face lit up. Flying? Oh shining, the thought rang beautifully.

"Only for height right now," Oramus added. He handed me the end of a rope. "When I tell you to go," he said, "hold this rope while flying straight up as high as you can. No swerving. Stay perpendicular to the ground." Each additional word felt like another line across my body, tightening.

"When you cannot go any higher, shoot a fireball parallel to the ground. When you feel a tug at the rope, come back down. While you are in the air, use your heat ability to stay warm. Understand?"

I nodded. I curled my toes, bobbed on my feet, anxious to get in the air before he said anything else. I clutched the rope in my hand like a lifeline.

"Ready then?" Oramus asked. I nodded again. He looked at the random others who nodded too. He turned back to me.

"All right? Go."

I sped off before his mouth closed. The cold slapped me over and over again in my face, on my chest, on my hands. It raced through my clothes, but the heat I gave off spread across my skin like a radiant glow.

The ground fled from me, rushed away from me until Oramus and the others were insignificant, indistinguishable.

It took a good thirty seconds at full speed to get to the point where I could go no further. The palace looked like a river stone and Oramus nothing more than a tiny pebble.

Automatically, without any decision on my part, I let out a burst of flame parallel to the ground. Immediately, with a great deal of purpose on my part, I let go of the rope.

It swiveled and snaked through the air as it fell, twisting and turning like a serpentine dragon. The sight was beautiful, the only connection between me and the ground running away from me, one less bond to think of.

I saw the dots below move, scurry around the great expanse of the ground. I smiled genuinely for the first time in weeks at the thought of spiting Oramus. I just didn't care. I couldn't hear a thing up there except for wind and self. Out of Oramus' control, finally. But not forever.

The plane of Falleon stretched out beneath me. I thought I saw it curve. I fancied I saw the ocean. One thing I saw for sure though, was the horizon.

I watched the sun set that evening. I followed its path across the sky with hungry eyes, even as I knew time was ticking. I drank with my eyes all the space before me, waiting for me.

Hours passed. The few times I looked down, I saw more dots on the ground, as well as three or four people circling in the air a hundred feet below me. I was unreachable. I was invincible.

For a little while, at least. As time marched on, hunger gnawed at my innards; thirst panted from my tongue. The first wobble scared even me as I fell about ten feet before catching myself. The end was nigh. I looked back at the horizon.

"Until we meet again," I whispered.

My strength gave out completely, and I plummeted downwards where fate awaited.

#

Two of the hoverers caught me about a hundred feet down. The force of hitting them knocked the wind out of me, and it was surely no better for the others.

As they brought me down, I considered what I did. Was it stupid? Maybe. Foolish? Yes. Did I regret it? Not a bit.

I struggled to stand when we landed. Oramus walked over to us, slowly. His face revealed nothing. He looked me over and then turned to a nearby group of nervous servants.

"Fetch Herb," he said equally slowly. The boys nodded and scurried off with such urgency that one would think Oramus had their heart essences too.

He said nothing else. I was brought inside, and Herb examined me. After a minute, he said all I needed was food, water, and rest.

"That can be arranged," Oramus said. "You are dismissed."

Herb bowed and took his leave. Oramus faced the servants once more.

"Have the cook make a soup and send it to Star's room. You, get a glass of water and bring it to mine."

He watched as all of the others left. Without saying anything, he put one hand around my waist and took my left hand in the other. Stiffly, he led me through the palace. At the grand stairs, we didn't turn right as I hoped. Instead, we turned left and walked to Oramus' suite.

"Sit down," he said and motioned toward a chair. I did of course, and waited, but Oramus said nothing more.

Another minute passed in silence, until a knock at the door broke it.

"Come in," Oramus said, not turning toward the door. The servant entered with obvious trepidation, glass of water in hand.

"I have your drink, Your Majesty," he said, hands shaking.

"Give it to her and leave," Oramus replied, facing the other way, hands behind his back.

I accepted the drink and gulped it down. Oramus watched the door close behind the servant. I finished the drink and placed the glass aside.

"Are you all right?" he asked finally.

"Yes, I think so," I replied. My fingers played with the condensation on the glass.

"Good," he said. He walked over to me and

looked down at me. I inwardly squirmed at his gaze but did nothing.

"Look at me," he said. I did as he said of course, square in the face. He studied me back, his mouth a solid line, his eyes stone, so stone. Quick as lightning, he raised his hand and slapped me hard across the face.

Lights burst in my vision, and I literally fell out of my chair. A cry of pain escaped my lips. Oramus' face was inches from mine when my sight cleared.

"How dare you," he roared, face contorted, "disrespect me like that? How dare you embarrass me in front of those people?"

The sheer fury on his face, the way he bared his teeth like a feral animal, the spit that flew with his words…terror gripped me from the inside, a vise-hold around my chest. Instinct, pure instinct coursed through my veins as I stood and tried to make a break for the exit. Oramus' voice ran faster.

"Stop!' he said. "Don't move." I stood there, unable to quell my quivering from head to toe. Oramus circled around me, the vulture he was, and sneered as he sought and found my terrified gaze.

"You're scared of me," he said. "As you should be. I hold my judgment from you out of respect for our future together. But let's not forget who is in charge." Oramus stretched his hand out toward my neck and grabbed the engagement pendant, his fingers grazing my throat. At the same time, he reached for the chain around his own neck, and pulled out the locket. He held it out, and I could feel its closeness.

"With this," he said face an inch away from mine, "With this, I own you. You are nothing more than who I say you are. I could, with one sentence, have you begging, screaming in pain, ready to kill your closest friend, ready to kill yourself if I so said."

He dropped the locket around his neck and moved his other hand to hold my chin.

"Remember," he said, "you are not indispensable."

My shaking intensified and leaked into my voice.

"I a–am if you want to go over the mountains," I said. I didn't know if I believed it, but I had to say something, something. And before I could stop, more words bubbled out. "As if there's anything there."

Oramus sneered again.

"You don't understand," he said, dropping his hand from my face. "But even so, if circumstances require it…" he paused, letting the words hang in the air, "I think I'll manage."

The memory of the words echoed in the air, and I dropped my gaze though I could still feel his eyes on me. My skin crawled with the threat, but I still couldn't move though every muscle in my body wanted to flee the scene, return to the horizon.

Oramus stepped back and took a deep breath in. I glanced up, and he lifted his head and stared me coldly in the face as he had before he struck me.

"Are we clear?" he asked. I nodded.

"That's right." Oramus looked away and began to circle me. "Never," he began, "talk back to me in front of others. Never question my judgment in front of anyone; never disobey the spirit of my commands." Each additional order he issued felt like another bond strapped across my body, another noose around my neck just waiting to choke me. My chest physically tightened with his words, and my breath came up short and ragged as he continued.

"And finally," he said as his voice fell to a whisper, coming around to face me head on again. "Never, ever disrespect me like that again. My kindness can only last so long." He peered into my face one last time.

"Do we understand each other?" he asked. I nodded, but he shook his head.

"Answer me, do we understand each other?" I gathered any saliva I had left in my mouth to rasp out an answer.

"Yes."

"That's right," he said, turning from me and walking to a bookcase nearby. "You may go now," he said, picking up a book and flipping to a bookmarked page. "Go back to your apartment and rest. Good night."

I rejoiced internally at the regained ability to move my legs.

"Good night, sir," I managed to say. He said nothing, and I turned to leave. As I did, though, I saw the thin leather book in his hands–*The Chronicles of Jusste Star*, the book I had lost to Corinth. His command made me leave the room, but my curiosity remained in there, wishing I had Corinth's ability, just so I could know what Oramus read.

Wishing didn't change anything.

CHAPTER THIRTY-NINE

The nights were lost to me. Dark, silent, oppressive. You would think that's better than days of servitude. At least during the day, the actions were automatic, trapped by Oramus' commands. As I tried to drift to sleep, however, I was trapped with my thoughts instead.

Many nights, Oramus would slip in sometime past midnight to find me still awake. Chiding me about needing my sleep, he would use his Void powers to drain my consciousness.

The sleep wasn't natural. That was for sure. But it never was to begin with.

#

One day, a month after everything went wrong, I sat in my usual chair in the library, blanket curled around my body like a death shroud. Nowhere in the castle was warm to me. The air felt infected, like it had contracted some sort of sickness. I shivered underneath the blanket, fur cape, and velvet dress.

Oramus walked in as he did every day to take me to training. This day, however, he stopped in front of me and looked me over with the appearance of concern.

"Pasin," he said, "you can't go on like this forever. You don't do anything besides eat and sleep."

I said nothing. Out of the corner of my eye, I saw his mouth turn down slightly into a frown.

"Look at me," he said. I obeyed and his grand visage met my gaze. Evidently what he saw did not please him.

"You need to do something," he said. "Take up a hobby perhaps. You shouldn't act like this before your wedding."

I felt an internal stirring with his suggestion, but nothing happened. It wasn't an order after all.

"I know," Oramus started, his eyes somehow lighting up. "We should go for a ride together. Leave the palace for a while, get some fresh air."

I said nothing. I guess he took that as assent.

"Put on your riding gear," he said, resting his hand on mine. "Meet me at the stables in twenty minutes." And he left.

I stood up to leave too. After all, that was an order.

#

Seeing the streets and shops of Falleon City made me realize I hadn't left the palace since I was taken. It also made me realize how little I knew about Falleon City.

I rode sidesaddle on the gray horse considered mine. My cape's hood draped over the crown of my head for two reasons. The day blew cold for one, but more importantly it hid my face from the people who looked at us with furtive curiosity.

"There's the girl," I imagined them whisper, "the

one who had everything—friends, freedom, ability—and lost it all. All because she couldn't get rid of him."

In my mind, others agreed.

"Who does that anyway?" they asked. "She had everything, everything—and now it's gone."

Absorbed with my thoughts, I barely registered the people moving out of our way. The shouts, the voices, the...clanking?

"Pasin!" A voice shouted from the noise. That voice...

"Pasin!" it shouted again.

I looked up and somehow, miraculously, Leyes stood twenty paces away, bound, chained, covered in ash. He lifted his hands to wave, and he smiled a large, tragic grin.

"Ley–"

"Don't speak to him," Oramus said quickly. The words bubbling up in my throat died, as did my smile when an overseer lashed Leyes with his whip.

"Keep forward steady," Oramus continued. "Don't look back." His order instantly whipped my head away from Leyes.

"Pasin!" I heard him cry. "Don't–"

"Shut up!" the overseer yelled. "Back in line!"

"Keep my pace," Oramus said, and he surged forward. I pushed my horse forward too, though my heart longed to stay back and tears rushed down my face.

#

We galloped through the rest of Falleon City until we reached the woods between the Inner and Andor sectors. Oramus slowed his horse down to a trot, and

I did the same.

Where he halted lay a secluded pond, hidden away by the weathered trees. Snow covered the ground beside the pond, but the space beneath the trees remained clear. Oramus dismounted, and I followed suit. Oramus even helped me step down from the saddle.

"I come here when I want to get away from the palace," he said, grasping my hand firmly as I descended. "Sometimes it's nice to be alone–or alone with someone."

We faced the frozen pond. Oramus looked at me, and I nodded half-heartedly. He sighed.

"Pasin," he said, turning me to face him. "You need to forget them. Forget what's happened before. Think about who you are, your rank, the people you're with."

He stepped closer to me, took both of my hands, and slowly moved me backwards.

"Our wedding is next month," he said in a lower tone. "I want us to be connected. To stand united before the crowd not just as power with power but as loving man with his loving wife."

He used both hands to move the hood back from my head. I felt exposed. I was exposed.

He placed my hands against his chest, where they rested uncomfortably. One of his hands grasped the back of my neck, while the other settled on my lower back. I drew in a quick breath as he pulled me in, closer to him. The hand at my neck moved, appeared beneath my chin. He directed my gaze toward him.

"Kiss me," he said, brushing a thumb across my lower lip and leaning forward. "With feeling," he whispered.

My mouth surged forward to meet his. Every fiber of my being screamed not to, but I didn't have a choice.

Each moment burst into a fresh reprise of embarrassment, shame, and heartbreak. His tongue in my mouth, his hand in my hair, his breath reaching down the back of my throat. And I reciprocated. Against every contrary thought, I gave back everything he did and more.

Oramus deepened the kiss, crushed me to his body. I drowned in his embrace, inwardly flailed against the black water closing in over my head. But it was no use.

Trapped, trapped, trapped between two arms, trapped in his embrace. Trapped by the locket around his neck and the necklace around mine. With my body moving automatically, my mind thought back to Leyes in chains. And where was Erise? Where was Filio? Dead, dead, trapped beneath the ground, cold and dead.

The heat between us heightened, and a pain near equal to my heart essence being ripped out shook my body. The pain of loss and failure tore open my heart, scalded the contents. It was nearly unbearable, burning me like a dying phoenix in my chest.

No. I looked at the raging creature inside—thrashing, flailing, burning. I looked at it one last time.

No.

And I closed the door.

I chose to ignore it, chose to let go, release—I chose to simply no longer care.

Immediately, I stopped. Stopped moving, stopped kissing, stopped groping. Warmth rushed through my body, and I felt possibility bounce on my fingertips. What? How?

After a moment, Oramus stopped too.

"What's wrong?" he asked. I could see the heat exuding from him. I could sense the warmth of the horses ten paces away.

"I…" Should I run? My heart jumped for joy with the thought of escape, and the warmth vanished. I felt all of the orders piling up on me again. No…that can't…

"I…" I willed myself to not care. Somehow, I managed to shut it off.

"What is it? Speak!" Oramus' face grew stern, his eyes searching for what?

"I realized," I started, though no invisible force spurred me on. "I realized that you're right."

His eyebrows rose.

"About what exactly?"

"About…" I began. About what?

"About moving on. I think—" I bit my lip, tried to look shy. "I think you convinced me."

His suspicion slowly melted into a sly smile.

"I did, did I?" he asked, his hand trailing up my arm. His touch sent waves of disgust in my mind, but somehow, I smiled.

"You sure did," I answered with my own sly smile. "Why don't you convince me some more?" I leaned forward and caught him square on the lips. His hands tightened around my hair, neck, waist. My mind fought revulsion, but my heart remained silent. Didn't even feel a thing.

CHAPTER FORTY

I spent the next few days slowly, cautiously testing out my powers in the moments I had alone. They were all there–the heat sensing, the fire, the flying, oh the flying! Even if it was only in a ten-foot tall room, my feet could leave the ground and stay suspended in the air! The beauty of it! The feeling of power again! It made me…it felt…oh shining.

One thing though–I could not entertain any feelings of kindness, of love, of anything like that. If I let these feelings stay in my mind, all of the power leaked away in a heartbeat. And so I couldn't think of Erise for the first two days. I couldn't think of Leyes or Filio at all. I let my heart lie dead and cold in my chest, so that the heat of power could flood through my veins.

Three days after forsaking my heart, I considered myself ready to make contact. The wedding was in two weeks; I had to get moving.

I located the dungeons deep under the palace. The entrance was near the back, below some of the administration offices. On a preliminary walk to see the surrounding area, I passed a door with a placard on it: "Head of Palace Security." So that was where Corinth's office was.

Oramus was gone for the day, off meeting with some group of people in Mint Leaf Bay. In fact, I was one of the highest-ranking people in the palace–me and Corinth. Imagine that. As such, I acted like it.

I walked to the entrance to the dungeons with purpose in my step, the cold exactness I felt in my heart reflected in my walk and on my face. People glanced at me and hurried away; it made me wonder what they knew about my powers. Did they know I wasn't allowed to use them? The sneer on my face must have scared them off.

The wall decorations shifted from the carved wood to stark stone. Ladies and gentlemen disappeared, and guards multiplied in number. I reached the entrance where three guards stood, armed and precise. I stopped in front of them and rose to my full height.

"Let me pass," I said. The three of them looked at each other, then the man in the middle spoke.

"I'm sorry, Your Highness, but only authorized persons are allowed to enter here," he replied.

"Right," I answered, looking him straight in the eyes. "And your name is?" Straight in the eyes.

"Garin Stone." I shifted my gaze to the others who hastily replied as well.

"Byrne Ice."

"Wess Gust."

"Thanks," I said in quite the ungrateful tone. "In case you are not aware, I am Pasin Star." I could tell from their faces that this wasn't news. "King Oramus has given me clearance to visit a prisoner."

The middle guard took a moment before replying. "I—I'm sorry. We can't…"

"Fine, fine," I interrupted. "I'll be sure to tell the king who exactly wasted our time getting him." I let this statement hang in the air as I stared them down. They twitched their lips, shifted their stances, but did nothing.

"I'll be back with my clearance in a moment. He will know what to do with those who disobey his orders." I turned and started to walk away.

"Wait!" The middle guard took a step forward, and I stopped. He hesitated.

"Well?" I let my impatience reverberate through my words.

"You…may enter," he said finally. I turned around and walked through the gap he left.

"Thanks," I said, only a trifle less ungrateful than before.

#

Once the guards were out of sight, I relaxed my posture and smiled to myself. If that wasn't the hugest bluff I could have pulled…I chose not to dwell on what could have happened had they called me out on it.

I searched the dungeons' coldness for pinpoints of warmth. The air nipped my skin as I walked; the warmths of humans were far milder here than they were above. I descended into the stone crypt, its dampness filling my nose, and stopped at the bottom of the steps.

I needed to see Light or Wood; one of them

would know what to do. I wanted to see Erise, but priorities had to be maintained. However, I did not want to see Leyes, if he was even there, that is. Would Oramus have killed him after the last incident? Fear tightened in my throat, and it took me a minute to regain myself.

I expanded my consciousness and focused on each pinprick of heat. Most of the presences were still, their warmths barely registering in my mind. Other, warmer presences paced the corridors, guards no doubt.

My heart jumped when I recognized Erise's shape, though far, far cooler than I had felt before, but I shook my head and refocused. I likewise ignored the familiar Air lying on another cell floor, trying not to let my relief overpower me.

After mentally sweeping the level twice, I expanded my focus even more, up and down, while keeping a metaphorical eye on the guard I felt coming closer with his strides. Twenty feet below, I sensed a collection of warmths, all three I recognized–Light, Wood, and Corinth.

Before I could register what that might mean, I felt the nearby guard about to turn the corner into my corridor. My feet moved away automatically in the opposite direction. Before I knew it, I found myself in front of Erise's cell.

I paused, steeling myself, making my heart as cold as the stone walls around us and the metal bars slicing through a small open space in the cell door. I stepped forward and peeked through the opening.

"Erise?" I whispered to the body curled up in the corner. A face darkened by dirt and shadow lifted itself from the person's chest.

"Pasin?" she whispered back. I nodded in the dim torchlight.

"Pasin!" She rose and came over to the door. I noticed she had to lift a length of chain attached to her foot to do so, and an Elemental Nullifier circled her wrist. Even this close, I could barely feel her warmth. "How did you get down here?"

"I don't have much time," I said. My mind stayed on the lookout for the roving guards, but none walked in our vicinity. "I would have gone to Light or Wood, but Corinth is with them. Do you know why?"

"No," she said. "He searched my mind after bringing me here, but I haven't seen him since."

I cast my focus back down, but Corinth remained on the same level. I snarled, shook my head.

"I have my powers back," I said. Erise's eyes widened. "Flight, fire, everything. Oramus doesn't know; no one does except us."

"That's great!"

"But I don't know what to do!" My voice rose and the heart inside me stirred. I stepped away from the window, closed my eyes, recollected myself. After a moment, I came back.

"That's the problem," I said. "I can't…it's not like before. I can only disobey him if…if I don't feel. If I control my emotions."

Erise looked away, chewed on her bottom lip.

"So if you don't use your heart," she said. "That has to be it. It's tied to the heart essence he took."

She fell silent. A guard ambled into the corridor one hallway over.

"We need to get rid of Oramus," she said, "Whether it's you who does it or someone else."

"I can do it," I said. My voice seemed to take on

the chill of the dungeons. "After what he's done, I can do it." Erise's face changed as I said this, though I couldn't precisely pin how.

"But we have to get you all out of here," I continued. "And I don't know how."

"We're not going to get out without getting these off." Erise lifted her hand so the nullifier glinted in the spare light. "We had enough trouble trying to get you out, and you weren't even in the dungeons."

"I don't think you'll be able to escape," I said. She nodded. "But we need to get you out, and soon, because Oramus and I are leaving the day of the wedding, right after the ceremony. And he means to have you executed, but I don't know when."

I looked away as I said the last bit, but I sensed her chest tighten. The guard nearby started walking again. Drick. I sensed down, but Corinth was still there.

"He's still with Light and Wood," I said, "but I need to go." I bounced on the balls of my feet.

"Hey, hey, calm down," Erise said, almost glaring at me through the barred window. "Stay focused, all right? Can you come back?"

"I think so," I said. I had to, somehow.

"All right, this is what you need to do. Come back and talk to Light and Wood. Try to figure out a plan, some kind of plan, and I will too." She glanced at her wrist. "And if you come across a nullifier key, pick it up, will you?"

Her body quivered in the cold, and I looked away, unwilling to see the trace of tragedy in her eyes.

"Of course," I said. I reached my hand through the opening to meet hers.

"And be on your guard, all right?" she said as she

grasped my hand. "If Corinth reads my mind again—"

"Don't say that."

"But still."

I warmed my hand quickly before letting go. Before I left, I sent a wave of heat into her cell as well.

"Be careful," she said.

"I will," I replied. The guard was about to turn the corner into our corridor, so I sped off in the opposite direction.

I knew the guards at the entrance would come for me if I didn't return soon. I turned my way toward the entrance, though through a different corridor. I wanted to believe it was random, but a familiar point of heat resonated in my mind. I crept up to the door and looked into his cell.

Leyes crouched on his hands and knees on the cold, stone floor, a feeble blanket draped over his back. He dragged his finger through the dirt with broad, sweeping motions. I couldn't tell what it was; whether he wrote words or drew pictures I had no idea. I tried to discern the markings and didn't notice his head move until it was too late.

Leyes looked my way, and I looked back without realizing the implications. His eyes widened as did mine; I disappeared from the window, rushed down the corridor, felt him bolt to the door.

"Pa—come back!" he strangled out in a loud whisper. "I know you're there! Come back!" He waited in silence, but I didn't move, didn't answer. A strange, guttural cry emitted from his throat.

"Come back!" he yelled, rattling his door. "Don't do this! I know you're there!"

"Hey, you!" a distant guard yelled back. "Shut it in

there!" Prisoners in other cells stirred. Against my better judgment, I crept up to his door and reached my hand up to meet his. He grasped wildly at my fingers, soaking my warmth into his freezing skin.

"Pasin," he whispered, almost gasping. "I…how…?"

"Shhh," I whispered, using all my will to stay indifferent. But the apathy was waning.

"Look at me, please," he said, grasping my hand even tighter. "Pasin, let me see you."

"Stop," I said. The warmth began to fade from my fingers. "I can't…"

I tried to jerk my hand away, but Leyes held fast.

"What's wrong?" he asked. "Don't leave, please."

"I can't!" I said, fear rising in me. I raged against his obstinacy and the flash of anger gave me the ability to retake my powers. I sent an explosion of heat through my hand, burning him, repelling his hand from mine.

"I'm sorry," I said as I fled down the corridor. "I can't—"

As I hurried back up to the entrance, I felt Leyes slowly pull away from the door and sit down on the floor. By the time I reached the entrance, he was dragging his fingers through the dirt once more, even more frantically than he had before.

I exited the dungeons without glancing at any of the entrance guards. Before I left entirely, though, I turned and did say one thing.

"I will be back in a week. I expect to be admitted on the same grounds."

I left before they could answer. If I had my heart, I might have cried. But my eyes remained dry.

CHAPTER FORTY-ONE

Over the next few days I spent almost all of my free time at the library, trying to think of some kind of strategy to get rid of Oramus. Of course, by the second day Oramus wanted to know what I was doing in there for so long, hunched over a stack of papers. I said the first thing I thought of.

"I'm writing a story," I said, draping my hand over the paper.

"A story?" Oramus walked up beside me and looked over my shoulder. "What's it about?"

"It's a secret," I said, turning to look up at him. In response to his raised eyebrows, I continued.

"It's actually a present for you," I said, "for our wedding. You've given me so much and I just wanted to give you something in return..."

"Ah," he said, a smile crossing his face. "You don't need to do that, darling. You are more than enough."

"But still," I said, looking into his eyes. "I want to give you something tangible, you know?"

"All right," he said, withdrawing his head. "I'll let you write then."

"And no peeking!" I added. His mouth curled again.

"No peeking," he repeated.

Oramus turned to leave when an idea flashed into my mind.

"Wait!"

He stopped and looked back at me.

"What?"

"I almost forgot. One of the finance ministers said I need you to sign and seal a letter authorizing the use of crystals on my dress."

"What? Fine." Oramus shook his head, as if he didn't want to be bothered by paltry things like fashion. "I'll have that sent up to your room later."

"Thank you," I said, smiling sweetly.

He left, but I remained hunched over my notebook. If someone had looked, they would have seen scene after scene of crossed out scenarios involving failed attempts of Pendra to free Espin, Luse, Lorvil, and Wytt from the clutches of Osten. But how to get them out all at once? How to get rid of Osten? What about the guards? What about Chriner? Would Pendra be able to kill him as well? Each new idea eventually succumbed to the strikethrough of my pencil.

Two hours passed, but I had little to show for it. Grass came up to me.

"You need to prepare for dinner, Your Highness."

"Right." I sighed and closed the notebook. "You can go ahead," I continued without looking at her. "I'll be there in a minute."

She curtsied and walked off. I peeked at her retreating form but hardened my heart against the sadness I associated with her. Her heart essence was probably locked up in that cabinet…but I couldn't think about that. I had to keep my mind on the task at hand. Only after getting rid of Oramus could we fix what he had done.

As I walked away from the library, a sudden…blip registered in my mind. A light mental prod confused me, like I was in a dream but touched by something from the conscious world. I stopped in the hallway and shook my head. I mentally searched, reasserting my focus, and felt Corinth just as I stepped around the corner.

We caught each other's gazes at the same time. Animosity brewed beneath his dead-leaf-brown eyes. I continued forward once more, and he stood there without saying a word. He didn't move a muscle as I walked past, but I felt him clench his fingers after he was out of sight.

#

A servant dropped Oramus' letter off at my room later that night. I took a piece of parchment from my desk and wrote my own letter on it, carefully copying his handwriting as well as I could. Then I picked up Oramus' letter and looked at the wax seal. OV, of course, but I could see the faint outline of a lion within the O. I concentrated on the heat in my index finger and slowly pried the seal of his paper and just as carefully reattached it to mine. I smiled to myself. I would be ready for the guards the next time I descended to the dungeons.

#

Three days later, rain hammered against the ceiling, a constant drumming like boots on stone, but I could still hear my pencil furiously scratching against the paper I hunched over.

If Pendra could get a hold of some Elemental Nullifier keys...if she got them to the others...if Espin and Luse came to the wedding...

Faster and faster the pencil moved, gouging black into the purity of the page...

And if Lorvil and Wytt stayed at the palace, then they could take it down from inside while most of the palace was away at the wedding!

I bolted upright, choked on my urge to laugh, but Oramus, not twenty feet away, still noticed the change.

"What is it?" he asked. I glanced down, noticed my hand shaking. I laid the pencil aside and put my hand in my lap.

"Oh, I just figured out a plot point," I said, barely keeping my voice stable.

"Is it good?"

"It's great," I said, grinning. "Absolutely great."

CHAPTER FORTY-TWO

The first step of implementing the plan meant getting a hold of some Element Nullifier keys. I didn't exactly know what they looked like, but I did know where they would be.

Around two in the morning I stole out of my room and crept downstairs, sensing and avoiding the guards on patrol. I made my way toward the dungeons but stopped short at the door with the plaque reading "Security Office." If those keys were anywhere in the palace, that would be the place.

I stood outside Corinth's office and focused my heat sensing on whatever lay beyond the door. No one occupied the office, but I did feel a familiar warmth in what must be a room adjoined to the office. It felt odd knowing Corinth was sleeping next door.

A smile crept onto my face as I stretched my hand toward the door, knowing I had at least three hours to find these keys and that by the time anyone realized they were missing it would be too late. I grabbed the handle, twisted it, and the smile disappeared.

Of course it would be locked. Had I really thought the security office would be left unlocked? I could hear a mental ghost of Filio berating me, telling me to use my head, but I shook him off.

I stood in front of the door for a good ten minutes as the frustration built. I was supposed to be some great Element, right? I could fly higher, shoot fire farther, all that stuff. And yet, I couldn't get past a locked door. I thought of melting the handle or the hinges, but that would be too shining obvious.

Corinth stirred in his bed next door, and I snorted. The keys would have to wait for another night.

#

About twelve hours later, Oramus and I returned to the palace after a horseback ride. The rain from the day before had dissipated, but moisture still hung in the air, cooling my face. He helped me dismount, and I kept my grasp on his hand once I was down.

"Can I talk to you in private?" I asked as two servants took the horses away.

"How long will it be?" he asked, though he didn't let go of my hand. "I have a meeting soon."

"Oh, not too long," I replied, gently rubbing my thumb against his fingers. "I have a problem, and I just wanted your opinion about it."

Oramus didn't answer for a moment, but then he looked down at me and smiled.

"All right," he said.

He squeezed my hand, and I, almost

automatically, squeezed it back.

#

"So what's wrong?" he asked as he shut his chamber door behind him. The closed door prevented any of the outside noise from invading the space. I made my way to the closest sofa and sat down.

"I've been thinking a lot about the wedding," I began. Oramus raised his eyebrows and walked toward me.

"That's good to hear," he replied. "Anything in particular?"

"Yes," I said, "yes there is." I glanced up at him. "Would you sit with me, please?"

Oramus hesitated, and I felt a catch in my throat. I didn't breathe for the seconds he didn't move, but the air released when he sat down.

"What is it?" he asked as he looked up to a nearby clock. Time to step it up, I thought.

"I've never been to a wedding," I said, "but I have heard about some of the traditions. Do you know which ones we're going to do, or…"

"That's really up to us," Oramus replied, leaning back from me. "I don't really care about doing a specific ceremony, but if you do—"

"Oh yes!" I answered before he finished. He looked down at me with a frown, and I corrected myself. "I'm sorry, but that's exactly what I was thinking!" His frown lessened, though it was no smile, and I continued.

"I was thinking," I said, looking down at my nails, a shy smile on my face, "I was hoping we could include the sacrifice ritual in the ceremony." The sacrifice was the symbolic moment when the bride and groom give up their past lives in exchange for their new life together.

Oramus' mouth twitched.

"That's standard," he said. "Already part of the plan."

"Not just the words," I continued, looking up, "but having the representatives as well." Now I knew that part wasn't standard. Usually it was just a string of words, but I knew sometimes people had family members or friends nearby representing the past being given up.

Oramus met my gaze.

"Whom did you have in mind?" he asked.

"That's the thing," I said, "I don't know yet." Oramus' eyebrows creased.

"Then why do it?" he asked, looking up at the clock again. I could feel the time slipping by, but this had to work out, it had to.

"Because I want to!" I said. Panic spilled into my words, made my voice rise. "I want to show you how much…how much of a difference you've been in my life! Something more meaningful, something more symbolic than words on a page or spoken out loud." My lips began to tremble with the outburst, but I continued.

"It would mean…so much to show you how much you mean to me," I said, feeling the corners of my eyes moisten. "For showing me what could be, instead of settling for what came to me." The moisture spilled over my eyelids and slid down my cheek. Oramus' gaze traced the tear's path.

"Does it really mean that much to you?" The

question hung in the air. His voice was quieter, though not softer, and his gaze remained on my face. I sniffed and let another tear fall.

"Of course," I replied, leaning forward. He raised one hand and let the second tear slip onto it. "I just want the representative to be right, to show it."

"What about that girl, Peridot?" he asked as the teardrop trailed down his finger.

"I still don't really know her," I said. Oramus took one of my hands into his free hand while looking at his other.

"And from Andor?" he asked, "Would anyone there work?" I shook my head.

"Nothing from before meeting you," I said, "could represent how much you are to me."

The water on his fingertip dropped onto his lap. Oramus followed it with his eyes and then looked back up at me.

"What about the others?" he asked, tilting his head ever so slightly. "The ones you travelled with?"

I opened my mouth just enough, as if it was such a surprise, as if it had never crossed my mind.

"The...Spark, right? And the Air?" Oramus continued. Now his gaze didn't break away from my face. "Unless that would be a problem..."

"No." I shook my head lightly and met his gaze fully. "No. That would be perfect." A smile broke across my face. "I knew you would know what to do."

Oramus smiled back and wiped the other tear from my face.

"I always do," he said.

"So we can do it?" I asked. "The sacrifices?" His hand moved from my face to my hair and started to spin a curl.

"If you want, darling," he replied. He wound the curl tighter. "But I know how to make it even more meaningful."

"How?"

"That is, if it means so much to you…"

"Of course."

He stopped spinning my hair but kept a hold of it.

"Let's make it more than symbolic," he said. "Your sacrifices, I mean."

"What do you—"

"They're going to be executed anyway," he said. A chill ran down my spine, the first chill in weeks. "And imagine how united we'll look after you dispatch them."

My mouth opened, a hundred different thoughts, protestations, questions tumbling through my mind until one came out.

"Me?" I asked, voice threatening to tremble. "Why me?"

"To prove to the people where your true loyalties lie," he said. letting his finger slip through my curl and come to rest on my knee. "I mean, I know how you've changed, but others may take some convincing." His gaze never wavered, and no warmth echoed in his eyes or voice. "Don't you agree?"

"I—"

"And it would be even better," he continued, "if you did it. As in," he said, in response to my confused look, "not just the act, but the choice of doing the act. Without this." He reached beneath his shirt and pulled out the heart essence locket. "Don't you agree?" he repeated.

His eyes searched my face, and the thoughts raced

through my mind. Kill Erise and Leyes? But I couldn't say no now, could I?

"Of course," I said. It won't come to that, I told myself. I'll kill him first, I thought.

"I understand it may be difficult," he added. "So if the day comes and you do feel hesitant, I'll be there if you need some…motivation." His fingers curled around the locket, and (was it my imagination?) I felt my throat tighten.

"I do have one request," I said, placing one hand on top of his on my knee. "If it's not too much."

"What?"

"This can be after the actual wedding ceremony, right? Not during—"

"Oh, oh no, don't worry," he said, replacing the locket and placing his other hand on top of our stacked ones. "That would be vulgar. It will be after. Right after."

Warmth had returned to his voice and even seemed to creep into his smile. I smiled back.

"Good," I said. If everything went according to plan, he wouldn't make it that far.

"Yes," he replied. "Now enough of this dreary talk."

He reached one hand up again, grabbed the curl, and began to guide me closer to him. I obeyed despite the disgust in my stomach and the absence of a command.

"You'll love the cliffs," he said. "You can see all the way to the horizon. And after the wedding ceremony, we can go directly to the mountains. Imagine what we'll see up there."

He trailed his lips across my face to my ear. I clutched his hand in mine and opened my mouth to reply, but he continued before I could get out a word.

When we separated, Oramus looked up to the clock again.

"Are you late?" I asked. The shadows of his kisses burned on my skin. He shook his head.

"If someone dares mention it," he said, "I'll say I was busy." He curled up one side of his mouth and I reciprocated.

"Come," he said, reaching out his hand. I took it and stood.

"I will see you later," he said as he led me out of the room. "Until then." He landed a soft kiss on my hand.

"Until then," I replied. As I walked back to my room, I didn't know whether to celebrate the victory or stew over the potential loss. Chill crept back into my fingertips, and I pushed the thoughts aside, felt heat rush back in, and focused my mind on what I had to do next.

CHAPTER FORTY-THREE

The plan to break into Corinth's office flooded my mind sometime between midnight and dawn. The next morning, I put this plan into action when Grass entered the library with lunch.

"Grass, I need you to do something." I looked at her directly and she looked blankly back.

"Go to Corinth's office. King Oramus wants him to mind search the grooms in the stable. The stable master lost his best whip and thinks one of them stole it. Tell him it needs to be done with utmost haste."

"Yes, Your Highness." Grass turned to leave.

"Also," I called out, "Go with him, have him tell you the results, and I'll tell King Oramus after you get back, understand?"

"Yes, Your Highness."

Grass left the library, and I sensed around. My new tutor sat at Water's desk, twitching with what I interpreted to be absorption in a towering stack of papers. I stood and hurried out the door in Grass' wake. Instead of turning right as she had, I went left and nearly ran through the corridor and down the back stairs toward Corinth's office. I took another moment to sense. Yes, Corinth sat in his office and after a few seconds of searching the masses in the forest hallway, I found Grass. She'd be there in only a minute, two minutes tops.

I positioned myself behind a tapestry at the end of the hall. I peered around until I found the right target. A vase stood on a nearby ledge, and it was easy to send a gust of wind towards it, toppling the vase. A loud crash resounded in the hall and I sensed Corinth lift his head, stand up, and glance outside his door. No one else stood in the hall.

Corinth let out a frustrated sigh and moved toward the sound source. Just as he reached the shattered remains of the vase, Grass turned the corner and approached him.

I couldn't hear her words, but it appeared from his body language that Corinth was vexed.

"He knows I have work to do," he said, his voice echoing down the hallway. "Why should he care about a whip?"

Once again, Grass' mouth moved, but I couldn't hear her reply. Corinth swayed on his feet, pursed his lips, but finally followed Grass out towards the stables. I emerged from my hiding place when I heard his voice once more.

"You there! Clean up that mess in my hallway!"

I scurried back behind the tapestry before the cleaning crew showed up. It took them at least ten minutes to clean up; I spent the entire time trying to sense the warmth of Corinth or Grass returning.

Finally, the hallway cleared out and I crept toward Corinth's office door, still slightly ajar from his departure. I pushed the door aside and entered.

Stacks of paper littered the room; open books were scattered across the desk and gaps in the bookshelves showed their displacement. A giant map of Falleon hung on the wall behind Corinth's desk, indecipherable marks covering many of the towns. Two lockets, like my essence locket but plainer, dangled on leather cords from a hook on the wall, light leaking from where the two halves clasped together. One shone brighter than the other. I took a quick breath at the sight but turned away.

I rummaged through the drawers, the bookcases, stopping every time I came across something metallic. I grabbed Erise's whip when I happened to see it.

As I searched his desk, my eyes darted toward the papers strewn across the top. Another map laid over all the other papers. At least, it looked like some sort of map, but it wasn't a map of Falleon. Strange names and shapes covered its surface, but it looked like nothing I'd seen before.

"Focus!" I seethed to myself. I shook my head and looked around again. A clock on the wall ticked out the time, and I could feel it slipping away. I searched less carefully, until finally, I heard the sound of metal on metal as I shook a pot. I peered into its depths and saw a pile of silver keys.

"Yes!" I hissed and grabbed four of them. They had the exact same finish as the silver bangles, the exact same coldness. I'd found them.

And just in time, too. I sensed Corinth marching back through a nearby corridor, his presence like an electric jolt in my mind. I clenched the keys in my fist, darted out into the hallway, and ran around the corner just as Corinth turned the corner on the opposite side. I kept walking, attempting my now-normal aloof bearing, but I felt Corinth stop. I went forward, but he stood still, head facing the corner I had just disappeared around, fingers twitching ever so slightly. I didn't like it; no, I hated it, but there was nothing I could do.

I hurried back to the library where Grass waited.

"Corinth found nothing," she said as I sat down. I nodded.

"I will be sure to tell King Oramus," I replied. "You are dismissed."

She left, and I took one more look at the keys. They represented so much—at the very least, the next step on my way to freedom.

#

After dinner, Oramus and I met with some of the men organizing our departure after the wedding. When the meeting ended, Oramus and I left first, of course, hand in hand. His hand squeezed mine, and I turned my head and flashed a smile. As soon as we left the room though, I felt Corinth stand and quickly follow us out of the room. He stopped for a split second and then jogged to catch up.

"Sire!" he called a good fifteen feet away. "Your Majesty!" he said, closing the gap. Oramus stopped, I with him, and turned to look at his second-in-command.

"What is it?" he asked. The other noblemen and councilors filed past us, splitting to accommodate our large bubble, parting around like a river around a stone.

Corinth bobbed on his feet for a moment, threw a

glance my way, and leaned toward Oramus.

"I need to speak to you, sir. Privately," he said. He glanced at me again, and I felt a tickle on the edge of my mind. Oramus snorted but didn't answer until the other people exited the hallway.

"Whatever you need to say, you can say it in front of Star," he said, rubbing a thumb across my fingers.

"I don't think that is…the best for—"

Oramus cut him off.

"Speak now or leave," he said. I sensed Corinth's muscles stiffen, but he didn't move.

"It's about her," he answered, looking straight at Oramus, eyes wide. "Something is different about her. If I'm doing a scan, I can't get into her mind. Even if I try only on her, I keep getting blocked. It's like before, after the nullifiers were off." My blood ran cold as he said these things to Oramus, but I managed to keep my face blank. Corinth's eyes stayed only on Oramus, as if begging him to believe him, but Oramus only shook his head.

"You're losing your touch Corinth," he said. "That's absolutely ridiculous." He turned to me this time.

"Is he right?" Oramus asked. "Tell me the truth."

"Of course not," I answered automatically. Corinth's face went pink, and I felt it heat up.

"Well obviously she's going to say that!" he said. "If she has her powers back, she must have found a way around the heart essence!"

"Are you implying I can't properly use my own Element?" Oramus asked, voice dropping dangerously low. He let go of my hand and stood more squarely before Corinth.

"No, no, I…"

"You're losing your touch Corinth," Oramus repeated. "If you keep this up, I don't know what we'll do with you." He smirked, but instead of anger, Corinth's voice and face reflected desperation.

"I'm not losing it!" he replied, voice getting higher with each word. "You have to believe me! I…she…"

Oramus started to turn, and Corinth looked at me. I practically saw the idea cross his mind. He jerked forward, grabbed me by the shoulders, and pressed his face within two inches of mine, staring into my eyes with the most force I had ever witnessed.

It felt like a brick hit my temple. I let out a small gasp of pain at the impact of his mind against mine, but he didn't get through. A manic smile lit up his face.

"See!" he nearly shouted, "She—"

But his body was thrown away from mine and Oramus stood between us.

"How dare you attack her like that?" he roared.

Corinth stood up quickly and pointed at me.

"No, no, sire she's hiding something! I used all I had and nothing! Nothing! She—"

"Corinth, you come in here, you accuse my fiancé, you insult my abilities, and now you attack my future queen? What the shriking is wrong with you?"

"But Oramus," he replied, still pointing at me. "She's hiding something! See how she acts! She—" He started walking toward me, but Oramus drew a knife.

"Take one more step and I'll cut that finger off."

Corinth stopped immediately and dropped his hand to his side. He said nothing, but his face showed a storm of anger, betrayal.

"You need to pull yourself together Corinth," Oramus said. "If you were anyone else…" He paused for a moment before continuing, "If you ever touch Star's mind without my permission, you will be aptly punished." Oramus turned back to me.

"Are you all right?"

"Yes," I answered. I rubbed my forehead, but the momentary pain had subsided. "I'm fine."

"Good," he replied. "If he ever tries that again, tell me immediately." I bobbed my head, and Oramus turned back to Corinth.

"You understand me too?" he asked. Corinth nodded as well.

"Yes, Your Majesty," he murmured.

"Even so, you will receive punishment." Oramus replaced the knife in his belt. "For the next week, you are to help the servants in the kitchen until we leave for the wedding. And while you're there, wear an Elemental Nullifier. On top of your sleeves." Corinth's eyes flashed at this, and his fingers twitched, but he didn't protest. Oramus continued.

"I don't want to see your face during this time," he said. "Are we clear?"

"Yes, sir."

"Now leave us."

Corinth bowed first to Oramus and then, after a moment, to me. If I had my heart, I'm sure I would have felt pity as he left for his punishment for speaking the truth. But I couldn't risk it–least of all for him.

Corinth left, and Oramus took my hands, softly.

"I'm sorry you had to go through that," he said. "He hasn't been right since you came back."

"It's fine," I replied. "I mean, it's not like…I

mean…" I didn't know what else to say. Oramus nodded, squeezed my hands, and leaned in closer.

"I'll take care of him. Let's not talk about it," he said. He tilted his head the slightest bit and parted his lips. I leaned in too without thought, pressed my lips against his. Corinth's warmth retreated into the depths of the palace and I focused on the warmth between me and my fiancé.

Oramus spoke after we parted.

"I need to check on the soldiers for our departure. I'll see you tomorrow."

"See you," I said. We walked down the hall and separated at the stairs. On the walk to my room, two things troubled me.

Corinth's punishment, for one. Punished for the truth. I held no love for the man, but it went against everything I fought for…before. Second–I might have been free from Oramus' commands, free from his orders. Even so, my body reacted to certain stimuli with the same speed and thoughtlessness as before. His orders were replaced by the ruthless efficiency of a body unhindered by feelings.

One week until the wedding. One week until the end.

CHAPTER FORTY-FOUR

The dungeon guards were far more accommodating the second time when I had my forged letter with Oramus' seal. I slipped it back under my cloak next to the nullifier keys as I entered the dungeons once again.

I strode sure and steady through the stone passageways, my warm breath creating clouds every time I breathed out though the cold didn't touch me. I followed a staircase down one more level, ready to tell Light and Wood what I'd been up to, ready to have everything fall into place.

I sensed their familiar warmths in the same place as before, but something was wrong, something. I walked up to Light's cell and peered inside.

The man sat on the floor, cross-legged and completely still. Unlike Erise, no chains held him to the ground. No nullifiers bound his wrist.

"Light?" I whispered.

He raised his head. It seemed like an eternity for the eyes to open, for them to squint through the darkness until they found mine. My heart dropped.

Those irises, once so bright as he discussed strategies and visions, lay dull in the face barely lit by torchlight. Dull like tarnished silver. Dull like a clouded pond. Dull like Grass' eyes.

He looked at me without recognition, and my mind flashed to the two essence lockets in Corinth's office, one so much brighter than the other. I turned, nearly stumbled up the steps and wound my way through the dungeon corridors to a familiar door.

"Erise!" I seethed through the barred window. My shoulders relaxed, though only slightly, when she turned her head my way and a smile lit her face.

"Pasin!" She stood and walked up to the door. I never thought I'd be so happy to see a chain around her ankle or a nullifier on her wrist.

"Here," I said, and stuffed two of the keys through the bars. "The other one's for Leyes. I can't see him." I didn't trust myself to see him. "Don't use them yet."

"Why not?"

"They're for the wedding," I said. "You and Leyes will be there. I can tell you how afterward," I added at her opening mouth. "The point is, I need you two for backup."

"What about Light and Wood?"

I took in a deep breath, steadying myself.

"Their heart essences are gone," I said. "I tried. I had a plan, but their heart essences are hanging in Corinth's office and there's no way I can get them without him noticing." Tears dotted the corners of my eyes.

"It was terrible," I said, "looking at him like that, seeing how empty…" My breath became less clouded, and the chill of the dungeons seeped into my skin.

"Stop," Erise said. She glared at me. "Focus," she said. "Don't lose yourself. We can do this."

"Right, right."

I stepped back from her door, collected myself, shut out the image of Light, his deadened eyes. Shut out the sound of Leyes' cry from before. Shut out the vision of Filio's still body splayed on the ground. When I stepped forward again, the heat had returned.

"All right," I said. "It's up to us."

I told her the plan, and she nodded.

"Leyes can't know beforehand," I said. "I don't think he's mentally ready." I gave Erise a look, silently begging her not to ask more.

"All right," she said.

"Because we have to get this right," I added, more to myself than her.

"But there's always after," she added. "If things don't work out." But I shook my head.

"Not for you," I said. I looked her square in the eyes as I spoke. "It won't come to that, but if it did, you and Leyes won't be there."

Erise's eyes widened.

"I have to go. Here," I said, stuffing her whip through the bars as well. Her eyes brightened.

"Tha—"

I cut her off, "I'll see you at the wedding." I turned away and began to walk down the corridor.

"Bye," her whisper floated through the air.

As I made my way back up to my room, my surroundings became warmer, but the chill stayed inside. I realized I never bothered to use my heat power to warm her cell. In the moment, however, it didn't bother me.

CHAPTER FORTY-FIVE

Over the next few days, Oramus, the others, and I travelled to our wedding destination. The wedding was to be held on the same cliffs that Erise, Leyes, Filio, and I had wandered by what seemed to be lifetimes ago.

We arrived, and the moment I woke up on the actual day of my wedding, my stomach clenched into a knot of nerves. I lay there, not moving, staring at the back of my eyelids for who knows how long. Shining shining pont pont drick! I heaved in a gasp of air and my eyes flew open. Two people stood over me, scrutinizing me.

"Good morning, milady," the first said. "We need to get you up and going–you have quite the big day today!"

As I raised my head, I felt sweat stick to my hair, head, pillow. Oh shining, my stomach hurt.

Two, three, four hours of bathing, dressing, being made up passed in excruciating slowness and terrifying speed. I kept replaying the plan, searching for any any any holes, mistakes, but why? It was too late. It had to work. Failure was not an option. Not an option...

Finally, they finished and propped me up in front of a mirror. I gasped.

As much as I didn't want to be there, in that dress, I was amazed at how stunning it was. Lace and beadwork mingled together down the front. A long train flowed from behind. White tulle and satin...it was just beyond...

"You need to eat something," one of the women told me. "You haven't eaten all morning." But I couldn't put the food in my mouth; the very thought of eating turned my still-clenched stomach.

So with an empty stomach, with more than sweaty palms, I waited in my tent for word to come that...

"It's time," the messenger said. He bowed to me and exited. I remained stone still for at least five seconds before the women hurried me out the door.

The messenger stood waiting. Upon my arrival, he led me through a small maze of tents. We met no one along the way, but I could feel the waiting crowd just around the corners—scores upon scores of lords, ladies, gentlemen, women, who knows who else. I sought for the two I cared most about, and I found them up near the front as they were supposed to be. Another pair stood at the front too.

The messenger left me in the hands of one more person right before the exact ceremony place.

"Wait here until the music starts," she said. I nodded blindly. It felt like an eternity passed and yet no time at all before the music began. The woman motioned, and I turned the corner.

The sheer gravity of what was happening hit me as a sea of heads turned the moment I set foot on the aisle. Heads upon heads upon heads stretched before me, and where they ended the sky emerged, breathless and blue as eternity.

The aisle lay eight feet wide and perhaps a hundred feet long. I began the trek, slowly, graciously, beaming like this was the best day of my life. Music filtered through the chilly March air, and with each step I took, destiny, fate, the future took one step closer as well.

Oramus stared me down all the way to the altar. His own eyes shone bright and a smile played on his lips. But it wasn't love dancing on his visage—I knew that for sure. It was pride that made him smile a close-lipped smile, pride that made his chin tilt up the more-than-slightest bit. He waited at the end of the aisle with pride and pompousness of a peacock. In his eyes, I was the prize for his victories—nothing more, nothing less.

He stood on the left of the end of the aisle. Behind him but closer to the crowd of sitting spectators stood Erise and Leyes. I could not look at them long though—I had to stay focused. Stay focused. Stay focused.

Across the lane from where Oramus stood, another person waited. Corinth occupied Leyes and Erise's counterpart spot. Corinth, finally out of his week of exile, stood stately in his black ensemble. Unlike the others in the area though, his face was one of barely-cloaked spite, emanating from his mouth, his eyes, his entirety.

But I had to stay focused. Stay focused. Stay focused.

I passed the rows and rows of people ecstatic to be privileged enough to witness a royal wedding. As Erise and Leyes drew closer, I averted my eyes, let the passion cool and die in my chest. Stay focused. Stay cool, stay focused. Do it.

The music faded, the crowd clapped as I reached the end of the aisle and took my place across from my betrothed. He opened his mouth enough to show his teeth as he smiled and let the clapping die down before doing anything else. After so, so long it did. He nodded to the dignified, white-haired man in the front row. The man picked himself up and joined us, between us and the ocean stretching all the way to the horizon. He blocked the ocean, he blocked the sky, blocked the horizon. He stood there, held his hands up (but not higher than Oramus' head, rest assured), and spoke.

"Here stand two people," he called out. "Not merely man and woman, but lover and beloved." His voice itched at my ears, tempted me to scratch it, but I resisted, somehow. I kept the smile plastered on my face instead.

"As one moves, the other moves too. As one stops, the other pauses."

Erise and Leyes stood right in my line of vision. I couldn't take them entirely out of my sight, and the expression on Leyes' face—oh! I looked even harder at the man directly opposite, let my smile simper on my face. His visible smugness swelled.

"As one smiles, let the other take heart. As one cries, let the other be the shield against sorrow."

The man took a deep breath and let his own smile light up his wrinkled face.

"Let your love shine, day and night, through

wind, rain, sun, darkness. May you be like the great heavenly light, the sun," he said, looking at Oramus, "and the moon," he said, looking at me. "Two parts of one whole, one illumination, one guiding light for the both." I heard an intake of breath and my eyes darted instinctively to the source. Leyes stared right at me, sweat on his forehead, pain clear on his face. But I turned away. Behind me, Corinth shifted.

"Let the days stretch out before you!" the man continued, speaking louder as in reverie. "May prosperity line your path. And may your lights shine on, past present, past life, past death." His part finished, the man lowered his arms, and spoke evenly once more.

"Now the couple will present their sacrifices," he said. I felt a jerk on my mental scan. Leyes again. I dared peek at him and saw Leyes nearly bent double, but I saw his lips move the same motion over and over and…

I shifted my focus back to Oramus. The man who gave the invocation retreated back to his seat and opened up the horizon once more. On my left, countless hordes of others, but on my right, free, clear space. And in front of me, my betrothed filled up the area with his presence, being, life.

Oramus put one hand in the space between us palm up, left it suspended in the air.

"With this hand," he said, voice loud and proud enough to reverberate through the air and infect the entire audience. "With his hand, I give up my past life. I forfeit my family, my friends, and offer them as a sacrifice to you."

A quiet whine leaked through the air. I couldn't even look at Leyes; he and I had to keep it together for just a minute more, just a minute…

"With this hand," I said, suspending my right hand above Oramus', palm up, about an inch above his. "I give up my past life."

Leyes' whine grew louder.

"I forfeit my family, my friends, and offer them as a sacrifice to you."

I lifted my other hand, began the second half, "With this hand…"

"STOP!" Leyes' shout echoed across the silent crowd. "What are you doing Pasin?" His voice cut me to the quick and I could feel my control leak from my chest–the cold of Oramus' control began to creep through my body…

"What are you doing?" he cried as guards scrambled to silence him. I tried to keep it in, but I couldn't, I couldn't—

"Oh, SHUT UP!" I shouted back at him, jerking my body to fully face him. "Don't you understand? You lost! You–are–done! And if you don't be quiet, I'll kill you myself right now!" I could look at Leyes as I said this; I looked at him as his entire face fell and the darkest gloom cast a pall over his countenance. I gained control through forfeiting any heart I had left. His pain meant nothing. But I turned back to Oramus.

"Only with your permission, that is," I said, smiling up at him with an adoration I almost believed. Even Oramus seemed surprised by my outburst, but after a moment he smiled back slyly and waved off the guards that were trying to take Leyes away.

"Leave him," he said. "He's been punished enough…for now." The guards retreated. I spared one last glance in that direction and saw Erise's face. I didn't dwell on her expression. Not yet.

Oramus and I replaced our hands–his right palm up and my right palm up above his. Finally, I slid my left-hand palm down between our right hands.

"With this hand, I accept your sacrifice and choose you. For now and forever." I even felt a shy blush creep through my face as my smile widened at my words. He smiled back, a grin full of lip and teeth. He placed his left hand on top of my right, completing the union.

"With this hand, I accept your sacrifice and choose you. For now and forever."

A cheer rose through the watching audience and I felt the smile on my face reach its peak. Oramus beamed back and I gazed into his face, letting the coldness of my loathing and the heat of my hatred clash together inside and finally, steadily come through my skin. My hands grew warm, slowly, slowly, then faster…

"Ladies and gentlemen," the officiant began.

…faster, faster…

"Let me introduce for the first time—"

BURST.

"Ah!" Oramus released my hands and jumped back from me, his hands red as the heat I felt inside. I blew him on his back and created a ring of fire surrounding us, separating us from the crowd. Despite the gasps and shouts in the crowd beyond, no one rose out of their chairs. Everyone stood still and watched through the dancing flames as a change of power happened before their very eyes. Even Corinth, Leyes, and Erise didn't shift from their positions though I sensed Erise doing something with her bonds.

I looked at Oramus, looked him square in the face. His feeble attempts to get up, to attack, to do anything were easily thwarted with a wave of my hands. I pulled one hand back, created a ball of fire dancing in my palm, and pushed it close to his throat.

"It's over," I said. All the hatred, the cold, burning hatred inside manifested itself in the raging creature in my hand. Oramus flinched back from the flame, seething and squirming.

"No," he choked. "No, you can't—"

"I can," I replied. "And I will." My hand moved forward, and—

"Wait–the heart essence!" He grabbed it from beneath his shirt, skirting around the flame in my hand. "If you kill me while I wear this, you die too." He looked at me this time right in my eyes, and a coy smile touched his lips. I reached out and snapped it from his hands, burning the rope that bound my heart to him. But as I took it…it was too easy. He gave it up too—

The moment my hand surrounded the locket, I gasped as a wave of, of feelings rushed into me. I rerealized all these things–myself, my joys, my cares, my loves. And as I had my heart again, I realized…I couldn't, I couldn't kill the man who stole it to begin with. Oramus knew it too.

He rose quickly and faced me.

"Get down!" I said, holding the fire still in front of me. But the heart was gone in my fury.

"You can't do it, can you?" he goaded, the smile slashed across his loathsome face. "Even after all of that, you still can't do it?"

"Get back!" I yelled, sending a gust of wind his way, but the force was gone. Tears formed at the edges of my eyes. Oramus laughed, sharp and derisive.

"You are so weak! You can't even kill your worst enemy!" Oramus stayed back, but he didn't back down. Behind him, I saw Erise moving her hands over to Leyes. But I didn't dare look at them, lest he notice. The audience remained silent.

"I can do it!" he roared. "I've killed, and I'll kill again!" Erise moved; she crept forward and I noticed out of the corner of my eye. I could sense her moving, but then–Corinth! I focused on him, but he didn't move. He could see just as easily as me, so why—

"That is why I am on top. That is why you will never win!" Oramus' proclamation echoed on the wind, his sheer will filling the air, and it was, for the moment, his.

But then Erise lashed out, let her iron whip flash through the air and hit Oramus square in the back. He jerked from the shock, turned with a yell toward his aggressor. Erise came at him, hand poised to deal the final attack, but Oramus was ready. His hand twitched toward his midsection, and I knew, I knew what he had there—

"NO!" I lunged at Oramus and pushed him with all my body's force. Two steps backwards, and the third didn't touch ground. Oramus' hands flailed in the empty air before him, and as he tipped backwards, an invisible, ethereal hook grabbed me and yanked me down with him. The locket slipped from my hands as I was pulled through the air.

Oramus' hand connected with my ankle as we tumbled. I caught myself, but his weight tried to drag me down, down, down.

"Pasin!" Erise ran to the edge of the cliff, but we were too far down to reach.

"If I die," Oramus snarled, nails digging into my skin, "you're coming t—"

"Pasin!" Leyes leapt over the cliff and grabbed my hand. I kicked frantically, trying to get rid of the parasite dangling from it, but he held on. With Leyes' help, we rose through the air, nearing the edge foot by foot and I felt it, felt him.

Corinth walked to the cliff's edge and watched us struggle to rise. Before anything else could happen, he slipped something from his sleeve and hurled it in our direction. I winced, waiting for the pierce of the man's weapon or for Leyes' cry of pain. The cry came, but it wasn't from Leyes.

I looked down at Oramus, but his eyes weren't on me. They stared without comprehension at the man looking back with his own coldness. Oramus' free hand jerked toward the needle in his neck and pulled it out, but his other hand loosened, lost its grip. He plummeted, hitting the cliffs on the way down, and disappeared into the ocean water below.

We landed on solid ground once more and stood up, looked around. Erise said the bystanders should bow to the new leader now, yes? Tradition. But everyone was on their feet, glancing between two people, me and Corinth. I turned to him, nerves catching my breath. He stared at a point past the cliff's edge. Finally he looked up, saw everyone waiting. A moment of realization, a moment of hesitation. He looked at me, and slowly, slowly kneeled and bowed his head.

The crowd followed suit. A sea of people rippled like the waves far below as each person recognized the new ruler. Me.

Wow.

Erise gave me a small smile and bowed as well. But I turned towards the one I had to speak to.

Leyes stood not two feet away from the cliff's edge where Oramus and I had fallen but a minute earlier. He stood, head lowered, not quite looking at me.

"Leyes," I started, "I...I didn't mean that back there...I—"

He shook his head and stepped forward, enveloping me in the warmth of his embrace, one hand on my back, one hand on my hair. I gave in to his warmth, almost sobbing into his neck.

"I'm so sorry," I choked out, letting everything I had felt, everything I had stuffed inside, out.

"Shh," he whispered. "It's all right." His voice didn't sound right yet, but I understood. And he did too.

"You dropped this," he said. One of his hands moved and he held it out to me. The locket.

"Thank you," I whispered. I took it back, felt the silver warm in my palm, and closed my hand around it. But the crowd waited.

"Please rise," I called to the onlookers. They obliged, obeyed, one or the other.

"I am not here to continue the tradition of tyranny. I am not here...to serve myself. What I want to do...is do what hasn't been done before and give up part of my leadership to others." I paused, then continued, "I will give a more detailed explanation in five days' time. Until then."

#

The next day Erise, Leyes, and I walked through the front gate of the palace. My palace, our palace. I realized, as I walked with purpose in my step, that this was the first time I entered through the main gate consciously and deliberately, of my own free will. I liked it.

CHAPTER FORTY-SIX

Back at the palace a week and a half later, I was in the library, my library, finally looking through the journal of Jusste Star. Well, the library wasn't really mine, but it was until the new government came into effect. Light and Wood had gone home for the time being, heart essence necklaces around their necks, but they would be back soon. Leyes had gone back to Fenicks to tell Water the news, all the news, and to fetch him as well. Until they all returned, however, the palace was mine.

Corinth entered the room and walked up to where I sat at the desk

"Star, I have something important to tell you."

He paused.

"Well it's actually two things," he said.

"Alright, let's hear it." I didn't mean to sound so sharp. Old habits die hard, I guess.

"May I sit?" he asked, gesturing toward a nearby seat. "This might take some time."

I raised my eyebrows.

"Sure, sure."

He sat like he talked, straight-backed and formal. I think he could feel some lingering tension as well.

"Oramus wasn't wrong," Corinth said. I furrowed my eyebrows. What did this have to do with anything? "About going over the mountains," he added. He sighed, twitched his mouth at my look of confusion, no doubt.

"Around six hundred years ago," he began. Six hundred? Recorded history didn't stretch that far back. "Elementals were a minority in the world. A tiny population in a world of people who were what we would call Absents.

"Even though the Elementals were more powerful, the sheer number of Absents overwhelmed them. The Absents were afraid of these strange people who could summon inexplicable powers at their will. They rose together and tried to eradicate the Elementals from their countries."

Countries? As in more than one? A world of Absents? Ludicrous.

"Among these Elementals, one stood out. He was a Psyche, a different sort of Element unknown today; he was also arguably one of the most powerful Elementals in history. As a Psyche, he could read minds, but his Element was so strong, he could even influence people's decisions.

"This Psyche gathered as many of the Elementals as he could and suggested a daring plan to rescue their people. He suggested a massive exodus across the ocean, an escape from their aggressors. Once they reached an empty land, they would claim it as their own.

"Many were ready for this next step as a people, but others were not. The Psyche mentally swayed them until everyone agreed. The Elementals were also joined by other creatures and peoples who could not fit into the Absent world. Elves, dragons, and similar beings came with the Elementals, all seeking their own asylum. When they reached this land, he had the foresight to know that Absents would eventually come across the ocean as well. He influenced the Elementals to work together—they created enormous mountains, a vast desert, and staggering cliffs to keep the Absents out. At the same time, they caged themselves in."

Corinth paused and only then did I realize I held my breath.

"When they were finished, the Psyche did two things. First, he went around the entire border of this…new world. He used his powers and actually focused them outside of himself so that he created a psychological barrier along the border. Should anyone encounter it, they would lose any desire to cross. Well, that was the plan anyway.

"The other thing he did, the last thing he did, was summon all of his powers and effectively destroyed all the memories the Elementals had of the outside world. However, this enormous display of power was the Psyche's downfall. He died from this act."

He paused again. I opened my mouth to speak, but he continued first.

"The interference of the Psyche explains many phenomena in this world. The disdain for Absents, for example, is a remnant of the hatred held by our ancestors. Though," he chuckled, "they really are the normal ones. Also, the few attempts to leave Falleon.

A person must have a strong will to evade the Psyche's legacy. But over the past few decades, this barrier has been deteriorating." Corinth chuckled again, though lower and darker this time. "This man changed history and history doesn't even remember his name."

The whole time Corinth spoke, he never quite looked at me squarely. Finally, he pulled his head up and looked me straight in the eyes.

"Unlike regular Elementals, the Psyche Element has a distinct recurring pattern. There is only ever one Psyche in existence; when one Psyche dies, another one is born immediately afterwards. Psyches retain the memories of all Psyches before them, though the power levels fluctuate. A transfer of memory, if you will. He or she is the link to the Elementals' true past."

Another moment's pause.

"I am the current Psyche, and I, Corinth Psyche, offer you my services."

It was my turn to pause as I pondered how in the world to respond to this revelation.

"Could you answer some questions?" Shining knew I had a lot of them.

"Of course," he replied.

"How did you and Oramus meet?" I asked. Corinth took in a breath and turned away for a moment.

"He…had heard rumors…about my Element," Corinth started again. "Some people knew the previous Psyche, though they didn't realize the extent of her powers. He's the one who studied myths and put two and two together."

Another pause. I wondered how this knowledge

weighed upon him.

"I was the outcast in my town, because I could hear what wasn't said out loud. People's thoughts would pop in my head if I looked at them long enough. And I had these stories in my head, of times before mine that I shouldn't know. I tried to share them with others, but they thought I was a lunatic. I thought so too.

"Oramus came looking for the freak in town. He asked about what I saw and gave me the information he knew. It all made sense when his words and my experience came together."

Where did Oramus learn his information to begin with? Would we ever know?

"What kind of things can you remember?" I asked. "Whose...lives can you see?"

"Well, the majority of other Psyches never grasped the full scope of the Element. Many others thought they were crazy or simply had odd dreams. A couple dozen others managed to read minds with the power, and only a handful recognized the history they knew. None have been nearly as strong as the Psyche who helped shape Falleon.

"The oddest ones," he continued. "Are the people who didn't even live in Falleon."

"What? There are Elementals beyond Falleon?"

Corinth looked up again.

"Yes," he said simply. "Most of these Psyches never realized their powers either, but there was one who discovered his abilities. He even found others like him, in the world outside Falleon—other people with powers they couldn't explain.

"Yes," he repeated. "There are people outside of Falleon...Elementals and otherwise. The only things dividing us are the mountains and the Psyche's will. And his will is waning."

I sat there, I the one looking down this time. Astounding…I didn't know what to do with this information.

"I need to tell Erise," I said, standing up to go. "Thank you for telling me Corinth…or Psyche I mean, I'll be right ba—"

"Wait, please," he said, standing as well.

"What?"

"I'd prefer if you would continue with Corinth, but…I also have something else to say."

What now?

CHAPTER FORTY-SEVEN

"What is it Corinth?"

He took a breath and answered.

"When you were here at the palace the first time, you told Oramus you were an orphan, right?"

I nodded.

"He sent me to verify your parents' identities and to come back to him with the results."

"He already told me they were dead," I said. I didn't need it reconfirmed.

"That was a lie," Corinth replied immediately. "Your parents are still alive."

"What?" The possibility of it, the sheer possibility hadn't entered my mind in ages. Corinth continued.

"I informed Oramus of their existence. He lied to you to make you more...dependent on him."

My parents were still alive? But that wasn't...couldn't...

I stood up, looked Corinth straight in the face. "Show me."

#

A few days later, once Leyes had returned, Leyes and I walked down a dimpled dirt road in the southeast Falleon City sector of Reden. As we approached the number Corinth told me, I slowed.

"I don't know if I can do this," I said, coming to a stop.

"You can do it," Leyes said automatically, taking my hand.

"Once I go in there, I'll know. Who they are, what they do...maybe even why..." I stopped again. "I don't know if I can handle that."

Leyes turned me toward him.

"Pasin," he said. "You have managed with much bigger truths than this. You have the strength. I know it."

He pulled me in for a hug.

"Do you want me to stay out here?" he asked.

"No, I want you with me. Please."

"All right."

We walked up the little path to the door of the cottage. It seemed in good shape—not a castle, but not a hovel. Leyes took a step back as I knocked on the door.

After some shuffling beyond the door, a large man pushed it aside. I stared openly. He was tall and large, not overweight, but burly.

"Well, what is it then?" he asked. His voice was like crackling leaves.

It took me a moment to realize he was talking to me.

"Um...are you Jost Copper?" I asked.

"Yes," he replied. "And you are?"

I turned to Leyes, who nodded.

"I'm Stella Smoke, and I..."

"Now if you're here for charity, you can just—"

"And I'm your daughter," I finished, looking him straight in his eyes. They widened.

"I was born on October fourteenth, sixteen years ago, and I was raised at the Andor Orphanage."

I knew my eyes challenged him. They challenged and threatened but begged, too.

Copper looked at Leyes and then back at me. After a moment and yet a lifetime, he spoke.

"Come in."

#

The home was cozy, with its blankets and trinkets lying about. Not stark, but not jam-packed either. A thin woman met us in the middle of the room.

"Who's this, Jost?" she asked.

"This is Stella Smoke," he said, looking at me with an expression of guilt mixed with sadness, "and she says she's...she's..."

"I'm your daughter," I repeated.

The woman looked from her husband to me and back again, her eyes wide with a hand over her mouth. She turned back to me, and her eyes held the same look that Copper's did. Slowly, she walked up to me, and slowly, she put her arms around me.

"I am so sorry," she whispered in my ear. I could feel her tears on my shoulder, and my own eyes clouded with moisture.

"Why," I choked. No one said anything for a moment. "Why did you do it?"

The woman let go of me and looked me straight

in the face, put a hand on my cheek, but said nothing. Jost came up behind her and put a hand on her shoulder.

"Why don't we sit down and talk," he said.

#

Over the next hour, I learned that Jost was a blacksmith. I learned that I had one set of grandparents still alive. I even learned that I had a brother. But the most important information, information I'd been waiting my entire life to hear, was finally revealed.

"It was a hard decision," the woman, my mother, Laina Fire said. "We had just gotten married, but it...it wasn't working. We were too young, not ready..." She looked at Jost who had been watching a point past the floor. He turned and nodded.

"When you were born," she continued. "We couldn't...hold on anymore. We separated and thought...thought that you would have a happier life...with a real family, not us." This time she stopped entirely. I saw tears in her eyes and felt them welling in my own.

"We came back together five years later," Jost said this time, taking Laina's hand in his. "But by then, we didn't know if you were still there..."

"We didn't even know your name," Laina added quietly.

"So we moved on," Jost ended. Silence fell. Laina opened her mouth to speak, but the noise of the door stopped her.

"I'm home!" someone called out. We all turned toward the door where a young boy stood stopped at the influx of visitors in his home.

"Who're they?" he asked, pointing to Leyes and myself.

"Reuler!" Laina started, stood up and walked over to the brown-haired schoolboy. "This," she said, gesturing toward me, "is Stella Smoke. Stella, this is Reuler Bronze." She paused and leaned over the still-confused boy. "This…is your older sister."

Reuler started at this, but he didn't look nearly as surprised as I expected.

"The one you and Dad talk about when you think I can't hear?" He raised his eyebrows. Laina laughed nervously at this.

"Yes, that one."

Reuler took a few steps forward closer to me.

"A Smoke? Can you do anything cool?" I heard Leyes let out the smallest, smallest snort at this. I smiled.

"Yeah," I replied. I held out my hands, wove my fingers through the air, and created a flower of fire.

"Whoa!" He smiled unabashedly, wide and large. "That was awesome!" He turned to his, our mother and father. "I like her. She can stay."

"Actually," I said, trying to avoid any more potential awkwardness. "I have somewhere I need to be."

Leyes rose at this and Reuler seemed to remember the other visitor.

"Wait, is that your boyfriend?" he asked, pointing at Leyes. Another light chuckle escaped from his lips. I felt a blush rise to my cheeks.

"Yeah," I replied again. "He is." Leyes reached out and took my right hand. Laina and Jost remained back, but interest showed in their eyes.

"Ew, gross!" Reuler recoiled with boyish instinct.

"Well, if you need to be going," Jost began, standing up and walking over to me "I guess this is goodbye for now." He patted my shoulder with his hand. "It's been good...to see you." He put his hand out to Leyes who shook it firmly. Jost nodded and stepped back. Laina took his place.

"You will come back, right?" she asked. I nodded.

"Of course."

She gave a small smile at my reply and carefully put her arms around me in another hug. On release, she looked at Leyes and nodded at him.

"It's been good to meet you as well," she said.

"You too, ma'am," Leyes replied.

Finally it was Reuler's turn.

"When are you coming back?" he asked excitedly. "Come back soon so you can show me more cool stuff!"

"Will do," I said, "within the month. As long as that's all right." I looked up at them, my parents who gave their own reserved smiles and nodded. Leyes and I walked through the door Reuler left open.

"Until then," I said.

"Until then," Jost and Laina replied.

"May Solluna light your path," Laina added with a smile.

As we walked back down the dimpled dirt road, we heard Reuler's voice float through the open door.

"Yes! Something exciting finally!" And then came Jost's voice.

"You know, she looked kind of familiar—I wonder if we've seen her somewhere..."

Leyes and I laughed once we were out of earshot.

"I guess government upheavals aren't very

interesting for boys," I said.

"I like your little brother," Leyes said. A beat and then he continued, "Are you going to tell them who you really are?"

"Yes," I said. "Eventually. But for now, I want to know them for them, and I want them to know me for me." Leyes gave me a look, but I held fast.

"Give me a few weeks. Let it be for now."

We held hands almost the entire way back, even the mile we flew in the air. Beautiful warmth in my hands, like the fire flower, but so much brighter.

CHAPTER FORTY-EIGHT

The cold air slapped across our faces as Leyes and I pushed up in the sky, farther than we had ever gone before. The snowy mountainside taunted us onward, daring us, but we challenged it back and kept climbing. Something itched at the back of my mind, but I ignored it and focused on the flight and the warm hand holding mine.

Leyes and I finally reached the lowest summit–only barely, but we reached it. I cleared an area of the snow, and we sat together, side to side.

Night was coming fast. The sun disappeared in the west and the dominant lights were the stars in the sky.

"I can feel it," Leyes said, grasping my hand, "The thing Corinth talked about. Like a nagging thought telling me to leave."

"He said that it's weaker now than it used to be," I replied. "And we know the truth about it. I wonder how it felt a century ago to a normal person."

We sat and pondered that for a minute. Leyes'

breath billowed out of his mouth like smoke.

"Look," he said, pointing with his free hand to a spot in the distance, on the far side of the mountains. Something was there besides darkness, something surely not noticeable during daylight. A group of lights shone in the distance, almost all the way at the edge of the horizon.

"Is that…a city?" I asked, incredulous. It looked like it, but how could one city be so bright?

"I think so." Leyes' voice sounded much more thoughtful.

"I mean, I believed Corinth," I said, gesticulating with my other hand, "but to think that it's really there! I mean—right…there."

Leyes didn't reply. Rather, he turned toward me.

"You can go," he said, gesturing to the new world in front of us. "I know you've always wanted to get out of here. I can tell the others."

I looked at him. His eyes shone with the overhead starlight and reflected the light in my eyes. I turned back to the far-off city. Its brightness rang through the night air like a siren's call.

"I will," I replied. Then I turned back to him. "But not today." I saw an outline of a smile creep across his face. "For now…I'm fine right here."

His smile widened and brightened and I felt it echo on my own face. We sat there in the dark, on the brink of who-knows-what, with no one but the stars as companions.

About the Author

H. C. Daria lives in South Carolina, USA. She began writing in 4th grade after reading *The Magician's Nephew* by C. S. Lewis. Daria's skill has greatly improved since then.

She runs a blog, hcdaria.blogspot.com, and even updates it occasionally.

About the Illustrator

Meilee Chao is a professional illustrator and character artist, also operating under the name "bkomae." The very first *Burst* fan, Chao was designated to be the cover artist for over ten years while they were hard at work, honing their craft. View their portfolio at meirii.com.

www.ingramcontent.com/pod-product-compliance
Lightning Source LLC
Chambersburg PA
CBHW030536260626
47157CB00006B/2063